PENGUIN CLASSICS

# THREE GOTHIC NOVELS

HORACE WALPOLE (1717–97), fourth earl of Orford, was the son of Robert Walpole, twice Prime Minister of Britain. In 1747 he moved to Strawberry Hill, Twickenham, his 'little Gothic castle', where he was at the centre of a literary and political society and arbiter of taste. *The Castle of Otranto* was published anonymously in 1764 and launched the Gothic novel in England. Walpole is also remembered for his witty letters to a wide circle of friends.

WILLIAM BECKFORD (1759–1844) was the son of a Lord Mayor of London and at one time was known as 'England's wealthiest son', with a fortune derived from the West Indies. He built Fonthill Abbey in Wiltshire, a prime example of Gothic architecture, where he lived until scandal and extravagance forced him to sell. *Vathek*, originally written in French, was published in 1786.

MARY SHELLEY (1797–1851) was the daughter of the philosopher and writer William Godwin and of Mary Wollstonecraft, author of *Vindication of the Rights of Woman*. In 1814 she eloped with the poet Shelley to the continent, marrying him on the death of his first wife. *Frankenstein* (1818) was written during a stay in Switzerland when she, Shelley and Byron each agreed to write a supernatural story.

MARIO PRAZ Professor of English Language and Literature at the University of Rome until 1966. He wrote a great many books on literature, many of them in English. He died in 1982.

PETER FAIRCLOUGH graduated with an English degree from Durham University and teaches English in Lancashire. He has also edited *Oliver Twist*, *Dombey and Son* and *The Last Chronicle of Barset* for the Penguin Classics.

# THREE Gothic NOVELS

*Edited by Peter Fairclough*
*with an Introductory Essay by*
*Mario Praz*

THE CASTLE OF OTRANTO
*Horace Walpole*

VATHEK
*William Beckford*

FRANKENSTEIN
*Mary Shelley*

PENGUIN BOOKS

PENGUIN BOOKS

Published by the Penguin Group
Penguin Books Ltd, 80 Strand, London WC2R 0RL, England
Penguin Putnam Inc., 375 Hudson Street, New York, New York 10014, USA
Penguin Books Australia Ltd, 250 Camberwell Road, Camberwell, Victoria 3124, Australia
Penguin Books Canada Ltd, 10 Alcorn Avenue, Toronto, Ontario, Canada M4V 3B2
Penguin Books India (P) Ltd, 11 Community Centre, Panchsheel Park, New Delhi – 110 017, India
Penguin Books (NZ) Ltd, Cnr Rosedale and Airborne Roads, Albany, Auckland, New Zealand
Penguin Books (South Africa) (Pty) Ltd, 24 Sturdee Avenue, Rosebank 2196, South Africa

Penguin Books Ltd, Registered Offices: 80 Strand, London WC2R 0RL, England

www.penguin.com

Published in the Penguin English Library 1968
Reprinted in Penguin Classics 1986
039



Printed in England by Clays Ltd, St Ives plc
Set in Monotype Scotch Roman



ISBN-13: 978–0–14–043036–3

www.greenpenguin.co.uk

# CONTENTS

# INTRODUCTORY ESSAY

THE favour recently enjoyed in some European countries (Italy for instance) by Gustav Meyrink's *The Golem* and Mikhail Bulgakov's *The Master and Margarita* makes one wonder whether the scanty fare provided by modern experimental novels and *anti-romans* has made readers so famished, that as soon as they happen to detect the smell of what the French romantics used to call the *roman-charogne*, they rush for it like mad. The terror and wonder which abound in those two novels have certainly profited also by the example of modern masters, but a reader familiar with the Gothic novels of the end of the eighteenth and the beginning of the nineteenth century will easily recognize in them themes and proceedings which were the stock-in-trade of the tales of terror. The terrific robot of the modern Prague banker is of the same lineage as Mary Shelley's monster, and the underground labyrinth through which the protagonist reaches the awesome room of the dark Jewish school is a commonplace of the Gothic tales, the double is a descendant of many a German *Doppelgänger*, the motif of the innocent accused and tried for a crime he has not committed, and incapable of proving his innocence, recalls episodes in *Frankenstein*, in *Melmoth the Wanderer* and in François Soulié's *Mémoires du diable*. In fact, though refined by the lesson of the later masters of the mysterious and the cruel, such as Kafka in fiction and Kubin in painting, the subject-matter of *The Golem* has such a distinct Gothic flavour that 'tracing its literary genealogy would take us very far, because on the one hand there is the Rosicrucian strain which begins with Godwin's later novels and gains in strength through Hawthorne's posthumous work, on the other hand there are Novalis's romanticism, certain inventions of Hoffmann (such as *Der Sandmann*), Jean Paul (such as *Der Komet oder Nikolaus Markgrat*), Arnim and Brentano, Balzac's and Gérard de Nerval's esoteric novels, etc.'[1] And in the posthumous work of the Russian novelist there is a devilish cat who descends from Hoffmann's Kater Murr, a man who lacks a shadow like Chamisso's Peter Schlemihl, besides obvious echoes of Goethe's *Faust*, of Gogol, and the Wandering Jew.

All this shows that the Gothic flame, as an Indian scholar has called it,[2] is far from extinguished. The appeal of terror and mystery no doubt existed also much earlier than the second half of the eighteenth century, witness the Hellenistic romances and the Elizabethan dramas, but it is in the last portion of that century that in fiction we meet with no less strange fashions than those of the *merveilleuses* and the *incroyables* of the Directory, which historians of costume quote as typical instances of the extravagant finery that usually either accompanies or follows epochs of great social revolutions. Thus about the time of the French Revolution there appeared in France the series of infernal novels of the Marquis de Sade, and in England a whole blossoming of Gothic novels, called tales of terror there and *romans noirs* abroad. The effect, in a survey of literary history, is not unlike the impression we receive in an air journey over Texas and New Mexico to the Grand Canyon, when we see a level plain suddenly interrupted by chains of craggy mountains, with rocks which have the aspect of ruined castles and ranges of convulsed peaks like a tumultuous barbaric horde.

And in the same way as such a full orchestra of the horrid

---

1. Elèmire Zolla's introduction to the Italian translation of *The Golem*, Milan, Bompiani, 1966.

2. Devendra P. Varma, *The Gothic Flame*, Being a History of the Gothic Novel in England, London, Arthur Barker, 1957; second edition, New York, Russell and Russell, 1966.

is announced by sporadic growths of strangely misshapen hills and grim outposts, so the novels of terror were announced by less fierce forerunners. An aesthetic theory of the Horrid and the Terrible had gradually developed in the course of the eighteenth century,[3] but why in the most polite and effeminate of centuries, in the century of *bergeries* and *fêtes galantes* and idyllic conversation pieces, the century of Watteau and Boucher and Zoffany, should people have begun to feel the horrible fascination of dark forests and lugubrious caverns, and cemeteries and thunderstorms? The answer is: just because of its feminine character. In no other century was woman such a dominating figure, the very essence of rococo being a feminine delicacy – just because of this the eighteenth century had *les nerfs à fleur de peau.* They discovered the *mal de vivre,* and the *vapeurs.* '*Les vapeurs, c'est l'ennui,*' said Madame d'Épinay. They had vague inklings of a metaphysical anxiety. Throughout her life Madame du Deffand experienced the oppressive feeling of an ultimate nothingness: '*Je suis tombée dans le néant . . . je retombe dans le néant*'.[4] Perhaps the origin of the painful pleasure imparted by the tales of terror is contained in two lines of Baudelaire ('*Au lecteur*' – *Les Fleurs du Mal*):

> *C'est l'Ennui! – L'oeil chargé d'un pleur involontaire*
> *Il rêve d'échafauds en fumant son houka.*[5]

The new sensibility had begun to find literary expression in compositions such as Collins's *Ode to Fear* and in *The Castle of Otranto,* written by Walpole as the whim of a dilettante mediaevalist; it had modified the conception of

3. Symptoms of this taste for the Horrid have been studied by D. Mornet, *Le Romantisme en France au XVIIIe siècle,* Paris, Hachette, 1912, ch. I, *Les premiers remous,* III, *Les grands ébranlements de l'âme.*

4. 'I fell into a void . . . and I am falling back into a void.'

5. Boredom – His eye filled with unwilled tears
He dreams of scaffolds as he smokes his hookah.

the Beautiful in Burke's famous *Philosophical Enquiry* (1757), where there occurs the startling statement: 'Whatever is fitted in any sort to excite the ideas of pain, that is to say, whatever is in any sort terrible . . . is a source of the sublime';[6] it had sought to analyse its own origins in such essays as that of J. and A. L. Aikin 'On the Pleasure derived from Objects of Terror', and the 'Enquiry into those kinds of Distress which excite agreeable sensations' (in *Miscellaneous Pieces in Prose*, London, 1773) and in Drake's essay 'On Objects of Terror' which precedes the fragment of *Montmorenci.* The discovery of Horror as a source of delight reacted on men's actual conception of Beauty itself: the Horrid, from being a category of the Beautiful, became eventually one of its essential elements, and the 'beautifully horrid' passed by insensible degrees into the 'horribly beautiful'.

Of course, as I was saying, the discovery of the beauty of the Horrid cannot be considered as belonging entirely to the eighteenth century, although it was only then that the idea came to full consciousness. That beauty and poetry may be extracted from such unpromising materials as the base and the repugnant, Shakespeare and the other Elizabethans had known long before this, though they did not theorize about it. In Lewis's *The Monk*, Agnes who, being with child, has been condemned to a slow and hideous death in a dungeon together with her offspring, says:

Sometimes I felt the bloated toad, hideous and pampered with the poisonous vapours of the dungeon, dragging its loathsome length along my bosom. Sometimes the quick cold lizard roused me, leaving its slimy track upon my face and entangling itself in the tresses of my wild and matted hair. Often have I at

6. For the effects of the new sensibility on the visual arts, see David Irwin, *English Neoclassical Art*, London, Faber, 1966, p. 135 ff., and Robert Rosenblum, *Transformations in Late Eighteenth Century Art*, Princeton University Press, 1967, pp. 11–19.

waking found my fingers ringed with the long worms which bred in the corrupted flesh of my infant.

These details, on which the *frénétique* romantics of a later date were to set store, where did Lewis find them but in Shakespeare's *Romeo and Juliet* (IV, i, 77 ff.)?

> O . . . rather than marry Paris
> . . . bid me lurk
> Where serpents are; chain me with roaring bears
> Or hide me nightly in a charnel-house,
> O'er cover'd quite with dead men's rattling bones,
> With reeky shanks, and yellow chapless skulls,
> Or bid me go into a new-made grave
> And hide me with a dead man in his shroud . . .

and in Otway's *The Orphan* (I, 209 ff., 446 ff.):

> When in some Cell distracted, as I shall be,
> Thou seest me lye; these unregarded Locks,
> Matted like Furies Tresses; my poor Limbs
> Chain'd to the Ground, &c.

On the other hand, the idea of pain as an integral part of desire had a certain novelty, if Novalis could remark (in *Psychologische Fragmente*): 'It is strange that the association of desire, religion and cruelty should not have immediately attracted men's attention to the intimate relationship which exists between them, and to the tendency which they have in common.' Novalis's *Fragments* appeared in 1798 in the *Athenäum*, one year after the publication of the definitive and complete edition of Sade's *Justine* and *Juliette* which had for the first time appeared respectively in 1791 and 1796.

A monster or a martyr, Donatien-Alphonse-François de Sade was certainly not the first to be endowed with an exceptional outlook on erotic matters, but the *siècle des lumières* supplied him with the torch of reason and the belief in the soundness of Nature's laws, and the newly undertaken exploration of the customs of primitive peoples who lived according to Nature made it clear to him that his 'apartness' from the feelings of his fellow-men was, in fact, not a shortcoming but a privilege; he was aware of the voice of Nature as nobody else was round him, hence he was the bearer of a message, the most daring philosopher of all. For Sade the whole history of civilized humanity was a mistake, and one had to revert to the condition of holy Nature. Nature taught destruction, murder, sexual promiscuity, and so far Sade was right. But had not the theory of original sin allowed for this? And was not the whole history of humanity an effort just to overcome that chaotic state of nature in order to create a liveable society? Sade would have us revert to private revenge for murder, to prostitution of boys and girls, to in-breeding, etc., stages and practices still instanced by primitive peoples, which mankind had to discard if it wanted to survive. The eighteenth century, through the work of Sade, saw the *reductio ad absurdum* of the return to Nature, because all the progress of man has consisted in getting further and further away from Nature, in creating an artificial ethical state, in evolving a new standard of values, as artificial as a city is artificial in comparison with the swamp which originally occupied the site. In his defective, unbalanced inner self, Sade was just a throw-back as most abnormal people and criminals are; he thought he was brandishing the torch of reason, it was only a searchlight into the remote den of the early stages of man.

And here is the connecting link between this isolated man, this curious relic of buried and forgotten pre-history, and the humanity of his day and of today. His writings are like the obscene scrawl one reads in a urinal, with the secret innuendo: '*Hypocrite lecteur, – mon semblable, – mon frère!*'[7] Because who has not been Sade once in his dreams? So that the deep caves and subterranean passage-ways of the inaccessible castles in which Sade's heroes stage their preposterous orgies are more than a symbol of his own

7. 'Hypocritical reader, – my fellow, – my brother!'

'apartness', of the isolation of his obsessive images; they are actually the symbol of the cave-man whose voice can be faintly heard in every Mr Earwicker's dream language, whose actions can at any moment, in the very midst of a civilized metropolis, startle us, in an imaginary Mr Hyde or in a real Mr Christie. And that is why notwithstanding his monotony, his lack of the detachment needed to recreate reality, and of skill in telling his tall stories, his pitiable clichés and 'philosophical' platitudes, Sade has been hailed as a unique writer and a great moralist who, in a different way than he thought, has contributed to the progress of enlightenment; he has torn the web of abstractions painfully woven by man through aeons, and presented him with a distorted mirror, which nevertheless contains his disturbing authentic image. He has recorded and made articulate for us the voice of the cave-man, that extinct species which still lingers at the bottom of our souls, and not unfrequently, in these troubled times, comes up to the surface.

Maurice Heine[8] advanced the supposition that 'Monk' Lewis while in Paris obtained a copy of Sade's *Justine*, whose third edition had appeared just then in Cazin's celebrated collection (1792). Sade's influence on Lewis seems probable to Heine, but Mrs Radcliffe, in this critic's view, would not have known him; rather, the reverse is possible, although before 1797 there were no French translations of Mrs Radcliffe's novels. In his *Idée sur les romans*, which precedes *Les Crimes de l'Amour* (1800), Sade thinks Lewis's *The Monk* '*supérieur, sous tous les rapports, aux bizarres élans de la brillante imagination de Radcliffe*'.[9] One may doubt, however, whether Sade spoke of Mrs Radcliffe more than

---

8. *Le Marquis de Sade et le roman noir*, Paris, Nouvelle Revue Française, 1933 (offprint from that review, August number for 1933).

9. 'Superior in all respects to the strange leaps of the brilliant imagination of Mrs Radcliffe.'

by hearsay. Anyhow it is curious to see how Sade, in his *Idée sur les romans*, tried to account for the tale of terror:

*Ce genre . . . devenait le fruit indispensable des secousses révolutionnaires, dont l'Europe entière se ressentait. Pour qui connaissait tous les malheurs dont les méchants peuvent accabler les hommes, le roman devenait assez difficile à faire, que monotone à lire: il n'y avait point d'individu qui n'eût plus éprouvé d'infortunes en quatre ou cinq ans que n'en pouvait peindre en un siècle le plus fameux romancier de la littérature: il fallait donc appeler l'enfer à son secours, pour se composer des titres à l'intérêt, et trouver dans le pays des chimères, ce qu'on savait couramment en ne fouillant que l'histoire de l'homme dans cet âge de fer. Mais que d'inconvénients presentait cette manière d'écrire! L'auteur du Moine ne les a plus évités que Radcliffe; ici nécessairement des deux choses l'une, ou il faut développer le sortilège, et dès lors vous n'intéressez plus, ou il ne faut jamais lever le rideau et vous voilà dans la plus affreuse invraisemblance.*[10]

What is chiefly worth noticing is that Lewis, Mrs Radcliffe and Sade belong to the same mental climate, the climate which produced so many incarnations of the theme of the

---

10. 'This genre was the inevitable product of the revolutionary shocks with which the whole of Europe resounded. For those who were acquainted with all the ills that are brought upon men by the wicked, the romantic novel was becoming somewhat difficult to write, and merely monotonous to read: there was nobody left who had not experienced more misfortunes in four or five years than could be depicted in a century by literature's most famous novelists: it was necessary to call upon hell for aid in order to arouse interest, and to find in the land of fantasies what was common knowledge from historical observation of man in this iron age. But this way of writing presented so many inconveniencies! The author of the *Moine* failed to avoid them no less than did Mrs Radcliffe; either of these two alternatives was unavoidable; either to explain away all the magic elements, and from then on to be interesting no longer, or never raise the curtain, and there you are in the most horrible unreality.'

persecuted maiden,[11] and found its chief pictorial expression in Goya.

If we take as a starting point for the history of the Gothic novel the external setting, emphasized in the very title of the first of them, *The Castle of Otranto*, we may feel tempted to see its genesis in the taste for ruins, a category of the picturesque which implied in itself the possibility of sinister developments, since old superstitions (those superstitions which 'call forth fresh delight to fancy's view', according to Collins's ode on them) believed ruins haunted. Indeed, for centuries ruins had been one of the favourite themes of devotional meditation;[12] they inspired the seventeenth-century bizarre painter Monsù Desiderio with his visions or rather stage-settings of lugubrious and catastrophic perspectives, until, in course of time, this strain acquired a deeper and more morbid significance, thanks, as we shall see in a moment, to Piranesi's *Carceri*. In the same way as shell-decorated grottoes and follies existed before Rousseau's *Promeneur solitaire*, Tempesta and Pomarancio had illustrated various kinds of torments on the walls of Santo Stefano Rotondo in Rome long before the torture chambers of the Marquis de Sade, and the picturesque groupings of ruins in the manner of Paul Brill, and fantastic sceneries in the manner of Agostino Tassi existed before Monsù Desiderio's ominous vistas.

But what begins as an arabesque, in time breeds teeth and nails, and after having pleasurably tickled the skin, gnaws through the very vitals. Subtle spirits discovered a

---

11. See M. Praz, *The Romantic Agony*, Oxford University Press, 1951 (second edition), Chapter III; L. A. Fiedler, *Love and Death in the American Novel*, New York, Criterion Books; London, Jonathan Cape, 1960.

12. See Rose Macaulay, *Pleasures of Ruins*, London, Thames and Hudson, 1966 (new edition) and R. Negri, *Gusto e poesia delle rovine in Italia tra il Sette e l'Ottocento*, Milan, Ceschina, 1965.

new sensation in the spectacle of ruins, the thrill caused by beauty threatened and dilapidated, a mixed charm of repulsion and attraction, '*quell'orror bello che attristando piace*',[13] as the Italian poet Ippolito Pindemonte said. In this way those ruins which in the seventeenth century had appealed to people because of the bizarre disorder of their aspect were invested in the eighteenth with vague aspirations towards infinity and the past, towards beauty undermined by death. From being a mere ornament in a garden a mock-Gothic castle became the background against which an idle and morbid mind projected its *rêves d'échafauds*.

In 1952 a Danish scholar, Jørgen Andersen,[14] found that 'there is a passage still unexplored leading from the *Carceri* into the strangely echoing vaults of the English Gothic novels'. He found that Piranesi's architectural settings 'often answer to Edmund Burke's analysis of the effect of "infinity and things multiplied without end" – Infinity has a tendency to fill the mind with that sort of delightful horror, which is the most genuine effect and truest test of the sublime'. It is well known that through the Adams, Piranesi's engraved work acquired a widespread influence on English interior decoration. Although Horace Walpole's appreciation of Piranesi is not without reserve, a passage in his advertisement to the fourth volume of the *Anecdotes of Painting in England* (1771) witnesses to his enthusiasm for the Italian engraver, when he advises the English artists to study:

the sublime dream of Piranesi, who seems to have conceived visions of Rome beyond what is boasted even in the meridian of its splendor. Savage as Salvator Rosa – fierce as Michael Angelo, and exuberant as Rubens, he has imagined scenes that

---

13. 'That beautiful horror which delights while it saddens.'
14. See his essay on 'Giant Dreams, Piranesi's Influence in England', in *English Miscellany*, 3, Rome, 1952.

would startle geometry, and exhaust the Indies to realize. He piles palaces on bridges, and temples on palaces, and scales Heaven with mountains of edifices. Yet what taste in his boldness! What labour and thought both in his rashness and details.

In the disproportion between Piranesi's mighty daedalean buildings and his little figures of men at the foot of them, is to be seen the germ of the ruling idea of *The Castle of Otranto*. But Dr Andersen has discovered a detail which leads to the very core of Walpole's inspiration: both in a scene of mighty arches and stairs in the *Opere varie* and in another of the *Carceri*, there appears a trophy surmounted by a monumental plumed helmet which in one case hangs threateningly over the dwarfed men below. Was it under an impression of such etchings that Walpole had the dream which (according to a letter of 9 March 1765) prompted him to write *The Castle of Otranto*?

'I waked one morning in the beginning of last June from a dream, of which all I could recover was, that I thought myself in an ancient castle (a very natural dream for a head filled like mine with Gothic story) and that on the uppermost bannister of a great staircase I saw a gigantic hand in armour. In the evening I sat down and began to write, without knowing in the least what I intended to say or relate.'

In the novel, which appeared in 1765, the hand in armour of the dream has become the gigantic helmet that in Piranesi's etching dominated the top of a great staircase. Unfortunately the spirit of Piranesi did not assist Walpole beyond the giant dream which opens the novel. There is no more real terror in the story than in Mozart's *Don Giovanni*: the idea of the terrible of those eighteenth-century works was of a melodramatic, stagey sort. Walpole's gigantic helmet and bleeding statue of Alfonso are no more horrifying than the stone effigy of the Commendatore in Mozart's opera. Leporello's comical comments are near at hand in the latter case; in *The Castle of Otranto* the answers of the silly frightened servants Diego and Jaquez to Manfred provide a similar sort of comic relief to the appalling apparition of the helmet. Of course *Don Giovanni* is a *dramma giocoso* and Walpole's aim was nothing of this kind, but there is no atmosphere of suspense and horror in the castle which, like Strawberry Hill, is only rococo in a Gothic disguise. Men had travelled far into the arts of evoking terror by the time of Mrs Shelley; there is a real sense of obsession in *Frankenstein*. Of the three panels of the polyptic which is offered in this volume, Walpole's Gothic, Beckford's exotic, and Mary Shelley's alpine and polar one, the Gothic panel is decidedly the weakest.

However, the merit of Walpole is to have first divined a potential source of the literary marvellous in the *Carceri*. The description of the secret passage through which Isabella hurries, calls those etchings to mind:

> The lower part of the castle was hollowed into several intricate cloisters; and it was not easy for one under so much anxiety to find the door that opened into the cavern. An awful silence reigned throughout those subterraneous regions, except now and then some blasts of wind that shook the doors she had passed, and which, grating on the rusty hinges, were re-echoed through that long labyrinth of darkness.

The hold of Piranesi's fantastic architectures on Beckford is even more manifest. In his *Dreams, Walking Thoughts and Incidents* (1783), Piranesi comes to his mind on his way to Bonn:

> I kept gazing at the azure irregular mountains which bounded the view, and in thought was already transported to their summits. Vast and wild were the prospects I surveyed from this imaginary exaltation, and innumerable the chimeras which trotted in my brain. Mounted on these fantastic quadrupeds, I shot visibly from rock to rock, and built castles in the style of Piranesi, upon most of their pinnacles. The magnificence and variety of my aërial towers hindered my thinking the way long.

Even more haunting is Piranesi's presence in Venice in the vicinity of the Piombi:

I left the courts, and stepping into my bark was rowed down a canal over which the lofty vaults of the palace cast a tremendous shade. Beneath these fatal waters the dungeons I have also been speaking of are situated . . . I shuddered whilst passing below [a marble bridge]; and believe it is not without cause, this structure is named Ponte dei Sospiri. Horrors and dismal prospects haunted my fancy upon my return. I could not dine in peace, so strongly was my imagination affected; but snatching my pencil, I drew chasms, and subterranean hollows, the domain of fear and torture, with chains, racks, wheels, and dreadful engines in the style of Piranesi.

The vast ruins and royal sepulchres of Istakar in *Vathek* seem inspired by the *Carceri:*

On the right rose the watch-towers, ranged before the ruins of an immense palace, whose walls were embossed with various figures. In front stood forth the colossal forms of four creatures, composed of the leopard and the griffin, and though but of stone, inspired emotions of terror.

So much had Piranesi's *Carceri* penetrated the spirit of the Gothic tales, that when De Quincey evoked them in a famous passage of the *Confessions of an English Opium-eater* he gave them a 'Gothic' character:

Many years ago, when I was looking over Piranesi's *Antiquities of Rome*, Coleridge, then standing by, described to me a set of plates from that artist, called his *Dreams*, and which record the scenery of his own visions during the delirium of a fever. Some of these (I describe only from memory of Coleridge's account) represented vast Gothic halls, on the floor of which stood mighty engines and machinery, wheels, cables, catapults, etc., expressive of enormous power put forth, or resistance overcome. Creeping along the sides of the walls, you perceived a staircase; and upon this, groping his way upwards was Piranesi himself. Follow the stairs a little farther, and you perceive them reaching an abrupt termination, without any balustrade, and allowing no step onwards to him who should reach the extremity, except into the depth below. Whatever is to become of poor Piranesi, at least you suppose that his labours must now in some way terminate. But raise your eyes, and behold a second flight of stairs still higher, on which again Piranesi is perceived, by this time standing on the very brink of the abyss. Once again elevate your eye, and a still more aërial flight is descried; and there, again, is the delirious Piranesi, busy on his aspiring labours: and so on, until the unfinished stairs and the hopeless Piranesi are lost in the upper gloom of the hall.

De Quincey grafts into Piranesi's etchings not only the Gothic strain but also a topos as ancient as Silius Italicus, who in the third book of his poem on the second Punic War speaks of the marching soldiers of Hannibal, who, having overcome a first mountain range, see another rise in front of them, and think they will never come to an end of their labours; a topos taken up by Pope in his *Essay on Criticism* in an image which Doctor Johnson proclaimed the most beautiful that ever appeared in English. In De Quincey, however, Piranesi's spiral stairs become the symbol of an anxiety which condensed the spirit of the Gothic tales and transmitted it to the French romantics.[15] Indeed, an anxiety with no possibility of escape is the main theme of the Gothic tales, and if *The Castle of Otranto* concludes with a conventional anagnorisis and a second-best marriage, there is no redemption at the end of the other two tales included in the present volume.

Perhaps the last biographer of Beckford, Marc Chadourne,[16] who has been able to utilize André Parreaux's standard work,[17] sees in Beckford a depth of *engagement* of which he had no capacity, for his soul was essentially a dilettante's. But how many anticipations there are in him, if one considers him in retrospect! A first impression of

15. See Luzius Keller, *Piranèse et les romantiques français, le mythe des escaliers en spirale*, Librairie José Corti, 1966.

16. *Eblis, ou l'enfer de William Beckford*, Jean-Jacques Pauvert Editeur, 1967.

17. *William Beckford*, Paris, Niget, 1960.

*Vathek* is of a pastiche of the *Arabian Nights* and of Voltaire's *Contes philosophiques*. Voltaire considered these just a trifle, while they are one of his major titles to fame; there is no reason to think that Beckford considered in a different way his Oriental story, in which enormous cruelties assume the ludicrous aspect of those in Voltaire's stories. The general impression is of an arabesque, a *scherzo*, a *scenario* in the manner of Loutherbourg. Vathek's murderous eye, the pact with the Powers of Darkness, the intervention of good angels under disguise (the episode of the shepherd with his magic flute), the torments of the damned (the burning heart seen through the crystal transparency of the breast), the admixture of the marvellous, the repulsive, the cruel and the grotesque, generally associated with the idea of the Orient, all these elements were known to the European tradition before Beckford. But if you consider *Vathek* in relation to the ferments seething at the end of the century, you soon discover to your surprise that this gay and gruesome *scenario* of Beckford lends itself to tempting parallels.

Chadourne sees the Hall of Eblis in the light of Sartre's *Huis-clos*:

*Leur huis-clos souterrain n'est que le prolongement, l'approfondissement de leur expérience terrestre par-delà le bien et le mal . . . Dans l'ombre souterraine comme au soleil des vivants, en bas comme en haut, dedans comme dehors, la même histoire toujours continue : la passion se change en dégoût, le bien engendre le mal, les amants qui s'étaient juré une éternité d'amour sont condamnés à se haïr et, la main sur le coeur, comme les ambitieux, les rebelles, les assoiffés de connaissances, à répéter : 'je souffre'. Notre enfer n'est qu'en ce monde; il n'est pas seulement les autres, il est en nous. A toute espérance il faut dire adieu. Telle paraît être, de* Vathek *au dernier des* Épisodes, *l'idée centrale, le noeud des thèmes du cycle. N'entrevoir en ces 'Contes arabes' que des licences de* Mille et une Nuits *plus ou moins roses, plus ou moins noires – inspirées par la lecture des* Mille et une Nuits, *de traités de magie, de la* Bibliothèque orientale *de d'Herbelot, à un jeune Anglais polyglotte, imaginatif, voltairianisé à seize ans par 'le vieux squelette aux yeux d'escarboucles' de Ferney, – ce serait s'interdire de pénétrer aux profondeurs où Beckford a conduit ses premiers lecteurs: Byron, Disraeli, Edgar Poe.*[18]

According to Chadourne, whatever was light and Voltairian in the early part of the tale vanishes at the very moment when Vathek and Nourinahar descend by torchlight the marble steps which lead to the palace of subterranean fire, when the Giaour has opened the ebony gate to take them to the presence of Eblis. Then 'the pen one had thought Voltairian is dipped into blacker and blacker ink: it is the pen of Edgar Poe, of Baudelaire, of Lautréamont'.

And as the shadow of the Divine Marquis hovered on these latter, do not we find in Beckford's own life striking parallels to *Justine*, not to mention *Les liaisons dangereuses*? Nourinahar's name in real life was Louisa, the wife of Beckford's cousin, Vathek – William himself, and Louisa in her letters calls him her infernal beloved, who

---

18. 'Their underground "*huis clos*" is merely the prolongation, the deepening, of their earthly experience, beyond good and evil . . . In the subterranean shades, as in the sunlight of the living, below as above, within as without, it is always the same story: passion is transformed into disgust, good engenders evil, lovers who swore eternal love are condemned to hating each other, and to repeating from the depths of their hearts, with the ambitious, the rebels, and those too thirsty for knowledge "I suffer". Our hell is in fact on earth, it does not consist only in the presence or impact of other people, it is within ourselves. We must say goodbye to all hope. This seems to be the central idea throughout the last of the Episodes of *Vathek*; the essence of the themes of the whole cycle. To see in these "*Contes arabes*" nothing else but variations of the *Arabian Nights*, sometimes rosy, sometimes black–inspired by reading the *Arabian Nights*, magical treatises, the *Bibliothèque orientale* of Herbelot, in an imaginative young English polyglot, "Voltairianized" at sixteen by Ferney's "old skeleton with carbuncle eyes": to see no more than this in them would amount to denying oneself the possibility of penetrating the depths into which Beckford led his first readers: Byron, Disraeli and Edgar Poe.'

knows how to speak of crimes gloriously; she compares him to a new Lucifer, she feels ripe for any criminal undertaking he may suggest, and miserable to have but a little victim (William Courtenay, 'Kitty', her five-years-old son) to sacrifice on his altar. It needs a good amount of naïveté to conclude with Guy Chapman[19] about the scandal, that 'the link is not, I believe, homosexual passion'! Chadourne seems closer to the real background of *Vathek* when he writes:[20]

*C'est donc bien dans les transes de voluptés sacrilèges que Vathek a jailli, l'oeil en flamme, de sa longue incubation, que le grand Hall égyptien de Splendens* [where the memorable orgy took place] *embaumé de vapeurs d'aloès s'est mué en Hall d'Eblis, que le dieu de cet empire souterrain s'est profilé avec la figure d'un jeune homme de vingt ans dont les traits nobles et réguliers semblaient avoir été flétris par des vapeurs malignes.*[21]

No wonder Byron called *Vathek* his Bible (as Oscar Wilde might have called Huysmans's *A rebours* his own Bible). And not only Byron's career, but even the career of Wilde is anticipated by the scandal centring on the trio Beckford–Louisa–William Courtenay. However the aristocracy in Beckford's time was still powerful enough to hush a scandal, and Beckford was only obliged to leave the country and suffer the destiny of the Wandering Jew. Henceforth his life took a less turbulent course, and his *Journal in Portugal and Spain for the years 1787–88*[22] is typical of

19. *Beckford*, London, Cape, 1937, p. 182 ff.

20. Op. cit., p. 53.

21. 'It was therefore from these sacrilegious and voluptuary trances that Vathek sprang, flaming eyed, from his long incubation; that the great Egyptian Hall of Splendens, balmy with the scent of aloes, became the Hall of Eblis; that the god of this subterranean empire became embodied as a young man of twenty, whose noble and regular features seemed to have been withered by the evil atmosphere.'

22. Edited with an Introduction and Notes by Boyd Alexander, London, Rupert Hart-Davis, 1954.

the eighteenth century in its vivacity and sense of intrigue. The background of a bigoted, pompous and decadent society, with debauched and tobacco-snuffing ecclesiastics, weak and demented sovereigns, angelically singing *castrati*, fireworks, chinoiseries, interminable ceremonies, sweetmeats of nuns, and ulcerous beggars, well might inspire an opera like Auden's and Stravinsky's *The Rake's Progress*. Against this background the *ci-devant* Lucifer Vathek softens into a figure of Watteau or Mozart, or – if we want a modern reference – of Ronald Firbank (indeed more than once that *Journal* calls to mind the *Eccentricities of Cardinal Pirelli*). Beckford had sublimated his passion for 'Kitty' into an adoration of Saint Anthony who is always represented either kneeling before, or hugging to his breast, the Infant Jesus. Portuguese music went straight to his heart with its plaintive and passionate cadences:

I went to the Martires – he writes on 26 November 1787 – to hear the famous Matins of Perez and the Dead Mass of Jommelli performed by all the principal musicians of the Royal Chapel, for the repose of the souls of their predecessors. Such august, such affecting music I never heard and perhaps may never hear again, for the flame of devout enthusiasm burns dim in almost every part of Europe and threatens total extinction in a very few years. As yet it glows at Lisbon and produced this day the most striking musical expression.

Also Beckford, for all his anticipations of Byron, Baudelaire and Wilde, remained one of the most striking expressions of something which, within a few years, would have become extinct in Europe. When, as an old man, he used to ride in the streets of Bath dressed in the style that had been in fashion when he had begun the building of Fonthill, with two grooms riding in front and one behind, and sometimes accompanied also by the dwarf, Piero, on a little grey pony, people would point him out as the relic of a fabulously remote age, the time of feudal aristocracy. He was an eccentric, like the Prince of Palagonia, who had peopled his villa at Bagheria with a crowd of quaint monsters of stone, and would pace the main street of Palermo – as Goethe saw him – solemnly, in court dress, well powdered and groomed, his hat under his arm, with elegant shoes whose buckles were studded with precious stones, preceded by a messenger carrying a silver salver to collect ransom-money for the Christians enslaved by the Saracens.

We are prepared to accept any improbability from *Vathek*, because it partakes of the nature of a fairy tale. We no more question the power of the Caliph's murderous eye than we would the capacity of angels to fly with a breast-bone ridiculously disproportionate to the magnitude of their wings. But Mary Shelley's *Frankenstein*, though it surpasses the other two Gothic stories in its capacity of stirring our sense of horror, has a fundamental weakness which seriously hampers the suspense of disbelief. In the fourth chapter we read that 'after days and nights of incredible labour and fatigue', the narrator has 'succeeded in discovering the cause of generation and life', nay more, he has become himself 'capable of bestowing animation upon lifeless matter'. He then addresses his friend thus:

I see by your eagerness, and the wonder and hope which your eyes express, my friend, that you expect to be informed of the secret with which I am acquainted; that cannot be: listen patiently until the end of my story, and you will easily perceive why I am reserved upon that subject. I will not lead you on, unguarded and ardent as I then was, to your destruction and infallible misery. Learn from me, if not by my precepts, at least by my example, how dangerous is the acquirement of knowledge.

Thus the manner of animating lifeless matter must be kept secret, but is the reader content with this blunt statement? Generally authors of pseudo-scientific novels try to lift the veil, be it only for a moment. So does M. P. Shiel in *The Purple Cloud*, a novel which appeared nearly a century later than Mrs Shelley's; so does his contemporary H. G. Wells, and so did Verne. In his study on '*Mary Shelley's Notes on Shelley's Poems and 'Frankenstein'*,[23] F. D. Fleck has called attention to 'Mary's continual emphasis upon Shelley's love of abstraction', and to the fact that '*Frankenstein* contains in an imaginative form her criticism of Shelley'. Certainly Frankenstein has many traits of young Shelley who also tried to pry into the hidden laws of Nature. The Shelleys had been reading *Vathek* in 1815 and they could not miss the hint at Vathek's 'insolent desire to penetrate the secrets of heaven'. The parallel passages from the novel and *Alastor* (1816), ll. 23–29, quoted by Fleck, seem indicative enough:

> I have made my bed
> In charnels and on coffins, where black death
> Keeps record of the trophies won from thee,
> Hoping to still these obstinate questionings
> Of thee and thine, by forcing some lone ghost
> Thy messenger, to render up the tale
> Of what we are.

Frankenstein also pursues his researches in churchyards (Chapter IV):

> Darkness had no effect upon my fancy; and a churchyard was to me merely the receptacle of bodies deprived of life, which, from being the seat of beauty and strength, had become food for the worm. Now I was led to examine the cause and progress of this decay, and forced to spend days and nights in vaults and charnel-houses. My attention was fixed upon every object the most insupportable to the delicacy of the human feelings. I saw how the fine form of man was degraded and wasted, I beheld the corruption of death succeed to the blossoming cheek of life, I saw how the worm inherited the wonders of the eye and brain . . . I pursued nature to her hiding-places. Who shall conceive the horrors of my secret toil, as I dabbled among the unhallowed damps of the grave, or tortured the living animal to

23. In *Studies in Romanticism*, VI, 4, Summer 1967.

animate the lifeless clay? My limbs now tremble and my eyes swim with the remembrance; but then a resistless, and almost frantic, impulse urged me forward, I seemed to have lost all soul of sensation but for this one pursuit. It was indeed but a passing trance, that only made me feel with renewed acuteness so soon as, the unnatural stimulus ceasing to operate, I had returned to my old habits. I collected bones from charnel-houses; and disturbed, with profane fingers, the tremendous secrets of the human frame. In a solitary chamber, or rather cell, at the top of the house, and separated from all the other apartments by a gallery and staircase, I kept my workshop of filthy creation: my eyeballs were starting from their sockets in attending to the details of my employment.

This is a mere expansion of Shelley's verse passage, but although Mrs Shelley has emphasized the Gothic horror of the quest, her grasp on reality is none the stronger. In the same way as Dickens, notwithstanding the wealth of adjectives at his command, in describing the London underworld never defines precisely the more repellent objects, but resorts to generic terms (such as: dirt, foul, impurity, filthy odours, etc.), Mrs Shelley uses words denoting the narrator's reaction to the materials of his experiments ('objects the most insupportable to the delicacy of the human feelings'), but never describes the objects themselves or the manner of the unholy operations.

The artificial creation of a human being had been the dream of centuries, but the problem was particularly alive in the eighteenth century and Goethe voiced it in the Homunculus in the second part of *Faust* which, however, was begun only in 1826, whereas *Frankenstein* was published in 1818. Sources have been pointed out,[24] in Godwin's novels, in Madame de Genlis's *Pygmalion et Galatée*, not to speak of *Paradise Lost*; Condillac may have

---

24. See Burton R. Pollin, *Philosophical and Literary Sources of 'Frankenstein'*, in *Comparative Literature*, XVII, no. 2, Spring 1966.

contributed his psychological sensationalism, Locke was meticulously read by Mrs Shelley through December 1816 and January 1817. Nobody, however, seems to have pointed out that a famous experiment in the creation of the artificial man had been tried in France. Jacques Vaucanson, who had constructed three famous automata, which had been shown throughout Europe and also in London (in 1742), a flute player, a drummer, and a digesting duck (*Canard digérateur*), is supposed to have been asked by Louis XV in 1739, whether he would be able to show in the same way the circulation of the blood. He then applied himself to '*construire une figure automate qui imitera dans ses mouvements les opérations animales, la circulation du sang, la respiration, la digestion, le jeu des muscles, tendons, nerfs, etc*'.[25] Vaucanson was not alone in his experiment; at the same time a physiocrat, François Quesnay, who had a no less keen interest in the problem of blood-circulation than in that of the circulation of wealth, a great minister, H. Jean-Baptiste Bertin, who was open to all curious inventions, and a surgeon, Claude-Nicolas Le Cat, pursued the same aim. Le Cat spoke of his own project at the inaugural session of the Rouen Académie des Sciences et Belles-Lettres, on 17 November 1744. The title of his Memoir runs: *Dissertation sur un homme artificiel dans lequel on verrait plusieurs phénomènes de l'homme vivant.* A contemporary report says that '*son automate aura respiration, circulation, quasi-digestion, secrétion et chile, coeur, poulmons, foye et vessie, et, Dieu nous le pardonne, tout ce qui s'ensuit. Mais il aura la fièvre, on le saignera, on le pur-*

---

25. 'construct an automated figure which would imitate in its movements the animal mechanisms, circulation of the blood, breathing, digestion, the play of muscles, tendons, nerves, etc.' *Procès-Verbal* of the Académie des Beaux-Arts at Lyon, 9 August 1741, reported in André Doyon and Lucien Liaigre, *Jacques Vaucanson, mécanicien de génie*, Presses Universitaires de France, 1966; p. 148.

*gera, et il ressemblera trop à un homme!'*[26] The report of the secretary of the Academy adds that the automaton would have even *'la parole même et l'articulation des mots, le tout par le moyen d'un nombre infini de grands et petits ressorts et de contrepoids'*.[27]

Jean-Baptiste Rodier, who frequented Vaucanson's workshop (*l'Hôtel de Mortagne*), maintains that in 1762 he saw there an automaton showing the blood-circulation. But trouble arose with the material of the conduits imitating the veins and arteries; tin proving unsatisfactory, someone thought of the recently discovered ductile properties of rubber, and a number of attempts were made to import this from Guyana in such a way that it would keep those properties; but it turned out that it was necessary to use rubber in its fresh state on the spot, and to this effect it was planned to construct the automaton there, but although the king himself had approved and ordered the expedition, the delays were such that Vaucanson became disgusted and the project came to nothing.

Attempts to reproduce the human voice were also made, a problem which in the seventeenth century had seemed almost sacrilegious. By the end of that century there spread throughout Germany a tale of Jews able to create *Golems*, or false likenesses of people. The famous Jesuit Anthanasius Kircher and others dreamed of harmonic machines capable of doing better than the speaking head attributed to Albertus Magnus (who by the way is mentioned among the books read by Frankenstein). A materialist philosopher, Julien de La Mettrie, in his *L'homme machine*

---

26. 'his automaton will have respiration, circulation, quasi-digestion, secretion and bile, heart, lungs, liver and bladder, and, God forgive us, everything that follows from that. But he will have fever, he will be bled and purged and be altogether too much like a man!'

27. 'even speech and the articulation of words, the whole made possible by an infinite number of large and small springs and balances'.

(Leyden, 1746) exhorted Vaucanson to construct a *parleur*, '*machine qui ne peut plus être regardée comme impossible surtout entre les mains d'un nouveau Prométhée*'.[28] And Jean Blanchet in his *Principes philosophiques* (1756) felt bold enough to indicate how to proceed for the construction of such an automaton, which would be capable '*de chanter, non seulement les airs les plus brillants, mais encore les plus beaux vers*'.[29] He concluded: '*Voilà un phénomène qui demanderait toute l' invention et l'industrie des Archimède, ou bien des Vaucanson, et qui étonnerait toute l'Europe sçavante.*'[30]

All these attempts seem rather to belong to the prehistory of cybernetics than to the sources of Mrs Shelley's Gothic novel. One wonders however whether those French precedents of the artificial man were at least mentioned in the conversation at Villa Diodati in 1816, when Polidori and Shelley talked about 'principles – whether man was to be thought merely an instrument', the primal source of life, Erasmus Darwin's theories, and galvanism, a discussion which may have given Mrs Shelley the idea of her novel. To be on the safe side, one should adopt Burton R. Pollin's view, that 'in the absence of further evidence it must be assumed that her tale first took the shape of her hideous dream, described in the preface, just before Shelley and Byron departed on their tour of Lake Leman, 23 June to 1 July'. We think, however, that the similarity of the *Frankenstein* theme to the attempts made in France to create an artificial man, may not be due to a mere coincidence; and we think also that the affinity of the theme of

28. 'A machine which can no longer be regarded as impossible especially in the hands of a new Prometheus'. See Doyon and Liaigre, op. cit., p. 164.

29. 'of singing not only the most brilliant tunes, but also the most beautiful verse'.

30. 'Here is a phenomenon which would demand all the invention and industry of Archimedes or the Vaucansons, and which would amaze all learned Europe.'

the innocent maiden accused of murdering a child, thanks to the infernal guile of the monster, to the fate of Sade's virtuous women cannot be coincidence either, the more so since the name of the innocent woman imprisoned, tried and executed, is none other than Justine.[31] Mrs Shelley's dream had been inspired by a passage she had read in Erasmus Darwin who, like the French scientists and makers of automata, was experimenting in the artificial creation of life. It is to be noticed that Walpole also claimed that a dream inspired his *The Castle of Otranto.*

There are in *Frankenstein* echoes of Coleridge's *Rime of the Ancient Mariner*,[32] witness the very appearance of the narrator ('his lustrous eyes dwell on me with all their melancholy sweetness', says Walton in the fourth preliminary letter), and the polar regions through which the last mad pursuit takes place; and certainly the image of the wounded deer in Chapter IX was inspired by William Cowper's famous passage (*The Task*, III, 108–20).[33] There are also anticipations of Poe's Imp of the Perverse ('Chance or rather the evil influence, the Angel of Destruction, which asserted omnipotent sway over me from the moment I turned my reluctant steps from my father's door – led me first to Mr Kempe, professor of natural philosophy'), and even of Ahab's pursuit of Moby Dick in Frankenstein's

31. However, the theme of the innocent accused of a murder must have become familiar to eighteenth-century people owing to Voltaire's intervention in the Calas case (1761).

32. Coleridge in his turn was influenced by Gothic fiction; there is a air of family relationship between *Vathek* and *Kubla Khan*, *The Castle of Otranto* and *Christabel.*

33. Echoes of contemporary motifs are present also in Mrs Shelley's other novel, *Valpurga, or the Life and Adventures of Castruccio, Prince of Lucca* (1823): Beatrice ends her days in the prison of the Inquisition (theme of the persecuted maiden), and Castruccio conforms to the type of Satanic hero of the *Vathek*-Byronic tradition: 'a majestic figure and a countenance beautiful but sad, tarnished by the expression of pride that animated it'.

relentless, Heaven-assigned chase of the monster. So that for the far-reaching implications of the main theme and for the grandiose scenery through which the mad chase takes place, Mrs Shelley's novel ranks as the greatest achievement of the Gothic school, notwithstanding its frequent clichés of phrasing and situation and the occasionally disarming naïveté. Because the way in which the monster acquires a remarkable degree of education, to the point of reading *Paradise Lost*, Plutarch's *Lives*, and the *Sorrows of Werther*, and of quoting Milton in his speeches ('Evil thenceforth became my good', 'It presented to me as exquisite and divine a retreat as Pandaemonium appeared to the daemons of hell after their suffering in the lake of fire', etc.), is a no less serious obstacle to the suspension of disbelief than the manner in which the monster is contrived by Frankenstein out of dead limbs.

There are in the novel all the elements of a good film, whatever one thinks of the one which was actually made; witness the very spectacular end, which reads like the script for a regular Hollywood finale:

He sprang from the cabin-window, as he said this, upon the ice-raft which lay close to the vessel. He was soon borne away by the waves and lost in darkness and distance.

Indeed, it was reserved for the film of our day to realize successfully effects[34] that the horror novelists tried to achieve, but crudely, so crudely indeed that they easily lent themselves to Jane Austen's and Thomas Love Peacock's satires. Can we refrain from smiling if we try with

34. Thus in the Polish film *Sister Joan of the Angels* we see fully realized the Radcliffe-inspired end of Stendhal's *Suora Scolastica* (*Chroniques italiennes*, II): '*Enfin il* [the Duke of Vargas] *arriva à la salle sombre dont nous avons parlé et qui était éclairée par quatre cierges placés sur un autel. Deux religieuses, jeunes encore, étaient couchées par terre et paraissaient mourir dans les convulsions du poison; trois autres, placées vingt pas plus loin, étaient aux genoux de leurs confesseurs. Le chanoine Cybo, assis sur un fauteuil placé contre l'autel, semblait impassible quoi-*

Dr Jane Lundblad[35] to recapitulate the principal traits of the tale of terror? An introductory story in order to produce an old manuscript where the happenings are written down, a Gothic castle forming a gloomy background with its secret corridors and labyrinthine network of subterranean passages, a mysterious crime frequently connected with illicit or incestuous love, and perpetrated by a person in holy orders, a villain (as a rule an Italian or a Spaniard) who has pledged himself to the devil, who finally hurls him into the abyss; ghosts, witches and sorcerers, nature conspiring to effects of terror and wonder, portraits endowed with a mysterious life, statues which suddenly are seen to bleed . . . all the paraphernalia and clichés which recur in the novels of the present volume and in other influential tales of terror (*The Monk; The Mysteries of Udolpho; Melmoth the Wanderer*, to mention only the chief ones) the effects of which were likely, we would imagine, to wear thin

---

*que fort pâle; deux grands jeunes gens, placés derrière lui, baissaient un peu la tête pour tâcher de ne pas voir les deux religieuses qui étaient au pied de l'autel et dont les longues robes de soie d'un vert foncé étaient agitées par des mouvements convulsifs.*' 'Finally he arrived in the gloomy chamber of which we have spoken, and which was lit by four candles placed on an altar. Two nuns, still young, were lying on the ground and seemed to be dying of convulsions from the poison; three others, twenty paces further on were at the knees of their confessors. The Canon Cybo, sitting in an armchair next to the altar, seemed unmoved though decidedly pale. Two young men behind him bowed their heads a little trying not to see the nuns who were at the foot of the altar and whose long green silk robes were agitated by convulsive movements.' The tale of terror, no less than historical painting as it was practised during the nineteenth century, has found its best medium in the film.

35. *Nathaniel Hawthorne and the Tradition of Gothic Romance*, Upsala, A.–B. Lundequistska Bokhandeln, Cambridge, Mass., Harvard University Press, 1946 (Essays and Studies on American Language and Literature ed. by S. B. Liljegren, IV).

before long, owing to their mechanical repetition. Do not we seem to catch Beckford himself smiling when he makes Carathis declare: 'I myself have a great desire to . . . visit the subterranean palace, which no doubt contains whatever can interest persons like us; there is nothing so pleasing as retiring to caverns; my taste for dead bodies and every thing like mummy is decided'?

The miracle is, instead, that the spell of such bugbears lasted so long. Perhaps because, as Charles Lamb remarked,[36] 'Gorgons, and Hydras, and Chimaeras – dire stories of Celaeno and the Harpies – may reproduce themselves in the brain of superstition – but they were there before. They are transcripts, types – the archetypes are in us, and eternal.' This is why the vampire still fascinates the cinema audience. Although the literary quality of the tales of terror is not very high, we must agree with Dr Lundblad that the Gothic romance grew into one of the most powerful currents in the general literature of the nineteenth century. Without exaggeration, the assertion may be made that no form of novel-writing has ever been as productive as the novel of terror and wonder. Its influence can be traced in E. T. A. Hoffmann, Tieck, La Motte-Fouqué, Spiess, Nodier, Gautier, the young Balzac, Brockden Brown, Poe, Hawthorne, and even Manzoni. Balzac, Baudelaire and Rossetti, among others, were admirers of Maturin who in *Melmoth the Wanderer* (1820) produced the synthesis of all the themes of the 'tales of terror' school, and in one of its episodes, a long story of a forced monastic vow derived from Diderot's *La religieuse*, showed a subtlety of penetration into the terrors of the soul such as is elsewhere only found in Poe.

Like the novels of the Marquis de Sade with which, as we have said, they had curious affinities, the Gothic tales were a powerful underground current (not, however, so concealed) in nineteenth-century fiction.

MARIO PRAZ

---

36. 'Witches, and Other Night-Fears', in *The Essays of Elia*.

# SUGGESTED FURTHER READING

### BOOKS ON THE INDIVIDUAL AUTHORS

Walpole's Selected and Collected Letters are edited by W. S. Lewis. The most recent books on Beckford are *Beckford* by G. Chapman (1952) and *The Caliph of Fonthill* by H. A. N. Brockman (1956). Mary Shelley's *Letters* (1944) and *Journal* (1947) are edited by F. L. Jones; other information is to be found in *Shelley, Godwin and their Circle* (1951) by N. H. Brailsford and *Child of Light* (1951) by Muriel Spark.

### GENERAL CRITICAL WORKS

The relevant Volumes in the *Oxford History of English Literature* are Volume 9 (1789–1815) by W. L. Renwick (1963), and Volume 10 (1815–32) by Ian Jack (1963); they contain full bibliographies. The Gothic Novel genre is examined by E. Birkhead in *The Tale of Terror* (1921); J. M. S. Tomkins places the Gothic Novel in its literary context in *The Popular Novel in England 1770–1800* (1932); and Louis James examines its Early Victorian decadence in '*Fiction for the Working Man 1830–50*' (1963). The European context is examined by Mario Praz in *The Romantic Agony* (1933, Fontana Paperback 1960), and Kenneth Clark discusses Strawberry Hill and Fonthill Abbey in *The Gothic Revival* (1928, Pelican Books 1964).

# A NOTE ON THE TEXTS

THIS text of *The Castle of Otranto*, which was first published in 1765, is that in *The Works of Horatio Walpole, Earl of Orford*, Volume 2, of 1798; it contains the author's final revisions. *Vathek* was written in French and first published in English in Samuel Henley's translation of 1786; this text is the fourth revised and corrected edition of that translation, of 1823. The text of *Frankenstein*, which was first published in 1818, is that of 1831, issued as the ninth in a series of Standard Novels and published by Colburn and Bentley; it contains the author's final revisions.

The heavy punctuation of *Vathek* and *Frankenstein* has frequently been omitted or lightened, and unnecessary dashes have been left out of *Vathek*.

P. F.

Facsimile of the title page of the first edition
of *The Castle of Otranto*

# THE
# CASTLE of OTRANTO,
## A
# STORY.

Tranſlated by

WILLIAM MARSHAL, Gent.

From the Original ITALIAN of

ONUPHRIO MURALTO,

CANON of the Church of St. NICHOLAS
at OTRANTO.

LONDON:
Printed for THO. LOWNDS in Fleet-Street.
MDCCLXV.

# PREFACE TO THE FIRST EDITION

THE following work was found in the library of an ancient catholic family in the north of England. It was printed at Naples, in the black letter, in the year 1529. How much sooner it was written does not appear. The principal incidents are such as were believed in the darkest ages of christianity; but the language and conduct have nothing that savours of barbarism. The style is the purest Italian. If the story was written near the time when it is supposed to have happened, it must have been between 1095, the æra of the first crusade, and 1243, the date of the last, or not long afterwards. There is no other circumstance in the work that can lead us to guess at the period in which the scene is laid: the names of the actors are evidently fictitious, and probably disguised on purpose: yet the Spanish names of the domestics seem to indicate that this work was not composed until the establishment of the Arragonian kings in Naples had made Spanish appellations familiar in that country. The beauty of the diction, and the zeal of the author, [moderated however by singular judgment] concur to make me think that the date of the composition was little antecedent to that of the impression. Letters were then in their most flourishing state in Italy, and contributed to dispel the empire of superstition, at that time so forcibly attacked by the reformers. It is not unlikely that an artful priest might endeavour to turn their own arms on the innovators; and might avail himself of his abilities as an author to confirm the populace in their ancient errors and superstitions. If this was his view, he has certainly acted with signal address. Such a work as the following would enslave a hundred vulgar minds beyond half the books of controversy that have been written from the days of Luther to the present hour.

The solution of the author's motives is however offered as a mere conjecture. Whatever his views were, or whatever effects the execution of them might have, his work can only be laid before the public at present as a matter of entertainment. Even as such, some apology for it is necessary. Miracles, visions, necromancy, dreams, and other preternatural events, are exploded now even from romances. That was not the case when our author wrote; much less when the story itself is supposed to have happened. Belief in every kind of prodigy was so established in those dark ages, that an author would not be faithful to the *manners* of the times who should omit all mention of them. He is not bound to believe them himself, but he must represent his actors as believing them.

If this *air* of the *miraculous* is excused, the reader will find nothing else unworthy of his perusal. Allow the possibility of the facts, and all the actors comport themselves as persons would do in their situation. There is no bombast, no similies, flowers, digressions, or unnecessary descriptions. Every thing tends directly to the catastrophe. Never is the reader's attention relaxed. The rules of the drama are almost observed throughout the conduct of the piece. The characters are well drawn, and still better maintained. Terror, the author's principal engine, prevents the story from ever languishing; and it is so often contrasted by pity, that the mind is kept up in a constant vicissitude of interesting passions.

Some persons may perhaps think the characters of the domestics too little serious for the general cast of the story; but besides their opposition to the principal personages, the art of the author is very observable in his conduct of the subalterns. They discover many passages essential to the story, which could not well be brought to light but by their *naïveté* and simplicity: in particular, the womanish terror and foibles of Bianca, in the last chapter, conduce essentially towards advancing the catastrophe.

It is natural for a translator to be prejudiced in favour of his adopted work. More impartial readers may not be so much struck with the beauties of this piece as I was. Yet I am not blind to my author's defects. I could wish he had grounded his plan on a more useful moral than this; that *the sins of fathers are visited on their children to the third and fourth generation.* I doubt whether in his time, any more than at present, ambition curbed its appetite of dominion from the dread of so remote a punishment. And yet this moral is weakened by that less direct insinuation, that even such anathema may be diverted by devotion to saint Nicholas. Here the interest of the monk plainly gets the better of the judgment of the author. However, with all its faults, I have no doubt but the English reader will be pleased with a sight of this performance. The piety that reigns throughout, the lessons of virtue that are inculcated, and the rigid purity of the sentiments, exempt this work from the censure to which romances are but too liable. Should it meet with the success I hope for, I may be encouraged to re-print the original Italian, though it will tend to depreciate my own labour. Our language falls far short of the charms of the Italian, both for variety and harmony. The latter is peculiarly excellent for simple narrative. It is difficult in English *to relate* without falling too low or rising too high; a fault obviously occasioned by the little care taken to speak pure language in common conversation. Every Italian or Frenchman of any rank piques himself on speaking his own tongue correctly and with choice. I cannot flatter myself with having done justice to my author in this respect; his style is as elegant as his conduct of the passions is masterly. It is pity that he did not apply his talents to what they were evidently proper for, the theatre.

I will detain the reader no longer but to make one short

remark. Though the machinery is invention, and the names of the actors imaginary, I cannot but believe that the groundwork of the story is founded on truth. The scene is undoubtedly laid in some real castle. The author seems frequently, without design, to describe particular parts. *The chamber*, says he, *on the right hand; the door on the left hand; the distance from the chapel to Conrad's apartment*: these and other passages are strong presumptions that the author had some certain building in his eye. Curious persons, who have leisure to employ in such researches, may possibly discover in the Italian writers the foundation on which our author has built. If a catastrophe, at all resembling that which he described, is believed to have given rise to this work, it will contribute to interest the reader, and will make *The Castle of Otranto* a still more moving story.

# PREFACE TO THE SECOND EDITION

THE favourable manner in which this little piece has been received by the public, calls upon the author to explain the grounds on which he composed it. But before he opens those motives, it is fit that he should ask pardon of his readers for having offered his work to them under the borrowed personage of a translator. As diffidence of his own abilities, and the novelty of the attempt, were his sole inducements to assume that disguise, he flatters himself he shall appear excusable. He resigned his performance to the impartial judgment of the public; determined to let it perish in obscurity, if disapproved; nor meaning to avow such a trifle, unless better judges should pronounce that he might own it without a blush.

It was an attempt to blend the two kinds of romance, the ancient and the modern. In the former all was imagination and improbability: in the latter, nature is always intended to be, and sometimes has been, copied with success. Invention has not been wanting; but the great resources of fancy have been dammed up, by a strict adherence to common life. But if in the latter species Nature has cramped imagination, she did but take her revenge, having been totally excluded from old romances. The actions, sentiments, conversations, of the heroes and heroines of ancient days were as unnatural as the machines employed to put them in motion.

The author of the following pages thought it possible to reconcile the two kinds. Desirous of leaving the powers of fancy at liberty to expatiate through the boundless realms of invention, and thence of creating more interesting situations, he wished to conduct the mortal agents in his drama according to the rules of probability; in short, to make them think, speak and act, as it might be supposed mere men and women would do in extraordinary positions. He had observed, that in all inspired writings, the personages under the dispensation of miracles, and witnesses to the most stupendous phoenomena, never lose sight of their human character: whereas in the productions of romantic story, an improbable event never fails to be attended by an absurd dialogue. The actors seem to lose their senses the moment the laws of nature have lost their tone. As the public have applauded the attempt, the author must not say he was entirely unequal to the task he had undertaken: yet if the new route he has struck out shall have paved a road for men of brighter talents, he shall own with pleasure and modesty, that he was sensible the plan was capable of receiving greater embellishments than his imagination or conduct of the passions could bestow on it.

With regard to the deportment of the domestics, on which I have touched in the former preface, I will beg leave to add a few words. The simplicity of their behaviour, almost tending to excite smiles, which at first seem not consonant to the serious cast of the work, appeared to me not only not improper, but was marked designedly in that manner. My rule was nature. However grave, important, or even melancholy, the sensations of princes and heroes may be, they do not stamp the same affections on their domestics: at least the latter do not, or should not be made to express their passions in the same dignified tone. In my humble opinion, the contrast between the sublime of the one, and the *naïveté* of the other, sets the pathetic of the former in a stronger light. The very impatience which a reader feels, while delayed by the coarse pleasantries of vulgar actors from arriving at the knowledge of the important catastrophe he expects, perhaps heightens, certainly proves that he has been artfully interested in, the depending event. But I had higher authority than my own opinion for this conduct. That great master of nature, Shakespeare, was the model I copied. Let me ask if his tragedies of Hamlet and Julius Caesar would not lose a considerable share of their spirit and wonderful beauties, if the humour of the grave-diggers, the fooleries of Polonius, and the clumsy jests of the Roman citizens were omitted, or vested in heroics? Is not the eloquence of Antony, the nobler and affectedly-unaffected oration of Brutus, artificially exalted by the rude bursts of nature from the mouths of their auditors? These touches remind one of the Grecian sculptor, who, to convey the idea of a Colossus within the dimensions of a seal, inserted a little boy measuring his thumb.

No, says Voltaire in his edition of Corneille, this mixture of buffoonery and solemnity is intolerable – Voltaire is a genius* – but not of Shakespeare's magnitude. Without recurring to disputable authority, I appeal from Voltaire to himself. I shall not avail myself of his former encomiums

---

*The following remark is foreign to the present question, yet excusable in an Englishman, who is willing to think that the severe criticisms of so masterly a writer as Voltaire on our immortal countryman, may have been the effusions of wit and precipitation, rather than the result of judgement and attention. May not the critic's skill in the force and powers of our language have been as incorrect and incompetent as his knowledge of our history? Of the latter his own pen has dropped glaring evidence. In his preface to Thomas Corneille's Earl of Essex, monsieur de Voltaire allows that the truth of history has been grossly perverted in that piece. In excuse he pleads, that when Corneille wrote, the noblesse of France were much unread in English story; but now, says the commentator, that they study it, such misrepresentation would not be suffered— Yet forgetting that the period of ignorance is lapsed, and that it is not very necessary to instruct the knowing, he undertakes from the overflowing of his own reading to give the nobility of his own country a detail of queen Elizabeth's favourites – of whom, says he, Robert Dudley was the first, and the earl of Leicester the second— Could one have believed that it could be necessary to inform monsieur de Voltaire himself, that Robert Dudley and the earl of Leicester were the same person?

on our mighty poet; though the French critic has twice translated the same speech in Hamlet, some years ago in admiration, latterly in derision; and I am sorry to find that his judgement grows weaker, when it ought to be farther matured. But I shall make use of his own words, delivered on the general topic of the theatre, when he was neither thinking to recommend or decry Shakespeare's practice; consequently at a moment when Voltaire was impartial. In the preface to his Enfant prodigue,[1] that exquisite piece of which I declare my admiration, and which, should I live twenty years longer, I trust I should never attempt to ridicule, he has these words, speaking of comedy, [but equally applicable to tragedy, if tragedy is, as surely it ought to be, a picture of human life; nor can I conceive why occasional pleasantry ought more to be banished from the tragic scene, than pathetic seriousness from the comic] *On y voit un melange de serieux et de plaisanterie, de comique et de touchant*; souvent même une seule avanture *produit tous ces contrastes. Rien n'est si commun qu'une maison dans laquelle* un pere gronde, une fille occupée de sa passion pleure; *le fils se moque des deux, et quelques parens prennent part differemment à la scene, &c. Nous n'inferons pas de là que toute comedie doive avoir des scenes de bouffonnerie et des scenes attendrissantes: il y a beaucoup de tres bonnes pieces où il ne regne que de la gayeté; d'autres toutes serieuses; d'autres melangées: d'autres où l'attendrissement va jusques aux larmes*: il ne faut donner l'exclusion à aucun genre: *et si l'on me demandoit, quel genre est le meilleur, je repondrois, celui qui est le mieux traité.*[2] Surely if a comedy may be *toute serieuse,*[3] tragedy may now and then, soberly, be indulged in a smile. Who shall proscribe it? Shall the critic, who in self-defence declares that *no kind* ought to be excluded from comedy, give laws to Shakespeare?

I am aware that the preface from whence I have quoted these passages does not stand in monsieur de Voltaire's name, but in that of his editor; yet who doubts that the editor and author were the same person? Or where is the editor, who has so happily possessed himself of his author's style and brilliant ease of argument? These passages were indubitably the genuine sentiments of that great writer. In his epistle to Maffei. prefixed to his Merope, he delivers almost the same opinion, though I doubt with a little irony. I will repeat his words, and then give my reason for quoting them. After translating a passage in Maffei's Merope, monsieur de Voltaire adds, *Tous ces traits sont naïfs: tout y est convenable à ceux que vous introduisez sur la scene*, et aux mœurs que vous leur donnez. *Ces familiarités naturelles eussent été, à ce que je crois, bien reçues dans Athenes; mais Paris et notre parterre veulent une autre espece de simplicité.*[4] I doubt, I say, whether there is not a grain of sneer in this and other passages of that epistle; yet the force of truth is not damaged by being tinged with ridicule. Maffei was to represent a Grecian story: surely the Athenians were as competent judges of Grecian manners, and of the propriety of introducing them, as the *parterre*[5] of Paris. On the contrary, says Voltaire [and I cannot but admire his reasoning] there were but ten thousand citizens at Athens, and Paris has near eight hundred thousand inhabitants, among whom one may reckon thirty thousand judges of dramatic works. – Indeed! – But allowing so numerous a tribunal, I believe this is the only instance in which it was ever pretended that thirty thousand persons, living near two thousand years after the æra in question, were, upon the mere face of the poll, declared better judges than the Grecians themselves of what ought to be the manners of a tragedy written on a Grecian story.

I will not enter into a discussion of the *espece de simplicité*,[6] which the *parterre* of Paris demands, nor of the shackles with which *the thirty thousand judges* have cramped their poetry, the chief merit of which, as I gather from repeated passages in The New Commentary on Corneille, consists in vaulting in spite of those fetters; a merit which, if true, would reduce poetry from the lofty effort of imagination, to a puerile and most contemptible labour –

*difficiles nugæ* [7] with a witness! I cannot help however mentioning a couplet, which to my English ears always sounded as the flattest and most trifling instance of circumstantial propriety; but which Voltaire, who has dealt so severely with nine parts in ten of Corneille's works, has singled out to defend in Racine;

*De son appartement cette porte est prochaine,*
*Et cette autre conduit dans celui de la* reine.

In English,

*To* Cæsar's *closet through this door you come,*
*And t'other leads to the queen's drawing-room.*

Unhappy Shakespeare! hadst thou made Rosencrans inform his compeer Guildenstern of the ichnography of the palace of Copenhagen, instead of presenting us with a moral dialogue between the prince of Denmark and the grave-digger, the illuminated pit of Paris would have been instructed a *second time* to adore thy talents.

The result of all I have said, is to shelter my own daring under the cannon of the brightest genius this country, at least, has produced. I might have pleaded, that having created a new species of romance, I was at liberty to lay down what rules I thought fit for the conduct of it: but I should be more proud of having imitated, however faintly, weakly, and at a distance, so masterly a pattern, than to enjoy the entire merit of invention, unless I could have marked my work with genius as well as with originality. Such as it is, the public have honoured it sufficiently, whatever rank their suffrages allot to it.

# SONNET

## TO THE RIGHT HONOURABLE

## LADY MARY COKE

The gentle maid, whose hapless tale
These melancholy pages speak;
Say, gracious lady, shall she fail
To draw the tear adown thy cheek?

No; never was thy pitying breast
Insensible to human woes;
Tender, though firm, it melts distrest
For weaknesses it never knows.

Oh! guard the marvels I relate
Of fell ambition scourg'd by fate,
From reason's peevish blame:
Blest with thy smile, my dauntless fail
I dare expand to fancy's gale,
For sure thy smiles are fame.

H. W.

# CHAPTER 1

Manfred, prince of Otranto, had one son and one daughter: the latter, a most beautiful virgin, aged eighteen, was called Matilda. Conrad, the son, was three years younger, a homely youth, sickly, and of no promising disposition; yet he was the darling of his father, who never showed any symptoms of affection to Matilda. Manfred had contracted a marriage for his son with the marquis of Vicenza's daughter, Isabella; and she had already been delivered by her guardians into the hands of Manfred, that he might celebrate the wedding as soon as Conrad's infirm state of health would permit. Manfred's impatience for their ceremonial was remarked by his family and neighbours. The former, indeed, apprehending the severity of their prince's disposition, did not dare to utter their surmises on this precipitation. Hippolita, his wife, an amiable lady, did sometimes venture to represent the danger of marrying their only son so early, considering his great youth, and greater infirmities; but she never received any other answer than reflections on her own sterility, who had given him but one heir. His tenants and subjects were less cautious in their discourses: they attributed this hasty wedding to the prince's dread of seeing accomplished an ancient prophecy, which was said to have pronounced, *That the castle and lordship of Otranto should pass from the present family, whenever the real owner should be grown too large to inhabit it*. It was difficult to make any sense of this prophecy; and still less easy to conceive what it had to do with the marriage in question. Yet these mysteries, or contradictions, did not make the populace adhere the less to their opinion.

Young Conrad's birth-day was fixed for his espousals.

The company was assembled in the chapel of the castle, and every thing ready for beginning the divine office, when Conrad himself was missing. Manfred, impatient of the least delay, and who had not observed his son retire, dispatched one of his attendants to summon the young prince. The servant, who had not staid long enough to have crossed the court to Conrad's apartment, came running back breathless, in a frantic manner, his eyes staring, and foaming at the mouth. He said nothing, but pointed to the court. The company were struck with terror and amazement. The princess Hippolita, without knowing what was the matter, but anxious for her son, swooned away. Manfred, less apprehensive than enraged at the procrastination of the nuptials, and at the folly of his domestic, asked imperiously, what was the matter? The fellow made no answer, but continued pointing towards the courtyard; and at last, after repeated questions put to him, cried out, Oh, the helmet! the helmet! In the mean time some of the company had run into the court, from whence was heard a confused noise of shrieks, horror, and surprise. Manfred, who began to be alarmed at not seeing his son, went himself to get information of what occasioned this strange confusion. Matilda remained endeavouring to assist her mother, and Isabella staid for the same purpose, and to avoid showing any impatience for the bridegroom, for whom, in truth, she had conceived little affection.

The first thing that struck Manfred's eyes was a group of his servants endeavouring to raise something that appeared to him a mountain of sable plumes. He gazed without believing his sight. What are ye doing? cried Manfred, wrathfully: Where is my son? A volley of voices replied, Oh, my lord! the prince! the prince! the helmet! the helmet! Shocked with these lamentable sounds, and dreading he knew not what, he advanced hastily – But what a sight for a father's eyes! – He beheld his child dashed to pieces, and almost buried under an enormous helmet, an hundred times more large than any casque ever made for human being, and shaded with a proportionable quantity of black feathers.

The horror of the spectacle, the ignorance of all around how this misfortune happened, and above all, the tremendous phænomenon before him, took away the prince's speech. Yet his silence lasted longer than even grief could occasion. He fixed his eyes on what he wished in vain to believe a vision; and seemed less attentive to his loss, than buried in meditation on the stupendous object that had occasioned it. He touched, he examined the fatal casque; nor could even the bleeding mangled remains of the young prince divert the eyes of Manfred from the portent before him. All who had known his partial fondness for young Conrad, were as much surprised at their prince's insensibility, as thunderstruck themselves at the miracle of the helmet. They conveyed the disfigured corse into the hall, without receiving the least direction from Manfred. As little was he attentive to the ladies who remained in the chapel: on the contrary, without mentioning the unhappy princesses his wife and daughter, the first sounds that dropped from Manfred's lips were, Take care of the lady Isabella.

The domestics, without observing the singularity of this direction, were guided by their affection to their mistress to consider it as peculiarly addressed to her situation, and flew to her assistance. They conveyed her to her chamber more dead than alive, and indifferent to all the strange circumstances she heard, except the death of her son. Matilda, who doted on her mother, smothered her own grief and amazement, and thought of nothing but assisting and comforting her afflicted parent. Isabella, who had been treated by Hippolita like a daughter, and who returned that tenderness with equal duty and affection, was scarce less assiduous about the princess; at the same time endeavouring to partake and lessen the weight of sorrow which she saw Matilda strove to suppress, for whom she had conceived the warmest sympathy of friendship. Yet her own situation could not help finding its place in her thoughts. She felt no concern for the death of young Conrad, except commiseration; and she was not sorry to be delivered from a marriage which had promised her little felicity, either from her destined bridegroom, or from the severe temper of Manfred, who, though he had distinguished her by great indulgence, had imprinted her mind with terror, from his causeless rigour to such amiable princesses as Hippolita and Matilda.

While the ladies were conveying the wretched mother to her bed, Manfred remained in the court, gazing on the ominous casque, and regardless of the crowd which the strangeness of the event had now assembled round him. The few words he articulated tended solely to enquiries, whether any man knew from whence it could have come? Nobody could give him the least information. However, as it seemed to be the sole object of his curiosity, it soon became so to the rest of the spectators, whose conjectures were as absurd and improbable as the catastrophe itself was unprecedented. In the midst of their senseless guesses a young peasant, whom rumour had drawn thither from a neighbouring village, observed that the miraculous helmet was exactly like that on the figure in black marble of Alfonso the Good, one of their former princes, in the church of St Nicholas. Villain! What sayest thou? cried Manfred, starting from his trance in a tempest of rage, and seizing the young man by the collar: How darest thou utter such treason? Thy life shall pay for it. The spectators, who as little comprehended the cause of the prince's fury as all the rest they had seen, were at a loss to unravel this new circumstance. The young peasant himself was still more astonished, not conceiving how he had offended the prince: yet recollecting himself, with a mixture of grace and humility, he disengaged himself from Manfred's gripe, and then, with an obeisance which discovered more jealousy of innocence, than dismay, he asked with respect, of what he was guilty! Manfred, more enraged at the vigour, however decently exerted, with which the young man had shaken off his hold, than appeased by his submission, ordered his attendants to seize him, and, if he had not been withheld by his friends whom he had invited to the nuptials, would have poignarded the peasant in their arms.

During this altercation some of the vulgar spectators had run to the great church which stood near the castle, and came back open-mouthed, declaring the helmet was missing from Alfonso's statue. Manfred, at this news, grew perfectly frantic; and, as if he sought a subject on which to vent the tempest within him, he rushed again on the young peasant, crying, Villain! monster! sorcerer! 'tis thou hast slain my son! The mob, who wanted some object within the scope of their capacities on whom they might discharge their bewildered reasonings, caught the words from the mouth of their lord, and re-echoed, Ay, ay, 'tis he: he has stolen the helmet from good Alfonso's tomb, and dashed out the brains of our young prince with it:—never reflecting how enormous the disproportion was between the marble helmet that had been in the church, and that of steel before their eyes; nor how impossible it was for a youth, seemingly not twenty, to wield a piece of armour of so prodigious a weight.

The folly of these ejaculations brought Manfred to himself: yet whether provoked at the peasant having observed the resemblance between the two helmets, and thereby led to the farther discovery of the absence of that in the church; or wishing to bury any fresh rumour under so impertinent a supposition; he gravely pronounced that the young man was certainly a necromancer, and that till the church could take cognizance of the affair, he would have the magician, whom they had thus detected, kept prisoner under the helmet itself, which he ordered his attendants to raise, and place the young man under it; declaring he should be kept there without food, with which his own infernal art might furnish him.

It was in vain for the youth to represent against this preposterous sentence: in vain did Manfred's friends endeavour to divert him from this savage and ill-grounded resolution. The generality were charmed with their lord's decision, which to their apprehensions carried great appearance of justice, as the magician was to be punished by the very instrument with which he had offended: nor were they struck with the least compunction at the probability of the youth being starved, for they firmly believed that by his diabolical skill he could easily supply himself with nutriment.

Manfred thus saw his commands even cheerfully obeyed; and appointing a guard with strict orders to prevent any food being conveyed to the prisoner, he dismissed his friends and attendants, and retired to his own chamber, after locking the gates of the castle, in which he suffered none but his domestics to remain.

In the mean time, the care and zeal of the young ladies had brought the princess Hippolita to herself, who amidst the transports of her own sorrow frequently demanded news of her lord, would have dismissed her attendants to watch over him, and at last enjoined Matilda to leave her, and visit and comfort her father. Matilda, who wanted no affectionate duty to Manfred, though she trembled at his austerity, obeyed the orders of Hippolita, whom she tenderly recommended to Isabella; and enquiring of the domestics for her father, was informed that he was retired to his chamber, and had commanded that nobody should have admittance to him. Concluding that he was immersed in sorrow for the death of her brother, and fearing to renew his tears by the sight of his sole remaining child, she hesitated whether she should break in upon his affliction; yet solicitude for him, backed by the commands of her mother, encouraged her to venture disobeying the orders he had given; a fault she had never been guilty of before. The gentle timidity of her nature made her pause for some minutes at his door. She heard him traverse his chamber backwards and forwards with disordered steps; a mood which increased her apprehensions. She was however just going to beg admittance, when Manfred suddenly opened the door; and as it was now twilight, concurring with the disorder of his mind, he did not distinguish the person, but asked angrily who it was? Matilda replied trembling, My dearest father, it is I, your daughter. Manfred, stepping back hastily, cried, Begone, I do not want a daughter; and, flinging back abruptly, clapped the door against the terrified Matilda.

She was too well acquainted with her father's impetuosity to venture a second intrusion. When she had a little recovered the shock of so bitter a reception, she wiped away her tears, to prevent the additional stab that the knowledge of it would give to Hippolita, who questioned her in the most anxious terms of the health of Manfred, and how he bore his loss. Matilda assured her he was well, and supported his misfortune with manly fortitude. But will he not let me see him? said Hippolita mournfully: Will he not permit me to blend my tears with his, and shed a mother's sorrows in the bosom of her lord? Or do you deceive me, Matilda? I know how Manfred doted on his son: Is not the stroke too heavy for him? Has he not sunk under it? – You do not answer me – Alas, I dread the worst! – Raise me, my maidens: I will, I will see my lord. Bear me to him instantly; he is dearer to me even than my children. Matilda made signs to Isabella to prevent Hippolita's rising; and both these lovely young women were using their gentle violence to stop and calm the princess, when a servant on the part of Manfred arrived, and told Isabella that his lord demanded to speak with her.

With me! cried Isabella. Go, said Hippolita, relieved by a message from her lord: Manfred cannot support the sight of his own family. He thinks you less disordered than we are, and dreads the shock of my grief. Console him, dear Isabella, and tell him I will smother my own anguish rather than add to his.

It was now evening; the servant who conducted Isabella bore a torch before her. When they came to Manfred, who was walking impatiently about the gallery, he started and said hastily, Take away that light, and begone. Then shutting the door impetuously, he flung himself upon a bench against the wall, and bade Isabella sit by him. She obeyed trembling. I sent for you, lady, said he,—and then stopped under great appearance of confusion. My lord! – Yes, I sent for you on a matter of great moment, resumed he:—Dry your tears, young lady – you have lost your bridegroom: – yes, cruel fate, and I have lost the hopes of my race! – But Conrad was not worthy of your beauty.—How! my lord, said Isabella; sure you do not suspect me of not feeling the concern I ought? My duty and affection would have always—Think no more of him, interrupted Manfred; he was a sickly puny child, and heaven has perhaps taken him away that I might not trust the honours of my house on so frail a foundation. The line of Manfred calls for numerous supports. My foolish fondness for that boy blinded the eyes of my prudence – but it is better as it is. I hope in a few years to have reason to rejoice at the death of Conrad.

Words cannot paint the astonishment of Isabella. At first she apprehended that grief had disordered Manfred's understanding. Her next thought suggested that this strange discourse was designed to ensnare her: she feared that Manfred had perceived her indifference for his son: and in consequence of that idea she replied, Good my lord, do not doubt my tenderness; my heart would have accompanied my hand. Conrad would have engrossed all my care; and wherever fate shall dispose of me, I shall always cherish his memory, and regard your highness and the virtuous Hippolita as my parents. Curse on Hippolita! cried Manfred: forget her from this moment, as I do. In short, lady, you have missed a husband undeserving of your charms: they shall now be better disposed of. Instead of a sickly boy, you shall have a husband in the prime of his age, who will know how to value your beauties, and who may expect a numerous offspring. Alas, my lord, said Isabella, my mind is too sadly engrossed by the recent catastrophe in your family to think of another marriage. If ever my father returns, and it shall be his pleasure, I shall obey, as I did when I consented to give my hand to your son: but until his return permit me to remain under your hospitable roof, and employ the melancholy hours in assuaging yours, Hippolita's, and the fair Matilda's affliction.

I desired you once before, said Manfred angrily, not to name that woman; from this hour she must be a stranger to you, as she must be to me: – in short, Isabella, since I cannot give you my son, I offer you myself—Heavens! cried Isabella, waking from her delusion, what do I hear! You, my lord! You! My father in law! the father of Conrad! the husband of the virtuous and tender Hippolita!—I tell you, said Manfred imperiously, Hippolita is no longer my wife; I divorce her from this hour. Too long has she cursed me by her unfruitfulness: my fate depends on having sons, – and this night I trust will give a new date to my hopes. At those words he seized the cold hand of Isabella, who was half-dead with fright and horror. She shrieked, and started from him. Manfred rose to pursue her; when the moon, which was now up, and gleamed in at the opposite casement, presented to his sight the plumes of the fatal helmet, which rose to the height of the windows, waving backwards and forwards in a tempestuous manner, and accompanied with a hollow and rustling sound. Isabella, who gathered courage from her situation, and who dreaded nothing so much as Manfred's pursuit of his declaration, cried, Look, my lord! see heaven itself declares against your impious intentions!—Heaven nor hell shall impede my designs, said Manfred, advancing again to seize the princess. At that instant the portrait of his grandfather, which hung over the bench where they had been sitting, uttered a deep sigh and heaved its breast. Isabella, whose back was turned to the picture, saw not the motion, nor knew whence the sound came, but started and said, Hark my lord! what sound was that? and at the same time made towards the door. Manfred, distracted between the flight of Isabella, who had now reached the stairs, and his inability to keep his eyes from the picture, which began to move, had however advanced some steps after her, still looking backwards on the portrait, when he saw it quit its pannel, and descend on the floor with a grave and melancholy air. Do I dream? cried Manfred returning, or are the devils themselves in league against me? Speak, infernal spectre! Or, if thou art my grand-sire, why dost thou too conspire against thy wretched descendant, who too dearly pays for—Ere he could finish the sentence the vision sighed again, and made a sign to Manfred to follow him. Lead on! cried Manfred; I will follow thee to the gulph of perdition. The spectre marched sedately, but dejected, to the end of the gallery, and turned into a chamber on the right hand. Manfred accompanied him at a little distance, full of anxiety and horror, but resolved. As he would have entered the chamber, the door was clapped-to with violence by an invisible hand. The prince, collecting courage from this delay, would have forcibly burst open the door with his foot, but found that it resisted his utmost efforts. Since hell will not satisfy my curiosity, said Manfred, I will use the human means in my power for preserving my race; Isabella shall not escape me.

That lady, whose resolution had given way to terror the moment she had quitted Manfred, continued her flight to the bottom of the principal staircase. There she stopped, not knowing whither to direct her steps, nor how to escape from the impetuosity of the prince. The gates of the castle she knew were locked, and guards placed in the court. Should she, as her heart prompted her, go and prepare Hippolita for the cruel destiny that awaited her, she did not doubt but Manfred would seek her there, and that his violence would incite him to double the injury he meditated, without leaving room for them to avoid the impetuosity of his passions. Delay might give him time to reflect on the horrid measures he had conceived, or produce some circumstance in her favour, if she could for that night at least avoid his odious purpose.—Yet where conceal herself! How avoid the pursuit he would infallibly make throughout the castle! As these thoughts passed rapidly through her mind, she recollected a subterraneous passage which led from the vaults of the castle to the church of saint Nicholas. Could she reach the altar before she was overtaken, she knew even Manfred's violence would not dare to profane the sacredness of the place; and she determined, if no other means of deliverance offered, to shut herself up for ever among the holy virgins, whose convent was contiguous to the cathedral. In this resolution, she seized a lamp that burned at the foot of the staircase, and hurried towards the secret passage.

The lower part of the castle was hollowed into several intricate cloisters; and it was not easy for one under so much anxiety to find the door that opened into the cavern. An awful silence reigned throughout those subterraneous regions, except now and then some blasts of wind that shook the doors she had passed, and which grating on the rusty hinges were re-echoed through that long labyrinth of darkness. Every murmur struck her with new terror;—yet more she dreaded to hear the wrathful voice of Manfred urging his domestics to pursue her. She trod as softly as impatience would give her leave,—yet frequently stopped and listened to hear if she was followed. In one of those moments she thought she heard a sigh. She shuddered, and recoiled a few paces. In a moment she thought she heard the step of some person. Her blood curdled; she concluded it was Manfred. Every suggestion that horror could inspire rushed into her mind. She condemned her rash flight, which had thus exposed her to his rage in a place where her cries were not likely to draw any body to her assistance.—Yet the sound seemed not to come from behind;—if Manfred knew where she was, he must have followed her: she was still in one of the cloisters, and the steps she had heard were too distinct to proceed from the way she had come. Cheered with this reflection, and hoping to find a friend in whoever was not the prince; she was going to advance, when a door that stood a-jar, at some distance to the left, was opened gently; but ere her lamp, which she held up, could discover who opened it, the person retreated precipitately on seeing the light.

Isabella, whom every incident was sufficient to dismay, hesitated whether she should proceed. Her dread of Manfred soon outweighed every other terror. The very circumstance of the person avoiding her, gave her a sort of courage. It could only be, she thought, some domestic belonging to the castle. Her gentleness had never raised her an enemy, and conscious innocence made her hope that, unless sent by the prince's order to seek her, his servants would rather assist than prevent her flight. Fortifying herself with these reflections, and believing, by what she could observe, that she was near the mouth of the subterraneous cavern, she approached the door that had been opened; but a sudden gust of wind that met her at the door extinguished her lamp, and left her in total darkness.

Words cannot paint the horror of the princess's situation. Alone in so dismal a place, her mind imprinted with all the terrible events of the day, hopeless of escaping, expecting every moment the arrival of Manfred, and far from tranquil on knowing she was within reach of somebody, she knew not whom, who for some cause seemed concealed thereabouts, all these thoughts crowded on her distracted mind, and she was ready to sink under her apprehensions. She addressed herself to every saint in heaven, and inwardly implored their assistance. For a considerable time she remained in an agony of despair. At last, as softly as was possible, she felt for the door, and, having found it, entered trembling into the vault from whence she had heard the sigh and steps. It gave her a kind of momentary joy to perceive an imperfect ray of clouded moonshine gleam from the roof of the vault, which seemed to be fallen in, and from whence hung a fragment of earth or building, she could not distinguish which, that appeared to have been crushed inwards. She advanced eagerly towards this chasm, when she discerned a human form standing close against the wall.

She shrieked, believing it the ghost of her betrothed Conrad. The figure advancing, said in a submissive voice, Be not alarmed, lady; I will not injure you. Isabella, a little encouraged by the words and tone of voice of the stranger, and recollecting that this must be the person who had opened the door, recovered her spirits enough to reply, Sir, whoever you are, take pity on a wretched princess standing on the brink of destruction: assist me to escape from this fatal castle, or in a few moments I may be made miserable for ever. Alas! said the stranger, what can I do to assist you? I will die in your defence; but I am unacquainted with the castle, and want—Oh! said Isabella, hastily interrupting him, help me but to find a trap-door that must be hereabout, and it is the greatest service you can do me; for I have not a minute to lose. Saying these words she felt about on the pavement, and directed the stranger to search likewise for a smooth piece of brass inclosed in one of the stones. That, said she, is the lock, which opens with a spring, of which I know the secret. If I can find that, I may escape – if not, alas, courteous stranger, I fear I shall have involved you in my misfortunes: Manfred will suspect you for the accomplice of my flight, and you will fall a victim to his resentment. I value not my life, said the stranger; and it will be some comfort to lose it in trying to deliver you from his tyranny. Generous youth, said Isabella, how shall I ever requite—As she uttered those words, a ray of moonshine streaming through a cranny of the ruin above shone directly on the lock they sought—Oh, transport! said Isabella, here is the trap-door! and taking out a key, she touched the spring, which starting aside discovered an iron ring. Lift up the door, said the princess. The stranger obeyed; and beneath appeared some stone steps descending into a vault totally dark. We must go down here, said Isabella: follow me; dark and dismal as it is, we cannot miss our way; it leads directly to the church of saint Nicholas—But perhaps, added the princess modestly, you have no reason to leave the castle, nor have I farther occasion for your service; in a few minutes I shall be safe from Manfred's rage – only let me know to whom I am so much obliged. I will never quit you, said the stranger eagerly, till I have placed you in safety – nor think me, princess, more generous than I am: though you are my principal care—The stranger was interrupted by a sudden noise of voices that seemed approaching, and they soon distinguished these words: Talk not to me of necromancers; I tell you she must be in the castle; I will find her in spite of enchantment.—Oh, heavens! cried Isabella, it is the voice of Manfred! Make haste, or we are ruined! and shut the trap-door after you. Saying this, she descended the steps precipitately; and as the stranger hastened to follow her, he let the door slip out of his hands: it fell, and the spring closed over it. He tried in vain to open it, not having observed Isabella's method of touching the spring, nor had he many moments to make an essay. The noise of the falling door had been heard by Manfred, who, directed by the sound, hastened thither, attended by his servants with torches. It must be Isabella, cried Manfred before he entered the vault; she is escaping by the subterraneous passage, but she cannot have got far.—What was the astonishment of the prince, when, instead of Isabella, the light of the torches discovered to him the young peasant, whom he thought confined under the fatal helmet! Traitor! said Manfred, how camest thou here! I thought thee in durance above in the court. I am no traitor, replied the young man boldly, nor am I answerable for your thoughts. Presumptuous villain! cried Manfred, dost thou provoke my wrath? Tell me; how hast thou escaped from above? Thou hast corrupted thy guards, and their lives shall answer it. My poverty, said the peasant calmly, will disculpate them: though the ministers of a tyrant's wrath, to thee they are faithful, and but too willing to execute the orders which you unjustly imposed upon them. Art thou so hardy as to dare my vengeance? said the prince – but tortures shall force the truth from thee. Tell me, I will know thy accomplices. There was my accomplice! said the youth smiling, and pointing to the roof. Manfred ordered the torches to be held up, and perceived that one of the cheeks of the enchanted casque had forced its way through the pavement of the court, as his servants had let it fall over the peasant, and had broken through into the vault, leaving a gap through which the peasant had pressed himself some minutes before he was found by Isabella. Was that the way by which thou didst descend? said Manfred. It was, said the youth. But what noise was that, said Manfred, which I heard as I entered the cloister? A door clapped, said the peasant: I heard it as well as you. What door? said Manfred hastily. I am not acquainted with your castle, said the peasant; this is the first time I ever entered it, and this vault the only part of it within which I ever was. But I tell thee, said Manfred, [wishing to find out if the youth had discovered the trap-door] it was this way I heard the noise: my servants heard it too.—My lord, interrupted one of them officiously,[1] to be sure it was the trap-door, and he was going to make his escape. Peace! blockhead, said the prince angrily; if he was going to escape, how should he come on this side? I will know from his own mouth what noise it was I heard. Tell me truly; thy life depends on thy veracity. My veracity is dearer to me than my life, said the peasant; nor would I purchase the one by forfeiting the other. Indeed! young philosopher! said Manfred contemptuously: tell me then, what was the noise I heard? Ask me what I can answer, said he, and put me to death instantly if I tell you a lie. Manfred, growing impatient at the steady valour and indifference of the youth, cried, Well then, thou man of truth! answer; was it the fall of the trap-door that I heard? It was, said the youth. It was! said the prince; and how didst thou come to know there was a trap-door here? I saw the plate of brass by a gleam of moonshine, replied he. But what told thee it was a lock? said Manfred: How didst thou discover the secret of opening it? Providence, that delivered me from the helmet, was able to direct me to the spring of a lock, said he. Providence should have gone a little farther, and have placed thee out of the reach of my resentment, said Manfred: when Providence had taught thee to open the lock, it abandoned thee for a fool, who did not know how to make use of its favours. Why didst thou not pursue the path pointed out for thy escape? Why didst thou shut the trap-door before thou hadst descended the steps? I might ask you, my lord, said the peasant, how I, totally unacquainted with your castle, was to know that those steps led to any outlet? but I scorn to evade your questions. Wherever those steps lead to, perhaps I should have explored the way – I could not have been in a worse situation than I was. But the truth is, I let the trap-door fall: your immediate arrival followed. I had given the alarm – what imported it to me whether I was seized a minute sooner or a minute later? Thou art a resolute villain for thy years, said Manfred – yet on reflection I suspect thou dost but trifle with me: thou hast not yet told me how thou didst open the lock. That I will show you, my lord, said the peasant; and taking up a fragment of stone that had fallen from above, he laid himself on the trap-door, and began to beat on the piece of brass that covered it; meaning to gain time for the escape of the princess. This presence of mind, joined to the frankness of the youth, staggered Manfred. He even felt a disposition towards pardoning one who had been guilty of no crime. Manfred was not one of those savage tyrants who wanton in cruelty unprovoked. The circumstances of his fortune had given an asperity to his temper, which was naturally humane;

and his virtues were always ready to operate, when his passion did not obscure his reason.

While the prince was in this suspense, a confused noise of voices echoed through the distant vaults. As the sound approached, he distinguished the clamour of some of his domestics, whom he had dispersed through the castle in search of Isabella, calling out, Where is my lord? Where is the prince? Here I am, said Manfred, as they came nearer; have you found the princess? The first that arrived replied, Oh, my lord! I am glad we have found you.—Found me! said Manfred: have you found the princess? We thought we had, my lord, said the fellow looking terrified - but— But what? cried the prince: has she escaped?—Jaquez and I, my lord—Yes, I and Diego, interrupted the second, who came up in still greater consternation—Speak one of you at a time, said Manfred; I ask you, where is the princess? We do not know, said they both together: but we are frightened out of our wits.—So I think, blockheads, said Manfred: what is it has scared you thus?—Oh, my lord! said Jaquez, Diego has seen such a sight! your highness would not believe your eyes.—What new absurdity is this? cried Manfred—Give me a direct answer, or by heaven—Why, my lord, if it please your highness to hear me, said the poor fellow; Diego and I—Yes, I and Jaquez, cried his comrade—Did not I forbid you to speak both at a time? said the prince: You, Jaquez, answer; for the other fool seems more distracted than thou art; what is the matter? My gracious lord, said Jaquez, if it please your highness to hear me; Diego and I, according to your highness's orders, went to search for the young lady; but being apprehensive that we might meet the ghost of my young lord, your highness's son, God rest his soul, as he has not received christian burial—Sot! cried Manfred in a rage, is it only a ghost then that thou hast seen? Oh, worse! worse! my lord! cried Diego: I had rather have seen ten whole ghosts.—Grant me patience! said Manfred; those blockheads distract me—Out of my sight,

Diego! And thou, Jaquez, tell me in one word, art thou sober? art thou raving? Thou wast wont to have some sense: has the other sot frightened himself and thee too? Speak; what is it he fancies he has seen? Why, my lord, replied Jaquez trembling, I was going to tell you highness, that since the calamitous misfortune of my young lord, God rest his soul! not one of us your highness's faithful servants, indeed we are, my lord, though poor men; I say, not one of us has dared to set a foot about the castle, but two together: so Diego and I, thinking that my young lady might be in the great gallery, went up there to look for her, and tell her your highness wanted something to impart to her.—O blundering fools! cried Manfred: and in the mean time she has made her escape, because you were afraid of goblins! Why, thou knave! she left me in the gallery; I came from thence myself.—For all that, she may be there still for aught I know, said Jaquez; but the devil shall have me before I seek her there again!—Poor Diego! I do not believe he will ever recover it! Recover what? said Manfred; am I never to learn what it is has terrified these rascals? But I lose my time; follow me, slave! I will see if she is in the gallery.—For heaven's sake, my dear good lord, cried Jaquez, do not go to the gallery! Satan himself I believe is in the great chamber next to the gallery.—Manfred, who hitherto had treated the terror of his servants as an idle panic, was struck at this new circumstance. He recollected the apparition of the portrait, and the sudden closing of the door at the end of the gallery – his voice faltered, and he asked with disorder, what is in the great chamber? My lord, said Jaquez, when Diego and I came into the gallery, he went first, for he said he had more courage than I. So when we came into the gallery, we found nobody. We looked under every bench and stool; and still we found nobody.—Were all the pictures in their places? said Manfred. Yes, my lord, answered Jaquez; but we did not think of looking behind them.—Well, well! said Manfred; proceed. When we came to the door of the great chamber, continued Jaquez, we found it shut.—And could not you open it? said Manfred. Oh! yes, my lord, would to heaven we had not! replied he—Nay, it was not I neither, it was Diego: he was grown foolhardy, and would go on, though I advised him not—If ever I open a door that is shut again—Trifle not, said Manfred shuddering, but tell me what you saw in the great chamber on opening the door.—I! my lord! said Jaquez,I saw nothing; I was behind Diego;—but I heard the noise.—Jaquez, said Manfred in a solemn tone of voice, tell me, I adjure thee by the souls of my ancestors, what it was thou sawest; what it was thou heardest? It was Diego saw it, my lord, it was not I, replied Jaquez; I only heard the noise. Diego had no sooner opened the door, than he cried out and ran back—I ran back too, and said, Is it the ghost? The ghost! No, no, said Diego, and his hair stood on end - it is a giant, I believe; he is all clad in armour, for I saw his foot and part of his leg, and they are as large as the helmet below in the court. As he said these words, my lord, we heard a violent motion and the rattling of armour, as if the giant was rising; for Diego has told me since, that he believes the giant was lying down, for the foot and leg were stretched at length on the floor. Before we could get to the end of the gallery, we heard the door of the great chamber clap behind us, but we did not dare turn back to see if the giant was following us—Yet now I think on it, we must have heard him if he had pursued us—But for heaven's sake, good my lord, send for the chaplain and have the castle exorcised, for, for certain, it is enchanted. Ay, pray do, my lord, cried all the servants at once, or we must leave your highness's service.—Peace, dotards! said Manfred, and follow me; I will know what all this means. We! my lord! cried they with one voice; we would not go up to the gallery for your highness's revenue. The young peasant, who had stood silent, now spoke. Will your highness, said he, permit me to try this adventure? My life is of consequence to nobody: I fear no bad angel, and have offended no good one. Your behaviour is above your seeming, said Manfred; viewing him with surprise and admiration—hereafter I will reward your bravery – but now, continued he with a sigh, I am so circumstanced, that I dare trust no eyes but my own—However, I give you leave to accompany me.

Manfred, when he first followed Isabella from the gallery, had gone directly to the apartment of his wife, concluding the princess had retired thither. Hippolita, who knew his step, rose with anxious fondness to meet her lord, whom she had not seen since the death of their son. She would have flown in a transport mixed of joy and grief to his bosom; but he pushed her rudely off, and said, Where is Isabella? Isabella! my lord! said the astonished Hippolita. Yes, Isabella; cried Manfred imperiously; I want Isabella: My lord, replied Matilda, who perceived how much his behaviour had shocked her mother, she has not been with us since your highness summoned her to your apartment. Tell me where she is, said the prince; I do not want to know where she has been. My good lord, said Hippolita, your daughter tells you the truth: Isabella left us by your command, and has not returned since:—but, my good lord, compose yourself: retire to your rest: this dismal day has disordered you. Isabella shall wait your orders in the morning. What, then you know where she is? cried Manfred: tell me directly, for I will not lose an instant—And you, woman, speaking to his wife, order your chaplain to attend me forthwith. Isabella, said Hippolita calmly, is retired I suppose to her chamber: she is not accustomed to watch at this late hour. Gracious my lord, continued she, let me know what has disturbed you: has Isabella offended you? Trouble me not with questions, said Manfred, but tell me where she is. Matilda shall call her, said the princess—sit down, my lord, and resume your wonted fortitude.—What, art thou jealous of Isabella, replied he, that you wish to be present at our interview? Good heavens! my lord, said Hippolita, what is it your highness means? Thou wilt know ere many minutes are passed, said the cruel prince. Send your chaplain to me, and wait my pleasure here. At these words he flung out of the room in search of Isabella; leaving the amazed ladies thunder-struck with his words and frantic deportment, and lost in vain conjectures on what he was meditating.

Manfred was now returning from the vault, attended by the peasant and a few of his servants whom he had obliged to accompany him. He ascended the stair-case without stopping till he arrived at the gallery, at the door of which he met Hippolita and her chaplain. When Diego had been dismissed by Manfred, he had gone directly to the princess's apartment with the alarm of what he had seen. That excellent lady, who no more than Manfred doubted of the reality of the vision, yet affected to treat it as a delirium of the servant. Willing, however, to save her lord from any additional shock, and prepared by a series of grief not to tremble at any accession to it; she determined to make herself the first sacrifice, if fate had marked the present hour for their destruction. Dismissing the reluctant Matilda to her rest, who in vain sued for leave to accompany her mother, and attended only by her chaplain, Hippolita had visited the gallery and great chamber: and now, with more serenity of soul than she had felt for many hours, she met her lord, and assured him that the vision of the gigantic leg and foot was all a fable; and no doubt an impression made by fear, and the dark and dismal hour of the night, on the minds of his servants: She and the chaplain had examined the chamber, and found every thing in the usual order.

Manfred, though persuaded, like his wife, that the vision had been no work of fancy, recovered a little from the tempest of mind into which so many strange events had thrown him. Ashamed too of his inhuman treatment of a princess, who returned every injury with new marks of tenderness and duty, he felt returning love forcing itself into his eyes – but not less ashamed of feeling remorse towards one, against whom he was inwardly meditating a yet more bitter outrage, he curbed the yearnings of his heart, and did not dare to lean even towards pity. The next transition of his soul was to exquisite villainy. Presuming on the unshaken submission of Hippolita, he flattered himself that she would not only acquiesce with patience to a divorce, but would obey, if it was his pleasure, in endeavouring to persuade Isabella to give him her hand—But ere he could indulge this horrid hope, he reflected that Isabella was not to be found. Coming to himself, he gave orders that every avenue to the castle should be strictly guarded, and charged his domestics on pain of their lives to suffer nobody to pass out. The young peasant, to whom he spoke favourably, he ordered to remain in a small chamber on the stairs, in which there was a pallet-bed, and the key of which he took away himself, telling the youth he would talk with him in the morning. Then dismissing his attendants, and bestowing a sullen kind of half-nod on Hippolita, he retired to his own chamber.

## CHAPTER 2

MATILDA, who by Hippolita's order had retired to her apartment, was ill-disposed to take any rest. The shocking fate of her brother had deeply affected her. She was surprised at not seeing Isabella: but the strange words which had fallen from her father, and his obscure menace to the princess his wife, accompanied by the most furious behaviour, had filled her gentle mind with terror and alarm. She waited anxiously for the return of Bianca, a young damsel that attended her, whom she had sent to learn what was become of Isabella. Bianca soon appeared, and informed her mistress of what she had gathered from the servants, that Isabella was no where to be found. She related the adventure of the young peasant, who had been discovered in the vault, though with many simple additions from the incoherent accounts of the domestics; and she dwelled principally on the gigantic leg and foot which had been seen in the gallery-chamber. This last circumstance had terrified Bianca so much, that she was rejoiced when Matilda told her that she would not go to rest, but would watch till the princess should rise.

The young princess wearied herself in conjectures on the flight of Isabella, and on the threats of Manfred to her mother. But what business could he have so urgent with the chaplain? said Matilda. Does he intend to have my brother's body interred privately in the chapel? Oh! madam, said Bianca, now I guess. As you are become his heiress, he is impatient to have you married: he has always been raving for more sons; I warrant he is now impatient for grandsons. As sure as I live, madam, I shall see you a bride at last. Good madam, you won't cast off your faithful Bianca: you won't put Donna Rosara over me, now you are a great princess? My poor Bianca, said Matilda, how fast your thoughts amble! I a great princess! What hast thou seen in Manfred's behaviour since my brother's death that bespeaks any increase of tenderness to me? No, Bianca, his heart was ever a stranger to me – but he is my father, and I must not complain. Nay, if heaven shuts my father's heart against me, it over-pays my little merit in the tenderness of my mother—O that dear mother! Yes, Bianca, 'tis there I feel the rugged temper of Manfred. I can support his harshness to me with patience; but it wounds my soul when I am witness to his causeless severity towards her. Oh, madam, said Bianca, all men use their wives so, when they are weary of them.—And yet you congratulated me but now, said Matilda, when you fancied my father intended to dispose of me. I would have you a great lady, replied Bianca, come what will. I do not wish to see you moped in a convent, as you would be if you had your will, and if my lady your mother, who knows that a bad husband is better than no husband at all, did not hinder you.—Bless me! what noise is that? Saint Nicholas forgive me! I was but in jest. It is the wind, said Matilda, whistling through the battlements in the tower above: you have heard it a thousand times. Nay, said Bianca, there was no harm neither in what I said: it is no sin to talk of matrimony—And so, madam, as I was saying; if my lord Manfred should offer you a handsome young prince for a bridegroom, you would drop him a curtsy, and tell him you would rather take the veil. Thank heaven! I am in no such danger, said Matilda: you know how many proposals for me he has rejected.—And you thank him, like a dutiful daughter, do you, madam?—But come, madam; suppose, to-morrow morning he was to send for you to the great council-chamber, and there you should find at his elbow a lovely young prince, with large black eyes, a smooth white forehead, and manly curling locks like jet; in short, madam, a young hero resembling the picture of the good Alfonso in the gallery, which you sit and gaze at for hours together.—Do not speak lightly of that picture, interrupted Matilda sighing: I know the adoration with which I look at that picture is uncommon – but I am not in love with a coloured pannel. The character of that virtuous prince, the veneration with which my mother has inspired me for his memory, the orisons[1] which I know not why she has enjoined me to pour forth at his tomb, all have concurred to persuade me that somehow or other my destiny is linked with something relating to him.—Lord! madam, how should that be? said Bianca: I have always heard that your family was no way related to his: and I am sure I cannot conceive why my lady, the princess, sends you in a cold morning, or a damp evening, to pray at his tomb: he is no saint by the almanack. If you must pray, why does not she bid you address yourself to our great saint Nicholas? I am sure he is the saint I pray to for a husband. Perhaps my mind would be less affected, said Matilda, if my mother would explain her reasons to me: but it is the mystery she observes, that inspires me with this – I know not what to call it. As she never acts from caprice, I am sure there is some fatal secret at bottom – nay, I know there is: in her agony of grief for my brother's death she dropped some words that intimated as much.—Oh, dear madam, cried Bianca, what were they? No, said Matilda: if a parent lets fall a word, and wishes it recalled, it is not for a child to utter it. What! was she sorry for what she had said? asked Bianca—I am sure, madam, you may trust me.—With my own little secrets, when I have any, I may, said Matilda; but never with my mother's: a child ought to have no ears or eyes but as a parent directs. Well! to be sure, madam, you was born to be a saint, said Bianca, and there's no resisting one's vocation: you will end in a convent at last. But there is my lady Isabella would not be so reserved to me: she will let me talk to her of young men; and when a handsome cavalier has come to the castle, she has owned to me that she wished your brother Conrad resembled him. Bianca, said the princess, I do not allow you to mention my friend disrespectfully. Isabella is of a cheerful disposition, but her soul is pure as virtue itself. She knows your idle babbling humour, and perhaps has now and then encouraged it, to divert melancholy, and to enliven the solitude in which my father keeps us.—Blessed Mary! said Bianca starting, there it is again!—Dear madam, do you hear nothing?—This castle is certainly haunted.—Peace! said Matilda, and listen! I did think I heard a voice – but it must be fancy; your terrors I suppose have infected me. Indeed! indeed! madam, said Bianca half-weeping with agony, I am sure I heard a voice. Does any body lie in the chamber beneath? said the princess. Nobody has dared to lie there, answered Bianca, since the great astrologer that was your brother's tutor drowned himself. For certain, madam, his ghost and the young prince's are now met in the chamber below – for heaven's sake let us fly to your mother's apartment! I charge you not to stir, said Matilda. If they are spirits in pain, we may ease their sufferings by questioning them. They can mean no hurt to us, for we have not injured them – and if they should, shall we be more safe in one chamber than in another? Reach me my beads; we will say a prayer, and then speak to them. Oh, dear lady, I would not speak to a ghost for the world, cried Bianca—As she said those words, they heard the casement of the little chamber below Matilda's open. They listened attentively, and in few minutes thought they heard a person sing, but could not distinguish the words. This can be no evil spirit, said the princess in a low voice: it is undoubtedly one of the family – open the window, and we shall know the voice. I dare not indeed, madam, said Bianca. Thou art a very fool, said Matilda, opening the window gently herself. The noise the princess made was however heard by the person beneath, who stopped, and, they concluded, had heard the casement open. Is any body below? said the princess: if there is, speak. Yes, said an unknown voice. Who is it? said Matilda. A stranger, replied the voice. What stranger? said she; and how didst thou come there at this unusual hour, when all the gates of the castle are locked? I am not here willingly, answered the voice—but pardon me, lady, if I have disturbed your rest: I knew not that I was overheard. Sleep had forsaken me: I left a restless couch, and came to waste the irksome hours with gazing on the fair approach of morning, impatient to be dismissed from this castle. Thy words and accents, said Matilda, are of a melancholy cast: if thou art unhappy, I pity thee. If poverty afflicts thee, let me know it; I will mention thee to the princess, whose beneficent soul ever melts for the distressed; and she will relieve thee. I am indeed unhappy, said the stranger; and I know not what wealth is: but I do not complain of the lot which heaven has cast for me: I am young and healthy, and am not ashamed of owing my support to myself – yet think me not proud, or that I disdain your generous offers. I will remember you in my orisons, and will pray for blessings on your gracious self and your noble mistress—If I sigh, lady, it is for others, not for myself. Now I have it, madam, said Bianca whispering the princess. This is certainly the young peasant; and by my conscience he is in love!—Well, this is a charming adventure!—Do, madam, let us sift him. He does not know you, but takes you for one of my lady Hippolita's women. Art thou not ashamed, Bianca? said the princess: what right have we to pry into the secrets of this young man's heart? He seems virtuous and frank, and tells us he is unhappy: are those circumstances that authorize us to make a property of him? How are we entitled to his confidence? Lord! madam, how little you know of love! replied Bianca: why, lovers have no pleasure equal to talking of their mistress. And would you have *me* become a peasant's confidante? said the princess. Well then, let me talk to him, said Bianca: though I have the honour of being your highness's maid of honour, I was not always so great: besides, if love levels ranks, it raises them too: I have a respect for any young man in love.—Peace, simpleton! said the princess. Though he said he was unhappy, it does not follow that he must be in love. Think of all that has happened today, and tell me if there are no misfortunes but what love causes. Stranger, resumed the princess, if thy misfortunes have not been occasioned by thy own fault, and are within the compass of the princess Hippolita's power to redress, I will take upon me to answer that she will be thy protectress. When thou art dismissed from this castle, repair to holy father Jerome at the convent adjoining the church of saint Nicholas, and make thy story known to him, as far as thou thinkest meet: he will not fail to inform the princess, who is the mother of all that want her assistance. Farewell: it is not seemly for me to hold farther converse with a man at this unwonted hour. May the saints guard thee, gracious lady! replied the peasant—but oh, if a poor and worthless stranger might presume to beg a minute's audience farther – am I so happy? – the casement is not shut – might I venture to ask—Speak quickly, said Matilda; the morning dawns apace: should the labourers come into the fields and perceive us—What wouldst thou ask?—I know not how – I know not if I dare, said the young stranger faltering – yet the humanity with which you have spoken to me emboldens—Lady! dare I trust you?—Heavens! said Matilda, what dost thou mean? with what wouldst thou trust me? Speak boldly, if thy secret is fit to be entrusted to a virtuous breast.—I would ask, said the peasant, recollecting himself, whether what I have heard from the domestics is true, that the princess is missing from the castle? What imports it to thee to know? replied Matilda. Thy first words bespoke a prudent and becoming gravity. Dost thou come hither to pry into the secrets of Manfred? Adieu. I have been mistaken in thee.—Saying these words, she shut the casement hastily, without giving the young man time to reply. I had acted more wisely, said the princess to Bianca with some sharpness, if I had let thee converse with this peasant: his inquisitiveness seems of a piece with thy own. It is not fit for me to argue with your highness, replied Bianca; but perhaps the questions I should have put to him, would have been more to the purpose, than those you have been pleased to ask him. Oh, no doubt, said Matilda; you are a very discreet personage! May I know what you would have asked him? A by-stander often sees more of the game than those that play, answered Bianca. Does your highness think, madam, that his question about my lady Isabella was the result of mere curiosity? No, no, madam; there is more in it than you great folks are aware of. Lopez told me, that all the servants believe this young fellow contrived my lady Isabella's escape—Now, pray, madam, observe— You and I both know that my lady Isabella never much fancied the prince your brother.— Well! he is killed just in the critical minute – I accuse nobody. A helmet falls from the moon – so my lord your father says; but Lopez and all the servants say that this young spark is a magician, and stole it from Alfonso's tomb.—Have done with this rhapsody of impertinence, said Matilda. Nay madam, as you please, cried Bianca— yet it is very particular though, that my lady Isabella should be missing the very same day, and that this young sorcerer should be found at the mouth of the trap-door— I accuse nobody – but if my young lord came honestly by his death—Dare not on thy duty, said Matilda, to breathe a suspicion on the purity of my dear Isabella's fame.— Purity, or not purity, said Bianca, gone she is: a stranger is found that nobody knows: you question him yourself: he tells you he is in love, or unhappy, it is the same thing – nay, he owned he was unhappy about others; and is any body unhappy about another, unless they are in love with them? And at the very next word he asks innocently, poor soul! if my lady Isabella is missing.—To be sure, said Matilda, thy observations are not totally without foundation – Isabella's flight amazes me: the curiosity of this stranger is very particular – yet Isabella never concealed a thought from me.—So she told you, said Bianca, to fish out your secrets – but who knows, madam, but this stranger may be some prince in disguise?—Do, madam, let me open the window, and ask him a few questions. No, replied Matilda, I will ask him myself, if he knows aught of Isabella: he is not worthy that I should converse farther with him. She was going to open the casement, when they heard the bell ring at the postern-gate of the castle, which is on the right hand of the tower, where Matilda lay. This prevented the princess from renewing the conversation with the stranger.

After continuing silent for some time; I am persuaded, said she to Bianca, that whatever be the cause of Isabella's flight, it had no unworthy motive. If this stranger was accessary to it, she must be satisfied of his fidelity and worth. I observed, did not you, Bianca? that his words were tinctured with an uncommon infusion of piety. It was no ruffian's speech: his phrases were becoming a man of gentle birth. I told you, madam, said Bianca, that I was sure he was some prince in disguise.—Yet, said Matilda, if he was privy to her escape, how will you account for his not accompanying her in her flight? Why expose himself unnecessarily and rashly to my father's resentment? As for that, madam, replied she, if he could get from under the helmet, he will find ways of eluding your father's anger. I do not doubt but he has some talisman or other about him.—You resolve every thing into magic, said Matilda—but a man who has any intercourse with infernal spirits does not dare to make use of those tremendous and holy words which he uttered. Didst thou not observe with what fervour he vowed to remember *me* to heaven in his prayers? Yes, Isabella was undoubtedly convinced of his piety.—Commend me to the piety of a young fellow and a damsel that consult to elope! said Bianca. No, no, madam; my lady Isabella is of another-guess mould than you take her for. She used indeed to sigh and lift up her eyes in your company, because she knows you are a saint – but when your back was turned—You wrong her, said Matilda; Isabella is no hypocrite: she has a due sense of devotion, but never affected a call she has not. On the contrary, she always combated my inclination for the cloister: and though I own the mystery she has made to me of her flight confounds me; though it seems inconsistent with the friendship between us; I cannot forget the disinterested warmth with which she always opposed my taking the veil: she wished to see me married, though my dower would have been a loss to her and my brother's children. For her sake I will believe well of this young peasant. Then you do think there is some liking between them? said Bianca.—While she was speaking, a servant came hastily into the chamber, and told the princess that the lady Isabella was found. Where? said Matilda. She has taken sanctuary in saint Nicholas's church, replied the servant: father Jerome has brought the news himself: he is below with his highness. Where is my mother? said Matilda. She is in her own chamber, madam, and has asked for you.

Manfred had risen at the first dawn of light, and gone to Hippolita's apartment, to enquire of she knew ought of Isabella. While he was questioning her, word was brought that Jerome demanded to speak with him. Manfred, little suspecting the cause of the friar's arrival, and knowing he was employed by Hippolita in her charities, ordered him to be admitted, intending to leave them together, while he pursued his search after Isabella. Is your business with me or the princess? said Manfred. With both, replied the holy man. The lady Isabella—What of her? interrupted Manfred eagerly—is at saint Nicholas's altar, replied Jerome. That is no business of Hippolita, said Manfred with confusion: let us retire to my chamber, father; and inform me how she came thither. No, my lord, replied the good man with an air of firmness and authority that daunted even the resolute Manfred, who could not help revering the saint-like virtues of Jerome: my commission is to both; and, with your highness's good-liking, in the presence of both I shall deliver it—But first, my lord, I must interrogate the princess, whether she is acquainted with the cause of the lady Isabella's retirement from your castle.—No, on my soul, said Hippolita; does Isabella charge me with being privy to it?—Father, interrupted Manfred, I pay due reverence to your holy profession; but I am sovereign here, and will allow no meddling priest to interfere in the affairs of my domestic. If you have aught to say, attend me to my chamber—I do not use to let my wife be acquainted with the secret affairs of my state; they are not within a woman's province. My lord, said the holy man, I am no intruder into the secrets of families. My office is to promote peace, to heal divisions, to preach repentance, and teach mankind to curb their headstrong passions. I forgive your highness's uncharitable apostrophe: I know my duty, and am the minister of a mightier prince than Manfred. Hearken to him who speaks through my organs. Manfred trembled with rage and shame. Hippolita's countenance declared her astonishment, and impatience to know where this would end: her silence more strongly spoke her observance of Manfred.

The lady Isabella, resumed Jerome, commends herself to both your highnesses; she thanks both for the kindness with which she has been treated in your castle: she deplores the loss of your son, and her own misfortune in not becoming the daughter of such wise and noble princes, whom she shall always respect as *parents*: she prays for uninterrupted union and felicity between you: [Manfred's colour changed] but as it is no longer possible for her to be allied to you, she entreats your consent to remain in sanctuary till she can learn news of her father; or, by the certainty of his death, be at liberty, with the approbation of her guardians, to dispose of herself in suitable marriage. I shall give no such consent, said the prince; but insist on her return to the castle without delay: I am answerable for her person to her guardians, and will not brook her being in any hands but my own. Your highness will recollect whether that can any longer be proper, replied the friar. I want no monitor, said Manfred colouring. Isabella's conduct leaves room for strange suspicions – and that young villain, who was at least the accomplice of her flight, if not the cause of it—The cause! interrupted Jerome: was a *young* man the cause? This is not to be borne! cried Manfred. Am I to be bearded in my own palace by an insolent monk! Thou art privy, I guess, to their amours. I would pray to heaven to clear up your uncharitable surmises, said Jerome, if your highness were not satisfied in your conscience how unjustly you accuse me. I do pray to heaven to pardon that uncharitableness: and I implore your highness to leave the princess at peace in that holy place, where she is not liable to be disturbed by such vain and worldly fantasies as discourses of love from any man. Cant not to me, said Manfred, but return, and bring the princess to her duty. It is my duty to prevent her return hither, said Jerome. She is where orphans and virgins are safest from the snares and wiles of this world; and nothing but a parent's authority shall take her thence. I am her parent, cried Manfred, and demand her. She wished to have you for her parent, said the friar; but heaven, that forbad that connexion, has for ever dissolved all ties betwixt you: and I announce to your highness—Stop! audacious man, said Manfred, and dread my displeasure. Holy father, said Hippolita, it is your office to be no respecter of persons: you must speak as your duty prescribes: but it is my duty to hear nothing that it pleases not my lord I should hear. I will retire to my oratory, and pray to the blessed Virgin to inspire you with her holy counsels, and to restore the heart of my gracious lord to its wonted peace and gentleness. Excellent woman! said the friar.—My lord, I attend your pleasure.

Manfred, accompanied by the friar, passed to his own apartment; where shutting the door, I perceive, father, said he, that Isabella has acquainted you with my purpose. Now hear my resolve, and obey. Reasons of state, most urgent reasons, my own and the safety of my people, demand that I should have a son. It is in vain to expect an heir from Hippolita. I have made choice of Isabella. You must bring her back; and you must do more. I know the influence you have with Hippolita; her conscience is in your hands. She is, I allow, a faultless woman: her soul is set on heaven, and scorns the little grandeur of this world: you can withdraw her from it entirely. Persuade her to consent to the dissolution of our marriage, and to retire into a monastery – she shall endow one if she will; and she shall have the means of being as liberal to your order as she or you can wish. Thus you will divert the calamities that are hanging over our heads, and have the merit of saving the principality of Otranto from destruction. You are a prudent man; and though the warmth of my temper betrayed me into some unbecoming expressions, I honour your virtue, and wish to be indebted to you for the repose of my life and the preservation of my family.

The will of heaven be done! said the friar. I am but its worthless instrument. It makes use of my tongue to tell thee, prince, of thy unwarrantable designs. The injuries of the virtuous Hippolita have mounted to the throne of pity. By me thou art reprimanded for thy adulterous intention of repudiating her: by me thou art warned not to pursue the incestuous design on thy contracted daughter. Heaven, that delivered her from thy fury, when the judgments so recently fallen on thy house ought to have inspired thee with other thoughts, will continue to watch over her. Even I, a poor and despised friar, am able to protect her from thy violence.—I, sinner as I am, and uncharitably reviled by your highness as an accomplice of I know not what amours, scorn the allurements with which it has pleased thee to tempt mine honesty. I love my order; I honour devout souls; I respect the piety of thy princess – but I will not betray the confidence she reposes in me, nor serve even the cause of religion by foul and sinful compliances—But forsooth! the welfare of the state depends on your highness having a son. Heaven mocks the short-sighted views of man. But yester-morn, whose house was so great, so flourishing as Manfred's?—Where is young Conrad now?—My lord, I respect your tears – but I mean not to check them—Let them flow, prince! they will weigh more with heaven towards the welfare of thy subjects, than a marriage, which, founded on lust or policy, could never prosper. The sceptre, which passed from the race of Alfonso to thine, cannot be preserved by a match which the church will never allow. If it is the will of the Most High that Manfred's name must perish, resign yourself, my lord, to its decrees; and thus deserve a crown that can never pass away.—Come, my lord, I like this sorrow—Let us return to the princess: she is not apprized of your cruel intentions; nor did I mean more than to alarm you. You saw with what gentle patience, with what efforts of love, she heard, she rejected hearing the extent of your guilt. I know she longs to fold you in her arms, and assure you of her unalterable affection. Father, said the prince, you mistake my compunction: true, I honour Hippolita's virtues; I think her a saint; and wish it were for my soul's health to tie faster the knot that has united us.—But alas! father, you know not the bitterest of my pangs! It is some time that I have had scruples on the legality of our union: Hippolita is related to me in the fourth degree—It is true, we had a dispensation; but I have been informed that she had also been contracted to another. This it is that sits heavy at my heart: to this state of unlawful wedlock I impute the visitation that has fallen on me in the death of Conrad!—Ease my conscience of this burden; dissolve our marriage, and accomplish the work of godliness which your divine exhortations have commenced in my soul.

How cutting was the anguish which the good man felt, when he perceived this turn in the wily prince! He trembled for Hippolita, whose ruin he saw was determined; and he feared, if Manfred had no hope of recovering Isabella, that his impatience for a son would direct him to some other object, who might not be equally proof against the temptation of Manfred's rank. For some time the holy man remained absorbed in thought. At length, conceiving some hope from delay, he thought the wisest conduct would be to prevent the prince from despairing of recovering Isabella. Her the friar knew he could dispose, from her affection to Hippolita, and from the aversion she had expressed to him for Manfred's addresses, to second his view, till the censures of the church could be fulminated against a divorce. With this intention, as if struck with the prince's scruples, he at length said, My lord, I have been pondering on what your highness has said; and if in truth it is delicacy of conscience that is the real motive of your repugnance to your virtuous lady, far be it from me to endeavour to harden your heart! The church is an indulgent mother; unfold your griefs to her: she alone can administer comfort to your soul, either by satisfying your conscience, or, upon examination of your scruples, by setting you at liberty, and indulging you in the lawful means of continuing your lineage. In the latter case, if the lady Isabella can be brought to consent— Manfred, who concluded that he had either over-reached the good man, or that his first warmth had been but a tribute paid to appearance, was overjoyed at this sudden turn, and repeated the most magnificent promises, if he should succeed by the friar's mediation. The well-meaning priest suffered him to deceive himself, fully determined to traverse his views, instead of seconding them.

Since we now understand one another, resumed the prince, I expect, father, that you satisfy me in one point. Who is the youth that we found in the vault? He must have been privy to Isabella's flight: tell me truly; is he her lover? or is he an agent for another's passion? I have often suspected Isabella's indifference to my son: a thousand circumstances crowd on my mind that confirm that suspicion. She herself was so conscious of it, that, while I discoursed her in the gallery, she outran my suspicions, and endeavoured to justify herself from coolness to Conrad. The friar, who knew nothing of the youth but what he had learnt occasionally from the princess, ignorant what was become of him, and not sufficiently reflecting on the impetuosity of Manfred's temper, conceived that it might not be amiss to sow the seeds of jealousy in his mind: they might be turned to some use hereafter, either by prejudicing the prince against Isabella, if he persisted in that union; or, by diverting his attention to a wrong scent, and employing his thoughts on a visionary intrigue, prevent his engaging in any new pursuit. With this unhappy policy, he answered in a manner to confirm Manfred in the belief of some connexion between Isabella and the youth. The prince, whose passions wanted little fuel to throw them into a blaze, fell into a rage at the idea of what the friar suggested. I will fathom to the bottom of this intrigue, cried he; and quitting Jerome abruptly, with a command to remain there till his return, he hastened to the great hall of the castle, and ordered the peasant to be brought before him.

Thou hardened young impostor! said the prince, as soon as he saw the youth; what becomes of thy boasted veracity now? It was Providence, was it, and the light of the moon, that discovered the lock of the trap-door to thee? Tell me, audacious boy, who thou art, and how long thou hast been acquainted with the princess – and take care to answer with less equivocation than thou didst last night, or tortures shall wring the truth from thee. The young man, perceiving that his share in the flight of the princess was discovered, and concluding that any thing he should say could no longer be of service or detriment to her, replied, I am no impostor, my lord; nor have I deserved opprobrious language. I answered to every question your highness put to me last night with the same veracity that I shall speak now: and that will not be from fear of your tortures, but because my soul abhors a falsehood. Please to repeat your questions, my lord; I am ready to give you all the satisfaction in my power. You know my questions, replied the prince, and only want time to prepare an evasion. Speak directly; who art thou? and how long hast thou been known to the princess? I am a labourer at the next village, said the peasant; my name is Theodore. The princess found me in the vault last night: before that hour I never was in her presence—I may believe as much or as little as I please of this, said Manfred; but I will hear thy own story, before I examine into the truth of it. Tell me, what reason did the princess give thee for making her escape? Thy life depends on thy answer. She told me, replied Theodore, that she was on the brink of destruction; and that, if she could not escape from the castle, she was in danger in a few moments of being made miserable for ever. And on this slight foundation, on a silly girl's report, said Manfred, thou didst hazard my displeasure? I fear no man's displeasure, said Theodore, when a woman in distress puts herself under my protection.—During this examination, Matilda was going to the apartment of Hippolita. At the upper end of the hall, where Manfred sat, was a boarded gallery with latticed windows, through which Matilda and Bianca were to pass. Hearing her father's voice, and seeing the servants assembled round him, she stopped to learn the occasion. The prisoner soon drew her attention: the steady and composed manner in which he answered, and the gallantry of his last reply, which were the first words she heard distinctly, interested her in his favour. His person was noble, handsome and commanding, even in that situation: but his countenance soon engrossed her whole care. Heavens! Bianca, said the princess softly, do I dream? or is not that youth the exact resemblance of Alfonso's picture in the gallery? She could say no more, for her father's voice grew louder at every word. This bravado, said he, surpasses all thy former insolence. Thou shalt experience the wrath with which thou darest to trifle. Seize him, continued Manfred, and bind him – the first news the princess hears of her champion shall be that he has lost his head for her sake. The injustice of which thou art guilty towards me, said Theodore, convinces me that I have done a good deed in delivering the princess from thy tyranny. May she be happy, whatever becomes of me!—This is a lover! cried Manfred in a rage: a peasant within sight of death is not animated by such sentiments. Tell me, tell me, rash boy, who thou art, or the rack shall force thy secret from thee. Thou hast threatened me with death already, said the youth, for the truth I have told thee: if that is all the encouragement I am to expect for sincerity, I am not tempted to indulge thy vain curiosity farther. Then thou wilt not speak? said Manfred. I will not, replied he. Bear him away into the court-yard, said Manfred; I will see his head this instant severed from his body.—Matilda fainted at hearing those words. Bianca shrieked, and cried, Help! help! the princess is dead! Manfred started at this ejaculation, and demanded what was the matter. The young peasant, who heard it too, was struck with horror, and asked eagerly the same question; but Manfred ordered him to be hurried into the court, and kept there for execution, till he had informed himself of the cause of Bianca's shrieks. When he learned the meaning, he treated it as a womanish panic; and ordering Matilda to be carried to her apartment, he rushed into the court, and, calling for one of his guards, bade Theodore kneel down and prepare to receive the fatal blow.

The undaunted youth received the bitter sentence with a resignation that touched every heart but Manfred's. He wished earnestly to know the meaning of the words he had heard relating to the princess; but, fearing to exasperate the tyrant more against her, he desisted. The only boon he deigned to ask was, that he might be permitted to have a confessor, and make his peace with heaven. Manfred, who hoped by the confessor's means to come at the youth's history, readily granted his request: and being convinced that father Jerome was now in his interest, he ordered him to be called and shrieve the prisoner. The holy man, who had little foreseen the catastrophe that his imprudence occasioned, fell on his knees to the prince, and adjured him in the most solemn manner not to shed innocent blood. He accused himself in the bitterest terms for his indiscretion, endeavoured to disculpate the youth, and left no method untried to soften the tyrant's rage. Manfred, more incensed than appeased by Jerome's intercession, whose retraction now made him suspect he had been imposed upon by both, commanded the friar to do his duty, telling him he would not allow the prisoner many minutes for confession. Nor do I ask many, my lord, said the unhappy young man. My sins, thank heaven! have not been numerous; nor exceed what might be expected at my years. Dry your tears, good father, and let us dispatch: this is a bad world; nor have I had cause to leave it with regret. Oh! wretched youth! said Jerome; how canst thou bear the sight of me with patience? I am thy murderer! It is I have brought this dismal hour upon thee!—I forgive thee from my soul, said the youth, as I hope heaven will pardon me. Hear my confession, father; and give me thy blessing. How can I prepare thee for thy passage, as I ought? said Jerome. Thou canst not be saved without pardoning thy foes – and canst thou forgive that impious man there? I can, said Theodore; I do.—And does not this touch thee, cruel prince? said the friar. I sent for thee to confess him, said Manfred sternly; not to plead for him. Thou didst first incense me against him – his blood be upon thy head!—It will! it will! said the good man in an agony of sorrow. Thou and I must never hope to go where this blessed youth is going.—Dispatch! said Manfred: I am no more to be moved by the whining of priests, than by the shrieks of women. What! said the youth, is it possible that my fate could have occasioned what I heard? Is the princess then again in thy power?—Thou dost but remember me of my wrath, said Manfred: prepare thee, for this moment is thy last. The youth, who felt his indignation rise, and who was touched with the sorrow which he saw he had infused into all the spectators, as well as into the friar, suppressed his emotions, and, putting off his doublet and unbuttoning his collar, knelt down to his prayers. As he stooped, his shirt flipped down below his shoulder, and discovered the mark of a bloody arrow. Gracious heaven! cried the holy man starting, what do I see? It is my child! my Theodore!

The passions that ensued must be conceived; they cannot be painted. The tears of the assistants were suspended by wonder, rather than stopped by joy. They seemed to enquire in the eyes of their lord what they ought to feel. Surprise, doubt, tenderness, respect, succeeded each other in the countenance of the youth. He received with modest submission the effusion of the old man's tears and embraces: yet afraid of giving a loose to hope, and suspecting from what had passed the inflexibility of Manfred's temper, he cast a glance towards the prince, as if to say, Canst thou be unmoved at such a scene as this?

Manfred's heart was capable of being touched. He forgot his anger in his astonishment; yet his pride forbad his owning himself affected. He even doubted whether this discovery was not a contrivance of the friar to save the youth. What may this mean! said he. How can he be thy son? Is it consistent with thy profession or reputed sanctity to avow a peasant's offspring for the fruit of thy irregular amours?—Oh God! said the holy man, dost thou question his being mine? Could I feel the anguish I do, if I were not his father? Spare him! good prince, spare him! and revile me as thou pleasest.—Spare him! spare him! cried the attendants, for this good man's sake!—Peace! said Manfred sternly: I must know more, ere I am disposed to pardon. A saint's bastard may be no saint himself—Injurious lord! said Theodore: add not insult to cruelty. If I am this venerable man's son, though no prince as thou art, know, the blood that flows in my veins—Yes, said the friar, interrupting him, his blood is noble: nor is he that abject thing, my lord, you speak him. He is my lawful son; and Sicily can boast of few houses more ancient than that of Falconara—But alas! my lord, what is blood? what is nobility? We are all reptiles, miserable sinful creatures. It is piety alone that can distinguish us from the dust whence we sprung, and whither we must return.—Truce to your sermon, said Manfred; you forget you are no longer friar Jerome but the count of Falconara. Let me know your history; you will have time to moralize hereafter, if you should not happen to obtain the grace of that sturdy criminal there. Mother of God! said the friar, is it possible my lord can refuse a father the life of his only, his long lost child? Trample me, my lord, scorn, afflict me, accept my life for his, but spare my son!—Thou canst feel then, said Manfred, what it is to lose an only son? A little hour ago thou didst preach up resignation to me: *my* house, if fate so pleased, must perish – but the count of Falconara—Alas! my lord, said Jerome, I confess I have offended; but aggravate not an old man's sufferings. I boast not of my family, nor think of such vanities – it is nature that pleads for this boy; it is the memory of the dear woman that bore him—Is she, Theodore, is she dead?—Her soul has long been with the blessed, said Theodore. Oh how? cried Jerome, tell me—No—she is happy! Thou art all my care now!—Most dread lord! will you – will you grant me my poor boy's life? Return to thy convent, answered Manfred; conduct the princess hither; obey me in what else thou knowest; and I promise thee the life of thy son.— Oh! my lord, said Jerome, is honesty the price I must pay for this dear youth's safety?—For me! cried Theodore: let me die a thousand deaths, rather than stain thy conscience. What is it the tyrant would exact of thee? Is the princess safe from his power? Protect her, thou venerable old man! and let all his wrath fall on me. Jerome endeavoured to check the impetuosity of the youth; and ere Manfred could reply, the trampling of horses was heard, and a brazen trumpet, which hung without the gate of the castle, was suddenly sounded. At the same instant the sable plumes on the enchanted helmet, which still remained at the other end of the court, were tempestuously agitated, and nodded thrice, as if bowed by some invisible wearer.

# CHAPTER 3

MANFRED's heart misgave him when he beheld the plumage on the miraculous casque shaken in concert with the sounding of the brazen trumpet. Father! said he to Jerome, whom he now ceased to treat as count of Falconara, what mean these portents? If I have offended—[the plumes were shaken with greater violence than before] Unhappy prince that I am! cried Manfred—Holy Father! will you not assist me with your prayers?—My lord, replied Jerome, heaven is no doubt displeased with your mockery of its servants. Submit yourself to the church; and cease to persecute her ministers. Dismiss this innocent youth; and learn to respect the holy character I wear: heaven will not be trifled with: you see—[the trumpet sounded again] I acknowledge I have been too hasty, said Manfred. Father, do you go to the wicket, and demand who is at the gate. Do you grant me the life of Theodore? replied the friar. I do, said Manfred; but enquire who is without.

Jerome, falling on the neck of his son, discharged a flood of tears, that spoke the fulness of his soul. You promised to go to the gate, said Manfred. I thought, replied the friar, your highness would excuse my thanking you first in this tribute of my heart. Go, dearest sir, said Theodore, obey the prince; I do not deserve that you should delay his satisfaction for me.

Jerome, enquiring who was without, was answered, A herald. From whom? said he. From the knight of the gigantic sabre, said the herald: and I must speak with the usurper of Otranto. Jerome returned to the prince, and did not fail to repeat the message in the very words it had been uttered. The first sounds struck Manfred with terror;

but when he heard himself styled usurper, his rage rekindled, and all his courage revived. Usurper!—Insolent villain! cried he, who dares to question my title? Retire, father; this is no business for monks: I will meet this presumptuous man myself. Go to your convent, and prepare the princess's return: your son shall be a hostage for your fidelity: his life depends on your obedience.—Good heaven! my lord, cried Jerome, your highness did but this instant freely pardon my child – have you so soon forgot the interposition of heaven?—Heaven, replied Manfred, does not send heralds to question the title of a lawful prince—I doubt whether it even notifies its will through friars – but that is your affair, not mine. At present you know my pleasure; and it is not a saucy herald that shall save your son, if you do not return with the princess.

It was in vain for the holy man to reply. Manfred commanded him to be conducted to the postern-gate, and shut out from the castle: and he ordered some of his attendants to carry Theodore to the top of the black tower, and guard him strictly; scarce permitting the father and son to exchange a hasty embrace at parting. He then withdrew to the hall, and, seating himself in princely state, ordered the herald to be admitted to his presence.

Well, thou insolent! said the prince, what wouldst thou with me? I come, replied he, to thee, Manfred, usurper of the principality of Otranto, from the renowned and invincible knight, the knight of the gigantic sabre: in the name of his lord, Frederic marquis of Vicenza, he demands the lady Isabella, daughter of that prince, whom thou hast basely and traitorously got into thy power, by bribing her false guardians during his absence: and he requires thee to resign the principality of Otranto, which thou hast usurped from the said lord Frederic, the nearest of blood to the last rightful lord Alfonso the Good. If thou dost not instantly comply with these just demands, he defies thee to single combat to the last extremity. And so saying, the herald cast down his warder.

And where is this braggart, who sends thee? said Manfred. At the distance of a league, said the herald: he comes to make good his lord's claim against thee, as he is a true knight, and thou an usurper and ravisher.

Injurious as this challenge was, Manfred reflected that it was not his interest to provoke the marquis. He knew how well-founded the claim of Frederic was; nor was this the first time he had heard of it. Frederic's ancestors had assumed the style of princes of Otranto, from the death of Alfonso the Good without issue: but Manfred, his father, and grandfather, had been too powerful for the house of Vicenza to dispossess them. Frederic, a martial and amorous young prince, had married a beautiful young lady, of whom he was enamoured, and who had died in childbed of Isabella. Her death affected him so much, that he had taken the cross and gone to the Holy Land, where he was wounded in an engagement against the infidels, made prisoner, and reported to be dead. When the news reached Manfred's ears, he bribed the guardians of the lady Isabella to deliver her up to him as a bride for his son Conrad; by which alliance he had purposed to unite the claims of the two houses. This motive, on Conrad's death, had co-operated to make him so suddenly resolve on espousing her himself; and the same reflection determined him now to endeavour at obtaining the consent of Frederic to this marriage. A like policy inspired him with the thought of inviting Frederic's champion into his castle, lest he should be informed of Isabella's flight, which he strictly enjoined his domestics not to disclose to any of the knight's retinue.

Herald, said Manfred, as soon as he had digested these reflections, return to thy master, and tell him, ere we liquidate our differences by the sword, Manfred would hold some converse with him. Bid him welcome to my castle, where, by my faith, as I am a true knight, he shall have courteous reception, and full security for himself and followers. If we cannot adjust our quarrel by amicable means,

I swear he shall depart in safety, and shall have full satisfaction according to the law of arms: so help me God and his holy Trinity!—The herald made three obeisances, and retired.

During this interview Jerome's mind was agitated by a thousand contrary passions. He trembled for the life of his son, and his first idea was to persuade Isabella to return to the castle. Yet he was scarce less alarmed at the thought of her union with Manfred. He dreaded Hippolita's unbounded submission to the will of her lord: and though he did not doubt but he could alarm her piety not to consent to a divorce, if he could get access to her; yet should Manfred discover that the obstruction came from him, it might be equally fatal to Theodore. He was impatient to know whence came the herald, who with so little management had questioned the title of Manfred: yet he did not dare absent himself from the convent, lest Isabella should leave it, and her flight be imputed to him. He returned disconsolately to the monastery, uncertain on what conduct to resolve. A monk, who met him in the porch and observed his melancholy air, said, Alas! brother, is it then true that we have lost our excellent princess Hippolita? The holy man started, and cried, What meanest thou, brother? I come this instant from the castle, and left her in perfect health. Martelli, replied the other friar, passed by the convent but a quarter of an hour ago on his way from the castle, and reported that her highness was dead. All our brethren are gone to the chapel to pray for her happy transit to a better life, and willed me to wait thy arrival. They know thy holy attachment to that good lady, and are anxious for the affliction it will cause in thee—Indeed we have all reason to weep; she was a mother to our house—But this life is but a pilgrimage; we must not murmur – we shall all follow her; may our end be like hers!—Good brother, thou dreamest, said Jerome: I tell thee I come from the castle, and left the princess well—Where is the lady Isabella?—Poor gentlewoman! replied the friar; I told her the sad news, and offered her spiritual comfort; I reminded her of the transitory condition of mortality, and advised her to take the veil: I quoted the example of the holy princess Sanchia of Arragon.—Thy zeal was laudable, said Jerome impatiently; but at present it was unnecessary: Hippolita is well – at least I trust in the Lord she is; I heard nothing to the contrary—Yet methinks the prince's earnestness—Well, brother, but where is the lady Isabella?—I know not, said the friar: she wept much, and said she would retire to her chamber. Jerome left his comrade abruptly, and hasted to the princess, but she was not in her chamber. He enquired of the domestics of the convent, but could learn no news of her. He searched in vain throughout the monastery and the church, and dispatched messengers round the neighbourhood, to get intelligence[1] if she had been seen; but to no purpose. Nothing could equal the good man's perplexity. He judged that Isabella, suspecting Manfred of having precipitated his wife's death, had taken the alarm, and withdrawn herself to some more secret place of concealment. This new flight would probably carry the prince's fury to the height. The report of Hippolita's death, though it seemed almost incredible, increased his consternation; and though Isabella's escape bespoke her aversion of Manfred for a husband, Jerome could feel no comfort from it, while it endangered the life of his son. He determined to return to the castle, and made several of his brethren accompany him, to attest his innocence to Manfred, and, if necessary, join their intercession with his for Theodore.

The prince, in the mean time, had passed into the court, and ordered the gates of the castle to be flung open for the reception of the stranger knight and his train. In a few minutes the cavalcade arrived. First came two harbingers with wands. Next a herald, followed by two pages and two trumpets. Then an hundred foot-guards. These were attended by as many horse. After them fifty footmen, clothed in scarlet and black, the colours of the knight. Then a led horse. Two heralds on each side of a gentleman on horseback bearing a banner with the arms of Vicenza and Otranto quarterly – a circumstance that much offended Manfred – but he stifled his resentment. Two more pages. The knight's confessor telling his beads. Fifty more footmen, clad as before. Two knights habited in complete armour, their beavers down, comrades to the principal knight. The 'squires of the two knights, carrying their shields and devices. The knight's own 'squire. An hundred gentlemen bearing an enormous sword, and seeming to faint under the weight of it. The knight himself on a chestnut steed, in complete armour, his lance in the rest, his face entirely concealed by his vizor, which was surmounted by a large plume of scarlet and black feathers. Fifty foot-guards with drums and trumpets closed the procession, which wheeled off to the right and left to make room for the principal knight.

As soon as he approached the gate, he stopped; and the herald advancing, read again the words of the challenge. Manfred's eyes were fixed on the gigantic sword, and he scarce seemed to attend to the cartel: but his attention was soon diverted by a tempest of wind that rose behind him. He turned, and beheld the plumes of the enchanted helmet agitated in the same extraordinary manner as before. It required intrepidity like Manfred's not to sink under a concurrence of circumstances that seemed to announce his fate. Yet scorning in the presence of strangers to betray the courage he had always manifested, he said boldly, Sir knight, whoever thou art, I bid thee welcome. If thou art of mortal mould, thy valour shall meet its equal: and if thou art a true knight, thou wilt scorn to employ sorcery to carry thy point. Be these omens from heaven or hell, Manfred trusts to the righteousness of his cause and to the aid of saint Nicholas, who has ever protected his house. Alight, sir knight, and repose thyself. To-morrow thou shalt have a fair field; and heaven befriend the juster side!

The knight made no reply, but, dismounting, was conducted by Manfred to the great hall of the castle. As they traversed the court, the knight stopped to gaze at the miraculous casque; and, kneeling down, seemed to pray inwardly for some minutes. Rising, he made a sign to the prince to lead on. As soon as they entered the hall, Manfred proposed to the stranger to disarm; but the knight shook his head in token of refusal. Sir knight, said Manfred, this is not courteous; but by my good faith I will not cross thee! nor shalt thou have cause to complain of the prince of Otranto. No treachery is designed on my part: I hope none is intended on thine. Here take my gage: [giving him his ring] your friends and you shall enjoy the laws of hospitality. Rest here until refreshments are brought: I will but give orders for the accommodation of your train, and return to you. The three knights bowed, as accepting his courtesy. Manfred directed the stranger's retinue to be conducted to an adjacent hospital, founded by the princess Hippolita for the reception of pilgrims. As they made the circuit of the court to return towards the gate, the gigantic sword burst from the supporters, and, falling to the ground opposite to the helmet, remained immoveable. Manfred, almost hardened to preternatural appearances, surmounted the shock of this new prodigy; and returning to the hall, where by this time the feast was ready, he invited his silent guests to take their places. Manfred, however ill his heart was at ease, endeavoured to inspire the company with mirth. He put several questions to them, but was answered only by signs. They raised their vizors but sufficiently to feed themselves, and that sparingly. Sirs, said the prince, ye are the first guests I ever treated within these walls, who scorned to hold any intercourse with me: nor has it oft been customary, I ween, for princes to hazard their state and dignity against strangers and mutes. You say you come in the name of Frederic of Vicenza: I have ever heard that he was a gallant and courteous knight; nor would he, I am bold to say, think it beneath him to mix in social converse with a prince that is his equal, and not unknown by deeds in arms.—Still ye are silent—Well! be it as it may – by the laws of hospitality and chivalry ye are masters under this roof: ye shall do your pleasure – but come, give me a goblet of wine; ye will not refuse to pledge me to the healths of your fair mistresses. The principal knight sighed and crossed himself, and was rising from the board—Sir knight, said Manfred, what I said was but in sport: I shall constrain you in nothing; use your good liking. Since mirth is not your mood, let us be sad. Business may hit your fancies better: let us withdraw; and hear if what I have to unfold may be better relished than the vain efforts I have made for your pastime.

Manfred, then, conducting the three knights into an inner chamber, shut the door, and, inviting them to be seated, began thus, addressing himself to the chief personage:

You come, sir knight, as I understand, in the name of the marquis of Vicenza, to re-demand the lady Isabella his daughter, who has been contracted in the face of holy church to my son, by the consent of her legal guardians; and to require me to resign my dominions to your lord, who gives himself for the nearest of blood to prince Alfonso, whose soul God rest! I shall speak to the latter article of your demands first. You must know, your lord knows, that I enjoy the principality of Otranto from my father Don Manuel, as he received it from his father Don Ricardo. Alfonso, their predecessor, dying childless in the Holy Land, bequeathed his estates to my grandfather Don Ricardo, in consideration of his faithful services – [The stranger shook his head] – Sir knight, said Manfred warmly, Ricardo was a valiant and upright man; he was a pious man; witness his munificent foundation of the adjoining church and two convents. He was peculiarly patronized by saint Nicholas—My grandfather was incapable—I say, sir, Don Ricardo was incapable—Excuse me, your interruption has disordered me—I venerate the memory of my grandfather—Well, sirs! he held this estate; he held it by his good sword, and by the favour of saint Nicholas – so did my father; and so, sirs, will I, come what will.—But Frederic, your lord, is nearest in blood – I have consented to put my title to the issue of the sword – does that imply a vitious[2] title? I might have asked, where is Frederic, your lord? Report speaks him dead in captivity. You say, your actions say, he lives – I question it not – I might, sirs, I might – but I do not. Other princes would bid Frederic take his inheritance by force, if he can: they would not stake their dignity on a single combat: they would not submit it to the decision of unknown mutes! Pardon me, gentlemen, I am too warm: but suppose yourselves in my situation: as ye are stout knights, would it not move your choler to have your own and the honour of your ancestors called in question?—But to the point. Ye require me to deliver up the lady Isabella—Sirs, I must ask if ye are authorized to receive her? [The knight nodded.] Receive her—continued Manfred: Well! you are authorized to receive her—But, gentle knight, may I ask if you have full powers? [The knight nodded.] 'Tis well, said Manfred: then hear what I have to offer—Ye see, gentlemen, before you the most unhappy of men! [he began to weep] afford me your compassion; I am entitled to it; indeed I am. Know, I have lost my only hope, my joy, the support of my house—Conrad died yester-morning. [The knights discovered signs of surprise.] Yes, sirs, fate has disposed of my son. Isabella is at liberty.—Do you then restore her, cried the chief knight, breaking silence. Afford me your patience, said Manfred. I rejoice to find, by this testimony of your good-will, that this matter may be adjusted without blood. It is no interest of mine dictates what little I have farther to say. Ye behold in me a man disgusted with the world: the loss of my son has weaned me from earthly cares. Power and greatness have no longer any charms in my eyes. I wished to transmit the sceptre I had received from my ancestors with honour to my son – but that is over! Life itself is so indifferent to me, that I accepted your defiance with joy: a good knight cannot go to the grave with more satisfaction than when falling in his vocation. Whatever is the will of heaven, I submit; for, alas! sirs, I am a man of many sorrows. Manfred is no object of envy – but no doubt you are acquainted with my story. [The knight made signs of ignorance, and seemed curious to have Manfred proceed.] Is it possible, sirs, continued the prince, that my story should be a secret to you? Have you heard nothing relating to me and the princess Hippolita? [They shook their heads]—No! Thus then, sirs, it is. You think me ambitious: ambition, alas, is composed of more rugged materials. If I were ambitious, I should not for so many years have been a prey to the hell of conscientious scruples—But I weary your patience: I will be brief. Know then, that I have long been troubled in mind on my union with the princess Hippolita.—Oh! sirs, if ye were acquainted with that excellent woman! if ye knew that I adore her like a mistress, and cherish her as a friend—But man was not born for perfect happiness! She shares my scruples, and with her consent I have brought this matter before the church, for we are related within the forbidden degrees. I expect every hour the definitive sentence that must separate us forever. I am sure you feel for me—I see you do—Pardon these tears! [The knights gazed on each other, wondering where this would end.] Manfred continued: The death of my son betiding while my soul was under this anxiety, I thought of nothing but resigning my dominions, and retiring forever from the sight of mankind. My only difficulty was to fix on a successor, who would be tender of my people, and to dispose of the lady Isabella, who is dear to me as my own blood. I was willing to restore the line of Alfonso, even in his most distant kindred: and though, pardon me, I am satisfied it was his will that Ricardo's lineage should take place of his own relations; yet, where was I to search for those relations? I knew of none but Frederic, your lord: he was a captive to the infidels, or dead; and were he living, and at home, would he quit the flourishing state of Vicenza for the inconsiderable principality of Otranto? If he would not, could I bear the thought of seeing a hard unfeeling viceroy set over my poor faithful people?—for, sirs, I love my people, and thank heaven am beloved by them.—But ye will ask, Whither tends this long discourse? Briefly then, thus, sirs. Heaven in your arrival seems to point out a remedy for these difficulties and my misfortunes. The lady Isabella is at liberty: I shall soon be so. I would submit to any thing for the good of my people—Were it not the best, the only way to extinguish the feuds between our families, if I were to take the lady Isabella to wife?—You start—But though Hippolita's virtues will ever be dear to me, a prince must not consider himself; he is born for his people.—A servant at that instant entering the chamber, apprized Manfred that Jerome and several of his brethren demanded immediate access to him.

The prince, provoked at this interruption, and fearing that the friar would discover to the strangers that Isabella had taken sanctuary, was going to forbid Jerome's entrance. But recollecting that he was certainly arrived to notify the princess's return, Manfred began to excuse himself to the knights for leaving them for a few moments, but was prevented by the arrival of the friars. Manfred angrily reprimanded them for their intrusion, and would have forced them back from the chamber; but Jerome was too much agitated to be repulsed. He declared aloud the flight of Isabella, with protestations of his own innocence. Manfred, distracted at the news, and not less at its coming to the knowledge of the strangers, uttered nothing but incoherent sentences, now upbraiding the friar, now apologizing to the knights, earnest to know what was become of Isabella, yet equally afraid of their knowing, impatient to pursue her, yet dreading to have them join in the pursuit. He offered to dispatch messengers in quest of her:—but the chief knight, no longer keeping silence, reproached Manfred in bitter terms for his dark and ambiguous dealing, and demanded the cause of Isabella's first absence from the castle. Manfred, casting a stern look at Jerome, implying a command of silence, pretended that on Conrad's death he had placed her in sanctuary until he could determine how to dispose of her. Jerome, who trembled for his son's life, did not dare contradict this falsehood; but one of his brethren, not under the same anxiety, declared frankly that she had fled to their church in the preceding night. The prince in vain endeavoured to stop this discovery, which overwhelmed him with shame and confusion. The principal stranger, amazed at the contradictions he heard, and more than half persuaded that Manfred had secreted the princess, notwithstanding the concern he expressed at her flight, rushing to the door, said, Thou traitor-prince! Isabella shall be found. Manfred endeavoured to hold him; but the other knights assisting their comrade, he broke from the prince, and hastened into the court, demanding his attendants. Manfred, finding it in vain to divert him from the pursuit, offered to accompany him; and summoning his attendants, and taking Jerome and some of the friars to guide them, they issued from the castle: Manfred privately giving orders to have the knight's company secured, while to the knight he affected to dispatch a messenger to require their assistance.

The company had no sooner quitted the castle, than Matilda, who felt herself deeply interested for the young peasant, since she had seen him condemned to death in the hall, and whose thoughts had been taken up with concerting measures to save him, was informed by some of the female attendants that Manfred had dispatched all his men various ways in pursuit of Isabella. He had in his hurry given this order in general terms, not meaning to extend it to the guard he had set upon Theodore, but forgetting it. The domestics, officious to obey so peremptory a prince, and urged by their own curiosity and love of novelty to join in any precipitate chace, had to a man left the castle. Matilda disengaged herself from her women, stole up to the black tower, and, unbolting the door, presented herself to the astonished Theodore. Young man, said she, though filial duty and womanly modesty condemn the step I am taking, yet holy charity, surmounting all other ties, justifies this act. Fly; the doors of thy prison are open: my father and his domestics are absent; but they may soon return: begone in safety; and may the angels of heaven direct thy course!—Thou art surely one of those angels! said the enraptured Theodore: none but a blessed saint could speak, could act, could look like thee!—May I not know the name of my divine protectress? Methought thou namedst thy father: is it possible? can Manfred's blood feel holy pity?—Lovely lady, thou answerest not— But how art thou here thyself? Why dost thou neglect thy own safety, and waste a thought on a wretch like Theodore? Let us fly together: the life thou bestowest shall be dedicated to thy defence. Alas! thou mistakest, said Matilda sighing: I am Manfred's daughter, but no dangers await me. Amazement! said Theodore: but last night I blessed myself for yielding thee the service thy gracious compassion so charitably returns me now. Still thou art in an error, said the princess; but this is no time for explanation. Fly, virtuous youth, while it is in my power to save thee: should my father return, thou and I both should indeed have cause to tremble. How? said Theodore: thinkest thou, charming maid, that I will accept of life at the hazard of aught calamitous to thee? Better I endured a thousand deaths— I run no risk, said Matilda, but by thy delay. Depart: it cannot be known that I assisted thy flight. Swear by the saints above, said Theodore, that thou canst not be suspected; else here I vow to await whatever can befall me. Oh! thou art too generous, said Matilda; but rest assured that no suspicion can alight on me. Give me thy beauteous hand in token that thou dost not deceive me, said Theodore; and let me bathe it with the warm tears of gratitude.—Forbear, said the princess: this must not be.—Alas! said Theodore, I have never known but calamity until this hour – perhaps shall never know other fortune again: suffer the chaste raptures of holy gratitude: 'tis my soul would print its effusions on thy hand.—Forbear, and begone, said Matilda: how would Isabella approve of seeing thee at my feet? Who is Isabella? said the young man with surprise. Ah me! I fear, said the princess, I am serving a deceitful one! Hast thou forgot thy curiosity this morning?—Thy looks, thy actions, all thy beauteous self seems an emanation of divinity, said Theodore, but thy words are dark and mysterious— Speak, lady, speak to thy servant's comprehension.—Thou understandest but too well, said Matilda: but once more I command thee to be gone: thy blood, which I may preserve, will be on my head, if I waste the time in vain discourse. I go, lady, said Theodore, because it is thy will, and because I would not bring the grey hairs of my father with sorrow to the grave. Say but, adored lady, that I have thy gentle pity—Stay, said Matilda; I will conduct thee to the subterraneous vault by which Isabella escaped; it will lead thee to the church of saint Nicholas, where thou mayst take sanctuary.—What! said Theodore, was it another, and not thy lovely self, that I assisted to find the subterraneous passage? It was, said Matilda: but ask no more; I tremble to see thee still abide here: fly to the sanctuary.—To sanctuary! said Theodore: No princess; sanctuaries are for helpless damsels, or for criminals. Theodore's soul is free from guilt, nor will wear the appearance of it. Give me a sword, lady, and thy father shall learn that Theodore scorns an ignominious flight. Rash youth! said Matilda, thou wouldst not dare to lift thy presumptuous arm against the prince of Otranto? Not against *thy* father; indeed I dare not, said Theodore: excuse me, lady; I had forgotten – but could I gaze on thee, and remember thou art sprung from the tyrant Manfred?—

But he is thy father, and from this moment my injuries are buried in oblivion. A deep and hollow groan, which seemed to come from above, startled the princess and Theodore. Good heaven! we are overheard! said the princess. They listened; but perceiving no farther noise, they both concluded it the effect of pent-up vapours: and the princess, preceding Theodore softly, carried him to her father's armoury; where equipping him with a complete suit, he was conducted by Matilda to the postern-gate. Avoid the town, said the princess, and all the western side of the castle: 'tis there the search must be making by Manfred and the strangers: but hie thee to the opposite quarter. Yonder, behind that forest to the east is a chain of rocks, hollowed into a labyrinth of caverns that reach to the sea-coast. There thou mayst lie concealed, till thou canst make signs to some vessel to put on shore and take thee off. Go! heaven be thy guide!—and sometimes in thy prayers remember—Matilda!—Theodore flung himself at her feet, and seizing her lily hand, which with struggles she suffered him to kiss, he vowed on the earliest opportunity to get himself knighted, and fervently entreated her permission to swear himself eternally her knight.—Ere the princess could reply, a clap of thunder was suddenly heard, that shook the battlements. Theodore, regardless of the tempest, would have urged his suit; but the princess, dismayed, retreated hastily into the castle, and commanded the youth to be gone, with an air that would not be disobeyed. He sighed, and retired, but with eyes fixed on the gate, until Matilda closing it put an end to an interview, in which the hearts of both had drunk so deeply of a passion which both now tasted for the first time.

Theodore went pensively to the convent, to acquaint his father with his deliverance. There he learned the absence of Jerome, and the pursuit that was making after the lady Isabella, with some particulars of whose story he now first became acquainted. The generous gallantry of his nature prompted him to wish to assist her; but the monks could lend him no lights to guess at the route she had taken. He was not tempted to wander far in search of her; for the idea of Matilda had imprinted itself so strongly on his heart, that he could not bear to absent himself at much distance from her abode. The tenderness Jerome had expressed for him concurred to confirm this reluctance; and he even persuaded himself that filial affection was the chief cause of his hovering between the castle and monastery. Until Jerome should return at night, Theodore at length determined to repair to the forest that Matilda had pointed out to him. Arriving there, he sought the gloomiest shades, as best suited to the pleasing melancholy that reigned in his mind. In this mood he roved insensibly to the caves which had formerly served as a retreat to hermits, and were now reported round the country to be haunted by evil spirits. He recollected to have heard this tradition; and being of a brave and adventurous disposition, he willingly indulged his curiosity in exploring the secret recesses of this labyrinth. He had not penetrated far before he thought he heard the steps of some person who seemed to retreat before him. Theodore, though firmly grounded in all our holy faith enjoins to be believed, had no apprehension that good men were abandoned without cause to the malice of the powers of darkness. He thought the place more likely to be infested by robbers, than by those infernal agents who are reported to molest and bewilder travellers. He had long burned with impatience to approve his valour. Drawing his sabre, he marched sedately onwards, still directing his steps as the imperfect rustling sound before him led the way. The armour he wore was a like indication to the person who avoided him. Theodore, now convinced that he was not mistaken, redoubled his pace, and evidently gained on the person that fled; whose haste increasing, Theodore came up just as a woman fell breathless before him. He hasted to raise her; but her terror was so great, that he apprehended she would faint in his arms. He used every gentle word to dispel her alarms, and assured her that, far from injuring, he would defend her at the peril of his life. The lady recovering her spirits from his courteous demeanour, and gazing on her protector, said, Sure I have heard that voice before?—Not to my knowledge, replied Theodore, unless, as I conjecture, thou art the lady Isabella.—Merciful heaven! cried she, thou art not sent in quest of me, art thou? And saying those words she threw herself at his feet, and besought him not to deliver her up to Manfred. To Manfred! cried Theodore—No, lady: I have once already delivered thee from his tyranny, and it shall fare hard with me now, but I will place thee out of the reach of his daring. Is it possible, said she, that thou shouldst be the generous unknown I met last night in the vault of the castle? Sure thou art not a mortal, but my guardian angel: on my knees let me thank— Hold, gentle princess, said Theodore, nor demean thyself before a poor and friendless young man. If heaven has selected me for thy deliverer, it will accomplish its work, and strengthen my arm in thy cause. But come, lady, we are too near the mouth of the cavern; let us seek its inmost recesses: I can have no tranquillity till I have placed thee beyond the reach of danger.—Alas! what mean you, sir? said she. Though all your actions are noble, though your sentiments speak the purity of your soul, is it fitting that I should accompany you alone into these perplexed retreats? Should we be found together, what would a censorious world think of my conduct?—I respect your virtuous delicacy, said Theodore; nor do you harbour a suspicion that wounds my honour. I meant to conduct you into the most private cavity of these rocks; and then, at the hazard of my life, to guard their entrance against every living thing. Besides, lady, continued he, drawing a deep sigh, beauteous and all perfect as your form is, and though my wishes are not guiltless of aspiring, know, my soul is dedicated to another; and although— A sudden noise prevented Theodore from proceeding. They soon distinguished these sounds, Isabella! What ho! Isabella!—

The trembling princess relapsed into her former agony of fear. Theodore endeavoured to encourage her, but in vain. He assured her he would die rather than suffer her to return under Manfred's power; and begging her to remain concealed, he went forth to prevent the person in search of her from approaching.

At the mouth of the cavern he found an armed knight discoursing with a peasant, who assured him he had seen a lady enter the passes of the rock. The knight was preparing to seek her, when Theodore, placing himself in his way, with his sword drawn, sternly forbad him at his peril to advance. And who are thou who darest to cross my way? said the knight haughtily. One who does not dare more than he will perform, said Theodore. I seek the lady Isabella, said the knight; and understand she has taken refuge among these rocks. Impede me not, or thou wilt repent having provoked my resentment.—Thy purpose is as odious as thy resentment is contemptible, said Theodore. Return whence thou camest, or we shall soon know whose resentment is most terrible.—The stranger, who was the principal knight that had arrived from the marquis of Vicenza, had galloped from Manfred as he was busied in getting information of the princess, and giving various orders to prevent her falling into the power of the three knights. Their chief had suspected Manfred of being privy to the princess's absconding; and this insult from a man who he concluded was stationed by that prince to secrete her, confirming his suspicions, he made no reply, but, discharging a blow with his sabre at Theodore, would soon have removed all obstruction, if Theodore, who took him for one of Manfred's captains, and who had no sooner given the provocation than prepared to support it, had not received the stroke on his shield. The valour that had so long been smothered in his breast, broke forth at once: he rushed impetuously on the knight, whose pride and wrath were not less powerful incentives to hardy deeds. The combat was furious, but not long. Theodore wounded the knight in three several places, and at last disarmed him as he fainted by the loss of blood. The peasant, who had fled on the first onset, had given the alarm to some of Manfred's domestics, who by his orders were dispersed through the forest in pursuit of Isabella. They came up as the knight fell, whom they soon discovered to be the noble stranger. Theodore, notwithstanding his hatred to Manfred, could not behold the victory he had gained without emotions of pity and generosity: but he was more touched, when he learned the quality of his adversary, and was informed that he was no retainer, but an enemy of Manfred. He assisted the servants of the latter in disarming the knight, and in endeavouring to staunch the blood that flowed from his wounds. The knight, recovering his speech, said in a faint and faltering voice, Generous foe, we have both been in an error: I took thee for an instrument of the tyrant; I perceive thou hast made the like mistake—It is too late for excuses—I faint.—If Isabella is at hand, call her—I have important secrets to—He is dying! said one of the attendants; has nobody a crucifix about them? Andrea, do thou pray over him.—Fetch some water, said Theodore, and pour it down his throat, while I hasten to the princess. Saying this, he flew to Isabella; and in a few words told her modestly, that he had been so unfortunate by mistake as to wound a gentleman from her father's court, who wished ere he died to impart something of consequence to her. The princess, who had been transported at hearing the voice of Theodore as he called her to come forth, was astonished at what she heard. Suffering herself to be conducted by Theodore, the new proof of whose valour recalled her dispersed spirits, she came where the bleeding knight lay speechless on the ground – but her fears returned when she beheld the domestics of Manfred. She would again have fled, if Theodore had not made her observe that they were unarmed, and had not threatened them with instant death, if they should dare to seize the princess. The stranger, opening his eyes, and beholding a woman, said, Art thou – pray tell me truly – art thou Isabella of Vicenza? I am, said she; good heaven restore thee!—Then thou – then thou—said the knight, struggling for utterance – seest – thy father!—Give me one— Oh! amazement! horror! what do I hear? what do I see? cried Isabella. My father! You my father! How come you here, sir? For heaven's sake speak!—Oh! run for help, or he will expire!—'Tis most true, said the wounded knight, exerting all his force; I am Frederic thy father—Yes, I came to deliver thee—It will not be—Give me a parting kiss, and take— Sir, said Theodore, do not exhaust yourself: suffer us to convey you to the castle.—To the castle! said Isabella: Is there no help nearer than the castle? Would you expose my father to the tyrant? If he goes thither, I dare not accompany him.—And yet, can I leave him?—My child, said Frederic, it matters not for me whither I am carried: a few minutes will place me beyond danger: but while I have eyes to dote on thee, forsake me not, dear Isabella! This brave knight – I know not who he is – will protect thy innocence. Sir, you will not abandon my child, will you?—Theodore, shedding tears over his victim, and vowing to guard the princess at the expence of his life, persuaded Frederic to suffer himself to be conducted to the castle. They placed him on a horse belonging to one of the domestics, after binding up his wounds as well as they were able. Theodore marched by his side; and the afflicted Isabella, who could not bear to quit him, followed mournfully behind.

# CHAPTER 4

THE sorrowful troop no sooner arrived at the castle, than they were met by Hippolita and Matilda, whom Isabella had sent one of the domestics before to advertise of their approach. The ladies, causing Frederic to be conveyed into the nearest chamber, retired, while the surgeons examined his wounds. Matilda blushed at seeing Theodore and Isabella together; but endeavoured to conceal it by embracing the latter, and condoling with her on her father's mischance. The surgeons soon came to acquaint Hippolita that none of the marquis's wounds were dangerous; and that he was desirous of seeing his daughter and the princesses. Theodore, under pretence of expressing his joy at being freed from his apprehensions of the combat being fatal to Frederic, could not resist the impulse of following Matilda. Her eyes were so often cast down on meeting his, that Isabella, who regarded Theodore as attentively as he gazed on Matilda, soon divined who the object was that he had told her in the cave engaged his affections. While this mute scene passed, Hippolita demanded of Frederic the cause of his having taken that mysterious course for reclaiming his daughter; and threw in various apologies to excuse her lord for the match contracted between their children. Frederic, however incensed against Manfred, was not insensible to the courtesy and benevolence of Hippolita: but he was still more struck with the lovely form of Matilda. Wishing to detain them by his bed-side, he informed Hippolita of his story. He told her, that, while prisoner to the infidels, he had dreamed that his daughter, of whom he had learned no news since his captivity, was detained in a castle, where she was in danger of the most dreadful misfortunes; and that if he obtained his liberty, and repaired to a wood near Joppa, he would learn more. Alarmed at this dream, and incapable of obeying the direction given by it, his chains became more grievous than ever. But while his thoughts were occupied on the means of obtaining his liberty, he received the agreeable news that the confederate princes, who were warring in Palestine, had paid his ransom. He instantly set out for the wood that had been marked in his dream. For three days he and his attendants had wandered in the forest without seeing a human form: but on the evening of the third they came to a cell, in which they found a venerable hermit in the agonies of death. Applying rich cordials, they brought the saint-like man to his speech. My sons, said he, I am bounden to your charity – but it is in vain – I am going to my eternal rest – yet I die with the satisfaction of performing the will of heaven. When first I repaired to this solitude, after seeing my country become a prey to unbelievers [it is, alas! above fifty years since I was witness to that dreadful scene!] saint Nicholas appeared to me, and revealed a secret, which he bade me never disclose to mortal man, but on my death-bed. This is that tremendous hour, and ye are no doubt the chosen warriors to whom I was ordered to reveal my trust. As soon as ye have done the last offices to this wretched corse, dig under the seventh tree on the left hand of this poor cave, and your pains will—Oh! good heaven receive my soul! With those words the devout man breathed his last. By break of day, continued Frederic, when we had committed the holy relics to earth, we dug according to direction—But what was our astonishment, when about the depth of six feet we discovered an enormous sabre – the very weapon yonder in the court! On the blade, which was then partly out of the scabbard, though since closed by our efforts in removing it, were written the following lines— No: excuse me, madam, added the marquis, turning to Hippolita, if I forbear to repeat them: I respect your sex and rank, and would not be guilty of offending your ear with sounds injurious to aught that is dear to you.—He paused. Hippolita trembled. She did not doubt but Frederic was destined by heaven to accomplish the fate that seemed to threaten her house. Looking with anxious fondness at Matilda, a silent tear stole down her cheek; but recollecting herself, she said, Proceed, my lord; heaven does nothing in vain: mortals must receive its divine behests with lowliness and submission. It is our part to deprecate its wrath, or bow to its decrees. Repeat the sentence, my lord: we listen resigned.—Frederic was grieved that he had proceeded so far. The dignity and patient firmness of Hippolita penetrated him with respect, and the tender silent affection, with which the princess and her daughter regarded each other, melted him almost to tears. Yet apprehensive that his forbearance to obey would be more alarming, he repeated in a faltering and low voice the following lines:

> Where'er a casque that suits this sword is found,
> With perils is thy daughter compass'd round:
> Alfonso's blood alone can save the maid,
> And quiet a long-restless prince's shade.

What is there in these lines, said Theodore impatiently, that affects these princesses? Why were they to be shocked by a mysterious delicacy, that has so little foundation? Your words are rude, young man, said the marquis; and though fortune has favoured you once—My honoured lord, said Isabella, who resented Theodore's warmth, which she perceived was dictated by his sentiments for Matilda, discompose not yourself for the glosing of a peasant's son: he forgets the reverence he owes you; but he is not accustomed—Hippolita, concerned at the heat that had arisen, checked Theodore for his boldness, but with an air acknowledging his zeal; and, changing the conversation, demanded of Frederic where he had left her lord? As the marquis was going to reply, they heard a noise without; and rising to enquire the cause, Manfred,

Jerome, and part of the troop, who had met an imperfect rumour of what had happened, entered the chamber. Manfred advanced hastily towards Frederic's bed to condole with him on his misfortune, and to learn the circumstances of the combat; when starting in an agony of terror and amazement, he cried, Ha! what art thou, thou dreadful spectre! Is my hour come?—My dearest, gracious lord, cried Hippolita, clasping him in her arms, what is it you see? Why do you fix your eye-balls thus?—What! cried Manfred breathless—dost thou see nothing, Hippolita? Is this ghastly phantom sent to me alone – to me, who did not— For mercy's sweetest self, my lord, said Hippolita, resume your soul, command your reason. There is none here but we, your friends.—What, is not that Alfonso? cried Manfred: dost thou not see him? Can it be my brain's delirium?—This! my lord, said Hippolita: this is Theodore, the youth who has been so unfortunate—Theodore! said Manfred mournfully, and striking his forehead—Theodore, or a phantom, he has unhinged the soul of Manfred.—But how comes he here? and how comes he in armour? I believe he went in search of Isabella, said Hippolita. Of Isabella? said Manfred, relapsing into rage—Yes, yes, that is not doubtful—But how did he escape from durance in which I left him? Was it Isabella, or this hypocritical old friar, that procured his enlargement?[1]—And would a parent be criminal, my lord, said Theodore, if he meditated the deliverance of his child? Jerome, amazed to hear himself in a manner accused by his son, and without foundation, knew not what to think. He could not comprehend how Theodore had escaped, how he came to be armed, and to encounter Frederic. Still he would not venture to ask any questions that might tend to inflame Manfred's wrath against his son. Jerome's silence convinced Manfred that he had contrived Theodore's release. —And is it thus, thou ungrateful old man, said the prince, addressing himself to the friar, that thou repayest mine and Hippolita's bounties? And not content with traversing my heart's nearest wishes, thou armest thy bastard, and bringest him into my own castle to insult me!—My lord, said Theodore, you wrong my father, nor he nor I is capable of harbouring a thought against your peace. Is it insolence thus to surrender myself to your highness's pleasure? added he, laying his sword respectfully at Manfred's feet. Behold my bosom; strike, my lord, if you suspect that a disloyal thought is lodged there. There is not a sentiment engraven on my heart, that does not venerate you and yours. The grace and fervour with which Theodore uttered these words, interested every person present in his favour. Even Manfred was touched—yet still possessed with his resemblance to Alfonso, his admiration was dashed with secret horror. Rise, said he; thy life is not my present purpose.—But tell me thy history, and how thou camest connected with this old traitor here. My lord! said Jerome eagerly.—Peace, impostor! said Manfred; I will not have him prompted. My lord, said Theodore, I want no assistance; my story is very brief. I was carried at five years of age to Algiers with my mother, who had been taken by corsairs from the coast of Sicily. She died of grief in less than a twelvemonth.—The tears gushed from Jerome's eyes, on whose countenance a thousand anxious passions stood expressed. Before she died, continued Theodore, she bound a writing about my arm under my garments, which told me I was the son of the count Falconara.—It is most true, said Jerome; I am that wretched father.—Again I enjoin thee silence, said Manfred: proceed. I remained in slavery, said Theodore, until within these two years, when attending on my master in his cruizes, I was delivered by a christian vessel, which overpowered the pirate; and discovering myself to the captain, he generously put me on shore in Sicily. But alas! instead of finding a father, I learned that his estate, which was situated on the coast, had during his absence been laid waste by the rover who had carried my mother and me into captivity: that his castle had been burnt to the ground:

and that my father on his return had sold what remained, and was retired into religion in the kingdom of Naples, but where, no man could inform me. Destitute and friendless, hopeless almost of attaining the transport of a parent's embrace, I took the first opportunity of setting sail for Naples; from whence within these six days I wandered into this province, still supporting myself by the labour of my hands; nor till yester-morn did I believe that heaven had reserved any lot for me but peace of mind and contented poverty. This, my lord, is Theodore's story. I am blessed beyond my hope in finding a father; I am unfortunate beyond my desert in having incurred your highness's displeasure. He ceased. A murmur of approbation gently arose from the audience. This is not all, said Frederic; I am bound in honour to add what he suppresses. Though he is modest, I must be generous – he is one of the bravest youths on christian ground. He is warm too; and from the short knowledge I have of him, I will pledge myself for his veracity: if what he reports of himself were not true, he would not utter it – and for me, youth, I honour a frankness which becomes thy birth. But now, and thou didst offend me; yet the noble blood which flows in thy veins may well be allowed to boil out, when it has so recently traced itself to its source. Come, my lord, [turning to Manfred] if I can pardon him, surely you may: it is not the youth's fault, if you took him for a spectre. This bitter taunt galled the soul of Manfred. If beings from another world, replied he haughtily, have power to impress my mind with awe, it is more than living man can do; nor could a stripling's arm— My lord, interrupted Hippolita, your guest has occasion for repose; shall we not leave him to his rest? Saying this, and taking Manfred by the hand, she took leave of Frederic, and led the company forth. The prince, not sorry to quit a conversation which recalled to mind the discovery he had made of his most secret sensations, suffered himself to be conducted to his own apartment, after permitting Theodore, though under engagement to return to the castle on the morrow, [a condition the young man gladly accepted] to retire with his father to the convent. Matilda and Isabella were too much occupied with their own reflections, and too little content with each other, to wish for farther converse that night. They separated each to her chamber, with more expressions of ceremony, and fewer of affection, than had passed between them since their childhood.

If they parted with small cordiality, they did but meet with greater impatience as soon as the sun was risen. Their minds were in a situation that excluded sleep, and each recollected a thousand questions which she wished she had put to the other overnight. Matilda reflected that Isabella had been twice delivered by Theodore in very critical situations, which she could not believe accidental. His eyes, it was true, had been fixed on her in Frederic's chamber; but that might have been to disguise his passion for Isabella from the fathers of both. It were better to clear this up. She wished to know the truth, lest she should wrong her friend by entertaining a passion for Isabella's lover. Thus jealousy prompted, and at the same time borrowed an excuse from friendship to justify its curiosity.

Isabella, not less restless, had better foundation for her suspicions. Both Theodore's tongue and eyes had told her his heart was engaged, it was true – yet perhaps Matilda might not correspond to his passion—She had ever appeared insensible to love; all her thoughts were set on heaven—Why did I dissuade her? said Isabella to herself; I am punished for my generosity—But when did they meet? where?—It cannot be; I have deceived myself.—Perhaps last night was the first time they ever beheld each other – it must be some other object that has prepossessed his affections—If it is, I am not so unhappy as I thought; if it is not my friend Matilda—How! can I stoop to wish for the affection of a man, who rudely and unnecessarily acquainted me with his indifference? and that at the very moment in which common courtesy demanded at least expressions of civility. I will go to my dear Matilda, who will confirm me in this becoming pride—Man is false—I will advise with her on taking the veil: she will rejoice to find me in this disposition; and I will acquaint her that I no longer oppose her inclination for the cloister. In this frame of mind, and determined to open her heart entirely to Matilda, she went to that princess's chamber, whom she found already dressed, and leaning pensively on her arm. This attitude, so correspondent to what she felt herself, revived Isabella's suspicions, and destroyed the confidence she had purposed to place in her friend. They blushed at meeting, and were too much novices to disguise their sensations with address. After some unmeaning questions and replies, Matilda demanded of Isabella the cause of her flight. The latter, who had almost forgotten Manfred's passion, so entirely was she occupied by her own, concluding that Matilda referred to her last escape from the convent, which had occasioned the events of the preceding evening, replied, Martelli brought word to the convent that your mother was dead.—Oh! said Matilda interrupting her, Bianca has explained that mistake to me: on seeing me faint, she cried out, The princess is dead! and Martelli, who had come for the usual dole to the castle— And what made you faint? said Isabella, indifferent to the rest. Matilda blushed, and stammered—My father—he was sitting in judgment on a criminal.—What criminal? said Isabella eagerly.— A young man, said Matilda—I believe —I think it was that young man that—What, Theodore? said Isabella. Yes, answered she; I never saw him before; I do not know how he had offended my father – but, as he has been of service to you, I am glad my lord has pardoned him. Served me? replied Isabella: do you term it serving me, to wound my father, and almost occasion his death? Though it is but since yesterday that I am blessed with knowing a parent, I hope Matilda does not think I am such a stranger to filial tenderness as not to resent the boldness of that audacious youth, and that it is impossible for me ever to feel any affection for one who dared to lift his arm against the author of my being. No, Matilda, my heart abhors him; and if you still retain the friendship for me that you have vowed from your infancy, you will detest a man who has been on the point of making me miserable for ever. Matilda held down her head, and replied, I hope my dearest Isabella does not doubt her Matilda's friendship: I never beheld that youth until yesterday; he is almost a stranger to me: but as the surgeons have pronounced your father out of danger, you ought not to harbour uncharitable resentment against one who I am persuaded did not know the marquis was related to you. You plead his cause very pathetically, said Isabella, considering he is so much a stranger to you! I am mistaken, or he returns your charity. What mean you? said Matilda. Nothing, said Isabella; repenting that she had given Matilda a hint of Theodore's inclination for her. Then changing the discourse, she asked Matilda what occasioned Manfred to take Theodore for a spectre? Bless me, said Matilda, did not you observe his extreme resemblance to the portrait of Alfonso in the gallery? I took notice of it to Bianca even before I saw him in armour; but with the helmet on, he is the very image of that picture. I do not much observe pictures, said Isabella; much less have I examined this young man so attentively as you seem to have done.— Ah! Matilda, your heart is in danger – but let me warn you as a friend—He has owned to me that he is in love: it cannot be with you, for yesterday was the first time you ever met – was it not? Certainly, replied Matilda. But why does my dearest Isabella conclude from any thing I have said, that—She paused—then continuing, He saw you first, and I am far from having the vanity to think that my little portion of charms could engage a heart devoted to you. May you be happy, Isabella, whatever is the fate of Matilda!—My lovely friend, said Isabella, whose heart was too honest to resist a kind expression, it is you that Theodore admires; I saw it; I am persuaded of it; nor shall a thought of my own happiness suffer me to interfere with yours. This frankness drew tears from the gentle Matilda; and jealousy, that for a moment had raised a coolness between these amiable maidens, soon gave way to the natural sincerity and candour of their souls. Each confessed to the other the impression that Theodore had made on her; and this confidence was followed by a struggle of generosity, each insisting on yielding her claim to her friend. At length, the dignity of Isabella's virtue reminding her of the preference which Theodore had almost declared for her rival, made her determine to conquer her passion, and cede the beloved object to her friend.

During this contest of amity, Hippolita entered her daughter's chamber. Madam, said she to Isabella, you have so much tenderness for Matilda, and interest yourself so kindly in whatever affects our wretched house, that I can have no secrets with my child, which are not proper for you to hear. The princesses were all attention and anxiety. Know then, madam, continued Hippolita, and you, my dearest Matilda, that being convinced by all the events of these two last ominous days, that heaven purposes the sceptre of Otranto should pass from Manfred's hands into those of the marquis Frederic, I have been perhaps inspired with the thought of averting our total destruction by the union of our rival houses. With this view I have been proposing to Manfred my lord to tender this dear dear child to Frederic your father—Me to lord Frederic! cried Matilda—Good heavens! my gracious mother – and have you named it to my father? I have, said Hippolita: he listened benignly to my proposal, and is gone to break it to the marquis. Ah! wretched princess! cried Isabella, what hast thou done? What ruin has thy inadvertent goodness been preparing for thyself, for me, and for Matilda! Ruin from me to you and to my child! said Hippolita: What can this mean? Alas! said Isabella, the purity of your own heart prevents your seeing the depravity of others. Manfred, your lord, that impious man— Hold, said Hippolita; you must not in my presence, young lady, mention Manfred with disrespect: he is my lord and husband, and—Will not be long so, said Isabella, if his wicked purposes can be carried into execution. This language amazes me, said Hippolita. Your feeling, Isabella, is warm; but until this hour I never knew it betray you into intemperance. What deed of Manfred authorizes you to treat him as a murderer, an assassin? Thou virtuous and too credulous princess! replied Isabella; it is not thy life he aims at – it is to separate himself from thee! to divorce thee! To – to divorce me! To divorce my mother! cried Hippolita and Matilda at once.—Yes, said Isabella; and to complete his crime, he meditates—I cannot speak it! What can surpass what thou hast already uttered? said Matilda. Hippolita was silent. Grief choked her speech: and the recollection of Manfred's late ambiguous discourses confirmed what she heard. Excellent, dear lady! madam! mother! cried Isabella, flinging herself at Hippolita's feet in a transport of passion; trust me, believe me, I will die a thousand deaths sooner than consent to injure you, than yield to so odious —oh!—This is too much! cried Hippolita: what crimes does one crime suggest! Rise, dear Isabella; I do not doubt your virtue. Oh! Matilda, this stroke is too heavy for thee! Weep not, my child; and not a murmur, I charge thee. Remember, he is *thy* father still.—But you are my mother too, said Matilda fervently; and *you* are virtuous, *you* are guiltless!—Oh! must not I, must not I complain? You must not, said Hippolita—Come, all will yet be well. Manfred, in the agony for the loss of thy brother, knew not what he said: perhaps Isabella misunderstood him: his heart is good – and, my child, thou knowest not all. There is a destiny hangs over us; the hand of Providence is stretched out—Oh! could I but save thee from the wreck! —Yes, continued she in a firmer tone, perhaps the sacrifice of myself may atone for all— I will go and offer myself to this divorce – it boots not what becomes of me. I will withdraw into the neighbouring monastery, and waste the remainder of life in prayers and tears for my child and – the prince! Thou art as much too good for this world, said Isabella, as Manfred is execrable—But think not, lady, that thy weakness shall determine for me. I swear – hear me, all ye angels— Stop, I adjure thee, cried Hippolita; remember, thou dost not depend on thyself; thou hast a father.—My father is too pious, too noble, interrupted Isabella, to command an impious deed. But should he command it, can a father enjoin a cursed act? I was contracted to the son; can I wed the father?—No, madam, no; force should not drag me to Manfred's hated bed. I loathe him, I abhor him: divine and human laws forbid.—And my friend, my dearest Matilda! would I wound her tender soul by injuring her adored mother? my own mother—I never have known another.— Oh! she is the mother of both! cried Matilda. Can we, can we, Isabella, adore her too much? My lovely children, said the touched Hippolita, your tenderness overpowers me – but I must not give way to it. It is not ours to make election for ourselves; heaven, our fathers, and our husbands, must decide for us. Have patience until you hear what Manfred and Frederic have determined. If the marquis accepts Matilda's hand, I know she will readily obey. Heaven may interpose and prevent the rest. What means my child? continued she, seeing Matilda fall at her feet with a flood of speechless tears—But no; answer me not, my daughter; I must not hear a word against the pleasure of thy father. Oh! doubt not my obedience, my dreadful obedience to him and to you! said Matilda. But can I, most respected of women, can I experience all this tenderness, this world of goodness, and conceal a thought from the best of mothers? What art thou going to utter? said Isabella trembling. Recollect thyself, Matilda. No, Isabella, said the princess, I should not deserve this incomparable parent, if the inmost recesses of my soul harboured a thought without her permission—Nay, I have offended her; I have suffered a passion to enter my heart without her avowal—But here I disclaim it; here I vow to heaven and her— My child! my child! said Hippolita, what words are these? What new calamities has fate in store for us? Thou, a passion! thou, in this hour of destruction— Oh! I see all my guilt! said Matilda. I abhor myself, if I cost my mother a pang. She is the dearest thing I have on earth—Oh! I will never, never behold him more! Isabella, said Hippolita, thou art conscious to this unhappy secret, whatever it is. Speak—What! cried Matilda, have I so forfeited my mother's love that she will not permit me even to speak my own guilt? Oh! wretched, wretched Matilda!—Thou art too cruel, said Isabella to Hippolita: canst thou behold this anguish of a virtuous mind, and not commiserate it? Not pity my child! said Hippolita, catching Matilda in her arms—Oh! I know she is good, she is all virtue, all tenderness, and duty. I do forgive thee, my excellent, my only hope! The princesses then revealed to Hippolita their mutual inclination for Theodore, and the purpose of Isabella to resign him to Matilda. Hippolita blamed their imprudence, and shewed them the improbability that either father would consent to bestow his heiress on so poor a man, though nobly born. Some comfort it gave her to find their passion of so recent a date, and that Theodore had but little cause to suspect it in either. She strictly enjoined them to avoid all correspondence with him. This Matilda fervently promised: but Isabella, who flattered herself that she meant no more than to promote his union with her friend, could not determine to avoid him; and made no reply. I will go to the convent, said Hippolita, and order new masses to be said for a deliverance from these calamities.—Oh! my mother, said Matilda, you mean to quit us: you mean to take sanctuary, and to give my father an opportunity of pursuing his fatal intention. Alas! on my knees I supplicate you to forbear—Will you leave me a prey to Frederic? I will follow you to the convent.—Be at peace, my child, said Hippolita: I will return instantly. I will never abandon thee, until I know it is the will of heaven, and for thy benefit. Do not deceive me, said Matilda. I will not marry Frederic until thou commandest it. Alas! what will become of me?—Why that exclamation? said Hippolita. I have promised thee to return.—Ah! my mother, replied Matilda, stay and save me from myself. A frown from thee can do more than all my father's severity. I have given away my heart, and you alone can make me recall it. No more, said Hippolita; thou must not relapse, Matilda. I can quit Theodore, said she, but must I wed another? Let me attend thee to the altar, and shut myself from the world forever. Thy fate depends on thy father, said Hippolita: I have ill bestowed my tenderness, if it has taught thee to revere aught beyond him. Adieu, my child! I go to pray for thee.

Hippolita's real purpose was to demand of Jerome, whether in conscience she might not consent to the divorce. She had oft urged Manfred to resign the principality, which the delicacy of her conscience rendered an hourly burthen to her. These scruples concurred to make the separation from her husband appear less dreadful to her than it would have seemed in any other situation.

Jerome, at quitting the castle overnight, had questioned Theodore severely why he had accused him to Manfred of being privy to his escape. Theodore owned it had been with design to prevent Manfred's suspicion from alighting on Matilda; and added, the holiness of Jerome's life and character secured him from the tyrant's wrath. Jerome was heartily grieved to discover his son's inclination for that princess; and, leaving him to his rest, promised in the morning to acquaint him with important reasons for conquering his passion. Theodore, like Isabella, was too recently acquainted with parental authority to submit to its decisions against the impulse of his heart. He had little curiosity to learn the friar's reasons, and less disposition to obey them. The lovely Matilda had made stronger impressions on him than filial affection. All night he pleased himself with visions of love; and it was not till late after the morning-office, that he recollected the friar's commands to attend him at Alfonso's tomb.

Young man, said Jerome, when he saw him, this tardiness does not please me. Have a father's commands already so little weight? Theodore made awkward excuses, and attributed his delay to having overslept himself. And on whom were thy dreams employed? said the friar sternly. His son blushed. Come, come, resumed the friar, inconsiderate youth, this must not be; eradicate this guilty passion from thy breast.—Guilty passion! cried Theodore: can guilt dwell with innocent beauty and virtuous modesty? It is sinful, replied the friar, to cherish those whom heaven has doomed to destruction. A tyrant's race must be swept from the earth to the third and fourth generation. Will heaven visit the innocent for the crimes of the guilty? said Theodore. The fair Matilda has virtues enough—To undo thee, interrupted Jerome. Hast thou so soon forgotten that twice the savage Manfred has pronounced thy sentence? Nor have I forgotten, sir, said Theodore, that the charity of his daughter delivered me from his power. I can forget injuries, but never benefits. The injuries thou hast received from Manfred's race, said the friar, are beyond what thou canst conceive.—Reply not, but view this holy image! Beneath this marble monument rest the ashes of good Alfonso; a prince adorned with every virtue: the father of his people! the delight of mankind! Kneel, headstrong boy, and list, while a father unfolds a tale of horror, that will expel every sentiment from thy soul, but sensations of sacred vengeance.—Alfonso! much-injured prince! let thy unsatisfied shade sit awful on the troubled air, while these trembling lips—Ha! who comes there?—The most wretched of women, said Hippolita, entering the choir. Good father, art thou at leisure?—But why this kneeling youth? what means the horror imprinted on each countenance? why at this venerable tomb

—Alas! hast thou seen aught? We were pouring forth our orisons to heaven, replied the friar with some confusion, to put an end to the woes of this deplorable province. Join with us, lady! thy spotless soul may obtain an exemption from the judgments which the portents of these days but too speakingly denounce against thy house. I pray fervently to heaven to divert them, said the pious princess. Thou knowest it has been the occupation of my life to wrest a blessing for my lord and my harmless children—One, alas! is taken from me! Would heaven but hear me for my poor Matilda! Father, intercede for her!—Every heart will bless her, cried Theodore with rapture.—Be dumb, rash youth! said Jerome. And thou, fond princess, contend not with the powers above! The Lord giveth, and the Lord taketh away: bless his holy name, and submit to his decrees. I do most devoutly, said Hippolita: but will he not spare my only comfort? must Matilda perish too? —Ah! father, I came—But dismiss thy son. No ear but thine must hear what I have to utter. May heaven grant thy every wish, most excellent princess! said Theodore retiring. Jerome frowned.

Hippolita then acquainted the friar with the proposal she had suggested to Manfred, his approbation of it, and the tender of Matilda that he was gone to make to Frederic. Jerome could not conceal his dislike of the motion, which he covered under pretence of the improbability that Frederic, the nearest of blood to Alfonso, and who was come to claim his succession, would yield to an alliance with the usurper of his right. But nothing could equal the perplexity of the friar, when Hippolita confessed her readiness not to oppose the separation, and demanded his opinion on the legality of her acquiescence. The friar catched eagerly at her request of his advice; and without explaining his aversion to the proposed marriage of Manfred and Isabella, he painted to Hippolita in the most alarming colours the sinfulness of her consent, denounced judgments against her if she complied, and enjoined her in the severest terms to treat any such proposition with every mark of indignation and refusal.

Manfred, in the mean time, had broken his purpose to Frederic, and proposed the double marriage. That weak prince, who had been struck with the charms of Matilda, listened but too eagerly to the offer. He forgot his enmity to Manfred, whom he saw but little hope of dispossessing by force; and flattering himself that no issue might succeed from the union of his daughter with the tyrant, he looked upon his own succession to the principality as facilitated by wedding Matilda. He made faint opposition to the proposal; affecting, for form only, not to acquiesce unless Hippolita should consent to the divorce. Manfred took that upon himself. Transported with his success, and impatient to see himself in a situation to expect sons, he hastened to his wife's apartment, determined to extort her compliance. He learned with indignation that she was absent at the convent. His guilt suggested to him that she had probably been informed by Isabella of his purpose. He doubted whether her retirement to the convent did not import an intention of remaining there, until she could raise obstacles to their divorce; and the suspicions he had already entertained of Jerome, made him apprehend that the friar would not only traverse his views, but might have inspired Hippolita with the resolution of taking sanctuary. Impatient to unravel this clue, and to defeat its success, Manfred hastened to the convent, and arrived there as the friar was earnestly exhorting the princess never to yield to the divorce.

Madam, said Manfred, what business drew you hither? Why did not you await my return from the marquis? I came to implore a blessing on your councils, replied Hippolita. My councils do not need a friar's intervention, said Manfred—and of all men living is that hoary traitor the only one whom you delight to confer with? Profane prince! said Jerome: is it at the altar that thou choosest to insult the servants of the altar?—But, Manfred, thy impious schemes are known. Heaven and this virtuous lady know them. Nay, frown not, prince. The church despises thy menaces. Her thunders will be heard above thy wrath. Dare to proceed in thy curst purpose of a divorce, until her sentence be known, and here I lance her anathema at thy head. Audacious rebel! said Manfred, endeavouring to conceal the awe with which the friar's words inspired him; dost thou presume to threaten thy lawful prince? Thou art no lawful prince, said Jerome; thou art no prince—Go, discuss thy claim with Frederic, and when that is done— It is done, replied Manfred: Frederic accepts Matilda's hand, and is content to wave his claim, unless I have no male issue.—As he spoke those words three drops of blood fell from the nose of Alfonso's statue. Manfred turned pale, and the princess sunk on her knees. Behold! said the friar: mark this miraculous indication that the blood of Alfonso will never mix with that of Manfred! My gracious lord, said Hippolita, let us submit ourselves to heaven. Think not thy ever obedient wife rebels against thy authority. I have no will but that of my lord and the church. To that revered tribunal let us appeal. It does not depend on us to burst the bonds that unite us. If the church shall approve the dissolution of our marriage, be it so— I have but few years, and those of sorrow, to pass. Where they be worn away so well as at the foot of this altar, in prayers for thine and Matilda's safety?—But thou shalt not remain here until then, said Manfred. Repair with me to the castle, and there I will advise on the proper measures for a divorce.—But this meddling friar comes not thither; my hospitable roof shall never more harbour a traitor – and for thy reverence's offspring, continued he, I banish him from my dominions. He, I ween, is no sacred personage, nor under the protection of the church. Whoever weds Isabella, it shall not be father Falconara's started-up son. They start up, said the friar, who are suddenly beheld in the seat of lawful princes; but they wither away like the grass, and their place knows them no more.

Manfred, casting a look of scorn at the friar, led Hippolita forth; but at the door of the church whispered one of his attendants to remain concealed about the convent, and bring him instant notice, if any one from the castle should repair thither.

## CHAPTER 5

EVERY reflection which Manfred made on the friar's behaviour, conspired to persuade him that Jerome was privy to an amour between Isabella and Theodore. But Jerome's new presumption, so dissonant from his former meekness, suggested still deeper apprehensions. The prince even suspected that the friar depended on some secret support from Frederic, whose arrival coinciding with the novel appearance of Theodore seemed to bespeak a correspondence. Still more was he troubled with the resemblance of Theodore to Alfonso's portrait. The latter he knew had unquestionably died without issue. Frederic had consented to bestow Isabella on him. These contradictions agitated his mind with numberless pangs. He saw but two methods of extricating himself from his difficulties. The one was to resign his dominions to the marquis.—Pride, ambition, and his reliance on ancient prophecies, which had pointed out a possibility of his preserving them to his posterity, combated that thought. The other was to press his marriage with Isabella. After long ruminating on these anxious thoughts, as he marched silently with Hippolita to the castle, he at last discoursed with that princess on the subject of his disquiet, and used every insinuating and plausible argument to extract her consent to, even her promise of promoting, the divorce. Hippolita needed little persuasion to bend her to his pleasure. She endeavoured to win him over to the measure of resigning his dominions; but finding her exhortations fruitless, she assured him, that as far as her conscience would allow, she would raise no opposition to a separation, though, without better founded scruples than what he yet alleged, she would not engage to be active in demanding it.

This compliance, though inadequate, was sufficient to raise Manfred's hopes. He trusted that his power and wealth would easily advance his suit at the court of Rome, whither he resolved to engage Frederic to take a journey on purpose. That prince had discovered so much passion for Matilda, that Manfred hoped to obtain all he wished by holding out or withdrawing his daughter's charms, according as the marquis should appear more or less disposed to co-operate in his views. Even the absence of Frederic would be a material point gained, until he could take farther measures for his security.

Dismissing Hippolita to her apartment, he repaired to that of the marquis; but crossing the great hall through which he was to pass, he met Bianca. That damsel he knew was in the confidence of both the young ladies. It immediately occurred to him to sift her on the subject of Isabella and Theodore. Calling her aside into the recess of the oriel window of the hall, and soothing her with many fair words and promises, he demanded of her whether she knew aught of the state of Isabella's affections. I! my lord? No, my lord—Yes, my lord—Poor lady! she is wonderfully alarmed about her father's wounds; but I tell her he will do well; don't your highness think so? I do not ask you, replied Manfred, what she thinks about her father: but you are in her secrets: come, be a good girl and tell me, is there any young man – ha? – you understand me. Lord bless me! understand your highness? No, not I: I told her a few vulnerary[1] herbs and repose— I am not talking, replied the prince impatiently, about her father: I know he will do well. Bless me, I rejoice to hear your highness say so; for though I thought it right not to let my young lady despond, methought his greatness had a wan look, and a something—I remember when young Ferdinand was wounded by the Venetian. Thou answerest from the point, interrupted Manfred; but here, take this jewel, perhaps that may fix thy attention—Nay, no reverences; my favour shall not stop here—Come, tell me truly; how stands Isabella's heart? Well, your highness has such a way, said Bianca—to be sure – but can your highness keep a secret? If it should ever come out of your lips— It shall not, it shall not, cried Manfred. Nay, but swear, your highness—by my halidame,[2] if it should ever be known that I said it—Why, truth is truth, I do not think my lady Isabella ever much affectioned my young lord, your son: yet he was a sweet youth as one should see. I am sure if I had been a princess—But bless me! I must attend my lady Matilda; she will marvel what is become of me.—Stay, cried Manfred, thou hast not satisfied my question. Hast thou ever carried any message, any letter?—I! Good gracious! cried Bianca: I carry a letter? I would not to be a queen. I hope your highness thinks, though I am poor, I am honest. Did your highness never hear what count Marsigli offered me, when he came a-wooing to my lady Matilda?—I have not leisure, said Manfred, to listen to thy tales. I do not question thy honesty; but it is thy duty to conceal nothing from me. How long has Isabella been acquainted with Theodore?—Nay, there is nothing can escape your highness, said Bianca—not that I know any thing of the matter. Theodore, to be sure, is a proper young man, and, as my lady Matilda says, the very image of good Alfonso: Has not your highness remarked it? Yes, yes—No—thou torturest me, said Manfred: Where did they meet? when?—Who, my lady Matilda? said Bianca. No, no, not Matilda; Isabella: When did Isabella first become acquainted with this Theodore?—Virgin Mary! said Bianca, how should I know? Thou dost know, said Manfred; and I must know; I will.—Lord! your highness is not jealous of young Theodore? said Bianca.—Jealous! No, no: why should I be jealous?—Perhaps I mean to unite them – if I was sure Isabella would have no repugnance.—Repugnance! No, I'll warrant her, said Bianca: he is as comely a youth as ever trod on christian ground: we are all in love with him: there is not a soul in the castle but would be rejoiced to have him for our prince – I mean, when it shall please heaven to call your highness to itself.—Indeed! said Manfred: has it gone so far? Oh! this cursed friar!—But I must not lose time—Go, Bianca, attend Isabella; but I charge thee, not a word of what has passed. Find out how she is affected towards Theodore; bring me good news, and that ring has a companion. Wait at the foot of the winding staircase: I am going to visit the marquis, and will talk farther with thee at my return.

Manfred, after some general conversation, desired Frederic to dismiss the two knights his companions, having to talk with him on urgent affairs. As soon as they were alone, he began in artful guise to sound the marquis on the subject of Matilda; and finding him disposed to his wish, he let drop hints on the difficulties that would attend the celebration of their marriage, unless— At that instant Bianca burst into the room, with a wildness in her look and gestures that spoke the utmost terror. Oh! my lord, my lord! cried she, we are all undone! It is come again! it is come again!—What is come again? cried Manfred amazed.—Oh! the hand! the giant! the hand!—Support me! I am terrified out of my senses, cried Bianca: I will not sleep in the castle to-night. Where shall I go? My things may come after me to-morrow.—Would I had been content to wed Francesco! This comes of ambition!—What has terrified thee thus, young woman? said the marquis: thou art safe here; be not alarmed. Oh! your greatness is wonderfully good, said Bianca, but I dare not—No, pray let me go—I had rather leave every thing behind me, than stay another hour under this roof. Go to, thou hast lost thy senses, said Manfred. Interrupt us not; we were communing on important matters.—My lord, this wench is subject to fits—Come with me, Bianca.—Oh! the saints! No, said Bianca—for certain it comes to warn your highness; why should it appear to me else? I say my prayers morning and evening—Oh! if your highness had believed Diego! 'Tis the same hand that he saw the foot to in the gallery-chamber—Father Jerome has often told us the prophecy would be out one of these days—Bianca, said he, mark my words.—Thou ravest, said Manfred in a rage: Begone, and keep these fooleries to frighten thy companions.—What! my lord, cried Bianca, do you think I have seen nothing? Go to the foot of the great stairs yourself—As I live I saw it. Saw what? Tell us fair maid, what thou hast seen, said Frederic. Can your highness listen, said Manfred, to the delirium of a silly wench, who has heard stories of apparitions until she believes them? This is more than fancy, said the marquis; her terror is too natural and too strongly impressed to be the work of imagination. Tell us, fair maiden, what it is has moved thee thus. Yes, my lord, thank your greatness, said Bianca —I believe I look very pale; I shall be better when I have recovered myself.—I was going to my lady Isabella's chamber by his highness's order—We do not want the circumstances, interrupted Manfred: since his highness will have it so, proceed; but be brief.—Lord, your highness thwarts one so! replied Bianca—I fear my hair—I am sure I never in my life—Well! as I was telling your greatness, I was going by his highness's order to my lady Isabella's chamber: she lies in the watchet-coloured chamber, on the right hand, one pair of stairs: so when I came to the great stairs—I was looking on his highness's present here. Grant me patience! said Manfred, will this wench never come to the point? What imports it to the marquis, that I gave thee a bawble for thy faithful attendance on my daughter? We want to know what thou sawest. I was going to tell your highness, said Bianca, if you would permit me.—So, as I was rubbing the ring—I am sure I had not gone up three steps, but I heard the rattling of armour; for all the world such a clatter, as Diego says he heard when the giant turned him about in the gallery-chamber.—What does she mean, my lord? said the marquis. Is your castle haunted by giants and goblins?—Lord, what, has not your greatness heard the story of the giant in the gallery-chamber? cried Bianca. I marvel his highness has not told you—mayhap you do not know there is a prophecy—This trifling is intolerable, interrupted Manfred. Let us dismiss this silly wench, my lord: we have more important affairs to discuss. By your favour, said Frederic, these are no trifles: the enormous sabre I was directed to in the wood, yon casque, its fellow - are these visions of this poor maiden's brain?—So Jaquez thinks, may it please your greatness, said Bianca. He says this moon will not be out without our seeing some strange revolution. For my part, I should not be surprised if it was to happen to-morrow; for, as I was saying, when I heard the clattering of armour, I was all in a cold sweat—I looked up, and, if your greatness will believe me, I saw upon the uppermost banister of the great stairs a hand in armour as big, as big—I thought I should have swooned—I never stopped until I came hither—Would I were well out of this castle! My lady Matilda told me but yester-morning that her highness Hippolita knows something—Thou art an insolent! cried Manfred—Lord marquis, it much misgives me that this scene is concerted to affront me. Are my own domestics suborned to spread tales injurious to my honour? Pursue your claim by manly daring; or let us bury our feuds, as was proposed, by the intermarriage of our children: but trust me, it ill becomes a prince of your bearing to practise on mercenary wenches. —I scorn your imputation, said Frederic; until this hour I never set eyes on this damsel: I have given her no jewel!—My lord, my lord, your conscience, your guilt accuses you, and would throw the suspicion on me—But keep your daughter, and think no more of Isabella: the judgments already fallen on your house forbid me matching into it.

Manfred, alarmed at the resolute tone in which Frederic delivered these words, endeavoured to pacify him. Dismissing Bianca, he made such submissions to the marquis, and threw in such artful encomiums on Matilda, that Frederic was once more staggered. However, as his passion was of so recent a date, it could not at once surmount the scruples he had conceived. He had gathered enough from Bianca's discourse to persuade him that heaven declared itself against Manfred. The proposed marriages too removed his claim to a distance: and the principality of Otranto was a stronger temptation, than the contingent reversion of it with Matilda. Still he would not absolutely recede from his engagements; but purposing to gain time, he demanded of Manfred if it was true in fact that Hippolita consented to the divorce. The prince, transported to find no other obstacle, and depending on his influence over his wife, assured the marquis it was so, and that he might satisfy himself of the truth from her own mouth.

As they were thus discoursing, word was brought that the banquet was prepared. Manfred conducted Frederic to the great hall, where they were received by Hippolita and the young princesses. Manfred placed the marquis next to Matilda, and seated himself between his wife and Isabella. Hippolita comported herself with an easy gravity; but the young ladies were silent and melancholy. Manfred, who was determined to pursue his point with the marquis in the remainder of the evening, pushed on the feast until it waxed late; affecting unrestrained gaiety, and plying Frederic with repeated goblets of wine. The latter, more upon his guard than Manfred wished, declined his frequent challenges, on pretence of his late loss of blood; while the prince, to raise his own disordered spirits, and to counterfeit unconcern, indulged himself in plentiful draughts, though not to the intoxication of his senses.

The evening being far advanced, the banquet concluded. Manfred would have withdrawn with Frederic; but the latter, pleading weakness and want of repose, retired to his chamber, gallantly telling the prince, that his daughter should amuse his highness until himself could attend him. Manfred accepted the party; and, to the no small grief of Isabella, accompanied her to her apartment. Matilda waited on her mother, to enjoy the freshness of the evening on the ramparts of the castle.

Soon as the company was dispersed their several ways, Frederic, quitting his chamber, enquired if Hippolita was alone; and was told by one of her attendants, who had not noticed her going forth, that at that hour she generally withdrew to her oratory, where he probably would find her. The marquis during the repast had beheld Matilda with increase of passion. He now wished to find Hippolita in the disposition her lord had promised. The portents that had alarmed him were forgotten in his desires. Stealing softly and unobserved to the apartment of Hippolita, he entered it with a resolution to encourage her acquiescence to the divorce, having perceived that Manfred was resolved to make the possession of Isabella an unalterable condition, before he would grant Matilda to his wishes.

The marquis was not surprised at the silence that reigned in the princess's apartment. Concluding her, as he had been advertised, in her oratory, he passed on. The door was a-jar; the evening gloomy and overcast. Pushing open the door gently, he saw a person kneeling before the altar. As he approached nearer, it seemed not a woman, but one in a long woollen weed, whose back was towards him. The person seemed absorbed in prayer. The marquis was about to return, when the figure rising, stood some moments fixed in meditation, without regarding him. The marquis, expecting the holy person to come forth, and meaning to excuse his uncivil interruption, said, Reverend father, I sought the lady Hippolita.—Hippolita! replied a hollow voice: camest thou to this castle to seek Hippolita?—And then the figure, turning slowly round, discovered to Frederic the fleshless jaws and empty sockets of a skeleton, wrapt in a hermit's cowl. Angels of grace, protect me! cried Frederic recoiling. Deserve their protection, said the spectre. Frederic, falling on his knees, adjured the phantom to take pity on him. Dost thou not remember me? said the apparition. Remember the wood of Joppa! Art thou that holy hermit? cried Frederic trembling—can I do aught for thy eternal peace?—Wast thou delivered from bondage, said the spectre, to pursue carnal delights? Hast thou forgotten the buried sabre, and the behest of heaven engraven on it?—I have not, I have not, said Frederic—But say, blest spirit, what is thy errand to me? what remains to be done? To forget Matilda! said the apparition – and vanished.

Frederic's blood froze in his veins. For some minutes he remained motionless. Then falling prostrate on his face before the altar, he besought the intercession of every saint for pardon. A flood of tears succeeded to this transport; and the image of the beauteous Matilda rushing in spite of him on his thoughts, he lay on the ground in a conflict of penitence and passion. Ere he could recover from this agony of his spirits, the princess Hippolita, with a taper in her hand, entered the oratory alone. Seeing a man without motion on the floor, she gave a shriek, concluding him dead. Her fright brought Frederic to himself. Rising suddenly, his face bedewed with tears, he would have rushed from her presence; but Hippolita, stopping him, conjured him in the most plaintive accents to explain the cause of his disorder, and by what strange chance she had found him there in that posture. Ah! virtuous princess! said the marquis, penetrated with grief – and stopped. For the love of heaven, my lord, said Hippolita, disclose the cause of this transport! What mean these doleful sounds, this alarming exclamation on my name? What woes has heaven still in store for the wretched Hippolita?—Yet silent?—By every pitying angel, I adjure thee, noble prince, continued she, falling at his feet, to disclose the purport of what lies at thy heart—I see thou feelest for me; thou feelest the sharp pangs that thou inflictest—Speak, for pity!—Does aught thou knowest concern my child?—I cannot speak, cried Frederic, bursting from her—Oh! Matilda!

Quitting the princess thus abruptly, he hastened to his own apartment. At the door of it he was accosted by Manfred, who, flushed by wine and love, had come to seek him, and to propose to waste some hours of the night in music and revelling. Frederic, offended at an invitation so dissonant from the mood of his soul, pushed him rudely aside, and, entering his chamber, flung the door intemperately against Manfred, and bolted it inwards. The haughty prince, enraged at this unaccountable behaviour, withdrew in a frame of mind capable of the most fatal excesses. As he crossed the court, he was met by the domestic whom he had planted at the convent as a spy on Jerome and Theodore. This man, almost breathless with the haste he had made, informed his lord, that Theodore and some lady from the castle were at that instant in private conference at the tomb of Alfonso in St Nicholas's church. He had dogged Theodore thither, but the gloominess of the night had prevented his discovering who the woman was.

Manfred, whose spirits were inflamed, and whom Isabella had driven from her on his urging his passion with too little reserve, did not doubt but the inquietude she had expressed had been occasioned by her impatience to meet Theodore. Provoked by this conjecture, and enraged at her father, he hastened secretly to the great church. Gliding softly between the aisles, and guided by an imperfect gleam of moonshine that shone faintly through the illuminated windows, he stole towards the tomb of Alfonso, to which he was directed by indistinct whispers of the persons he sought. The first sounds he could distinguish were —Does it, alas, depend on me? Manfred will never permit our union.—No, this shall prevent it! cried the tyrant, drawing his dagger, and plunging it over her shoulder into the bosom of the person that spoke—Ah me, I am slain! cried Matilda sinking: Good heaven, receive my soul!—Savage, inhuman monster! what hast thou done? cried Theodore, rushing on him, and wrenching his dagger from him.—Stop, stop thy impious hand, cried Matilda; it is my father!—Manfred, waking as from a trance, beat his breast, twisted his hands in his locks, and endeavoured to recover his dagger from Theodore to dispatch himself. Theodore, scarce less distracted, and only mastering the transports of his grief to assist Matilda, had now by his cries drawn some of the monks to his aid. While part of them endeavoured in concert with the afflicted Theodore to stop the blood of the dying princess, the rest prevented Manfred from laying violent hands on himself.

Matilda, resigning herself patiently to her fate, acknowledged with looks of grateful love the zeal of Theodore. Yet oft as her faintness would permit her speech its way, she begged the assistants to comfort her father. Jerome by this time had learnt the fatal news, and reached the church. His looks seemed to reproach Theodore; but turning to Manfred, he said, Now, tyrant! behold the completion of woe fulfilled on thy impious and devoted head! The blood of Alfonso cried to heaven for vengeance; and heaven has permitted its altar to be polluted by assassination, that thou mightest shed thy own blood at the foot of that prince's sepulchre!—Cruel man! cried Matilda, to aggravate the woes of a parent! May heaven bless my father, and forgive him as I do! My lord, my gracious sire, dost thou forgive thy child? Indeed I came not hither to meet Theodore! I found him praying at this tomb, whither my mother sent me to intercede for thee, for her—Dearest father, bless your child, and say you forgive her.—Forgive thee! Murderous monster! cried Manfred—can assassins forgive? I took thee for Isabella; but heaven directed my bloody hand to the heart of my child!—Oh! Matilda—I cannot utter it – canst thou forgive the blindness of my rage?—I can, I do, and may heaven confirm it! said Matilda—But while I have life to ask it – oh, my mother! what will she feel!—Will you comfort her, my lord? Will you not put her away? Indeed she loves you—Oh, I am faint! bear me to the castle – can I live to have her close my eyes?

Theodore and the monks besought her earnestly to suffer herself to be borne into the convent; but her instances were so pressing to be carried to the castle, that, placing her on a litter, they conveyed her thither as she requested.

Theodore supporting her head with his arm, and hanging over her in an agony of despairing love, still endeavoured to inspire her with hopes of life. Jerome on the other side comforted her with discourses of heaven, and holding a crucifix before her, which she bathed with innocent tears, prepared her for her passage to immortality. Manfred, plunged in the deepest affliction, followed the litter in despair.

Ere they reached the castle, Hippolita, informed of the dreadful catastrophe, had flown to meet her murdered child; but when she saw the afflicted procession, the mightiness of her grief deprived her of her senses, and she fell lifeless to the earth in a swoon. Isabella and Frederic, who attended her, were overwhelmed in almost equal sorrow. Matilda alone seemed insensible to her own situation: every thought was lost in tenderness for her mother. Ordering the litter to stop, as soon as Hippolita was brought to herself, she asked for her father. He approached, unable to speak. Matilda, seizing his hand and her mother's, locked them in her own, and then clasped them to her heart. Manfred could not support this act of pathetic piety. He dashed himself on the ground, and cursed the day he was born. Isabella, apprehensive that these struggles of passion were more than Matilda could support, took upon herself to order Manfred to be borne to his apartment, while she caused Matilda to be conveyed to the nearest chamber. Hippolita, scarce more alive than her daughter, was regardless of every thing but her: but when the tender Isabella's care would have likewise removed her, while the surgeons examined Matilda's wound, she cried, Remove me? Never! never! I lived but in her, and will expire with her. Matilda raised her eyes at her mother's voice, but closed them again without speaking. Her sinking pulse, and the damp coldness of her hand, soon dispelled all hopes of recovery. Theodore followed the surgeons into the outer chamber, and heard them pronounce the fatal sentence with a transport equal to phrensy—

Since she cannot live mine, cried he, at least she shall be mine in death!—Father! Jerome! will you not join our hands? cried he to the friar, who with the marquis had accompanied the surgeons. What means thy distracted rashness? said Jerome: is this an hour for marriage? It is, it is, cried Theodore: alas, there is no other! Young man, thou art too unadvised, said Frederic: dost thou think we are to listen to thy fond transports in this hour of fate? What pretensions hast thou to the princess? Those of a prince, said Theodore; of the sovereign of Otranto. This reverend man, my father, has informed me who I am. Thou ravest, said the marquis: there is no prince of Otranto but myself, now Manfred by murder, by sacrilegious murder, has forfeited all pretensions. My lord, said Jerome, assuming an air of command, he tells you true. It was not my purpose the secret should have been divulged so soon; but fate presses onward to its work. What his hot-headed passion has revealed, my tongue confirms. Know, prince, that when Alfonso set sail for the Holy Land—Is this a season for explanations? cried Theodore. Father, come and unite me to the princess: she shall be mine – in every other thing I will dutifully obey you. My life! my adored Matilda! continued Theodore, rushing back into the inner chamber, will you not be mine? will you not bless your— Isabella made signs to him to be silent, apprehending the princess was near her end. What, is she dead? cried Theodore: is it possible? The violence of his exclamations brought Matilda to herself. Lifting up her eyes she looked round for her mother—Life of my soul! I am here, cried Hippolita: think not I will quit thee! —Oh! you are too good, said Matilda—but weep not for me, my mother! I am going where sorrow never dwells.— Isabella, thou hast loved me; wot thou not supply my fondness to this dear, dear woman? Indeed I am faint!— Oh! my child! my child! said Hippolita in a flood of tears, can I not withhold thee a moment?—It will not be, said Matilda—Commend me to heaven—Where is my father?

Forgive him, dearest mother—forgive him my death; it was an error—Oh! I had forgotten—Dearest mother, I vowed never to see Theodore more—Perhaps that has drawn down this calamity—but it was not intentional—can you pardon me?—Oh! wound not my agonizing soul! said Hippolita; thou never couldst offend me.—Alas, she faints! Help! help!—I would say something more, said Matilda struggling, but it wonnot be – Isabella – Theodore – for my sake – oh!—She expired. Isabella and her women tore Hippolita from the corse; but Theodore threatened destruction to all who attempted to remove him from it. He printed a thousand kisses on her clay-cold hands, and uttered every expression that despairing love could dictate.

Isabella, in the mean time, was accompanying the afflicted Hippolita to her apartment; but in the middle of the court they were met by Manfred, who, distracted with his own thoughts, and anxious once more to behold his daughter, was advancing to the chamber where she lay. As the moon was now at its height, he read in the countenances of this unhappy company the event he dreaded. What! is she dead? cried he in wild confusion—A clap of thunder at that instant shook the castle to its foundations; the earth rocked, and the clank of more than mortal armour was heard behind. Frederic and Jerome thought the last day was at hand. The latter, forcing Theodore along with them, rushed into the court. The moment Theodore appeared, the walls of the castle behind Manfred were thrown down with a mighty force, and the form of Alfonso, dilated to an immense magnitude, appeared in the centre of the ruins. Behold in Theodore, the true heir of Alfonso! said the vision: and having pronounced those words, accompanied by a clap of thunder, it ascended solemnly towards heaven, where the clouds parting asunder, the form of saint Nicholas was seen; and receiving Alfonso's shade, they were soon wrapt from mortal eyes in a blaze of glory.

The beholders fell prostrate on their faces, acknowledging the divine will. The first that broke silence was Hippolita. My lord, said she to the desponding Manfred, behold the vanity of human greatness! Conrad is gone! Matilda is no more! in Theodore we view the true prince of Otranto. By what miracle he is so, I know not – suffice it to us, our doom is pronounced! Shall we not, can we but dedicate the few deplorable hours we have to live, in deprecating the farther wrath of heaven? Heaven ejects us – whither can we fly, but to yon holy cells that yet offer us a retreat? —Thou guiltless but unhappy woman! unhappy by my crimes! replied Manfred, my heart at last is open to thy devout admonitions. Oh! could – but it cannot be – ye are lost in wonder – let me at last do justice on myself! To heap shame on my own head is all the satisfaction I have left to offer to offended heaven. My story has drawn down these judgments: let my confession atone—But ah! what can atone for usurpation and a murdered child? a child murdered in a consecrated place!— List, sirs, and may this bloody record be a warning to future tyrants!

Alfonso, ye all know, died in the Holy Land—Ye would interrupt me; ye would say he came not fairly to his end—It is most true – why else this bitter cup which Manfred must drink to the dregs? Ricardo, my grandfather, was his chamberlain—I would draw a veil over my ancestor's crimes – but it is in vain: Alfonso died by poison. A fictitious will declared Ricardo his heir. His crimes pursued him – yet he lost no Conrad, no Matilda! I pay the price of usurpation for all! A storm overtook him. Haunted by his guilt, he vowed to saint Nicholas to found a church and two convents if he lived to reach Otranto. The sacrifice was accepted: the saint appeared to him in a dream, and promised that Ricardo's posterity should reign in Otranto until the rightful owner should be grown too large to inhabit the castle, and as long as issue-male from Ricardo's loins should remain to enjoy it.—Alas! alas! nor male nor female, except myself, remains of all his wretched race!—I have done – the woes of these three days speak the rest. How this young man can be Alfonso's heir I know not – yet I do not doubt it. His are these dominions; I resign them – yet I knew not Alfonso had an heir – I question not the will of heaven – poverty and prayer must fill up the woeful space, until Manfred shall be summoned to Ricardo.

What remains is my part to declare, said Jerome. When Alfonso set sail for the Holy Land, he was driven by a storm on the coast of Sicily. The other vessel, which bore Ricardo and his train, as your *lordship* must have heard, was separated from him. It is most true, said Manfred; and the title you give me is more than an out-cast can claim—Well, be it so – proceed. Jerome blushed, and continued. For three months lord Alfonso was wind-bound in Sicily. There he became enamoured of a fair virgin named Victoria. He was too pious to tempt her to forbidden pleasures. They were married. Yet deeming this amour incongruous with the holy vow of arms by which he was bound, he was determined to conceal their nuptials until his return from the crusade, when he purposed to seek and acknowledge her for his lawful wife. He left her pregnant. During his absence she was delivered of a daughter: but scarce had she felt a mother's pangs, ere she heard the fatal rumour of her lord's death, and the succession of Ricardo. What could a friendless, helpless woman do? would her testimony avail?—Yet, my lord, I have an authentic writing.—It needs not, said Manfred; the horrors of these days, the vision we have but now seen, all corroborate thy evidence beyond a thousand parchments. Matilda's death and my expulsion—Be composed, my lord, said Hippolita; this holy man did not mean to recall your griefs. Jerome proceeded.

I shall not dwell on what is needless. The daughter of which Victoria was delivered, was at her maturity bestowed in marriage on me. Victoria died; and the secret remained locked in my breast. Theodore's narrative has told the rest.

The friar ceased. The disconsolate company retired to the remaining part of the castle. In the morning Manfred signed his abdication of the principality, with the approbation of Hippolita, and each took on them the habit of religion in the neighbouring convents. Frederic offered his daughter to the new prince, which Hippolita's tenderness for Isabella concurred to promote: but Theodore's grief was too fresh to admit the thought of another love; and it was not till after frequent discourses with Isabella, of his dear Matilda, that he was persuaded he could know no happiness but in the society of one with whom he could forever indulge the melancholy that had taken possession of his soul.

**Facsimile of the first authorized edition (in French) of *Vathek***

# VATHEK.

A LAUSANNE,

Chez ISAAC HIGNOU & Comp^e.

M. DCC. LXXXVII.

VATHEK, ninth Caliph of the race of the Abassides, was the son of Motassem, and the grandson of Haroun al Raschid. From an early accession to the throne, and the talents he possessed to adorn it, his subjects were induced to expect that his reign would be long and happy. His figure was pleasing and majestic; but when he was angry, one of his eyes became so terrible, that no person could bear to behold it; and the wretch upon whom it was fixed instantly fell backward, and sometimes expired. For fear, however, of depopulating his dominions and making his palace desolate, he but rarely gave way to his anger.

Being much addicted to women and the pleasures of the table, he sought by his affability to procure agreeable companions; and he succeeded the better as his generosity was unbounded and his indulgences unrestrained: for he did not think, with the Caliph Omar Ben Abdalaziz, that it was necessary to make a hell of this world to enjoy Paradise in the next.

He surpassed in magnificence all his predecessors. The palace of Alkoremi, which his father, Motassem, had erected on the hill of Pied Horses, and which commanded the whole city of Samarah, was, in his idea, far too scanty: he added, therefore, five wings, or rather other palaces, which he destined for the particular gratification of each of the senses.

In the first of these were tables continually covered with the most exquisite dainties; which were supplied both by night and by day, according to their constant consumption; whilst the most delicious wines and the choicest cordials flowed forth from a hundred fountains that were never exhausted. This palace was called *The Eternal or Unsatiating Banquet.*

The second was styled *The Temple of Melody, or the Nectar of the Soul.* It was inhabited by the most skilful musicians and admired poets of the time; who not only displayed their talents within, but dispersing in bands without, caused every surrounding scene to reverberate their songs, which were continually varied in the most delightful succession.

The palace named *The Delight of the Eyes, or the Support of Memory*, was one entire enchantment. Rarities, collected from every corner of the earth, were there found in such profusion as to dazzle and confound, but for the order in which they were arranged. One gallery exhibited the pictures of the celebrated Mani, and statues that seemed to be alive. Here a well-managed perspective attracted the sight; there the magic of optics agreeably deceived it: whilst the naturalist, on his part, exhibited in their several classes the various gifts that Heaven had bestowed on our globe. In a word, Vathek omitted nothing in this palace that might gratify the curiosity of those who resorted to it, although he was not able to satisfy his own; for, of all men, he was the most curious.

*The Palace of Perfumes*, which was termed likewise *The Incentive to Pleasure*, consisted of various halls, where the different perfumes which the earth produces were kept perpetually burning in censers of gold. Flambeaux and aromatic lamps were here lighted in open day. But the too powerful effects of this agreeable delirium might be alleviated by descending into an immense garden, where an assemblage of every fragrant flower diffused through the air the purest odours.

The fifth palace, denominated *The Retreat of Mirth, or the Dangerous*, was frequented by troops of young females, beautiful as the Houris, and not less seducing; who never failed to receive, with caresses, all whom the Caliph allowed to approach them and enjoy a few hours of their company.

Notwithstanding the sensuality in which Vathek indulged, he experienced no abatement in the love of his people, who thought that a sovereign giving himself up to pleasure was as able to govern as one who declared himself an enemy to it. But the unquiet and impetuous disposition of the Caliph would not allow him to rest there. He had studied so much for his amusement in the lifetime of his father, as to acquire a great deal of knowledge, though not a sufficiency to satisfy himself; for he wished to know every thing; even sciences that did not exist. He was fond of engaging in disputes with the learned, but did not allow them to push their opposition with warmth. He stopped with presents the mouths of those whose mouths could be stopped; whilst others, whom his liberality was unable to subdue, he sent to prison to cool their blood; a remedy that often succeeded.

Vathek discovered also a predilection for theologica controversy; but it was not with the orthodox that he usually held. By this means he induced the zealots to oppose him, and then persecuted them in return; for he resolved, at any rate, to have reason on his side.

The great prophet, Mahomet, whose vicars the Caliphs are, beheld with indignation from his abode in the seventh heaven the irreligious conduct of such a vicegerent. 'Let us leave him to himself,' said he to the Genii, who are always ready to receive his commands: 'let us see to what lengths his folly and impiety will carry him: if he run into excess, we shall know how to chastise him. Assist him, therefore, to complete the tower which, in imitation of Nimrod, he hath begun; not, like that great warrior, to escape being drowned, but from the insolent curiosity of penetrating the secrets of heaven: – he will not divine the fate that awaits him.'

The Genii obeyed; and, when the workmen had raised their structure a cubit in the daytime, two cubits more were added in the night. The expedition with which the fabric arose was not a little flattering to the vanity of Vathek: he fancied that even insensible matter shewed a forwardness to subserve his designs; not considering that the successes of the foolish and wicked form the first rod of their chastisement.

His pride arrived at its height when, having ascended, for the first time, the fifteen hundred stairs of his tower, he cast his eyes below, and beheld men not larger than pismires; mountains, than shells; and cities, than bee-hives. The idea which such an elevation inspired of his own grandeur completely bewildered him: he was almost ready to adore himself; till, lifting his eyes upward, he saw the stars as high above him as they appeared when he stood on the surface of the earth.

He consoled himself, however, for this intruding and unwelcome perception of his littleness, with the thought of being great in the eyes of others; and flattered himself that the light of his mind would extend beyond the reach of his sight, and extort from the stars the decrees of his destiny.

With this view, the inquisitive Prince passed most of his nights on the summit of his tower, till becoming an adept in the mysteries of astrology, he imagined that the planets had disclosed to him the most marvellous adventures, which were to be accomplished by an extraordinary personage, from a country altogether unknown. Prompted by motives of curiosity, he had always been courteous to strangers; but, from this instant, he redoubled his attention, and ordered it to be announced, by sound of trumpet, through all the streets of Samarah, that no one of his subjects, on peril of his displeasure, should either lodge or detain a traveller, but forthwith bring him to the palace.

Not long after this proclamation, arrived in his metropolis a man so abominably hideous that the very guards who arrested him were forced to shut their eyes as they led him along: the Caliph himself appeared startled at so horrible a visage; but joy succeeded to this emotion of terror, when the stranger displayed to his view such rarities as he had never before seen, and of which he had no conception.

In reality, nothing was ever so extraordinary as the merchandise this stranger produced; most of his curiosities, which were not less admirable for their workmanship than splendor, had, besides, their several virtues described on a parchment fastened to each. There were slippers, which, by spontaneous springs, enabled the feet to walk; knives, that cut without motion of the hand; sabres, that dealt the blow at the person they were wished to strike; and the whole enriched with gems that were hitherto unknown.

The sabres especially, the blades of which emitted a dazzling radiance, fixed, more than all the rest, the Caliph's attention; who promised himself to decipher, at his leisure, the uncouth characters engraven on their sides. Without, therefore, demanding their price, he ordered all the coined gold to be brought from his treasury, and commanded the merchant to take what he pleased. The stranger obeyed, took little, and remained silent.

Vathek, imagining that the merchant's taciturnity was occasioned by the awe which his presence inspired, encouraged him to advance, and asked him, with an air of condescension, who he was? whence he came? and where he obtained such beautiful commodities? The man, or rather monster, instead of making a reply, thrice rubbed his forehead, which, as well as his body, was blacker than ebony; four times clapped his paunch, the projection of which was enormous; opened wide his huge eyes, which glowed like firebrands; began to laugh with a hideous noise, and discovered[1] his long amber-coloured teeth, bestreaked with green.

The Caliph, though a little startled, renewed his enquiries, but without being able to procure a reply. At which, beginning to be ruffled, he exclaimed, 'Knowest thou, wretch, who I am, and at whom thou art aiming thy gibes?' – Then, addressing his guards, 'Have ye heard him speak? – is he dumb?' – 'He hath spoken,' they replied, 'but to no purpose.' 'Let him speak then again,' said Vathek, 'and tell me who he is, from whence he came, and where he procured these singular curiosities; or I swear, by the ass of Balaam, that I will make him rue his pertinacity.'

This menace was accompanied by one of the Caliph's angry and perilous glances, which the stranger sustained without the slightest emotion; although his eyes were fixed on the terrible eye of the Prince.

No words can describe the amazement of the courtiers, when they beheld this rude merchant withstand the encounter unshocked. They all fell prostrate with their faces on the ground, to avoid the risk of their lives; and would have continued in the same abject posture, had not the Caliph exclaimed, in a furious tone, 'Up, cowards! seize the miscreant! see that he be committed to prison, and guarded by the best of my soldiers! Let him, however, retain the money I gave him; it is not my intent to take from him his property; I only want him to speak.'

No sooner had he uttered these words, than the stranger was surrounded, pinioned, and bound with strong fetters, and hurried away to the prison of the great tower, which was encompassed by seven empalements of iron bars, and armed with spikes in every direction, longer and sharper than spits. The Caliph, nevertheless, remained in the most violent agitation. He sat down indeed to eat; but, of the three hundred dishes that were daily placed before him, he could taste of no more than thirty-two.

A diet to which he had been so little accustomed was sufficient of itself to prevent him from sleeping; what then must be its effect when joined to the anxiety that preyed upon his spirits? At the first glimpse of dawn he hastened to the prison, again to importune this intractable stranger; but the rage of Vathek exceeded all bounds on finding the prison empty, the grates burst asunder, and his guards lying lifeless around him. In the paroxysm of his passion he fell furiously on the poor carcases, and kicked them till evening without intermission. His courtiers and vizirs exerted their efforts to soothe his extravagance; but, finding every expedient ineffectual, they all united in one vociferation, 'The Caliph is gone mad! the Caliph is out of his senses!'

This outcry, which soon resounded through the streets of Samarah, at length reached the ears of Carathis, his mother, who flew in the utmost consternation to try her ascendency on the mind of her son. Her tears and caresses called off his attention; and he was prevailed upon, by her intreaties, to be brought back to the palace.

Carathis, apprehensive of leaving Vathek to himself, had him put to bed; and, seating herself by him, endeavoured by her conversation to appease and compose him. Nor could any one have attempted it with better success; for the Caliph not only loved her as a mother, but respected her as a person of superior genius. It was she who had induced him, being a Greek herself, to adopt the sciences and systems of her country, which all good Mussulmans hold in such thorough abhorrence.

Judicial astrology was one of those sciences in which Carathis was a perfect adept. She began, therefore, with reminding her son of the promise which the stars had made him; and intimated an intention of consulting them again. 'Alas!' said the Caliph as soon as he could speak, 'what a fool I have been! not for having bestowed forty thousand kicks on my guards, who so tamely submitted to death; but for never considering that this extraordinary man was the same that the planets had foretold; whom, instead of ill-treating, I should have conciliated by all the arts of persuasion.'

'The past,' said Carathis, 'cannot be recalled; but it behoves us to think of the future: perhaps you may again see the object you so much regret: it is possible the inscriptions on the sabres will afford information. Eat, therefore, and take thy repose, my dear son. We will consider, to-morrow, in what manner to act.'

Vathek yielded to her counsel as well as he could, and arose in the morning with a mind more at ease. The sabres he commanded to be instantly brought; and, poring upon them, through a coloured glass, that their glittering might not dazzle, he set himself in earnest to decipher the inscriptions; but his reiterated attempts were all of them nugatory: in vain did he beat his head, and bite his nails; not a letter of the whole was he able to ascertain. So unlucky a disappointment would have undone him again, had not Carathis, by good fortune, entered the apartment.

'Have patience, my son!' said she: 'you certainly are possessed of every important science; but the knowledge of languages is a trifle at best, and the accomplishment of none but a pedant. Issue a proclamation, that you will confer such rewards as become your greatness upon any one that shall interpret what you do not understand, and what is beneath you to learn; you will soon find your curiosity gratified.'

'That may be,' said the Caliph; 'but, in the mean time, I shall be horribly disgusted by a crowd of smatterers, who will come to the trial as much for the pleasure of retailing their jargon as from the hope of gaining the reward. To avoid this evil, it will be proper to add, that I will put every candidate to death, who shall fail to give satisfaction; for, thank Heaven! I have skill enough to distinguish, whether one translates or invents.'

'Of that I have no doubt,' replied Carathis; 'but to put the ignorant to death is somewhat severe, and may be productive of dangerous effects. Content yourself with commanding their beards to be burnt: beards in a state are not quite so essential as men.'

The Caliph submitted to the reasons of his mother; and, sending for Morakanabad, his prime vizir, said, 'Let the common criers proclaim, not only in Samarah, but throughout every city in my empire, that whosoever will repair hither and decipher certain characters which appear to be inexplicable, shall experience that liberality for which I am renowned; but that all who fail upon trial shall have their beards burnt off to the last hair. Let them add, also, that I will bestow fifty beautiful slaves, and as many jars of apricots from the Isle of Kirmith, upon any man that shall bring me intelligence[2] of the stranger.'

The subjects of the Caliph, like their sovereign, being great admirers of women and apricots from Kirmith, felt their mouths water at these promises, but were totally unable to gratify their hankering; for no one knew what had become of the stranger.

As to the Caliph's other requisition, the result was different. The learned, the half learned, and those who were neither, but fancied themselves equal to both, came boldly to hazard their beards, and all shamefully lost them. The exaction of these forfeitures, which found sufficient employment for the eunuchs, gave them such a smell of singed hair as greatly to disgust the ladies of the seraglio, and to make it necessary that this new occupation of their guardians should be transferred to other hands.

At length, however, an old man presented himself, whose beard was a cubit and a half longer than any that had appeared before him. The officers of the palace whispered to each other, as they ushered him in, 'What a pity, oh! what a great pity that such a beard should be burnt!' Even the Caliph, when he saw it, concurred with them in opinion; but his concern was entirely needless. This venerable personage read the characters with facility, and explained them verbatim as follows: 'We were made where every thing is well made: we are the least of the wonders of a place where all is wonderful, and deserving the sight of the first potentate on earth.'

'You translate admirably!' cried Vathek; 'I know to what these marvellous characters allude. Let him receive as many robes of honour and thousands of sequins of gold as he hath spoken words. I am in some measure relieved from the perplexity that embarrassed me!' Vathek invited the old man to dine, and even to remain some days in the palace.

Unluckily for him, he accepted the offer; for the Caliph,

having ordered him next morning to be called, said: 'Read again to me what you have read already; I cannot hear too often the promise that is made me – the completion of which I languish to obtain.' The old man forthwith put on his green spectacles, but they instantly dropped from his nose, on perceiving that the characters he had read the day preceding had given place to others of different import. 'What ails you?' asked the Caliph; 'and why these symptoms of wonder?' – 'Sovereign of the world!' replied the old man, 'these sabres hold another language to-day from that they yesterday held.' – 'How say you?' returned Vathek: – 'but it matters not; tell me, if you can, what they mean.' – 'It is this, my lord,' rejoined the old man: '"Woe to the rash mortal who seeks to know that of which he should remain ignorant; and to undertake that which surpasseth his power!"' – 'And woe to thee!' cried the Caliph, in a burst of indignation, 'to-day thou art void of understanding: begone from my presence, they shall burn but the half of thy beard, because thou wert yesterday fortunate in guessing: – my gifts I never resume.' The old man, wise enough to perceive he had luckily escaped, considering the folly of disclosing so disgusting a truth, immediately withdrew and appeared not again.

But it was not long before Vathek discovered abundant reason to regret his precipitation; for, though he could not decipher the characters himself, yet, by constantly poring upon them, he plainly perceived that they every day changed; and, unfortunately, no other candidate offered to explain them. This perplexing occupation inflamed his blood, dazzled his sight, and brought on such a giddiness and debility that he could hardly support himself. He failed not, however, though in so reduced a condition, to be often carried to his tower, as he flattered himself that he might there read in the stars, which he went to consult, something more congruous to his wishes: but in this his hopes were deluded; for his eyes, dimmed by the vapours of his head, began to subserve his curiosity so ill, that he beheld nothing but a thick, dun cloud, which he took for the most direful of omens.

Agitated with so much anxiety, Vathek entirely lost all firmness; a fever seized him, and his appetite failed. Instead of being one of the greatest eaters, he became as distinguished for drinking. So insatiable was the thirst which tormented him, that his mouth, like a funnel, was always open to receive the various liquors that might be poured into it, and especially cold water, which calmed him more than any other.

This unhappy Prince, being thus incapacitated for the enjoyment of any pleasure, commanded the palaces of the five senses to be shut up; forbore to appear in public, either to display his magnificence or administer justice, and retired to the inmost apartment of his harem. As he had ever been an excellent husband, his wives, overwhelmed with grief at his deplorable situation, incessantly supplied him with prayers for his health, and water for his thirst.

In the mean time the Princess Carathis, whose affliction no words can describe, instead of confining herself to sobbing and tears, was closeted daily with the vizir Morakanabad, to find out some cure, or mitigation, of the Caliph's disease. Under the persuasion that it was caused by enchantment, they turned over together, leaf by leaf, all the books of magic that might point out a remedy; and caused the horrible stranger, whom they accused as the enchanter, to be every where sought for with the strictest diligence.

At the distance of a few miles from Samarah stood a high mountain, whose sides were swarded with wild thyme and basil, and its summit overspread with so delightful a plain, that it might have been taken for the Paradise destined for the faithful. Upon it grew a hundred thickets of eglantine and other fragrant shrubs; a hundred arbours of roses, entwined with jessamine and honeysuckle; as many clumps of orange trees, cedar, and citron; whose branches, interwoven with the palm, the pomegranate, and the vine, presented every luxury that could regale the eye or the taste. The ground was strewed with violets, harebells, and pansies; in the midst of which numerous tufts of jonquils, hyacinths, and carnations perfumed the air. Four fountains, not less clear than deep, and so abundant as to slake the thirst of ten armies, seemed purposely placed here, to make the scene more resemble the garden of Eden watered by four sacred rivers. Here, the nightingale sang the birth of the rose, her well-beloved, and, at the same time, lamented its short-lived beauty: whilst the dove deplored the loss of more substantial pleasures; and the wakeful lark hailed the rising light that reanimates the whole creation. Here, more than anywhere, the mingled melodies of birds expressed the various passions which inspired them; and the exquisite fruits, which they pecked at pleasure, seemed to have given them a double energy.

To this mountain Vathek was sometimes brought, for the sake of breathing a purer air; and, especially, to drink at will of the four fountains. His attendants were his mother, his wives, and some eunuchs, who assiduously employed themselves in filling capacious bowls of rock crystal, and emulously presenting them to him. But it frequently happened that his avidity exceeded their zeal, insomuch that he would prostrate himself upon the ground to lap the water, of which he could never have enough.

One day, when this unhappy Prince had been long lying in so debasing a posture, a voice, hoarse but strong, thus addressed him: 'Why dost thou assimilate thyself to a dog, O Caliph, proud as thou art of thy dignity and power?' At this apostrophe, he raised up his head, and beheld the stranger that had caused him so much affliction. Inflamed with anger at the sight, he exclaimed, 'Accursed Giaour! what comest thou hither to do? – is it not enough to have transformed a Prince remarkable for his agility into a water budget? Perceivest thou not, that I may perish by drinking to excess, as well as by thirst?'

'Drink, then, this draught,' said the stranger, as he presented to him a phial of a red and yellow mixture: 'and, to satiate the thirst of thy soul as well as of thy body, know that I am an Indian; but from a region of India which is wholly unknown.'

The Caliph, delighted to see his desires accomplished in part, and flattering himself with the hope of obtaining their entire fulfilment, without a moment's hesitation swallowed the potion, and instantaneously found his health restored, his thirst appeased, and his limbs as agile as ever. In the transports of his joy, Vathek leaped upon the neck of the frightful Indian, and kissed his horrid mouth and hollow cheeks, as though they had been the coral lips and the lilies and roses of his most beautiful wives.

Nor would these transports have ceased had not the eloquence of Carathis repressed them. Having prevailed upon him to return to Samarah, she caused a herald to proclaim as loudly as possible: 'The wonderful stranger hath appeared again; he hath healed the Caliph; he hath spoken! he hath spoken!'

Forthwith, all the inhabitants of this vast city quitted their habitations, and ran together in crowds to see the procession of Vathek and the Indian, whom they now blessed as much as they had before execrated, incessantly shouting, 'He hath healed our sovereign; he hath spoken! he hath spoken!' Nor were these words forgotten in the public festivals which were celebrated the same evening, to testify the general joy; for the poets applied them as a chorus to all the songs they composed on this interesting subject.

The Caliph, in the meanwhile, caused the palaces of the senses to be again set open; and, as he found himself naturally prompted to visit that of Taste in preference to the rest, immediately ordered a splendid entertainment, to which his great officers and favourite courtiers were all invited. The Indian, who was placed near the Prince, seemed to think that, as a proper acknowledgment of so distinguished a privilege, he could neither eat, drink, nor talk too much. The various dainties were no sooner served up than they vanished, to the great mortification of Vathek, who piqued himself on being the greatest eater alive, and at this time in particular was blessed with an excellent appetite.

The rest of the company looked round at each other in amazement; but the Indian, without appearing to observe it, quaffed large bumpers to the health of each of them; sung in a style altogether extravagant; related stories, at which he laughed immoderately, and poured forth extemporaneous verses, which would not have been thought bad, but for the strange grimaces with which they were uttered. In a word, his loquacity was equal to that of a hundred astrologers; he ate as much as a hundred porters, and caroused in proportion.

The Caliph, notwithstanding the table had been thirty-two times covered, found himself incommoded by the voraciousness of his guest, who was now considerably declined in the Prince's esteem. Vathek, however, being unwilling to betray the chagrin he could hardly disguise, said in a whisper to Bababalouk, the chief of his eunuchs: 'You see how enormous his performances are in every way; what would be the consequence should he get at my wives! – Go! redouble your vigilance, and be sure look well to my Circassians, who would be more to his taste than all of the rest.'

The bird of the morning had thrice renewed his song, when the hour of the Divan[3] was announced. Vathek, in gratitude to his subjects having promised to attend, immediately arose from table and repaired thither, leaning upon his vizir, who could scarcely support him; so disordered was the poor Prince by the wine he had drunk, and still more by the extravagant vagaries of his boisterous guest.

The vizirs, the officers of the crown and of the law, arranged themselves in a semicircle about their sovereign, and preserved a respectful silence; whilst the Indian, who looked as cool as if he had been fasting, sat down without ceremony on one of the steps of the throne, laughing in his sleeve at the indignation with which his temerity had filled the spectators.

The Caliph, however, whose ideas were confused, and whose head was embarrassed, went on administering justice at haphazard; till at length the prime vizir, perceiving his situation, hit upon a sudden expedient to interrupt the audience and rescue the honour of his master, to whom he said in a whisper, 'My lord, the Princess Carathis, who hath passed the night in consulting the planets, informs you that they portend you evil, and the danger is urgent. Beware lest this stranger, whom you have so lavishly recompensed for his magical gewgaws, should make some attempt on your life: his liquor, which at first had the appearance of effecting your cure, may be no more than a poison, the operation of which will be sudden. Slight not this surmise; ask him, at least, of what it was compounded, whence he procured it; and mention the sabres which you seem to have forgotten.'

Vathek, to whom the insolent airs of the stranger became every moment less supportable, intimated to his vizir, by a wink of acquiescence, that he would adopt his advice; and, at once turning towards the Indian, said, 'Get up, and declare in full Divan of what drugs was compounded the liquor you enjoined me to take, for it is suspected to be poison: give also that explanation I have so earnestly desired concerning the sabres you sold me, and thus shew your gratitude for the favours heaped on you.'

Having pronounced these words in as moderate a tone as he well could, he waited in silent expectation for an answer. But the Indian, still keeping his seat, began to renew his loud shouts of laughter, and exhibit the same horrid grimaces he had shewn them before, without vouchsafing a word in reply. Vathek, no longer able to brook such insolence, immediately kicked him from the steps; instantly descending, repeated his blow; and persisted, with such assiduity, as incited all who were present to follow his example. Every foot was up and aimed at the Indian, and no sooner had any one given him a kick, than he felt himself constrained to reiterate the stroke.

The stranger afforded them no small entertainment; for, being both short and plump, he collected himself into a ball, and rolled on all sides at the blows of his assailants, who pressed after him, wherever he turned, with an eagerness beyond conception, whilst their numbers were every moment increasing. The ball, indeed, in passing from one apartment to another, drew every person after it that came in its way: insomuch that the whole palace was thrown into confusion and resounded with a tremendous clamour. The women of the harem, amazed at the uproar, flew to their blinds to discover the cause; but no sooner did they catch a glimpse of the ball than, feeling themselves unable to refrain, they broke from the clutches of their eunuchs, who, to stop their flight, pinched them till they bled; but in vain: whilst themselves, though trembling with terror at the escape of their charge, were as incapable of resisting the attraction.

After having traversed the halls, galleries, chambers, kitchens, gardens, and stables of the palace, the Indian at last took his course through the courts; whilst the Caliph, pursuing him closer than the rest, bestowed as many kicks as he possibly could; yet not without receiving now and then a few which his competitors, in their eagerness, designed for the ball.

Carathis, Morakanabad, and two or three old vizirs, whose wisdom had hitherto withstood the attraction, wishing to prevent Vathek from exposing himself in the presence of his subjects, fell down in his way to impede the pursuit: but he, regardless of their obstruction, leaped over their heads, and went on as before. They then ordered the Muezins[4] to call the people to prayers; both for the sake of getting them out of the way, and of endeavouring, by their petitions, to avert the calamity: but neither of these expedients was a whit more successful. The sight of this fatal ball was alone sufficient to draw after it every beholder. The Muezins themselves, though they saw it but at a distance, hastened down from their minarets, and mixed with the crowd; which continued to increase in so surprising a manner that scarcely an inhabitant was left in Samarah except the aged; the sick, confined to their beds; and infants at the breast, whose nurses could run more nimbly without them. Even Carathis, Morakanabad, and the rest, were all become of the party. The shrill screams of the females, who had broken from their apartments and were unable to extricate themselves from the pressure of the crowd, together with those of the eunuchs jostling after them, and terrified lest their charge should escape from their sight; the execrations of husbands, urging forward and menacing each other; kicks given and received; stumblings and overthrows at every step; in a word, the confusion that universally prevailed, rendered Samarah like a city taken by storm, and devoted to absolute plunder. At last, the cursed Indian, who still preserved his rotundity of figure, after passing through all the streets and public places, and leaving them empty, rolled onwards to the plain of Catoul, and entered the valley at the foot of the mountain of the four fountains.

As a continual fall of water had excavated an immense gulph in the valley, whose opposite side was closed in by a steep acclivity, the Caliph and his attendants were apprehensive lest the ball should bound into the chasm, and, to prevent it, redoubled their efforts, but in vain. The Indian persevered in his onward direction; and, as had been apprehended, glancing from the precipice with the rapidity of lightning, was lost in the gulph below.

Vathek would have followed the perfidious Giaour, had not an invisible agency arrested his progress. The multitude that pressed after him were at once checked in the same manner, and a calm instantaneously ensued. They all gazed at each other with an air of astonishment; and notwithstanding that the loss of veils and turbans, together with torn habits, and dust blended with sweat, presented a most laughable spectacle, yet there was not one smile to be seen. On the contrary, all with looks of confusion and sadness returned in silence to Samarah, and retired to their inmost apartments, without ever reflecting, that they had been impelled by an invisible power into the extravagance for which they reproached themselves: for it is but just that men, who so often arrogate to their own merit the good of which they are but instruments, should also attribute to themselves absurdities which they could not prevent.

The Caliph was the only person who refused to leave the valley. He commanded his tents to be pitched there, and stationed himself on the very edge of the precipice, in spite of the representations of Carathis and Morakanabad, who pointed out the hazard of its brink giving way, and the vicinity to the magician that had so cruelly tormented him. Vathek derided all their remonstances; and having ordered a thousand flambeaux to be lighted, and directed his attendants to proceed in lighting more, lay down on the slippery margin, and attempted, by the help of this artificial splendor, to look through that gloom, which all the fires of the empyrean had been insufficient to pervade. One while he fancied to himself voices arising from the depth of the gulph; at another, he seemed to distinguish the accents of the Indian; but all was no more than the hollow murmur of waters, and the din of the cataracts that rushed from steep to steep down the sides of the mountain.

Having passed the night in this cruel perturbation, the Caliph, at daybreak, retired to his tent: where, without taking the least sustenance, he continued to doze till the dusk of evening began again to come on. He then resumed his vigils as before, and persevered in observing them for many nights together. At length, fatigued with so fruitless an employment, he sought relief from change. To this end, he sometimes paced with hasty strides across the plain;

and as he wildly gazed at the stars, reproached them with having deceived him; but, lo! on a sudden, the clear blue sky appeared streaked over with streams of blood, which reached from the valley even to the city of Samarah. As this awful phœnomenon seemed to touch his tower, Vathek at first thought of repairing thither to view it more distinctly; but, feeling himself unable to advance, and being overcome with apprehension, he muffled up his face in the folds of his robe.

Terrifying as these prodigies were, this impression upon him was no more than momentary, and served only to stimulate his love of the marvellous. Instead, therefore, of returning to his palace, he persisted in the resolution of abiding where the Indian had vanished from his view. One night, however, while he was walking as usual on the plain, the moon and stars were eclipsed at once, and a total darkness ensued. The earth trembled beneath him, and a voice came forth, the voice of the Giaour, who, in accents more sonorous than thunder, thus addressed him: 'Wouldest thou devote thyself to me? adore the terrestrial influences, and abjure Mahomet? On these conditions I will bring thee to the Palace of Subterranean Fire. There shalt thou behold, in immense depositories, the treasures which the stars have promised thee; and which will be conferred by those Intelligences whom thou shalt thus render propitious. It was from thence I brought my sabres, and it is there that Soliman Ben Daoud reposes, surrounded by the talismans that control the world.'

The astonished Caliph trembled as he answered, yet he answered in a style that shewed him to be no novice in preternatural adventures: 'Where art thou? be present to my eyes; dissipate the gloom that perplexes me, and of which I deem thee the cause. After the many flambeaux I have burnt to discover thee, thou mayest at least grant a glimpse of thy horrible visage.' – 'Abjure then Mahomet!' replied the Indian, 'and promise me full proofs of thy sincerity: otherwise, thou shalt never behold me again.'

The unhappy Caliph, instigated by insatiable curiosity, lavished his promises in the utmost profusion. The sky immediately brightened; and, by the light of the planets which seemed almost to blaze, Vathek beheld the earth open; and, at the extremity of a vast black chasm, a portal of ebony, before which stood the Indian, holding in his hand a golden key which he sounded against the lock.

'How,' cried Vathek, 'can I descend to thee? Come, take me, and instantly open the portal.' – 'Not so fast,' replied the Indian, 'impatient Caliph! Know that I am parched with thirst, and cannot open this door, till my thirst be thoroughly appeased; I require the blood of fifty children. Take them from among the most beautiful sons of thy vizirs and great men; or neither can my thirst nor thy curiosity be satisfied. Return to Samarah; procure for me this necessary libation; some back hither; throw it thyself into this chasm, and then shalt thou see!'

Having thus spoken, the Indian turned his back on the Caliph, who, incited by the suggestions of daemons, resolved on the direful sacrifice. He now pretended to have regained his tranquillity, and set out for Samarah amidst the acclamations of a people who still loved him, and forbore not to rejoice when they believed him to have recovered his reason. So successfully did he conceal the emotion of his heart, that even Carathis and Morakanabad were equally deceived with the rest. Nothing was heard of but festivals and rejoicings. The fatal ball, which no tongue had hitherto ventured to mention, was brought on the tapis.[5] A general laugh went round, though many, still smarting under the hands of the surgeon from the hurts received in that memorable adventure, had no great reason for mirth.

The prevalence of this gay humour was not a little grateful to Vathek, who perceived how much it conduced to his project. He put on the appearance of affability to every one; but especially to his vizirs and the grandees of his court, whom he failed not to regale with a sumptuous banquet; during which he insensibly directed the conversation to the children of his guests. Having asked, with a good-natured air, which of them were blessed with the handsomest boys, every father at once asserted the pretensions of his own; and the contest imperceptibly grew so warm, that nothing could have withholden them from coming to blows but their profound reverence for the person of the Caliph. Under the pretence, therefore, of reconciling the disputants, Vathek took upon him to decide; and, with this view, commanded the boys to be brought.

It was not long before a troop of these poor children made their appearance, all equipped by their fond mothers with such ornaments as might give the greatest relief to their beauty, or most advantageously display the graces of their age. But, whilst this brilliant assemblage attracted the eyes and hearts of every one besides, the Caliph scrutinized each, in his turn, with a malignant avidity that passed for attention, and selected from their number the fifty whom he judged the Giaour would prefer.

With an equal shew of kindness as before, he proposed to celebrate a festival on the plain, for the entertainment of his young favourites, who, he said, ought to rejoice still more than all at the restoration of his health, on account of the favours he intended for them.

The Caliph's proposal was received with the greatest delight, and soon published through Samarah. Litters, camels, and horses were prepared. Women and children, old men and young, every one placed himself as he chose. The cavalcade set forward, attended by all the confectioners in the city and its precincts; the populace, following on foot, composed an amazing crowd, and occasioned no little noise. All was joy; nor did any one call to mind what most of them had suffered when they lately travelled the road they were now passing so gaily.

The evening was serene, the air refreshing, the sky clear, and the flowers exhaled their fragrance. The beams of the declining sun, whose mild splendour reposed on the summit of the mountain, shed a glow of ruddy light over its green declivity, and the white flocks sporting upon it. No sounds were heard, save the murmurs of the four fountains, and the reeds and voices of shepherds calling to each other from different eminences.

The lovely innocents destined for the sacrifice added not a little to the hilarity of the scene. They approached the plain full of sportiveness, some coursing butterflies, others culling flowers, or picking up the shining little pebbles that attracted their notice. At intervals they nimbly started from each other for the sake of being caught again and mutually imparting a thousand caresses.

The dreadful chasm, at whose bottom the portal of ebony was placed, began to appear at a distance. It looked like a black streak that divided the plain. Morakanabad and his companions took it for some work which the Caliph had ordered. Unhappy men! little did they surmise for what it was destined. Vathek, unwilling that they should examine it too nearly, stopped the procession, and ordered a spacious circle to be formed on this side, at some distance from the accursed chasm. The body-guard of eunuchs was detached, to measure out the lists intended for the games, and prepare the rings for the arrows of the young archers. The fifty competitors were soon stripped, and presented to the admiration of the spectators the suppleness and grace of their delicate limbs. Their eyes sparkled with a joy, which those of their fond parents reflected. Every one offered wishes for the little candidate nearest his heart, and doubted not of his being victorious. A breathless suspense awaited the contests of these amiable and innocent victims.

The Caliph, availing himself of the first moment to retire from the crowd, advanced towards the chasm; and there heard, yet not without shuddering, the voice of the Indian; who, gnashing his teeth, eagerly demanded, 'Where are they? – where are they? – perceivest thou not how my mouth waters?' – 'Relentless Giaour!' answered Vathek, with emotion; 'can nothing content thee but the massacre of these lovely victims? Ah! wert thou to behold their beauty, it must certainly move thy compassion.' – 'Perdition on thy compassion, babbler!' cried the Indian: 'give them me; instantly give them, or my portal shall be closed against thee for ever!' – 'Not so loudly,' replied the Caliph, blushing. – 'I understand thee,' returned the Giaour with the grin of an Ogre; 'thou wantest no presence of mind: I will for a moment forbear.'

During this exquisite dialogue, the games went forward with all alacrity, and at length concluded, just as the twilight began to overcast the mountains. Vathek, who was still standing on the edge of the chasm, called out, with all his might, 'Let my fifty little favourites approach me, separately; and let them come in the order of their success. To the first, I will give my diamond bracelet; to the second, my collar of emeralds; to the third, my aigret of rubies; to the fourth, my girdle of topazes; and to the rest, each a part of my dress, even down to my slippers.'

This declaration was received with reiterated acclamations; and all extolled the liberality of a Prince who would thus strip himself for the amusement of his subjects and the encouragement of the rising generation. The Caliph, in the meanwhile, undressed himself by degrees, and, raising his arm as high as he was able, made each of the prizes glitter in the air; but whilst he delivered it with one hand to the child who sprung forward to receive it, he with the other pushed the poor innocent into the gulph, where the Giaour, with a sullen muttering, incessantly repeated, 'More! more!'

This dreadful device was executed with so much dexterity, that the boy who was approaching him remained unconscious of the fate of his forerunner; and, as to the spectators, the shades of evening, together with their distance, precluded them from perceiving any object distinctly. Vathek, having in this manner thrown in the last of the fifty, and, expecting that the Giaour, on receiving him, would have presented the key, already fancied himself as great as Soliman, and consequently above being amenable for what he had done; when, to his utter amazement, the chasm closed, and the ground became as entire as the rest of the plain.

No language could express his rage and despair. He execrated the perfidy of the Indian; loaded him with the most infamous invectives; and stamped with his foot, as resolving to be heard. He persisted in this till his strength failed him, and then fell on the earth like one void of sense. His vizirs and grandees, who were nearer than the rest, supposed him at first to be sitting on the grass, at play with their amiable children; but at length, prompted by doubt, they advanced towards the spot, and found the Caliph alone, who wildly demanded what they wanted? 'Our children! our children!' cried they. 'It is assuredly pleasant,' said he, 'to make me accountable for accidents. Your children, while at play, fell from the precipice, and I should have experienced their fate, had I not suddenly started back.'

At these words, the fathers of the fifty boys cried out aloud; the mothers repeated their exclamations an octave higher; whilst the rest, without knowing the cause, soon drowned the voices of both with still louder lamentations of their own. 'Our Caliph,' said they, and the report soon circulated, 'our Caliph has played us this trick, to gratify his accursed Giaour. Let us punish him for perfidy! let us avenge ourselves! let us avenge the blood of the innocent! let us throw this cruel Prince into the gulph that is near, and let his name be mentioned no more!'

At this rumour and these menaces, Carathis, full of consternation, hastened to Morakanabad, and said: 'Vizir, you have lost two beautiful boys, and must necessarily be the most afflicted of fathers; but you are virtuous; save your master.' – 'I will brave every hazard,' replied the vizir, 'to rescue him from his present danger, but afterwards will abandon him to his fate. Bababalouk,' continued he, 'put yourself at the head of your eunuchs: disperse the mob, and, if possible, bring back this unhappy Prince to his palace.' Bababalouk and his fraternity, felicitating each other in a low voice on their having been spared the cares as well as the honour of paternity, obeyed the mandate of the vizir; who, seconding their exertions to the utmost of his power, at length accomplished his generous enterprize; and retired, as he resolved, to lament at his leisure.

No sooner had the Caliph re-entered his palace than Carathis commanded the doors to be fastened; but perceiving the tumult to be still violent, and hearing the imprecations which resounded from all quarters, she said to her son, 'Whether the populace be right or wrong, it behoves you to provide for your safety; let us retire to your own apartment, and from thence through the subterranean passage, known only to ourselves, into your tower: there, with the assistance of the mutes who never leave it, we may be able to make a powerful resistance. Bababalouk, supposing us to be still in the palace, will guard its avenues for his own sake; and we shall soon find, without the counsels of that blubberer Morakanabad, what expedient may be the best to adopt.'

Vathek, without making the least reply, acquiesced in his mother's proposal, and repeated as he went, 'Nefarious Giaour! where art thou? hast thou not yet devoured those poor children? where are thy sabres? thy golden key? thy talismans?' Carathis, who guessed from these interrogations a part of the truth, had no difficulty to apprehend in getting at the whole as soon as he should be a little composed in his tower. The Princess was so far from being influenced by scruples, that she was as wicked as woman could be, which is not saying a little; for the sex pique themselves on their superiority in every competition. The recital of the Caliph, therefore, occasioned neither terror nor surprize to his mother: she felt no emotion but from the promises of the Giaour, and said to her son, 'This Giaour, it must be confessed, is somewhat sanguinary in his taste; but the terrestrial powers are always terrible; nevertheless, what the one hath promised, and the others can confer, will prove a sufficient indemnification. No crimes should be thought too dear for such a reward: forbear, then, to revile the Indian; you have not fulfilled the conditions to which his services are annexed: for instance, is not a sacrifice to the subterranean Genii required? and should we not be prepared to offer it as soon as the tumult is subsided? This charge I will take on myself, and have no doubt of succeeding, by means of your treasures, which, as there are now so many others in store, may without fear be exhausted.' Accordingly, the Princess, who possessed the most consummate skill in the art of persuasion, went immediately back through the subterranean passage; and, presenting herself to the populace from a window of the palace, began to harangue them with all the address of which she was mistress; whilst Bababalouk showered money from both hands amongst the crowd, who by these united means were soon appeased. Every person retired to his home, and Carathis returned to the tower.

Prayer at break of day was announced, when Carathis and Vathek ascended the steps which led to the summit of the tower, where they remained for some time though the weather was lowering and wet. This impending gloom corresponded with their malignant dispositions; but when the sun began to break through the clouds, they ordered a pavilion to be raised, as a screen against the intrusion of his beams. The Caliph, overcome with fatigue, sought refreshment from repose, at the same time hoping that significant dreams might attend on his slumbers; whilst the indefatigable Carathis, followed by a party of her mutes, descended to prepare whatever she judged proper for the oblation of the approaching night.

By secret stairs, contrived within the thickness of the wall, and known only to herself and her son, she first repaired to the mysterious recesses in which were deposited the mummies that had been wrested from the catacombs of the ancient Pharaohs. Of these she ordered several to be taken. From thence she resorted to a gallery where, under the guard of fifty female negroes, mute and blind of the right eye, were preserved the oil of the most venomous serpents, rhinoceros' horns, and woods of a subtile and penetrating odour procured from the interior of the Indies, together with a thousand other horrible rarities. This collection had been formed for a purpose like the present, by Carathis herself, from a presentiment that she might one day enjoy some intercourse with the infernal powers, to whom she had ever been passionately attached, and to whose taste she was no stranger.

To familiarize herself the better with the horrors in view, the Princess remained in the company of her negresses, who squinted in the most amiable manner from the only eye they had, and leered, with exquisite delight, at the sculls and skeletons which Carathis had drawn forth from her cabinets: all of them making the most frightful contortions and uttering such shrill chatterings, that the Princess, stunned by them and suffocated by the potency of the exhalations, was forced to quit the gallery, after stripping it of a part of its abominable treasures.

Whilst she was thus occupied, the Caliph, who, instead of the visions he expected, had acquired in these unsubstantial regions a voracious appetite, was greatly provoked at the mutes. For having totally forgotten their deafness, he had impatiently asked them for food; and seeing them regardless of his demand, he began to cuff, pinch, and bite them, till Carathis arrived to terminate a scene so indecent, to the great content of these miserable creatures. 'Son! what means all this?' said she, panting for breath. 'I thought I heard as I came up the shrieks of a thousand bats, torn from their crannies in the recesses of a cavern; and it was the outcry only of these poor mutes, whom you were so unmercifully abusing. In truth, you but ill deserve the admirable provision I have brought you.' – 'Give it me instantly,' exclaimed the Caliph; 'I am perishing for hunger!' – 'As to that,' answered she, 'you must have an excellent stomach if it can digest what I have brought.' – 'Be quick,' replied the Caliph; – 'but, oh heavens! what horrors! what do you intend?' – 'Come, come,' returned Carathis, 'be not so squeamish; but help me to arrange every thing properly; and you shall see that what you reject with such symptoms of disgust will soon complete your felicity. Let us get ready the pile for the sacrifice of to-night; and think not of eating till that is performed: know you not, that all solemn rites ought to be preceded by a rigorous abstinence?'

The Caliph, not daring to object, abandoned himself to grief and the wind that ravaged his entrails, whilst his mother went forward with the requisite operations. Phials of serpents' oil, mummies, and bones, were soon set in order on the balustrade of the tower. The pile began to rise and in three hours was twenty cubits high. At length darkness approached, and Carathis, having stripped herself to her inmost garment, clapped her hands in an impulse of ecstasy; the mutes followed her example; but Vathek, extenuated with hunger and impatience, was unable to support himself, and fell down in a swoon. The sparks had already kindled the dry wood; the venomous oil burst into a thousand blue flames; the mummies, dissolving, emitted a thick dun vapour; and the rhinoceros' horns, beginning to consume, all together diffused such a stench, that the Caliph, recovering, started from his trance, and gazed wildly on the scene in full blaze around him. The oil gushed forth in a plenitude of streams; and the negresses, who supplied it without intermission, united their cries to those of the Princess. At last the fire became so violent, and the flames reflected from the polished marble so dazzling, that the Caliph, unable to withstand the heat and the blaze, effected his escape, and took shelter under the imperial standard.

In the mean time, the inhabitants of Samarah, scared at the light which shone over the city, arose in haste, ascended their roofs, beheld the tower on fire, and hurried, half naked, to the square. Their love for their sovereign immediately awoke; and, apprehending him in danger of perishing in his tower, their whole thoughts were occupied with the means of his safety. Morakanabad flew from his retirement, wiped away his tears, and cried out for water like the rest. Bababalouk, whose olfactory nerves were more familiarized to magical odours, readily conjecturing that Carathis was engaged in her favourite amusements, strenuously exhorted them not to be alarmed. Him, however, they treated as an old poltroon, and styled him a rascally traitor. The camels and dromedaries were advancing with water; but no one knew by which way to enter the tower. Whilst the populace was obstinate in forcing the doors, a violent north-east wind drove an immense volume of flame against them. At first they recoiled, but soon came back with redoubled zeal. At the same time, the stench of the horns and mummies increasing, most of the crowd fell backwards in a state of suffocation. Those that kept their feet mutually wondered at the cause of the smell, and admonished each other to retire. Morakanabad, more sick than the rest, remained in a piteous condition. Holding his nose with one hand, every one persisted in his efforts with the other to burst open the doors and obtain admission. A hundred and forty of the strongest and most resolute at length accomplished their purpose. Having gained the stair-case, by their violent exertions, they attained a great height in a quarter of an hour.

Carathis, alarmed at the signs of her mutes, advanced to the stair-case, went down a few steps, and heard several voices calling out from below, 'You shall in a moment have water!' Being rather alert, considering her age, she presently regained the top of the tower, and bade her son suspend the sacrifice for some minutes; adding, 'We shall soon be enabled to render it more grateful. Certain dolts of your subjects, imagining, no doubt, that we were on fire, have been rash enough to break through those doors which had hitherto remained inviolate, for the sake of bringing up water. They are very kind, you must allow, so soon to forget the wrongs you have done them; but that is of little moment. Let us offer them to the Giaour; let them come up; our mutes, who neither want strength nor experience, will soon dispatch them, exhausted as they are with fatigue.' – 'Be it so,' answered the Caliph, 'provided we finish, and I dine.' In fact, these good people, out of breath from ascending fifteen hundred stairs in such haste, and chagrined at having spilt by the way the water they had taken, were no sooner arrived at the top, than the blaze of the flames and the fumes of the mummies at once overpowered their senses. It was a pity! for they beheld not the agreeable smile with which the mutes and negresses adjusted the cord to their necks: these amiable personages rejoiced, however, no less at the scene. Never before had the ceremony of strangling been performed with so much facility. They all fell, without the least resistance or struggle: so that Vathek, in the space of a few moments, found himself surrounded by the dead bodies of the most faithful of his subjects; all which were thrown on the top of the pile. Carathis, whose presence of mind never forsook her, perceiving that she had carcases sufficient to complete her oblation, commanded the chains to be stretched across the stair-case, and the iron doors barricadoed, that no more might come up.

No sooner were these orders obeyed, than the tower shook; the dead bodies vanished in the flames, which at once changed from a swarthy crimson to a bright rose colour; an ambient vapour emitted the most exquisite fragrance; the marble columns rang with harmonious sounds, and the liquefied horns diffused a delicious perfume. Carathis, in transports, anticipated the success of her enterprize; whilst her mutes and negresses, to whom these sweets had given the colic, retired grumbling to their cells.

Scarcely were they gone, when, instead of the pile, horns, mummies, and ashes, the Caliph both saw and felt, with a degree of pleasure which he could not express, a table covered with the most magnificent repast: flagons of wine and vases of exquisite sherbet reposing on snow. He availed himself, without scruple, of such an entertainment; and had already laid hands on a lamb stuffed with pistachios, whilst Carathis was privately drawing from a filigree urn a parchment that seemed to be endless, and which had escaped the notice of her son. Totally occupied in gratifying an importunate appetite, he left her to peruse it without interruption; which having finished, she said to him, in an authoritative tone, 'Put an end to your gluttony, and hear the splendid promises with which you are favoured!' She then read as follows: 'Vathek, my well-beloved, thou hast surpassed my hopes: my nostrils have been regaled by the savour of thy mummies, thy horns, and, still more, by the lives devoted on the pile. At the full of the moon, cause the bands of thy musicians, and thy tymbals, to be heard; depart from thy palace, surrounded by all the pageants of majesty – thy most faithful slaves, thy best beloved wives, thy most magnificent litters, thy richest loaden camels – and set forward on thy way to Istakhar. There I await thy coming: that is the region of wonders: there shalt thou receive the diadem of Gian Ben Gian, the talismans of Soliman, and the treasures of the pre-Adamite sultans:[6] there shalt thou be solaced with all kinds of delight. – But beware how thou enterest any dwelling on thy route; or thou shalt feel the effects of my anger.'

The Caliph, notwithstanding his habitual luxury, had never before dined with so much satisfaction. He gave full scope to the joy of these golden tidings; and betook himself to drinking anew. Carathis, whose antipathy to wine was by no means insuperable, failed not to pledge him at every bumper he ironically quaffed to the health of Mahomet. This infernal liquor completed their impious temerity, and prompted them to utter a profusion of blasphemies. They gave a loose to their wit, at the expense of the ass of Balaam, the dog of the seven sleepers, and the other animals admitted into the Paradise of Mahomet.[7] In this sprightly humour, they descended the fifteen hundred stairs, diverting themselves as they went, at the anxious faces they saw on the square, through the barbacans and loopholes of the tower; and at length arrived at the royal apartments, by the subterranean passage. Bababalouk was parading to and fro, and issuing his mandates with great pomp to the eunuchs, who were snuffing the lights and painting the eyes of the Circassians. No sooner did he catch sight of the Caliph and his mother, than he exclaimed, 'Hah! you have then, I perceive, escaped from the flames; I was not, however, altogether out of doubt.' – 'Of what moment is it to us what you thought or think?' cried Carathis: 'go, speed; tell Morakanabad that we immediately want him; and take care not to stop by the way to make your insipid reflections.'

Morakanabad delayed not to obey the summons, and was received by Vathek and his mother with great solemnity. They told him, with an air of composure and commiseration, that the fire at the top of the tower was extinguished; but that it had cost the lives of the brave people who sought to assist them.

'Still more misfortunes!' cried Morakanabad, with a sigh. 'Ah, commander of the faithful, our holy Prophet is certainly irritated against us! it behoves you to appease him.' 'We will appease him hereafter,' replied the Caliph, with a smile that augured nothing of good. 'You will have leisure sufficient for your supplications during my absence, for this country is the bane of my health. I am disgusted with the mountain of the four fountains, and am resolved to go and drink of the stream of Rocnabad. I long to refresh myself in the delightful valleys which it waters. Do you, with the advice of my mother, govern my dominions, and take care to supply whatever her experiments may demand; for you well know that our tower abounds in materials for the advancement of science.'

The tower but ill suited Morakanabad's taste. Immense treasures had been lavished upon it; and nothing had he ever seen carried thither but female negroes, mutes, and abominable drugs. Nor did he know well what to think of Carathis, who, like a cameleon, could assume all possible colours. Her cursed eloquence had often driven the poor Mussulman to his last shifts. He considered, however, that if she possessed but few good qualities, her son had still fewer; and that the alternative, on the whole, would be in her favour. Consoled, therefore, with this reflection, he went, in good spirits, to soothe the populace, and make the proper arrangements for his master's journey.

Vathek, to conciliate the Spirits of the subterranean palace, resolved that his expedition should be uncommonly splendid. With this view he confiscated, on all sides, the property of his subjects; whilst his worthy mother stripped the seraglios she visited of the gems they contained. She collected all the sempstresses and embroiderers of Samarah and other cities, to the distance of sixty leagues, to prepare pavilions, palanquins, sofas, canopies, and litters for the train of the monarch. There was not left, in Masulipatan, a single piece of chintz; and so much muslin had been brought up to dress out Bababalouk and the other black eunuchs, that there remained not an ell of it in the whole Irak of Babylon.

During these preparations, Carathis, who never lost sight of her great object, which was to obtain favour with the powers of darkness, made select parties of the fairest and most delicate ladies of the city; but in the midst of their gaiety, she contrived to introduce vipers amongst them, and to break pots of scorpions under the table. They all bit to a wonder, and Carathis would have left her friends to die, were it not that, to fill up the time, she now and then amused herself in curing their wounds, with an excellent anodyne of her own invention: for this good Princess abhorred being indolent.

Vathek, who was not altogether so active as his mother, devoted his time to the sole gratification of his senses, in the palaces which were severally dedicated to them. He disgusted himself no more with the Divan, or the mosque. One half of Samarah followed his example, whilst the other lamented the progress of corruption.

In the midst of these transactions, the embassy returned, which had been sent, in pious times, to Mecca. It consisted of the most reverend Moullahs[8] who had fulfilled their commission, and brought back one of those precious besoms which are used to sweep the sacred Cahaba:[9] a present truly worthy of the greatest potentate on earth!

The Caliph happened at this instant to be engaged in an apartment by no means adapted to the reception of embassies. He heard the voice of Bababalouk, calling out from between the door and the tapestry that hung before it, 'Here are the excellent Edris al Shafei, and the seraphic Al Mouhateddin, who have brought the besom from Mecca, and, with tears of joy, intreat they may present it to your majesty in person.' – 'Let them bring the besom hither; it may be of use,' said Vathek. – 'How!' answered Bababalouk, half aloud and amazed. 'Obey,' replied the Caliph, 'for it is my sovereign will; go instantly, vanish! for here will I receive the good folk who have thus filled thee with joy.'

The eunuch departed muttering, and bade the venerable train attend him. A sacred rapture was diffused amongst these reverend old men. Though fatigued with the length of their expedition, they followed Bababalouk with an alertness almost miraculous, and felt themselves highly flattered, as they swept along the stately porticoes, that the Caliph would not receive them like ambassadors in ordinary in his hall of audience. Soon reaching the interior of the harem (where, through blinds of Persian, they perceived large soft eyes, dark and blue, that came and went like lightning), penetrated with respect and wonder, and full of their celestial mission, they advanced in procession towards the small corridors that appeared to terminate in nothing, but, nevertheless, led to the cell where the Caliph expected their coming.

'What! is the commander of the faithful sick?' said Edris al Shafei in a low voice to his companion. – 'I rather think he is in his oratory,' answered Al Mouhateddin. Vathek, who heard the dialogue, cried out, 'What imports it you, how I am employed? approach without delay.' They advanced, whilst the Caliph, without shewing himself, put forth his hand from behind the tapestry that hung before the door, and demanded of them the besom. Having prostrated themselves as well as the corridor would permit, and even in a tolerable semicircle, the venerable Al Shafei, drawing forth the besom from the embroidered and perfumed scarves in which it had been enveloped and secured from the profane gaze of vulgar eyes,[10] arose from his associates, and advanced, with an air of the most awful solemnity, towards the supposed oratory; but with what astonishment! with what horror was he seized! Vathek, bursting out into a villainous laugh, snatched the besom from his trembling hand, and, fixing upon some cobwebs, that hung from the ceiling, gravely brushed them away till not a single one remained. The old men, overpowered with amazement, were unable to lift their beards from the ground; for, as Vathek had carelessly left the tapestry between them half drawn, they were witnesses of the whole transaction. Their tears bedewed the marble. Al Mouhateddin swooned through mortification and fatigue, whilst the Caliph, throwing himself backward on his seat, shouted and clapped his hands without mercy. At last, addressing himself to Bababalouk, 'My dear black,' said he, 'go, regale these pious poor souls with my good wine from Schiraz, since they can boast of having seen more of my palace than any one besides.' Having said this, he threw the besom in their face, and went to enjoy the laugh with Carathis. Bababalouk did all in his power to console the ambassadors; but the two most infirm expired on the spot: the rest were carried to their beds, from whence, being heartbroken with sorrow and shame, they never arose.

The succeeding night, Vathek, attended by his mother, ascended the tower to see if every thing were ready for his journey; for he had great faith in the influence of the stars. The planets appeared in their most favourable aspects. The Caliph, to enjoy so flattering a sight, supped gaily on the roof; and fancied that he heard, during his repast, loud shouts of laughter resound through the sky, in a manner that inspired the fullest assurance.

All was in motion at the palace; lights were kept burning through the whole of the night: the sound of implements, and of artizans finishing their work; the voices of women, and their guardians, who sung at their embroidery: all conspired to interrupt the stillness of nature, and infinitely delighted the heart of Vathek who imagined himself going in triumph to sit upon the throne of Soliman. The people were not less satisfied than himself: all assisted to accelerate the moment which should rescue them from the wayward caprices of so extravagant a master.

The day preceding the departure of this infatuated Prince was employed by Carathis in repeating to him the decrees of the mysterious parchment, which she had thoroughly gotten by heart; and in recommending him not to enter the habitation of any one by the way: 'For well thou knowest,' added she, 'how liquorish thy taste is after good dishes and young damsels: let me, therefore, enjoin thee to be content with thy old cooks, who are the best in the world; and not to forget that, in thy ambulatory seraglio, there are at least three dozen of pretty faces which Bababalouk has not yet unveiled. I myself have a great desire to watch over thy conduct, and visit the subterranean palace, which, no doubt, contains whatever can interest persons like us. There is nothing so pleasing as retiring to caverns: my taste for dead bodies, and every thing like mummy, is decided; and, I am confident, thou wilt see the most exquisite of their kind. Forget me not then, but the moment thou art in possession of the talismans which are to open the way to the mineral kingdoms and the centre of the earth itself, fail not to dispatch some trusty Genius to take me and my cabinet; for the oil of the serpents I have pinched to death will be a pretty present to the Giaour, who cannot but be charmed with such dainties.'

Scarcely had Carathis ended this edifying discourse, when the sun, setting behind the mountain of the four fountains, gave place to the rising moon. This planet, being that evening at full, appeared of unusual beauty and magnitude in the eyes of the women, the eunuchs and the pages, who were all impatient to set forward. The city re-echoed with shouts of joy and flourishing of trumpets. Nothing was visible but plumes nodding on pavilions, and aigrets shining in the mild lustre of the moon. The spacious square resembled an immense parterre variegated with the most stately tulips of the East.

Arrayed in the robes which were only worn at the most distinguished ceremonials, and supported by his vizir and Bababalouk, the Caliph descended the great staircase of the tower in the sight of all his people. He could not forbear pausing, at intervals, to admire the superb appearance which every where courted his view; whilst the whole multitude, even to the camels with their sumptuous burdens, knelt down before him. For some time a general stillness prevailed, which nothing happened to disturb but the shrill screams of some eunuchs in the rear. These vigilant guards, having remarked certain cages of the ladies swagging somewhat awry, and discovered that a few adventurous gallants had contrived to get in, soon dislodged the enraptured culprits and consigned them, with good commendations, to the surgeons of the serail. The majesty of so magnificent a spectacle was not, however, violated by incidents like these. Vathek, meanwhile, saluted the moon with an idolatrous air, that neither pleased Morakanabad, nor the doctors of the law, any more than the vizirs and grandees of his court, who were all assembled to enjoy the last view of their sovereign.

At length, the clarions and trumpets from the top of the tower announced the prelude of departure. Though the instruments were in unison with each other, yet a singular dissonance was blended with their sounds. This proceeded from Carathis who was singing her direful orisons[11] to the Giaour, whilst the negresses and mutes supplied thorough-bass, without articulating a word. The good Mussulmans fancied that they heard the sullen hum of those nocturnal insects which presage evil, and importuned Vathek to beware how he ventured his sacred person.

On a given signal, the great standard of the Califat was displayed: twenty thousand lances shone around it; and the Caliph, treading royally on the cloth of gold which had been spread for his feet, ascended his litter amidst the general acclamations of his subjects.

The expedition commenced with the utmost order and so entire a silence, that even the locusts were heard from the thickets on the plain of Catoul. Gaiety and good humour prevailing, they made full six leagues before the dawn; and the morning star was still glittering in the firmament, when the whole of this numerous train had halted on the banks of the Tigris, where they encamped to repose for the rest of the day.

The three days that followed were spent in the same manner; but on the fourth the heavens looked angry: lightnings broke forth in frequent flashes; re-echoing peals of thunder succeeded; and the trembling Circassians clung with all their might to their ugly guardians. The Caliph himself was greatly inclined to take shelter in the large town of Ghulchissar, the governor of which came forth to meet him, and tendered every kind of refreshment the place could supply. But, having examined his tablets, he suffered the rain to soak him almost to the bone, notwithstanding the importunity of his first favourites. Though he began to regret the palace of the senses, yet he lost not sight of his enterprize, and his sanguine expectation confirmed his resolution. His geographers were ordered to attend him; but the weather proved so terrible that these poor people exhibited a lamentable appearance: and their maps of the different countries, spoiled by the rain, were in a still worse plight than themselves. As no long journey had been undertaken since the time of Haroun al Raschid, every one was ignorant which way to turn; and Vathek, though well versed in the course of the heavens, no longer knew his situation on earth. He thundered even louder than the elements; and muttered forth certain hints of the bow-string, which were not very soothing to literary ears. Disgusted at the toilsome weariness of the way, he determined to cross over the craggy heights and follow the guidance of a peasant, who undertook to bring him in four days to Rocnabad. Remonstrances were all to no purpose: his resolution was fixed.

The females and eunuchs uttered shrill wailings at the sight of the precipices below them, and the dreary prospects that opened in the vast gorges of the mountains. Before they could reach the ascent of the steepest rock, night overtook them, and a boisterous tempest arose, which, having rent the awnings of the palanquins and cages, exposed to the raw gusts the poor ladies within, who had never before felt so piercing a cold. The dark clouds that overcast the face of the sky deepened the horrors of this disastrous night, insomuch that nothing could be heard distinctly but the mewling of pages and lamentations of sultanas.

To increase the general misfortune, the frightful uproar of wild beasts resounded at a distance; and there were soon perceived in the forest they were skirting the glaring of eyes, which could belong only to devils or tigers. The pioneers, who, as well as they could, had marked out a track, and a part of the advanced guard, were devoured before they had been in the least apprized of their danger. The confusion that prevailed was extreme. Wolves, tigers, and other carnivorous animals, invited by the howling of their companions, flocked together from every quarter. The crashing of bones was heard on all sides, and a fearful rush of wings over head; for now vultures also began to be of the party.

The terror at length reached the main body of the troops which surrounded the monarch and his harem at the distance of two leagues from the scene. Vathek (voluptuously reposed in his capacious litter upon cushions of silk, with two little pages beside him of complexions more fair than the enamel of Franguistan, who were occupied in keeping off flies) was soundly asleep, and contemplating in his dreams the treasures of Soliman. The shrieks, however, of his wives awoke him with a start; and, instead of the Giaour with his key of gold, he beheld Bababalouk full of consternation. 'Sire,' exclaimed this good servant of the most potent of monarchs, 'misfortune is arrived at its height; wild beasts, who entertain no more reverence for your sacred person than for a dead ass, have beset your camels and their drivers; thirty of the most richly laden are already become their prey, as well as your confectioners, your cooks, and purveyors; and unless our holy Prophet should protect us, we shall have all eaten our last meal.' At the mention of eating, the Caliph lost all patience. He began to bellow, and even beat himself (for there was no seeing in the dark). The rumour every instant increased; and Bababalouk, finding no good could be done with his master, stopped both his ears against the hurly-burly of the harem, and called out aloud, 'Come, ladies and brothers! all hands to work: strike light in a moment! never shall it be said, that the commander of the faithful served to regale these infidel brutes.' Though there wanted not, in this bevy of beauties, a sufficient number of capricious and wayward, yet, on the present occasion, they were all compliance. Fires were visible, in a twinkling, in all their cages. Ten thousand torches were lighted at once. The Caliph himself seized a large one of wax; every person followed his example; and by kindling ropes' ends, dipped in oil and fastened on poles, an amazing blaze was spread. The rocks were covered with the splendour of sunshine. The trails of sparks, wafted by the wind, communicated to the dry fern, of which there was plenty. Serpents were observed to crawl forth from their retreats, with amazement and hissings; whilst the horses snorted, stamped the ground, tossed their noses in the air, and plunged about without mercy.

One of the forests of cedar that bordered their way took fire; and the branches that overhung the path, extending their flames to the muslins and chintzes which covered the cages of the ladies, obliged them to jump out, at the peril of their necks. Vathek, who vented on the occasion a thousand blasphemies, was himself compelled to touch, with his sacred feet, the naked earth.

Never had such an incident happened before. Full of mortification, shame, and despondence, and not knowing how to walk, the ladies fell into the dirt. 'Must I go on foot?' said one. 'Must I wet my feet?' cried another. 'Must I soil my dress?' asked a third. 'Execrable Bababalouk!' exclaimed all. 'Outcast of hell! what hast thou to do with torches? Better were it to be eaten by tigers, than to fall into our present condition! we are for ever undone! Not a porter is there in the army, nor a currier of camels, but hath seen some part of our bodies; and, what is worse, our very faces!' On saying this the most bashful amongst them hid their foreheads on the ground, whilst such as had more boldness flew at Bababalouk; but he, well apprized of their humour, and not wanting in shrewdness, betook himself to his heels along with his comrades, all dropping their torches and striking their tymbals.

It was not less light than in the brightest of the dog-days, and the weather was hot in proportion; but how degrading was the spectacle, to behold the Caliph bespattered, like an ordinary mortal! As the exercise of his faculties seemed to be suspended, one of his Ethiopian wives (for he delighted in variety) clasped him in her arms, threw him upon her shoulder like a sack of dates, and, finding that the fire was hemming them in, set off with no small expedition, considering the weight of her burden. The other ladies, who had just learned the use of their feet, followed her; their guards galloped after; and the camel-drivers brought up the rear, as fast as their charge would permit.

They soon reached the spot where the wild beasts had commenced the carnage, but which they had too much good sense not to leave at the approaching of the tumult, having made besides a most luxurious supper. Bababalouk, nevertheless, seized on a few of the plumpest, which were unable to budge from the place, and began to flay them with admirable adroitness. The cavalcade having proceeded so far from the conflagration that the heat felt rather grateful than violent, it was immediately resolved on to halt. The tattered chintzes were picked up; the scraps, left by the wolves and tigers, interred; and vengeance was taken on some dozens of vultures, that were too much glutted to rise on the wing. The camels, which had been left unmolested to make sal ammoniac, being numbered, and the ladies once more enclosed in their cages, the imperial tent was pitched on the levellest ground they could find.

Vathek, reposing upon a mattress of down, and tolerably recovered from the jolting of the Ethiopian, who, to his feelings, seemed the roughest trotting jade he had hitherto mounted, called out for something to eat. But, alas! those delicate cakes which had been baked in silver ovens for his royal mouth, those rich manchets,[12] amber comfits, flagons of Schiraz wine, porcelain vases of snow, and grapes from the banks of the Tigris, were all irremediably lost!

And nothing had Bababalouk to present in their stead but a roasted wolf, vultures *à la daube*,[13] aromatic herbs of the most acrid poignancy, rotten truffles, boiled thistles, and such other wild plants as much ulcerate the throat and parch up the tongue. Nor was he better provided in the article of drink; for he could procure nothing to accompany these irritating viands but a few phials of abominable brandy which had been secreted by the scullions in their slippers. Vathek made wry faces at so savage a repast, and Bababalouk answered them with shrugs and contortions. The Caliph, however, ate with tolerable appetite, and fell into a nap that lasted six hours.

The splendor of the sun, reflected from the white cliffs of the mountains, in spite of the curtains that enclosed Vathek, at length disturbed his repose. He awoke terrified, and stung to the quick by wormwood-colour flies, which emitted from their wings a suffocating stench. The miserable monarch was perplexed how to act, though his wits were not idle in seeking expedients; whilst Bababalouk lay snoring amidst a swarm of those insects that busily thronged to pay court to his nose. The little pages, famished with hunger, had dropped their fans on the ground, and exerted their dying voices in bitter reproaches on the Caliph, who now, for the first time, heard the language of truth.

Thus stimulated, he renewed his imprecations against the Giaour, and bestowed upon Mahomet some soothing expressions. 'Where am I?' cried he: 'What are these dreadful rocks? these valleys of darkness? Are we arrived at the horrible Kaf?[14] Is the Simurgh[15] coming to pluck out my eyes, as a punishment for undertaking this impious enterprize?' Having said this he turned himself towards an outlet in the side of his pavilion; but, alas! what objects occurred to his view? on one side, a plain of black sand that appeared to be unbounded; and, on the other, perpendicular crags, bristled over with those abominable thistles which had so severely lacerated his tongue. He fancied, however, that he perceived amongst the brambles and briars some gigantic flowers, but was mistaken; for these were only the dangling palampores and variegated tatters of his gay retinue. As there were several clefts in the rock from whence water seemed to have flowed, Vathek applied his ear with the hope of catching the sound of some latent torrent; but could only distinguish the low murmurs of his people, who were repining at their journey, and complaining for the want of water. 'To what purpose,' asked they, 'have we been brought hither? hath our Caliph another tower to build? or have the relentless afrits[16] whom Carathis so much loves, fixed their abode in this place?'

At the name of Carathis, Vathek recollected the tablets he had received from his mother, who assured him they were fraught with preternatural qualities, and advised him to consult them as emergencies might require. Whilst he was engaged in turning them over, he heard a shout of joy and a loud clapping of hands. The curtains of his pavilion were soon drawn back and he beheld Bababalouk, followed by a troop of his favourites, conducting two dwarfs, each a cubit high; who had brought between them a large basket of melons, oranges, and pomegranates. They were singing in the sweetest tones the words that follow: 'We dwell on the top of these rocks, in a cabin of rushes and canes; the eagles envy us our nest: a small spring supplies us with water for the Abdest,[17] and we daily repeat prayers, which the Prophet approves. We love you, O commander of the faithful! our master, the good Emir Fakreddin, loves you also: he reveres, in your person, the vicegerent of Mahomet. Little as we are, in us he confides: he knows our hearts to be as good as our bodies are contemptible; and hath placed us here to aid those who are bewildered on these dreary mountains. Last night, whilst we were occupied within our cell in reading the holy Koran, a sudden hurricane blew out our lights, and rocked our habitation. For two whole hours a palpable darkness prevailed; but we heard sounds at a distance, which we conjectured to proceed from the bells of a Cafila,[18] passing over the rocks. Our ears were soon filled with deplorable shrieks, frightful roarings, and the sound of tymbals. Chilled with terror, we concluded that the Deggial,[19] with his exterminating angels, had sent forth his plagues on the earth. In the midst of these melancholy reflections, we perceived flames of the deepest red glow in the horizon; and found ourselves, in a few moments, covered with flakes of fire. Amazed at so strange an appearance, we took up the volume dictated by the blessed Intelligence, and, kneeling, by the light of the fire that surrounded us, we recited the verse which says, "Put no trust in any thing but the mercy of Heaven: there is no help, save in the holy Prophet: the mountain of Kaf itself may tremble; it is the power of Alla only that cannot be moved." After having pronounced these words, we felt consolation, and our minds were hushed into a sacred repose. Silence ensued, and our ears clearly distinguished a voice in the air, saying: "Servants of my faithful servant! go down to the happy valley of Fakreddin: tell him that an illustrious opportunity now offers to satiate the thirst of his hospitable heart. The commander of true believers is, this day, bewildered amongst these mountains, and stands in need of thy aid." – We obeyed with joy the angelic mission; and our master, filled with pious zeal, hath culled with his own hands these melons, oranges, and pomegranates. He is following us, with a hundred dromedaries, laden with the purest waters of his fountains; and is coming to kiss the fringe of your consecrated robe, and implore you to enter his humble habitation, which, placed amidst these barren wilds, resembles an emerald set in lead.' The dwarfs, having ended their address, remained still standing, and, with bands crossed upon their bosoms, preserved a respectful silence.

Vathek, in the midst of this curious harangue, seized the basket; and, long before it was finished, the fruits had dissolved in his mouth. As he continued to eat, his piety increased; and, in the same breath, he recited his prayers and called for the Koran and sugar.

Such was the state of his mind when the tablets, which were thrown by at the approach of the dwarfs, again attracted his eye. He took them up; but was ready to drop on the ground when he beheld, in large red characters, inscribed by Carathis, these words – which were, indeed, enough to make him tremble: 'Beware of old doctors and their puny messengers of but one cubit high: distrust their pious frauds; and, instead of eating their melons, impale on a spit the bearers of them. Shouldest thou be such a fool as to visit them, the portal of the subterranean palace will shut in thy face, with such force as shall shake thee asunder: thy body shall be spit upon, and bats will nestle in thy belly.'

'To what tends this ominous rhapsody?' cried the Caliph; 'and must I, then, perish in these deserts with thirst, whilst I may refresh myself in the delicious valley of melons and cucumbers? Accursed be the Giaour with his portal of ebony! he hath made me dance attendance too long already. Besides, who shall prescribe laws to me? I, forsooth, must not enter any one's habitation! Be it so; but what one can I enter that is not my own?' Bababalouk, who lost not a syllable of this soliloquy, applauded it with all his heart; and the ladies, for the first time, agreed with him in opinion.

The dwarfs were entertained, caressed, and seated, with great ceremony, on little cushions of satin. The symmetry of their persons was a subject of admiration; not an inch of them was suffered to pass unexamined. Knick-knacks and dainties were offered in profusion; but all were declined with respectful gravity. They climbed up the sides of the Caliph's seat, and, placing themselves each on one of his shoulders, began to whisper prayers in his ears. Their tongues quivered like aspen leaves; and the patience of Vathek was almost exhausted, when the acclamations of the troops announced the approach of Fakreddin, who was come with a hundred old grey-beards, and as many Korans and dromedaries. They instantly set about their ablutions, and began to repeat the Bismillah.[20] Vathek, to get rid of these officious[21] monitors, followed their example, for his hands were burning.

The good emir, who was punctiliously religious, and likewise a great dealer in compliments, made an harangue five times more prolix and insipid than his little harbingers had already delivered. The Caliph, unable any longer to refrain, exclaimed, 'For the love of Mahomet, my dear Fakreddin, have done! let us proceed to your valley, and enjoy the fruits that Heaven hath vouchsafed you.' The hint of proceeding put all into motion. The venerable attendants of the emir set forward somewhat slowly, but Vathek having ordered his little pages, in private, to goad on the dromedaries, loud fits of laughter broke forth from the cages; for the unwieldy curvetting of these poor beasts, and the ridiculous distress of their superannuated riders, afforded the ladies no small entertainment.

They descended, however, unhurt into the valley, by the easy slopes which the emir had ordered to be cut in the rock; and already the murmuring of streams and the rustling of leaves began to catch their attention. The cavalcade soon entered a path, which was skirted by flowering shrubs, and extended to a vast wood of palm trees, whose branches overspread a vast building of freestone. This edifice was crowned with nine domes, and adorned with as many portals of bronze, on which was engraven the following inscription: 'This is the asylum of pilgrims, the refuge of travellers, and the depository of secrets from all parts of the world.'

Nine pages, beautiful as the day, and decently clothed in robes of Egyptian linen, were standing at each door. They received the whole retinue with an easy and inviting air. Four of the most amiable placed the Caliph on a magnificent tecthtrevan;[22] four others, somewhat less graceful, took charge of Bababalouk, who capered for joy at the snug little cabin that fell to his share: the pages that remained waited on the rest of the train.

Every man being gone out of sight, the gate of a large enclosure on the right turned on its harmonious hinges; and a young female, of a slender form, came forth. Her light brown hair floated in the hazy breeze of the twilight. A troop of young maidens, like the Pleiades, attended her on tiptoe. They hastened to the pavilions that contained the sultanas; and the young lady, gracefully bending, said to them, 'Charming princesses! every thing is ready; we have prepared beds for your repose, and strewed your apartments with jasmine. No insects will keep off slumber from visiting your eyelids; we will dispel them with a thousand plumes. Come, then, amiable ladies! refresh your delicate feet and your ivory limbs in baths of rose water; and, by the light of perfumed lamps, your servants will amuse you with tales.' The sultanas accepted with pleasure these obliging offers, and followed the young lady to the emir's harem; where we must, for a moment, leave them and return to the Caliph.

Vathek found himself beneath a vast dome, illuminated by a thousand lamps of rock crystal: as many vases of the same material, filled with excellent sherbet, sparkled on a large table, where a profusion of viands were spread. Amongst others, were rice boiled in milk of almonds, saffron soups, and lamb *à la crême*; of all which the Caliph was amazingly fond. He took of each as much as he was able; testified his sense of the emir's friendship by the gaiety of his heart; and made the dwarfs dance against their will, for these little devotees durst not refuse the commander of the faithful. At last, he spread himself on the sofa, and slept sounder than he ever had before.

Beneath this dome a general silence prevailed; for there was nothing to disturb it but the jaws of Bababalouk, who had untrussed himself to eat with greater advantage, being anxious to make amends for his fast in the mountains. As his spirits were too high to admit of his sleeping, and hating to be idle, he proposed with himself to visit the harem and repair to his charge of the ladies: to examine if they had been properly lubricated with the balm of Mecca; if their eyebrows and tresses were in order; and, in a word, to perform all the little offices they might need. He sought for a long time together but without being able to find out the door. He durst not speak aloud for fear of disturbing the Caliph; and not a soul was stirring in the precincts of the palace. He almost despaired of effecting his purpose, when a low whispering just reached his ear. It came from the dwarfs, who were returned to their old occupation, and, for the nine hundred and ninety-ninth time in their lives, were reading over the Koran. They very politely invited Bababalouk to be of their party; but his head was full of other concerns. The dwarfs, though not a little scandalized at his dissolute morals, directed him to the apartments he wanted to find. His way thither lay through a hundred dark corridors, along which he groped as he went, and at last began to catch, from the extremity of a passage, the charming gossiping of the women, which not a little delighted his heart. 'Ah, ha! what, not yet asleep?' cried he; and, taking long strides as he spoke, 'did you not suspect me of abjuring my charge?' Two of the black eunuchs, on hearing a voice so loud, left their party in haste, sabre in hand, to discover the cause; but presently was repeated on all sides, ' 'Tis only Bababalouk! no one but Bababalouk!' This circumspect guardian, having gone up to a thin veil of carnation-colour silk that hung before the doorway, distinguished, by means of the softened splendor that shone through it, an oval bath of dark porphyry, surrounded by curtains, festooned in large folds. Through the apertures between them, as they were not drawn close, groups of young slaves were visible; amongst whom Bababalouk perceived his pupils, indulgingly expanding their arms, as if to embrace the perfumed water and refresh themselves after their fatigues. The looks of tender languor; their confidential whispers, and the enchanting smiles with which they were imparted; the exquisite fragrance of the roses: all combined to inspire a voluptuousness, which even Bababalouk himself was scare able to withstand.

He summoned up, however, his usual solemnity; and in the peremptory tone of authority, commanded the ladies instantly to leave the bath. Whilst he was issuing these mandates, the young Nouronihar, daughter of the emir, who was as sprightly as an antelope, and full of wanton gaiety, beckoned one of her slaves to let down the great swing which was suspended to the ceiling by cords of silk; and whilst this was doing, winked to her companions in the bath, who, chagrined to be forced from so soothing a state of indolence, began to twist and entangle their hair to plague and detain Bababalouk, and teased him, besides, with a thousand vagaries.

Nouronihar, perceiving that he was nearly out of patience, accosted him, with an arch air of respectful concern, and said, 'My lord! it is not by any means decent that the chief eunuch of the Caliph, our sovereign, should thus continue standing; deign but to recline your graceful person upon this sofa, which will burst with vexation if it have not the honour to receive you.' Caught by these flattering accents, Bababalouk gallantly replied, 'Delight of the apple of my eye! I accept the invitation of your honeyed lips; and, to say truth, my senses are dazzled with the radiance that beams from your charms.' – 'Repose, then, at your ease,' replied the beauty, as she placed him on the pretended sofa, which, quicker than lightning, flew up all at once. The rest of the women, having aptly conceived her design, sprang naked from the bath, and plied the swing with such unmerciful jerks that it swept through the whole compass of a very lofty dome, and took from the poor victim all power of respiration. Sometimes his feet razed the surface of the water; and, at others, the skylight almost flattened his nose. In vain did he fill the air with the cries of a voice that resembled the ringing of a cracked jar; the peals of laughter were still predominant.

Nouronihar, in the inebriety of youthful spirits, being used only to eunuchs of ordinary harems, and having never seen any thing so eminently disgusting, was far more diverted than all the rest. She began to parody some Persian verses and sang, with an accent most demurely piquant, 'Oh, gentle white dove! as thou soar'st through the air, vouchsafe one kind glance on the mate of thy love: melodious Philomel, I am thy rose; warble some couplet to ravish my heart!'

The sultanas and their slaves, stimulated by these pleasantries, persevered at the swing with such unremitted assiduity, that at length the cord which had secured it snapt suddenly asunder; and Bababalouk fell, floundering like a turtle, to the bottom of the bath. This accident occasioned an universal shout. Twelve little doors, till now unobserved, flew open at once; and the ladies, in an instant, made their escape; but not before having heaped all the towels on his head and put out the lights that remained.

The deplorable animal, in water to the chin, overwhelmed with darkness, and unable to extricate himself from the wrappers that embarrassed him, was still doomed to hear, for his further consolation, the fresh bursts of merriment his disaster occasioned He bustled, but in vain, to get from the bath; for the margin was become so slippery with the oil spilt in breaking the lamps, that, at every effort, he slid back with a plunge which resounded aloud through the hollow of the dome. These cursed peals of laughter were redoubled at every relapse, and he, who thought the place infested rather by devils than women, resolved to cease groping, and abide in the bath; where he amused himself with soliloquies, interspersed with imprecations, of which his malicious neighbours, reclining on down, suffered not an accent to escape. In this delectable plight the morning surprized him. The Caliph, wondering at his absence, had caused him to be sought for every where. At last he was drawn forth almost smothered from under the wisp of linen, and wet even to the marrow. Limping, and his teeth chattering with cold, he approached his master, who enquired what was the matter, and how he came soused in so strange a pickle. – 'And why did you enter this cursed lodge?' answered Bababalouk gruffly. 'Ought a monarch like you to visit with his harem the abode of a grey-bearded emir, who knows nothing of life? – And with what gracious damsels doth the place too abound! Fancy to yourself how they have soaked me like a burnt crust; and made me dance like a jack-pudding, the livelong night through, on their damnable swing. What an excellent lesson for your sultanas, into whom I had instilled such reserve and decorum!' Vathek, comprehendng not a syllable of all this invective, obliged him to relate minutely the transaction: but, instead of sympathizing with the miserable sufferer, he laughed immoderately at the device of the swing and the figure of Bababalouk mounted upon it. The stung eunuch could scarcely preserve the semblance of respect. 'Ay, laugh, my lord! laugh,' said he; 'but I wish this Nouronihar would play some trick on you; she is too wicked to spare even majesty itself.' These words made, for the present, but a slight impression on the Caliph; but they not long after recurred to his mind.

This conversation was cut short by Fakreddin, who came to request that Vathek would join in the prayers and ablutions, to be solemnized on a spacious meadow watered by innumerable streams. The Caliph found the waters refreshing, but the prayers abominably irksome. He diverted himself, however, with the multitude of calenders, santons, and derviches, who were continually coming and going; but especially with the bramins, faquirs,[23] and other enthusiasts, who had travelled from the heart of India, and halted on their way with the emir. These latter had each of them some mummery peculiar to himself. One dragged a huge chain wherever he went; another an orang-outang; whilst a third was furnished with scourges; and all performed to a charm. Some would climb up trees, holding one foot in the air; others poise themselves over a fire, and without mercy fillip their noses. There were some amongst them that cherished vermin, which were not ungrateful in requiting their caresses. These rambling fanatics revolted the heart of the derviches, the calenders, and santons; however, the vehemence of their aversion soon subsided, under the hope that the presence of the Caliph would cure their folly, and convert them to the Mussulman faith. But, alas! how great was their disappointment! for Vathek, instead of preaching to them, treated them as buffoons, bade them present his compliments to Visnow and Ixhora, and discovered a predilection for a squat old man from the Isle of Serendib, who was more ridiculous than any of the rest. 'Come!' said he, 'for the love of your gods, bestow a few slaps on your chops to amuse me.' The old fellow, offended at such an address, began loudly to weep; but, as he betrayed a villainous drivelling in shedding tears, the Caliph turned his back and listened to Bababalouk, who whispered, whilst he held the umbrella over him, 'Your majesty should be cautious of this odd assembly, which hath been collected I know not for what. Is it necessary to exhibit such spectacles to a mighty potenate, with interludes of talapoins more mangy than dogs? Were I you, I would command a fire to be kindled, and at once rid the estates of the emir, of his harem, and all his menagerie.' – 'Tush, dolt,' answered Vathek, 'and know that all this infinitely charms me. Nor shall I leave the meadow till I have visited every hive of these pious mendicants.'

Wherever the Caliph directed his course, objects of pity were sure to swarm round him; the blind, the purblind, smarts without noses, damsels without ears, each to extol the munificence of Fakreddin, who, as well as his attendant grey-beards, dealt about, gratis, plasters and cataplasms to all that applied. At noon, a superb corps of cripples made its appearance; and soon after advanced, by platoons, on the plain, the completest association of invalids that had ever been embodied till then. The blind went groping with the blind, the lame limped on together, and the maimed made gestures to each other with the only arm that remained. The sides of a considerable waterfall were crowded by the deaf; amongst whom were some from Pegû, with ears uncommonly handsome and large, but who were still less able to hear than the rest. Nor were there wanting others in abundance with hump-backs, wenny necks, and even horns of an exquisite polish.

The emir, to aggrandize the solemnity of the festival, in honour of his illustrious visitant, ordered the turf to be spread on all sides with skins and table-cloths; upon which were served up for the good Mussulmans pilaus of every hue, with other orthodox dishes; and, by the express order of Vathek, who was shamefully tolerant, small plates of abominations were prepared, to the great scandal of the faithful. The holy assembly began to fall to. The Caliph, in spite of every remonstrance from the chief of his eunuchs, resolved to have a dinner dressed on the spot. The complaisant emir immediately gave orders for a table to be placed in the shade of the willows. The first service consisted of fish, which they drew from a river, flowing over sands of gold at the foot of a lofty hill. These were broiled as fast as taken, and served up with a sauce of vinegar and small herbs that grew on Mount Sinai; for every thing with the emir was excellent and pious.

The dessert was not quite set on, when the sound of lutes from the hill was repeated by the echoes of the neighbouring mountains. The Caliph, with an emotion of pleasure and surprize, had no sooner raised up his head, than a handful of jasmine dropped on his face. An abundance of tittering succeeded the frolic, and instantly appeared, through the bushes, the elegant forms of several young females, skipping and bounding like roes. The fragrance diffused from their hair struck the sense of Vathek, who, in an ecstasy, suspending his repast, said to Bababalouk, 'Are the Peris[24] come down from their spheres? Note her, in particular, whose form is so perfect; venturously running on the brink of the precipice, and turning back her head, as regardless of nothing but the graceful flow of her robe. With what captivating impatience doth she contend with the bushes for her veil? could it be she who threw the jasmine at me?' – 'Ay! she it was; and you too would she throw, from the top of the rock,' answered Bababalouk, 'for that is my good friend Nouronihar, who so kindly lent me her swing. My dear lord and master,' added he, wresting a twig from a willow, 'let me correct her for her want of respect: the emir will have no reason to complain; since (bating what I owe to his piety) he is much to be blamed for keeping a troop of girls on the mountains, where the sharpness of the air gives their blood too brisk a circulation.'

'Peace! blasphemer,' said the Caliph; 'speak not thus of her, who, over these mountains, leads my heart a willing captive. Contrive, rather, that my eyes may be fixed upon hers; that I may respire her sweet breath as she bounds panting along these delightful wilds!' On saying these words, Vathek extended his arms towards the hill; and directing his eyes with an anxiety unknown to him before, endeavoured to keep within view the object that enthralled his soul; but her course was as difficult to follow as the flight of one of those beautiful blue butterflies of Cachmere which are at once, so volatile and rare.

The Caliph, not satisfied with seeing, wished also to hear Nouronihar, and eagerly turned to catch the sound of her voice. At last, he distinguished her whispering to one of her companions behind the thicket from whence she had thrown the jasmine: 'A Caliph, it must be owned, is a fine thing to see; but my little Gulchenrouz is much more amiable: one lock of his hair is of more value to me than the richest embroidery of the Indies. I had rather that his teeth should mischievously press my finger, than the richest ring of the imperial treasure. Where have you left him, Sutlememe? and why is he not here?'

The agitated Caliph still wished to hear more; but she immediately retired with all her attendants. The fond monarch pursued her with his eyes till she was gone out of sight; and then continued like a bewildered and benighted traveller, from whom the clouds had obscured the constellation that guided his way. The curtain of night seemed dropped before him: every thing appeared discoloured. The falling waters filled his soul with dejection, and his tears trickled down the jasmines he had caught from Nouronihar, and placed in his inflamed bosom. He snatched up a few shining pebbles, to remind him of the scene where he felt the first tumults of love. Two hours were elapsed, and evening drew on, before he could resolve to depart from the place. He often, but in vain, attempted to go: a soft languor enervated the powers of his mind. Extending himself on the brink of the stream, he turned his eyes towards the blue summits of the mountain, and exclaimed, 'What concealest thou behind thee, pitiless rock? what is passing in thy solitudes? Whither is she gone? O heaven! perhaps she is now wandering in thy grottoes with her happy Gulchenrouz!'

In the mean time, the damps began to descend; and the emir, solicitous for the health of the Caliph, ordered the imperial litter to be brought. Vathek, absorbed in his reveries, was imperceptibly removed and conveyed back to the saloon that received him the evening before. But let us leave the Caliph immersed in his new passion, and attend Nouronihar beyond the rocks where she had again joined her beloved Gulchenrouz.

This Gulchenrouz was the son of Ali Hassan, brother to the emir; and the most delicate and lovely creature in the world. Ali Hassan, who had been absent ten years on a voyage to the unknown seas, committed, at his departure, this child, the only survivor of many, to the care and protection of his brother. Gulchenrouz could write in various characters with precision, and paint upon vellum the most elegant arabesques that fancy could devise. His sweet voice accompanied the lute in the most enchanting manner; and when he sang the loves of Megnoun and Leilah, or some unfortunate lovers of ancient days, tears insensibly overflowed the cheeks of his auditors. The verses he composed (for, like Megnoun, he, too, was a poet) inspired that unresisting languor, so frequently fatal to the female heart. The women all doated upon him; and, though he had passed his thirteenth year, they still detained him in the harem. His dancing was light as the gossamer waved by the zephyrs of spring; but his arms, which twined so gracefully with those of the young girls in the dance, could neither dart the lance in the chace, nor curb the steeds that pastured in his uncle's domains. The bow, however, he drew with a certain aim, and would have excelled his competitors in the race, could he have broken the ties that bound him to Nouronihar.

The two brothers had mutually engaged their children to each other; and Nouronihar loved her cousin more than her own beautiful eyes. Both had the same tastes and amusements; the same long, languishing looks; the same tresses; the same fair complexions; and, when Gulchenrouz appeared in the dress of his cousin, he seemed to be more feminine than even herself. If, at any time, he left the harem to visit Fakreddin, it was with all the bashfulness of a fawn, that consciously ventures from the lair of its dam: he was, however, wanton enough to mock the solemn old grey-beards, though sure to be rated without mercy in return. Whenever this happened, he would hastily plunge into the recesses of the harem; and, sobbing, take refuge in the fond arms of Nouronihar, who loved even his faults beyond the virtues of others.

It fell out this evening, that, after leaving the Caliph in the meadow, she ran with Gulchenrouz over the green sward of the mountain that sheltered the vale where Fakreddin had chosen to reside. The sun was dilated on the edge of the horizon; and the young people, whose fancies were lively and inventive, imagined they beheld, in the gorgeous clouds of the west, the domes of Shaddukian and Amberabad, where the Peris have fixed their abode. Nouronihar, sitting on the slope of the hill, supported on her knees the perfumed head of Gulchenrouz. The unexpected arrival of the Caliph, and the splendor that marked his appearance, had already filled with emotion the ardent soul of Nouronihar. Her vanity irresistibly prompted her to pique the Prince's attention; and this she before took good care to effect, whilst he picked up the jasmine she had thrown upon him. But when Gulchenrouz asked after the flowers he had culled for her bosom, Nouronihar was all in confusion. She hastily kissed his forehead, arose in a flutter, and walked with unequal steps on the border of the precipice. Night advanced, and the pure gold of the setting sun had yielded to a sanguine red, the glow of which, like the reflection of a burning furnace, flushed Nouronihar's animated countenance. Gulchenrouz, alarmed at the agitation of his cousin, said to her, with a supplicating accent, 'Let us begone; the sky looks portentous, the tamarisks tremble more than common, and the raw wind chills my very heart. Come! let us begone; 'tis a melancholy night!' Then taking hold of her hand, he drew it towards the path he besought her to go. Nouronihar unconsciously followed the attraction; for a thousand strange imaginations occupied her spirits. She passed the large round of honeysuckles, her favourite resort, without ever vouchsafing it a glance; yet Gulchenrouz could not help snatching off a few shoots in his way, though he ran as if a wild beast were behind.

The young females seeing them approach in such haste, and, according to custom, expecting a dance, instantly assembled in a circle and took each other by the hand; but Gulchenrouz, coming up out of breath, fell down at once on the grass. This accident struck with consternation the whole of this frolicsome party; whilst Nouronihar, half distracted and overcome, both by the violence of her exercise and the tumult of her thoughts, sunk feebly down at his side, cherished his cold hands in her bosom, and chafed his temples with a fragrant perfume. At length he came to himself, and wrapping up his head in the robe of his cousin, intreated that she would not return to the harem. He was afraid of being snapped at by Shaban his tutor, a wrinkled old eunuch of a surly disposition; for, having interrupted the wonted walk of Nouronihar, he dreaded lest the churl should take it amiss. The whole of this sprightly group, sitting round upon a mossy knoll, began to entertain themselves with various pastimes, whilst their superintendents, the eunuchs, were gravely conversing at a distance. The nurse of the emir's daughter, observing her pupil sit ruminating with her eyes on the ground, endeavoured to amuse her with diverting tales; to which Gulchenrouz, who had already forgotten his inquietudes, listened with a breathless attention. He laughed, he clapped his hands, and passed a hundred little tricks on the whole of the company, without omitting the eunuchs, whom he provoked to run after him, in spite of their age and decrepitude.

During these occurrences, the moon arose, the wind subsided, and the evening became so serene and inviting, that a resolution was taken to sup on the spot. One of the eunuchs ran to fetch melons whilst others were employed in showering down almonds from the branches that overhung this amiable party. Sutlememe, who excelled in dressing a salad, having filled large bowls of porcelain with eggs of small birds, curds turned with citron juice, slices of cucumber, and the inmost leaves of delicate herbs, handed it round from one to another and gave each their shares with a large spoon of cocknos.[25] Gulchenrouz, nestling, as usual, in the bosom of Nouronihar, pouted out his vermilion little lips against the offer of Sutlememe; and would take it only from the hand of his cousin, on whose mouth he hung, like a bee inebriated with the nectar of flowers.

In the midst of this festive scene, there appeared a light on the top of the highest mountain, which attracted the notice of every eye. This light was not less bright than the moon when at full, and might have been taken for her, had not the moon already risen. The phaenomenon occasioned a general surprize, and no one could conjecture the cause. It could not be a fire, for the light was clear and bluish; nor had meteors ever been seen of that magnitude or splendor. This strange light faded for a moment, and immediately renewed its brightness. It first appeared motionless, at the foot of the rock; whence it darted in an instant, to sparkle in a thicket of palm-trees: from thence it glided along the torrent; and at last fixed in a glen that was narrow and dark. The moment it had taken its direction, Gulchenrouz, whose heart always trembled at any thing sudden or rare, drew Nouronihar by the robe and anxiously requested her to return to the harem. The women were importunate in seconding the intreaty; but the curiosity of the emir's daughter prevailed. She not only refused to go back, but resolved at all hazards, to pursue the appearance.

Whilst they were debating what was best to be done, the light shot forth so dazzling a blaze that they all fled away shrieking. Nouronihar followed them a few steps; but, coming to the turn of a little byepath, stopped, and went back alone. As she ran with an alertness peculiar to herself, it was not long before she came to the place where they had just been supping. The globe of fire now appeared stationary in the glen, and burned in majestic stillness. Nouronihar, pressing her hands upon her bosom, hesitated, for some moments, to advance. The solitude of her situation was new, the silence of the night awful, and every object inspired sensations which, till then, she never had felt. The affright of Gulchenrouz recurred to her mind, and she a thousand times turned to go back; but this luminous appearance was always before her. Urged on by an irresistible impulse, she continued to approach it, in defiance of every obstacle that opposed her progress.

At length she arrived at the opening of the glen; but, instead of coming up to the light, she found herself surrounded by darkness; excepting that, at a considerable distance, a faint spark glimmered by fits. She stopped a second time: the sound of waterfalls mingling their murmurs, the hollow rustlings among the palm-branches and the funereal screams of the birds from their rifted trunks, all conspired to fill her soul with terror. She imagined, every moment, that she trod on some venomous reptile. All the stories of malignant dives and dismal Ghoules thronged into her memory; but her curiosity was, notwithstanding, more predominant than her fears. She therefore firmly entered a winding track that led towards the spark; but, being a stranger to the path, she had not gone far, till she began to repent of her rashness. 'Alas!' said she, 'that I were but in those secure and illuminated apartments, where my evenings glided on with Gulchenrouz! Dear child! how would thy heart flutter with terror, wert thou wandering in these wild solitudes, like me!' Thus speaking, she advanced, and coming up to steps hewn in the rock, ascended them undismayed. The light which was now gradually enlarging, appeared above her on the summit of the mountain, and as if proceeding from a cavern. At length, she distinguished a plaintive and melodious union of voices, that resembled the dirges which are sung over tombs. A sound like that which arises from the filling of baths struck her ear at the same time. She continued ascending, and discovered large wax torches in full blaze, planted here and there in the fissures of the rock. This appearance filled her with fear, whilst the subtile and potent odour which the torches exhaled caused her to sink, almost lifeless, at the entrance of the grot.

Casting her eyes within in this kind of trance, she beheld

a large cistern of gold, filled with a water, the vapour of which distilled on her face a dew of the essence of roses. A soft symphony resounded through the grot. On the sides of the cistern she noticed appendages of royalty, diadems and feathers of the heron, all sparkling with carbuncles. Whilst her attention was fixed on this display of magnificence, the music ceased, and a voice instantly demanded, 'For what monarch are these torches kindled, this bath prepared, and these habiliments which belong not only to the sovereigns of the earth, but even to the talismanic powers?' To which a second voice answered, 'They are for the charming daughter of the emir Fakreddin.' – 'What,' replied the first, 'for that trifler, who consumes her time with a giddy child, immersed in softness, and who, at best, can make but a pitiful husband?' – 'And can she,' rejoined the other voice, 'be amused with such empty toys, whilst the Caliph, the sovereign of the world, he who is destined to enjoy the treasures of the pre-Adamite sultans, a Prince six feet high, and whose eyes pervade the inmost soul of a female, is inflamed with love for her? No! she will be wise enough to answer that passion alone that can aggrandize her glory. No doubt she will, and despise the puppet of her fancy. Then all the riches this place contains, as well as the carbuncle of Giamschid, shall be hers.' – 'You judge right,' returned the first voice; 'and I haste to Istakhar to prepare the palace of subterranean fire for the reception of the bridal pair.'

The voices ceased; the torches were extinguished; the most entire darkness succeeded; and Nouronihar, recovering with a start, found herself reclined on a sofa in the harem of her father. She clapped her hands, and immediately came together Gulchenrouz and her women, who, in despair at having lost her, had dispatched eunuchs to seek her in every direction. Shaban appeared with the rest, and began to reprimand her, with an air of consequence: 'Little impertinent,' said he, 'have you false keys, or are you beloved of some Genius that hath given you a picklock? I will try the extent of your power: come to the dark chamber, and expect not the company of Gulchenrouz: be expeditious! I will shut you up, and turn the key twice upon you!' At these menaces, Nouronihar indignantly raised her head, opened on Shaban her black eyes, which, since the important dialogue of the enchanted grot, were considerably enlarged, and said, 'Go, speak thus to slaves; but learn to reverence her who is born to give laws and subject all to her power.'

Proceeding in the same style, she was interrupted by a sudden exclamation of, 'The Caliph! the Caliph!' All the curtains were thrown open, the slaves prostrated themselves in double rows, and poor little Gulchenrouz went to hide beneath the couch of a sofa. At first appeared a file of black eunuchs trailing after them long trains of muslin embroidered with gold, and holding in their hands censers, which dispensed, as they passed, the grateful perfume of the wood of aloes. Next marched Bababalouk with a solemn strut, and tossing his head, as not overpleased at the visit. Vathek came close after, superbly robed: his gait was unembarrassed and noble; and his presence would have engaged admiration, though he had not been the sovereign of the world. He approached Nouronihar with a throbbing heart, and seemed enraptured at the full effulgence of her radiant eyes, of which he had before caught but a few glimpses; but she instantly depressed them, and her confusion augmented her beauty.

Bababalouk, who was a thorough adept in coincidences of this nature, and knew that the worst game should be played with the best face, immediately made a signal for all to retire; and no sooner did he perceive beneath the sofa the little one's feet, than he drew him forth without ceremony, set him upon his shoulders, and lavished him, as he went off, a thousand unwelcome caresses. Gulchenrouz cried out, and resisted till his cheeks became the colour of the blossom of pomegranates, and his tearful eyes sparkled with indignation. He cast a significant glance at

Nouronihar, which the Caliph noticing, asked, 'Is that, then, your Gulchenrouz?' – 'Sovereign of the world!' answered she, 'spare my cousin, whose innocence and gentleness deserve not your anger!' – 'Take comfort,' said Vathek, with a smile: 'he is in good hands. Bababalouk is fond of children, and never goes without sweetmeats and comfits.' The daughter of Fakreddin was abashed, and suffered Gulchenrouz to be borne away without adding a word. The tumult of her bosom betrayed her confusion, and Vathek, becoming still more impassioned, gave a loose to his frenzy; which had only not subdued the last faint strugglings of reluctance, when the emir, suddenly bursting in, threw his face upon the ground at the feet of the Caliph, and said, 'Commander of the faithful! abase not yourself to the meanness of your slave.' – 'No, emir,' replied Vathek, 'I raise her to an equality with myself: I declare her my wife; and the glory of your race shall extend from one generation to another.' – 'Alas! my lord,' said Fakreddin, as he plucked off a few grey hairs of his beard, 'cut short the days of your faithful servant, rather than force him to depart from his word. Nouronihar is solemnly promised to Gulchenrouz, the son of my brother Ali Hassan: they are united, also, in heart; their faith is mutually plighted; and affiances, so sacred, cannot be broken.' – 'What then!' replied the Caliph bluntly; 'would you surrender this divine beauty to a husband more womanish than herself? and can you imagine that I will suffer her charms to decay in hands so inefficient and nerveless? No! she is destined to live out her life within my embraces: such is my will; retire, and disturb not the night I devote to the worship of her charms.'

The irritated emir drew forth his sabre, presented it to Vathek, and stretching out his neck, said, in a firm tone of voice, 'Strike your unhappy host, my lord: he has lived long enough, since he hath seen the Prophet's vicegerent violate the rights of hospitality.' At his uttering these words, Nouronihar, unable to support any longer the conflict of her passions, sunk down into a swoon. Vathek, both terrified for her life and furious at an opposition to his will, bade Fakreddin assist his daughter, and withdrew; darting his terrible look at the unfortunate emir, who suddenly fell backward, bathed in a sweat as cold as the damp of death.

Gulchenrouz, who had escaped from the hands of Bababalouk, and was at that instant returned, called out for help as loudly as he could, not having strength to afford it himself. Pale and panting, the poor child attempted to revive Nouronihar by caresses; and it happened, that the thrilling warmth of his lips restored her to life. Fakreddin, beginning also to recover from the look of the Caliph, with difficulty tottered to a seat; and, after warily casting round his eye, to see if this dangerous Prince were gone, sent for Shaban and Sutlememe; and said to them apart, 'My friends! violent evils require violent remedies; the Caliph has brought desolation and horror into my family; and how shall we resist his power? Another of his looks will send me to the grave. Fetch, then, that narcotic powder which a dervich brought me from Aracan. A dose of it, the effect of which will continue three days, must be administered to each of these children. The Caliph will believe them to be dead; for they will have all the appearance of death. We shall go as if to inter them in the cave of Meimouné, at the entrance of the great desert of sand and near the bower of my dwarfs. When all the spectators shall be withdrawn, you, Shaban, and four select eunuchs, shall convey them to the lake; where provision shall be ready to support them a month: for one day allotted to the surprize this event will occasion, five to the tears, a fortnight to reflection, and the rest to prepare for renewing his progress, will, according to my calculation, fill up the whole time that Vathek will tarry; and I shall then be freed from his intrusion.'

'Your plan is good,' said Sutlememe, 'if it can but be effected. I have remarked that Nouronihar is well able to support the glances of the Caliph, and that he is far from being sparing of them to her; be assured, therefore, that, notwithstanding her fondness for Gulchenrouz, she will never remain quiet, while she knows him to be here. Let us persuade her that both herself and Gulchenrouz are really dead, and that they were conveyed to those rocks, for a limited season, to expiate the little faults of which their love was the cause. We will add that we killed ourselves in despair; and that your dwarfs, whom they never yet saw, will preach to them delectable sermons. I will engage that every thing shall succeed to the bent of your wishes.' – 'Be it so!' said Fakreddin: 'I approve your proposal: let us lose not a moment to give it effect.'

They hastened to seek for the powder, which, being mixed in a sherbet was immediately administered to Gulchenrouz and Nouronihar. Within the space of an hour, both were seized with violent palpitations, and a general numbness gradually ensued. They arose from the floor where they had remained ever since the Caliph's departure, and, ascending to the sofa, reclined themselves upon it, clasped in each other's embraces. 'Cherish me, my dear Nouronihar!' said Gulchenrouz: 'put thy hand upon my heart; it feels as if it were frozen. Alas! thou art as cold as myself! hath the Caliph murdered us both, with his terrible look?' – 'I am dying!' cried she, in a faltering voice: 'press me closer; I am ready to expire!' – 'Let us die, then, together,' answered the little Gulchenrouz, whilst his breast laboured with a convulsive sigh; 'let me, at least, breathe forth my soul on thy lips!' They spoke no more, and became as dead.

Immediately the most piercing cries were heard through the harem; whilst Shaban and Sutlememe personated, with great adroitness, the parts of persons in despair. The emir, who was sufficiently mortified to be forced into such untoward expedients, and had now, for the first time, made a trial of his powder, was under no necessity of counterfeiting grief. The slaves, who had flocked together from all quarters, stood motionless at the spectacle before them. All lights were extinguished, save two lamps, which shed a wan glimmering over the faces of these lovely flowers that seemed to be faded in the spring-time of life. Funeral vestments were prepared; their bodies were washed with rose-water; their beautiful tresses were braided and incensed; and they were wrapped in symars whiter than alabaster.

At the moment that their attendants were placing two wreaths of their favourite jasmines on their brows, the Caliph, who had just heard the tragical catastrophe, arrived. He looked not less pale and haggard than the Ghoules that wander at night among the graves. Forgetful of himself and every one else, he broke through the midst of the slaves; fell prostrate at the foot of the sofa; beat his bosom; called himself 'atrocious murderer!' and invoked upon his head a thousand imprecations. With a trembling hand he raised the veil that covered the countenance of Nouronihar, and uttering a loud shriek, fell lifeless on the floor. The chief of the eunuchs dragged him off, with horrible grimaces, and repeated as he went, 'Ay, I foresaw she would play you some ungracious turn!'

No sooner was the Caliph gone, than the emir commanded biers to be brought, and forbade that any one should enter the harem. Every window was fastened; all instruments of music were broken; and the Imans[26] began to recite their prayers. Towards the close of this melancholy day, Vathek sobbed in silence; for they had been forced to compose with anodynes his convulsions of rage and desperation.

At the dawn of the succeeding morning, the wide folding doors of the palace were set open, and the funeral procession moved forward for the mountain. The wailful cries of 'La Ilah illa Alla!'[27] reached the Caliph, who was eager to cicatrize himself and attend the ceremonial; nor could he have been dissuaded, had not his excessive weakness disabled him from walking. At the few first steps he fell on the ground, and his people were obliged to lay him on a bed, where he remained many days in such a state of insensibility as excited compassion in the emir himself.

When the procession was arrived at the grot of Meimouné, Shaban and Sutlememe dismissed the whole of the train, excepting the four confidential eunuchs who were appointed to remain. After resting some moments near the biers, which had been left in the open air, they caused them to be carried to the brink of a small lake, whose banks were overgrown with a hoary moss. This was the great resort of herons and storks which preyed continually on little blue fishes. The dwarfs, instructed by the emir, soon repaired thither, and, with the help of the eunuchs, began to construct cabins of rushes and reeds, a work in which they had admirable skill. A magazine also was contrived for provisions, with a small oratory for themselves, and a pyramid of wood, neatly piled to furnish the necessary fuel: for the air was bleak in the hollows of the mountains.

At evening two fires were kindled on the brink of the lake, and the two lovely bodies, taken from their biers, were carefully deposited upon a bed of dried leaves within the same cabin. The dwarfs began to recite the Koran, with their clear shrill voices; and Shaban and Sutlememe stood at some distance, anxiously waiting the effects of the powder. At length Nouronihar and Gulchenrouz faintly stretched out their arms; and, gradually opening their eyes, began to survey, with looks of increasing amazement, every object around them. They even attempted to rise; but, for want of strength, fell back again. Sutlememe, on this, administered a cordial, which the emir had taken care to provide.

Gulchenrouz, thoroughly aroused, sneezed out aloud; and, raising himself with an effort that expressed his surprize, left the cabin and inhaled the fresh air with the greatest avidity. 'Yes,' said he, 'I breathe again! again do I exist! I hear sounds! I behold a firmament, spangled over with stars!' Nouronihar, catching these beloved accents, extricated herself from the leaves and ran to clasp Gulchenrouz to her bosom. The first objects she remarked were their long simars, their garlands of flowers, and their naked feet: she hid her face in her hands to reflect. The vision of the enchanted bath, the despair of her father, and, more vividly than both, the majestic figure of Vathek, recurred to her memory. She recollected, also, that herself and Gulchenrouz had been sick and dying; but all these images bewildered her mind. Not knowing where she was, she turned her eyes on all sides, as if to recognize the surrounding scene. This singular lake, those flames reflected from its glassy surface, the pale hues of its banks, the romantic cabins, the bulrushes that sadly waved their drooping heads, the storks whose melancholy cries blended with the shrill voices of the dwarfs – every thing conspired to persuade her that the angel of death had opened the portal of some other world.

Gulchenrouz, on his part, lost in wonder, clung to the neck of his cousin. He believed himself in the region of phantoms, and was terrified at the silence she preserved. At length addressing her: 'Speak,' said he; 'where are we? Do you not see those spectres that are stirring the burning coals? Are they Monker and Nekir[28] who are come to throw us into them? Does the fatal bridge across this lake, whose solemn stillness perhaps conceals from us an abyss, in which for whole ages we shall be doomed incessantly to sink?'

'No, my children,' said Sutlememe, going towards them; 'take comfort! the exterminating angel, who conducted our souls hither after yours, hath assured us, that the chastisement of your indolent and voluptuous life shall be restricted to a certain series of years, which you must pass in this dreary abode; where the sun is scarcely visible, and where the soil yields neither fruits nor flowers. These,' continued she, pointing to the dwarfs, 'will provide for our wants; for souls so mundane as ours retain too strong a tincture of their earthly extraction. Instead of meats, your food will be nothing but rice; and your bread shall be moistened in the fogs that brood over the surface of the lake.'

At this desolating prospect, the poor children burst into tears, and prostrated themselves before the dwarfs; who perfectly supported their characters, and delivered an excellent discourse, of a customary length, upon the sacred camel which, after a thousand years, was to convey them to the paradise of the faithful.

The sermon being ended, and ablutions performed, they praised Alla and the Prophet, supped very indifferently, and retired to their withered leaves. Nouronihar and her little cousin consoled themselves on finding that the dead might lie in one cabin. Having slept well before, the remainder of the night was spent in conversation on what had befallen them; and both, from a dread of apparitions, betook themselves for protection to one another's arms.

In the morning, which was lowering and rainy, the dwarfs mounted high poles, like minarets, and called them to prayers. The whole congregation, which consisted of Sutlememe, Shaban, the four eunuchs, and a few storks that were tired of fishing, was already assembled. The two children came forth from their cabin with a slow and dejected pace. As their minds were in a tender and melancholy mood, their devotions were performed with fervour. No sooner were they finished than Gulchenrouz demanded of Sutlememe and the rest, 'how they happened to die so opportunely for his cousin and himself?' – 'We killed ourselves,' returned Sutlememe, 'in despair at your death.' On this, Nouronihar, who, notwithstanding what had passed, had not yet forgotten her vision, said, 'And the Caliph! is he also dead of his grief? and will he likewise come hither?' The dwarfs, who were prepared with an answer, most demurely replied, 'Vathek is damned beyond all redemption!' – 'I readily believe so,' said Gulchenrouz; 'and am glad, from my heart, to hear it; for I am convinced it was his horrible look that sent us hither, to listen to sermons, and mess upon rice.' One week passed away on the side of the lake unmarked by any variety; Nouronihar ruminating on the grandeur of which death had deprived her, and Gulchenrouz applying to prayers and basket-making with the dwarfs, who infinitely pleased him.

Whilst this scene of innocence was exhibiting in the mountains, the Caliph presented himself to the emir in a new light. The instant he recovered the use of his senses, with a voice that made Bababalouk quake, he thundered out, 'Perfidious Giaour! I renounce thee for ever! it is thou who hast slain my beloved Nouronihar! and I supplicate the pardon of Mahomet, who would have preserved her to me had I been more wise. Let water be brought to perform my ablutions, and let the pious Fakreddin be called to offer up his prayers with mine, and reconcile me to him. Afterwards, we will go together and visit the sepulchre of the unfortunate Nouronihar. I am resolved to become a hermit, and consume the residue of my days on this mountain, in hope of expiating my crimes.' – 'And what do you intend to live upon there?' enquired Bababalouk. – 'I hardly know,' replied Vathek, 'but I will tell you when I feel hungry – which, I believe, will not soon be the case.'

The arrival of Fakreddin put a stop to this conversation. As soon as Vathek saw him, he threw his arms around his neck, bedewed his face with a torrent of tears, and uttered things so affecting, so pious, that the emir, crying for joy, congratulated himself in his heart upon having performed so admirable and unexpected a conversion. As for the pilgrimage to the mountain, Fakreddin had his reasons not to oppose it; therefore, each ascending his own litter, they started.

Notwithstanding the vigilance with which his attendants watched the Caliph, they could not prevent his harrowing his cheeks with a few scratches, when on the place where he was told Nouronihar had been buried; they were even obliged to drag him away, by force of hands, from the melancholy spot. However, he swore, with a solemn oath, that he would return thither every day. This resolution did not exactly please the emir – yet he flattered himself that the Caliph might not proceed farther, and would merely perform his devotions in the cavern of Meimouné. Besides, the lake was so completely concealed within the solitary bosom of those tremendous rocks, that he thought it utterly impossible any one could ever find it. This security of Fakreddin was also considerably strengthened by the conduct of Vathek, who performed his vow most scrupulously, and returned daily from the hill so devout, and so contrite, that all the grey-beards were in a state of ecstasy on account of it.

Nouronihar was not altogether so content; for though she felt a fondness for Gulchenrouz, who, to augment the attachment, had been left at full liberty with her, yet she still regarded him as but a bawble that bore no competition with the carbuncle of Giamschid. At times, she indulged doubts on the mode of her being; and scarcely could believe that the dead had all the wants and the whims of the living. To gain satisfaction, however, on so perplexing a topic, one morning, whilst all were asleep, she arose with a breathless caution from the side of Gulchenrouz; and, after having given him a soft kiss, began to follow the windings of the lake, till it terminated with a rock, the top of which was accessible, though lofty. This she climbed with considerable toil; and having reached the summit, set forward in a run, like a doe before the hunter. Though she skipped with the alertness of an antelope, yet, at intervals, she was forced to desist, and rest beneath the tamarisks to recover her breath. Whilst she, thus reclined, was occupied with her little reflections on the apprehension that she had some knowledge of the place, Vathek, who, finding himself that morning but ill at ease, had gone forth before the dawn, presented himself on a sudden to her view. Motionless with surprise, he durst not approach the figure before him trembling and pale, but yet lovely to behold. At length Nouronihar, with a mixture of pleasure and affliction, raising her fine eyes to him, said, 'My lord! are you then come hither to eat rice and hear sermons with me?' – 'Beloved phantom!' cried Vathek, 'thou dost speak; thou hast the same graceful form; the same radiant features; art thou palpable likewise?' and, eagerly embracing her, added, 'Here are limbs and a bosom animated with a gentle warmth! – What can such a prodigy mean?'

Nouronihar, with indifference, answered, – 'You know, my lord, that I died on the very night you honoured me with your visit. My cousin maintains it was from one of your glances; but I cannot believe him; for to me they seem not so dreadful. Gulchenrouz died with me, and we were both brought into a region of desolation, where we are fed with a wretched diet. If you be dead also, and are come hither to join us, I pity your lot; for you will be stunned with the clang of the dwarfs and the storks. Besides, it is mortifying in the extreme, that you, as well as myself, should have lost the treasures of the subterranean palace.'

At the mention of the subterranean palace, the Caliph suspended his caresses (which, indeed, had proceeded pretty far), to seek from Nouronihar an explanation of her meaning. She then recapitulated her vision, what immediately followed, and the history of her pretended death; adding, also, a description of the place of expiation from whence she had fled; and all in a manner that would have extorted his laughter, had not the thoughts of Vathek been too deeply engaged. No sooner, however, had she ended, than he again clasped her to his bosom and said, 'Light of my eyes, the mystery is unravelled; we both are alive! Your father is a cheat, who, for the sake of dividing us, hath deluded us both; and the Giaour, whose design, as far as I can discover, is that we shall proceed together, seems scarce a whit better. It shall be some time at least before he finds us in his palace of fire. Your lovely little person in my estimation is far more precious than all the treasures of the pre-Adamite sultans; and I wish to possess it at pleasure, and in open day, for many a moon, before I go to burrow underground, like a mole. Forget this little trifler, Gulchenrouz; and—' – 'Ah, my lord!' interposed Nouronihar, 'let me intreat that you do him no evil.' – 'No, no!' replied Vathek; 'I have already bid you forbear to alarm yourself for him. He has been brought up too much on milk and sugar to stimulate my jealousy. We will leave him with the dwarfs; who, by the bye, are my old acquaintances: their company will suit him far better than yours. As to other matters, I will return no more to your father's. I want not to have my ears dinned by him and his dotards with the violation of the rights of hospitality, as if it were less an honour for you to espouse the sovereign of the world than a girl dressed up like a boy.'

Nouronihar could find nothing to oppose in a discourse so eloquent. She only wished the amorous monarch had discovered more ardour for the carbuncle of Giamschid; but flattered herself it would gradually increase, and therefore yielded to his will with the most bewitching submission.

When the Caliph judged it proper, he called for Bababalouk, who was asleep in the cave of Meimouné, and dreaming that the phantom of Nouronihar, having mounted him once more on her swing, had just given him such a jerk, that he one moment soared above the mountains, and the next sunk into the abyss. Starting from his sleep at the sound of his master, he ran, gasping for breath, and had nearly fallen backward at the sight, as he believed, of the spectre by whom he had so lately been haunted in his dream. 'Ah, my lord!' cried he, recoiling ten steps, and covering his eyes with both hands, 'do you then perform the office of a Ghoule? have you dug up the dead? Yet hope not to make her your prey; for, after all she hath caused me to suffer, she is wicked enough to prey even upon you.'

'Cease to play the fool,' said Vathek, 'and thou shalt

soon be convinced that it is Nouronihar herself, alive and well, whom I clasp to my breast. Go and pitch my tents in the neighbouring valley. There will I fix my abode, with this beautiful tulip, whose colours I soon shall restore. There exert thy best endeavours to procure whatever can augment the enjoyments of life, till I shall disclose to thee more of my will.'

The news of so unlucky an event soon reached the ears of the emir, who abandoned himself to grief and despair, and began, as did his old grey-beards, to begrime his visage with ashes. A total supineness ensued; travellers were no longer entertained; no more plasters were spread; and, instead of the charitable activity that had distinguished this asylum, the whole of its inhabitants exhibited only faces of half a cubit long, and uttered groans that accorded with their forlorn situation.

Though Fakreddin bewailed his daughter as lost to him for ever, yet Gulchenrouz was not forgotten. He dispatched immediate instructions to Sutlememe, Shaban, and the dwarfs, enjoining them not to undeceive the child in respect to his state, but, under some pretence, to convey him far from the lofty rock at the extremity of the lake, to a place which he should appoint, as safer from danger, for he suspected that Vathek intended him evil.

Gulchenrouz, in the mean while, was filled with amazement at not finding his cousin; nor were the dwarfs less surprized: but Sutlememe, who had more penetration, immediately guessed what had happened. Gulchenrouz was amused with the delusive hope of once more embracing Nouronihar in the interior recesses of the mountains, where the ground, strewed over with orange blossoms and jasmines, offered beds much more inviting than the withered leaves in their cabin; where they might accompany with their voices the sounds of their lutes, and chase butterflies. Sutlememe was far gone in this sort of description, when one of the four eunuchs beckoned her aside, to apprize her of the arrival of a messenger from their fraternity, who had explained the secret of the flight of Nouronihar, and brought the commands of the emir. A council with Shaban and the dwarfs was immediately held. Their baggage being stowed in consequence of it, they embarked in a shallop, and quietly sailed with the little one, who acquiesced in all their proposals. Their voyage proceeded in the same manner, till they came to the place where the lake sinks beneath the hollow of a rock: but as soon as the bark had entered it, and Gulchenrouz found himself surrounded with darkness, he was seized with a dreadful consternation, and incessantly uttered the most piercing outcries; for he now was persuaded he should actually be damned for having taken too many little freedoms in his lifetime with his cousin.

But let us return to the Caliph, and her who ruled over his heart. Bababalouk had pitched the tents, and closed up the extremities of the valley with magnificent screens of India cloth, which were guarded by Ethiopian slaves with their drawn sabres. To preserve the verdure of this beautiful enclosure in its natural freshness, white eunuchs went continually round it with gilt water vessels. The waving of fans was heard near the imperial pavilion; where, by the voluptuous light that glowed through the muslins, the Caliph enjoyed, at full view, all the attractions of Nouronihar. Inebriated with delight, he was all ear to her charming voice, which accompanied the lute; while she was not less captivated with his descriptions of Samarah, and the tower full of wonders, but especially with his relation of the adventure of the ball, and the chasm of the Giaour, with its ebony portal.

In this manner they conversed the whole day, and at night they bathed together in a basin of black marble, which admirably set off the fairness of Nouronihar. Bababalouk, whose good graces this beauty had regained, spared no attention that their repasts might be served up with the minutest exactness: some exquisite rarity was ever placed before them; and he sent even to Schiraz, for that fragrant and delicious wine which had been hoarded up in bottles, prior to the birth of Mahomet. He had excavated little ovens in the rock, to bake the nice manchets which were prepared by the hands of Nouronihar, from whence they had derived a flavour so grateful to Vathek, that he regarded the ragouts of his other wives as entirely mawkish: whilst they would have died of chagrin at the emir's, at finding themselves so neglected, if Fakreddin, notwithstanding his resentment, had not taken pity upon them.

The Sultana Dilara, who, till then, had been the favourite, took this dereliction of the Caliph to heart, with a vehemence natural to her character; for, during her continuance in favour, she had imbibed from Vathek many of his extravagant fancies, and was fired with impatience to behold the superb tombs of Istakhar, and the palace of forty columns; besides, having been brought up amongst the Magi, she had fondly cherished the idea of the Caliph's devoting himself to the worship of fire: thus his voluptuous and desultory life with her rival was to her a double source of affliction. The transient piety of Vathek had occasioned her some serious alarms; but the present was an evil of far greater magnitude. She resolved, therefore, without hesitation, to write to Carathis, and acquaint her that all things went ill; that they had eaten, slept, and revelled at an old emir's, whose sanctity was very formidable; and that, after all, the prospect of possessing the treasures of the pre-Adamite sultans was no less remote than before. This letter was entrusted to the care of two woodmen, who were at work in one of the great forests of the mountains, and who, being acquainted with the shortest cuts, arrived in ten days at Samarah.

The Princess Carathis was engaged at chess with Morakanabad, when the arrival of these woodfellers was announced. She, after some weeks of Vathek's absence, had forsaken the upper regions of her tower, because every thing appeared in confusion among the stars, which she consulted relative to the fate of her son. In vain did she renew her fumigations, and extend herself on the roof, to obtain mystic visions; nothing more could she see in her dreams, than pieces of brocade, nosegays of flowers, and other unmeaning gewgaws. These disappointments has thrown her into a state of dejection, which no drug in her power was sufficient to remove. Her only resource was in Morakanabad, who was a good man, and endowed with a decent share of confidence; yet whilst in her company he never thought himself on roses.

No person knew aught of Vathek, and, of course, a thousand ridiculous stories were propagated at his expense. The eagerness of Carathis may be easily guessed at receiving the letter, as well as her rage at reading the dissolute conduct of her son. 'It is so?' said she; 'either I will perish, or Vathek shall enter the palace of fire. Let me expire in flames, provided he may reign on the throne of Soliman!' Having said this, and whirled herself round in a magical manner, which struck Morakanabad with such terror as caused him to recoil, she ordered her great camel Alboufaki to be brought, and the hideous Nerkes, with the unrelenting Cafour, to attend. 'I require no other retinue,' said she to Morakanabad; 'I am going on affairs of emergency; a truce, therefore, to parade! Take you care of the people: fleece them well in my absence; for we shall expend large sums, and one knows not what may betide.'

The night was uncommonly dark, and a pestilential blast blew from the plain of Catoul, that would have deterred any other traveller, however urgent the call: but Carathis enjoyed most whatever filled others with dread. Nerkes concurred in opinion with her; and Cafour had a particular predilection for a pestilence. In the morning this accomplished caravan, with the woodfellers, who directed their route, halted on the edge of an extensive marsh, from whence so noxious a vapour arose as would have destroyed any animal but Alboufaki, who naturally inhaled these malignant fogs with delight. The peasants intreated their convoy not to sleep in this place. 'To sleep,' cried Carathis, 'what an excellent thought! I never sleep, but for visions; and, as to my attendants, their occupations are too many to close the only eye they have.' The poor peasants, who were not overpleased with their party, remained open-mouthed with surprize.

Carathis alighted, as well as her negresses; and, severally stripping off their outer garments, they all ran to cull from those spots where the sun shone fiercest the venomous plants that grew on the marsh. This provision was made for the family of the emir, and whoever might retard the expedition to Istakhar. The woodmen were overcome with fear, when they beheld these three horrible phantoms run; and, not much relishing the company of Alboufaki, stood aghast at the command of Carathis to set forward, notwithstanding it was noon, and the heat fierce enough to calcine even rocks. In spite, however, of every remonstrance, they were forced implicitly to submit.

Alboufaki, who delighted in solitude, constantly snorted whenever he perceived himself near a habitation; and Carathis, who was apt to spoil him with indulgence, as constantly turned him aside: so that the peasants were precluded from procuring subsistence; for the milch goats and ewes, which Providence had sent towards the district they traversed to refresh travellers with their milk, all fled at the sight of the hideous animal and his strange riders. As to Carathis, she needed no common aliment; for her invention had previously furnished her with an opiate to stay her stomach, some of which she imparted to her mutes.

At dusk Alboufaki, making a sudden stop, stampt with his foot; which, to Carathis, who knew his ways, was a certain indication that she was near the confines of some cemetery. The moon shed a bright light on the spot, which served to discover a long wall with a large door in it, standing ajar, and so high that Alboufaki might easily enter. The miserable guides, who perceived their end approaching, humbly implored Carathis, as she had now so good an opportunity, to inter them, and immediately gave up the ghost. Nerkes and Cafour, whose wit was of a style peculiar to themselves, were by no means parsimonious of it on the folly of these poor people; nor could anything have been found more suited to their taste than the site of the burying-ground, and the sepulchres which its precincts contained. There were at least two thousand of them on the declivity of a hill. Carathis was too eager to execute her plan to stop at the view, charming as it appeared in her eyes. Pondering the advantages that might accrue from her present situation, she said to herself, 'So beautiful a cemetery must be haunted by Ghoules! they never want for intelligence: having heedlessly suffered my stupid guides to expire, I will apply for directions to them; and, as an inducement, will invite them to regale on these fresh corpses.' After this wise soliloquy, she beckoned to Nerkes and Cafour, and made signs with her fingers, as much as to say, 'Go; knock against the sides of the tombs and strike up your delightful warblings.'

The negresses, full of joy at the behests of their mistress, and promising themselves much pleasure from the society of the Ghoules, went with an air of conquest, and began their knockings at the tombs. As their strokes were repeated, a hollow noise was made in the earth; the surface hove up into heaps; and the Ghoules, on all sides, protruded their noses to inhale the effluvia which the carcases of the woodmen began to emit. They assembled before a sarcophagus of white marble, where Carathis was seated between the bodies of her miserable guides. The Princess received her visitants with distinguished politeness; and, supper being ended, they talked of business. Carathis soon learned from them every thing she wanted to discover; and, without loss of time, prepared to set forward on her journey. Her negresses, who were forming tender connexions with the Ghoules, importuned her, with all their fingers, to wait at least till the dawn. But Carathis, being chastity in the abstract, and an implacable enemy to love intrigues and sloth, at once rejected their prayer, mounted Alboufaki, and commanded them to take their seats instantly. Four days and four nights she continued her route without interruption. On the fifth, she traversed craggy mountains and half-burnt forests; and arrived on the sixth before the beautiful screens which concealed from all eyes the voluptuous wanderings of her son.

It was daybreak, and the guards were snoring on their posts in careless security, when the rough trot of Alboufaki awoke them in consternation. Imagining that a group of spectres, ascended from the abyss, was approaching, they all, without ceremony, took to their heels. Vathek was at that instant with Nouronihar in the bath, hearing tales, and laughing at Bababalouk who related them; but, no sooner did the outcry of his guards reach him, than he flounced from the water like a carp, and as soon threw himself back at the sight of Carathis; who, advancing with her negresses upon Alboufaki, broke through the muslin awnings and veils of the pavilion. At this sudden apparition, Nouronihar (for she was not at all times free from remorse) fancied that the moment of celestial vengeance was come, and clung about the Caliph in amorous despondence.

Carathis, still seated on her camel, foamed with indignation at the spectacle which obtruded itself on her chaste view. She thundered forth without check or mercy, 'Thou double-headed and four-legged monster! what means all this winding and writhing? Art thou not ashamed to be seen grasping this limber sapling, in preference to the sceptre of the pre-Adamite sultans? Is it then for this paltry doxy that thou hast violated the conditions in the parchment of our Giaour? Is it on her thou hast lavished thy precious moments? Is this the fruit of the knowledge I have taught thee? Is this the end of thy journey? Tear thyself from the arms of this little simpleton; drown her in the water before me, and instantly follow my guidance.'

In the first ebullition of his fury, Vathek had resolved to rip open the body of Alboufaki and to stuff it with those of the negresses and of Carathis herself; but the remembrance of the Giaour, the palace of Istakhar, the sabres, and the talismans, flashing before his imagination with the simultaneousness of lightning, he became more moderate, and said to his mother in a civil, but decisive tone, 'Dread lady, you shall be obeyed; but I will not drown Nouronihar. She is sweeter to me than a Myrabolan comfit; and is enamoured of carbuncles, especially that of Giamschid, which hath also been promised to be conferred upon her: she, therefore, shall go along with us; for I intend to repose with her upon the sofas of Soliman: I can sleep no more without her.' – 'Be it so,' replied Carathis, alighting, and at the same time committing Alboufaki to the charge of her black women.

Nouronihar, who had not yet quitted her hold, began to take courage; and said, with an accent of fondness to the Caliph, 'Dear sovereign of my soul! I will follow thee, if it be thy will, beyond the Kaf, in the land of the afrits. I will not hesitate to climb, for thee, the nest of the Simurgh; who, this lady excepted, is the most awful of created beings.' – 'We have here, then,' subjoined Carathis, 'a girl both of courage and science!' Nouronihar had certainly both; but, notwithstanding all her firmness, she could not help casting back a thought of regret upon the graces of her little Gulchenrouz, and the days of tender endearments she had participated with him. She even dropped a few tears, which the Caliph observed; and inadvertently breathed out with a sigh, 'Alas! my gentle cousin, what will become of thee?' Vathek, at this apostrophe, knitted up his brows, and Carathis enquired what it could mean. 'She is preposterously sighing after a stripling with languishing eyes and soft hair, who loves her,' said the Caliph. – 'Where is he?' asked Carathis. 'I must be acquainted with this pretty child; for,' added she, lowering her voice, 'I design, before I depart, to regain the favour of the Giaour. There is nothing so delicious, in his estimation, as the heart of a delicate boy palpitating with the first tumults of love.'

Vathek, as he came from the bath, commanded Bababalouk to collect the women and other movables of his harem, embody his troops, and hold himself in readiness to march within three days; whilst Carathis retired alone to a tent, where the Giaour solaced her with encouraging visions: but at length waking, she found at her feet Nerkes and Cafour, who informed her, by their signs, that having led Alboufaki to the borders of a lake, to browse on some grey moss that looked tolerably venomous, they had discovered certain blue fishes, of the same kind with those in the reservoir on the top of the tower. 'Ah! ha!' said she, 'I will go thither to them. These fish are, past doubt, of a species that, by a small operation, I can render oracular. They may tell me where this little Gulchenrouz is, whom I am bent upon sacrificing.' Having thus spoken, she immediately set out with her swarthy retinue.

It being but seldom that time is lost in the accomplishment of a wicked enterprize, Carathis and her negresses soon arrived at the lake; where, after burning the magical drugs with which they were always provided, they stripped themselves naked, and waded to their chins; Nerkes and Cafour waving torches around them, and Carathis pronouncing her barbarous incantations. The fishes, with one accord, thrust forth their heads from the water, which was violently rippled by the flutter of their fins; and at length finding themselves constrained by the potency of the charm, they opened their piteous mouths, and said, 'From gills to tail, we are yours; what seek ye to know?' – 'Fishes,' answered she, 'I conjure you, by your glittering scales, tell me where now is Gulchenrouz?' – 'Beyond the rock,' replied the shoal, in full chorus; 'will this content you? for we do not delight in expanding our mouths.' – 'It will,' returned the Princess; 'I am not to learn that you are not used to long conversations; I will leave you therefore to repose, though I had other questions to propound.' The instant she had spoken, the water became smooth, and the fishes at once disappeared.

Carathis, inflated with the venom of her projects, strode hastily over the rock, and found the amiable Gulchenrouz asleep in an arbour, whilst the two dwarfs were watching at his side, and ruminating their accustomed prayers. These diminutive personages possessed the gift of divining whenever an enemy to good Mussulmans approached; thus they anticipated the arrival of Carathis, who, stopping short, said to herself, 'How placidly doth he recline his lovely little head! how pale and languishing are his looks! it is just the very child of my wishes!' The dwarf inter-rupted this delectable soliloquy by leaping instantly upon her, and scratching her face with their utmost zeal. But Nerkes and Cafour, betaking themselves to the succour of their mistress, pinched the dwarfs so severely in return, that they both gave up the ghost, imploring Mahomet to inflict his sorest vengeance upon this wicked woman and all her household.

At the noise which this strange conflict occasioned in the valley, Gulchenrouz awoke, and bewildered with terror, sprung impetuously and climbed an old fig-tree that rose against the acclivity of the rocks; from thence he gained their summits, and ran for two hours without once looking back. At last, exhausted with fatigue, he fell senseless into the arms of a good old Genius, whose fondness for the company of children had made it his sole occupation to protect them. Whilst performing his wonted rounds through the air, he had pounced on the cruel Giaour, at the instant of his growling in the horrible chasm, and had rescued the fifty little victims which the impiety of Vathek had devoted to his voracity. These the Genius brought up in nests still higher than the clouds, and himself fixed his abode in a nest more capacious than the rest, from which he had expelled the rocs that had built it.

These inviolable asylums were defended against the

dives and the afrits by waving streamers; on which were inscribed in characters of gold, that flashed like lightning, the names of Alla and the Prophet. It was there that Gulchenrouz, who as yet remained undeceived with respect to his pretended death, thought himself in the mansions of eternal peace. He admitted without fear the congratulations of his little friends, who were all assembled in the nest of the venerable Genius, and vied with each other in kissing his serene forehead and beautiful eyelids. Remote from the inquietudes of the world, the impertinence of harems, the brutality of eunuchs, and the inconstancy of women, there he found a place truly congenial to the delights of his soul. In this peaceable society his days, months, and years glided on; nor was he less happy than the rest of his companions: for the Genius, instead of burdening his pupils with perishable riches and vain sciences, conferred upon them the boon of perpetual childhood.

Carathis, unaccustomed to the loss of her prey, vented a thousand execrations on her negresses, for not seizing the child, instead of amusing themselves with pinching to death two insignificant dwarfs from which they could gain no advantage. She returned into the valley murmuring; and, finding that her son was not risen from the arms of Nouronihar, discharged her ill-humour upon both. The idea, however, of departing next day for Istakhar, and of cultivating, through the good offices of the Giaour, an intimacy with Eblis himself, at length consoled her chagrin. But fate had ordained it otherwise.

In the evening, as Carathis was conversing with Dilara, who through her contrivance had become of the party, and whose taste resembled her own, Bababalouk came to acquaint her that the sky towards Samarah looked of a fiery red, and seemed to portend some alarming disaster. Immediately recurring to her astrolabes and instruments of magic, she took the altitude of the planets, and discovered, by her calculations, to her great mortification, that a formidable revolt had taken place at Samarah, that Motavakel, availing himself of the disgust which was inveterate against his brother, had incited commotions amongst the populace, made himself master of the palace, and actually invested the great tower, to which Morakanabad had retired, with a handful of the few that still remained faithful to Vathek.

'What!' exclaimed she; 'must I lose, then, my tower! my mutes! my negresses! my mummies! and, worse than all, the laboratory, the favourite resort of my nightly lucubrations, without knowing, at least, if my hare-brained son will complete his adventure? No! I will not be the dupe! immediately will I speed to support Morakanabad. By my formidable art, the clouds shall pour grape-shot in the faces of the assailants and shafts of red-hot iron on their heads. I will let loose my stores of hungry serpents and torpedoes from beneath them; and we shall soon see the stand they will make against such an explosion!'

Having thus spoken, Carathis hasted to her son who was tranquilly banqueting with Nouronihar in his superb carnation-coloured tent. 'Glutton that thou art!' cried she; 'were it not for me, thou wouldst soon find thyself the mere commander of savoury pies. Thy faithful subjects have abjured the faith they swore to thee. Motavakel, thy brother, now reigns on the hill of Pied Horses, and, had I not some slight resources in the tower, would not be easily persuaded to abdicate. But, that time may not be lost, I shall only add a few words: Strike tent to-night; set forward; and beware how thou loiterest again by the way. Though thou hast forfeited the conditions of the parchment, I am not yet without hope; for it cannot be denied that thou hast violated, to admiration, the laws of hospitality by seducing the daughter of the emir, after having partaken of his bread and his salt. Such a conduct cannot but be delightful to the Giaour; and if, on thy march, thou canst signalize thyself by an additional crime, all will still go well, and thou shalt enter the palace of Soliman in triumph. Adieu! Alboufaki and my negresses are waiting at the door.'

The Caliph had nothing to offer in reply: he wished his mother a prosperous journey, and ate on till he had finished his supper. At midnight the camp broke up, amidst the flourishing of trumpets and other martial instruments; but loud indeed must have been the sound of the tymbals, to overpower the blubbering of the emir and his grey-beards; who, by an excessive profusion of tears, had so far exhausted the radical moisture, that their eyes shrivelled up in their sockets, and their hairs dropped off by the roots. Nouronihar, to whom such a symphony was painful, did not grieve to get out of hearing. She accompanied the Caliph in the imperial litter, where they amused themselves with imagining the splendor which was soon to surround them. The other women, overcome with dejection, were dolefully rocked in their cages; whilst Dilara consoled herself with anticipating the joy of celebrating the rites of fire on the stately terraces of Istakhar.

In four days they reached the spacious valley of Rocnabad. The season of spring was in all its vigour, and the grotesque branches of the almond trees in full blossom, fantastically chequered with hyacinths and jonquils, breathed forth a delightful fragrance. Myriads of bees, and scarce fewer of santons, had there taken up their abode. On the banks of the stream, hives and oratories were alternately ranged; and their neatness and whiteness were set off by the deep green of the cypresses that spired up amongst them. These pious personages amused themselves with cultivating little gardens, that abounded with flowers and fruits; especially musk-melons of the best flavour that Persia could boast. Sometimes dispersed over the meadow, they entertained themselves with feeding peacocks whiter than snow, and turtles more blue than the sapphire. In this manner were they occupied when the harbingers of the imperial procession began to proclaim,

'Inhabitants of Rocnabad! prostrate yourselves on the brink of your pure waters; and tender your thanksgivings to Heaven, that vouchsafeth to shew you a ray of its glory: for, lo! the commander of the faithful draws near.'

The poor santons, filled with holy energy, having bustled to light up wax torches in their oratories, and expand the Koran on their ebony desks, went forth to meet the Caliph with baskets of honeycomb, dates, and melons. But, whilst they were advancing in solemn procession and with measured steps, the horses, camels, and guards wantoned over their tulips and other flowers, and made a terrible havoc amongst them. The santons could not help casting from one eye a look of pity on the ravages committing around them; whilst the other was fixed upon the Caliph and heaven. Nouronihar, enraptured with the scenery of a place which brought back to her remembrance the pleasing solitudes where her infancy had passed, entreated Vathek to stop: but he, suspecting that these oratories might be deemed by the Giaour an habitation, commanded his pioneers to level them all. The santons stood motionless with horror at the barbarous mandate, and at last broke out into lamentations; but these were uttered with so ill a grace, that Vathek bade his eunuchs to kick them from his presence. He then descended from the litter with Nouronihar. They sauntered together in the meadow; and amused themselves with culling flowers, and passing a thousand pleasantries on each other. But the bees, who were staunch Mussulmans, thinking it their duty to revenge the insult offered to their dear masters the santons, assembled so zealously to do it with good effect, that the Caliph and Nouronihar were glad to find their tents prepared to receive them.

Bababalouk, who, in capacity of purveyor, had acquitted himself with applause as to peacocks and turtles, lost no time in consigning some dozens to the spit, and as many more to be fricasseed. Whilst they were feasting, laughing, carousing, and blaspheming at pleasure on the banquet so liberally furnished, the Moullahs, the sheiks, the cadis[29] and Imans of Schiraz (who seemed not to have met the santons) arrived; leading by bridles of riband, inscribed from the Koran, a train of asses which were loaded with the choicest fruits the country could boast. Having presented their offerings to the Caliph, they petitioned him to honour their city and mosques with his presence. 'Fancy not,' said Vathek, 'that you can detain me. Your presents I condescend to accept, but beg you will let me be quiet, for I am not over-fond of resisting temptation. Retire, then; yet, as it is not decent for personages so reverend to return on foot, and as you have not the appearance of expert riders, my eunuchs shall tie you on your asses, with the precaution that your backs be not turned towards me; for they understand etiquette.' – In this deputation were some high-stomached sheiks who, taking Vathek for a fool, scrupled not to speak their opinion. These Bababalouk girded with double cords; and having well disciplined their asses with nettles behind, they all started, with a preternatural alertness, plunging, kicking, and running foul of one another, in the most ludicrous manner imaginable.

Nouronihar and the Caliph mutually contended who should most enjoy so degrading a sight. They burst out in peals of laughter to see the old men and their asses fall into the stream. The leg of one was fractured; the shoulder of another dislocated; the teeth of a third dashed out; and the rest suffered still worse.

Two days more, undisturbed by fresh embassies, having been devoted to the pleasures of Rocnabad, the expedition proceeded; leaving Schiraz on the right, and verging towards a large plain; from whence were discernible, on the edge of the horizon, the dark summits of the mountains of Istakhar.

At this prospect the Caliph and Nouronihar were unable to repress their transports. They bounded from their litter to the ground, and broke forth into such wild exclamations, as amazed all within hearing. Interrogating each other, they shouted, 'Are we not approaching the radiant palace of light? or gardens, more delightful than those of Sheddad?' – Infatuated mortals! they thus indulged delusive conjecture, unable to fathom the decrees of the Most High!

The good Genii, who had not totally relinquished the superintendence of Vathek, repairing to Mahomet in the seventh heaven, said, 'Merciful Prophet! stretch forth thy propitious arms towards thy vicegerent; who is ready to fall, irretrievably, into the snare which his enemies, the dives, have prepared to destroy him. The Giaour is awaiting his arrival, in the abominable palace of fire; where, if he once set his foot, his perdition will be inevitable.' Mahomet answered, with an air of indignation, 'He hath too well deserved to be resigned to himself; but I permit you to try if one effort more will be effectual to divert him from pursuing his ruin.'

One of these beneficent Genii, assuming, without delay, the exterior of a shepherd, more renowned for his piety than all the derviches and santons of the region, took his station near a flock of white sheep, on the slope of a hill; and began to pour forth from his flute such airs of pathetic melody, as subdued the very soul, and, wakening remorse, drove far from it every frivolous fancy. At these energetic sounds, the sun hid himself beneath a gloomy cloud; and the waters of two little lakes, that were naturally clearer than crystal, became of a colour like blood. The whole of this superb assembly was involuntarily drawn towards the declivity of the hill. With downcast eyes, they all stood abashed; each upbraiding himself with the evil he had done. The heart of Dilara palpitated; and the chief of the eunuchs, with a sigh of contrition, implored pardon of the women, whom, for his own satisfaction, he had so often tormented.

Vathek and Nouronihar turned pale in their litter; and regarding each other with haggard looks, reproached themselves – the one with a thousand of the blackest crimes, a thousand projects of impious ambition; the other with the desolation of her family, and the perdition of the amiable Gulchenrouz. Nouronihar persuaded herself that she heard, in the fatal music, the groans of her dying father; and Vathek, the sobs of the fifty children he had sacrificed to the Giaour. Amidst these complicated pangs of anguish, they perceived themselves impelled towards the shepherd, whose countenance was so commanding that Vathek, for the first time, felt overawed; whilst Nouronihar concealed her face with her hands. The music paused; and the Genius, addressing the Caliph, said, 'Deluded prince! to whom Providence hath confided the care of innumerable subjects, is it thus that thou fulfillest thy mission? Thy crimes are already completed; and art thou now listening towards thy punishment? Thou knowest that, beyond these mountains, Eblis[30] and his accursed dives hold their infernal empire; and seduced by a malignant phantom, thou art proceeding to surrender thyself to them! This moment is the last of grace allowed thee: abandon thy atrocious purpose: return: give back Nouronihar to her father, who still retains a few sparks of life: destroy thy tower with all its abominations: drive Carathis from thy councils: be just to thy subjects: respect the ministers of the Prophet: compensate for thy impieties by an exemplary life; and, instead of squandering thy days in voluptuous indulgence, lament thy crimes on the sepulchres of thy ancestors. Thou beholdest the clouds that obscure the sun: at the instant he recovers his splendor, if thy heart be not changed, the time of mercy assigned thee will be past for ever.'

Vathek, depressed with fear, was on the point of prostrating himself at the feet of the shepherd, whom he perceived to be of a nature superior to man: but, his pride prevailing, he audaciously lifted his head, and, glancing at him one of his terrible looks, said, 'Whoever thou art, withhold thy useless admonitions: thou wouldst either delude me, or art thyself deceived. If what I have done be so criminal as thou pretendest, there remains not for me a moment of grace. I have traversed a sea of blood to acquire a power which will make thy equals tremble; deem not that I shall retire when in view of the port, or that I will relinquish her who is dearer to me than either my life or thy mercy. Let the sun appear! let him illume my career! it matters not where it may end.' On uttering these words, which made even the Genius shudder, Vathek threw himself into the arms of Nouronihar, and commanded that his horses should be forced back to the road.

There was no difficulty in obeying these orders, for the attraction had ceased: the sun shone forth in all his glory, and the shepherd vanished with a lamentable scream.

The fatal impression of the music of the Genius remained, notwithstanding, in the heart of Vathek's attendants. They viewed each other with looks of consternation. At the approach of night almost all of them escaped; and of this numerous assemblage there only remained the chief of the eunuchs, some idolatrous slaves, Dilara, and a few other women who, like herself, were votaries of the religion of the Magi.

The Caliph, fired with the ambition of prescribing laws to the powers of darkness, was but little embarrassed at this dereliction. The impetuosity of his blood prevented him from sleeping; nor did he encamp any more as before. Nouronihar, whose impatience, if possible, exceeded his own, importuned him to hasten his march, and lavished on him a thousand caresses, to beguile all reflection. She fancied herself already more potent than Balkis,[31] and pictured to her imagination the Genii falling prostrate at the foot of her throne. In this manner they advanced by moonlight till they came within view of the two towering rocks that form a kind of portal to the valley, at the extremity of which rose the vast ruins of Istakhar. Aloft on the mountain glimmered the fronts of various royal mausoleums, the horror of which was deepened by the shadows of night. They passed through two villages almost deserted, the only inhabitants remaining being a few feeble old men, who, at the sight of horses and litters, fell upon their knees, and cried out, 'O Heaven! is it then by these phantoms that we have been for six months tormented? Alas! it was from the terror of these spectres and the noise beneath the mountains, that our people have fled, and left us at the mercy of the maleficent spirits!' The Caliph, to whom these complaints were but unpromising auguries, drove over the bodies of these wretched old men, and at length arrived at the foot of the terrace of black marble. There he descended from his litter, handing down Nouronihar. Both with beating hearts stared wildly around them, and expected, with an apprehensive shudder, the approach of the Giaour; but nothing as yet announced his appearance.

A death-like stillness reigned over the mountain and through the air; the moon dilated on a vast platform the shades of the lofty columns, which reached from the terrace almost to the clouds; the gloomy watch-towers, whose number could not be counted, were covered by no roof; and their capitals, of an architecture unknown in the records of the earth, served as an asylum for the birds of night, which, alarmed at the approach of such visitants, fled away croaking.

The chief of the eunuchs, trembling with fear, besought Vathek that a fire might be kindled. 'No,' replied he, 'there is no time left to think of such trifles. Abide where thou art, and expect my commands.' Having thus spoken, he presented his hand to Nouronihar; and ascending the steps of a vast stair-case, reached the terrace, which was flagged with squares of marble, and resembled a smooth expanse of water, upon whose surface not a blade of grass ever dared to vegetate. On the right rose the watch-towers, ranged before the ruins of an immense palace, whose walls were embossed with various figures. In front stood forth the colossal forms of four creatures, composed of the leopard and the griffin, and though but of stone, inspired emotions of terror. Near these were distinguished, by the splendor of the moon, which streamed full on the place, characters like those on the sabres of the Giaour, and which possessed the same virtue of changing every moment. These, after vacillating for some time, fixed at last in Arabic letters, and prescribed to the Caliph the following words: 'Vathek, thou hast violated the conditions of my parchment, and deserveth to be sent back; but in favour to thy companion, and as the meed for what thou hast done to obtain it, Eblis permitteth that the portal of his palace shall be opened, and the subterranean fire will receive thee into the number of its adorers.'

He scarcely had read these words before the mountain, against which the terrace was reared, trembled, and the watch-towers were ready to topple headlong upon them; the rock yawned, and disclosed within it a stair-case of polished marble, that seemed to approach the abyss. Upon each stair were planted two large torches, like those Nouronihar had seen in her vision, the camphorated vapour of which ascended and gathered itself into a cloud under the hollow of the vault.

This appearance, instead of terrifying, gave new courage to the daughter of Fakreddin. Scarcely deigning to bid adieu to the moon and the firmament, she abandoned without hesitation the pure atmosphere, to plunge into these infernal exhalations. The gait of those impious personages was haughty and determined. As they descended, by the effulgence of the torches, they gazed on each other with mutual admiration, and both appeared so resplendent that they already esteemed themselves spiritual Intelligences. The only circumstance that perplexed them was their not arriving at the bottom of the stairs: on hastening their descent with an ardent impetuosity, they felt their steps accelerated to such a degree, that they seemed not walking but falling from a precipice. Their progress, however, was at length impeded by a vast portal of ebony, which the Caliph without difficulty recognized. Here the Giaour awaited them with the key in his hand. 'Ye are welcome!' said he to them, with a ghastly smile, 'in spite of Mahomet and all his dependents. I will now usher you into that palace where you have so highly merited a place.' Whilst he was uttering these words he touched the enamelled lock with his key, and the doors at once flew open with a noise still louder than the thunder of the dog-days, and as suddenly recoiled the moment they had entered.

The Caliph and Nouronihar beheld each other with amazement at finding themselves in a place which, though roofed with a vaulted ceiling, was so spacious and lofty, that at first they took it for an immeasurable plain. But their eyes at length growing familiar to the grandeur of the surrounding objects, they extended their view to those at a distance, and discovered rows of columns and arcades, which gradually diminished, till they terminated in a point radiant as the sun when he darts his last beams athwart the ocean. The pavement, strewed over with gold dust and saffron, exhaled so subtle an odour as almost overpowered them. They, however, went on, and observed an infinity of censers, in which ambergris and the wood of aloes were continually burning. Between the several columns were placed tables, each spread with a profusion of viands, and wines of every species sparkling in vases of crystal. A throng of Genii and other fantastic spirits of either sex danced lasciviously at the sound of music which issued from beneath.

In the midst of this immense hall, a vast multitude was incessantly passing, who severally kept their right hands on their hearts, without once regarding any thing around them: they had all the livid paleness of death. Their eyes, deep sunk in their sockets, resembled those phosphoric meteors that glimmer by night in places of interment. Some stalked slowly on, absorbed in profound reverie; some, shrieking with agony, ran furiously about like tigers wounded with poisoned arrows; whilst others, grinding their teeth in rage, foamed along more frantic than the wildest maniac. They all avoided each other; and, though surrounded by a multitude that no one could number, each wandered at random unheedful of the rest, as if alone on a desert where no foot had trodden.

Vathek and Nouronihar, frozen with terror at a sight so baleful, demanded of the Giaour what these appearances might mean, and why these ambulating spectres never withdrew their hands from their hearts? 'Perplex not yourselves with so much at once,' replied he bluntly; 'you will soon be acquainted with all: let us haste and present you to Eblis.' They continued their way through the multitude: but, notwithstanding their confidence at first, they were not sufficiently composed to examine with attention the various perspectives of halls and of galleries that opened on the right hand and left; which were all illuminated by torches and braziers, whose flames rose in pyramids to the centre of the vault. At length they came to a place where long curtains, brocaded with crimson and gold, fell from all parts in solemn confusion. Here the choirs and dances were heard no longer. The light which glimmered came from afar.

After some time, Vathek and Nouronihar perceived a gleam brightening through the drapery, and entered a vast tabernacle hung round with the skins of leopards. An infinity of elders with streaming beards, and afrits in complete armour, had prostrated themselves before the ascent of a lofty eminence; on the top of which, upon a globe of fire, sat the formidable Eblis. His person was that of a young man, whose noble and regular features seemed to have been tarnished by malignant vapours. In his large eyes appeared both pride and despair: his flowing hair retained some resemblance to that of an angel of light. In his hand, which thunder had blasted, he swayed the iron sceptre that causes the monster Ouranbad, the afrits, and all the powers of the abyss to tremble. At his presence, the heart of the Caliph sunk within him; and he fell prostrate on his face. Nouronihar, however, though greatly dismayed, could not help admiring the person of Eblis; for she expected to have seen some stupendous giant. Eblis, with a voice more mild than might be imagined, but such as penetrated the soul and filled it with the deepest melancholy, said, 'Creatures of clay, I receive you into mine empire: ye are numbered amongst my adorers: enjoy whatever this palace affords: the treasures of the pre-Adamite sultans, their fulminating sabres, and those talismans that compel the dives to open the subterranean expanses of the mountain of Kaf, which communicate with these. There, insatiable as your curiosity may be, shall you find sufficient objects to gratify it. You shall possess the exclusive privilege of entering the fortresses of Aherman, and the halls of Argenk, where are pourtrayed all creatures endowed with intelligence; and the various animals that inhabited the earth prior to the creation of that contemptible being whom ye denominate the father of mankind.'

Vathek and Nouronihar, feeling themselves revived and encouraged by this harangue, eagerly said to the Giaour, 'Bring us instantly to the place which contains these precious talismans.' – 'Come,' answered this wicked dive, with his malignant grin – 'come and possess all that my sovereign hath promised, and more.' He then conducted them into a long aisle adjoining the tabernacle; preceding them with hasty steps, and followed by his disciples with the utmost alacrity. They reached, at length, a hall of great extent, and covered with a lofty dome; around which appeared fifty portals of bronze, secured with as many fastenings of iron. A funereal gloom prevailed over the whole scene. Here, upon two beds of incorruptible cedar, lay recumbent the fleshless forms of the pre-Adamite kings, who had been monarchs of the whole earth. They still possessed enough of life to be conscious of their deplorable condition. Their eyes retained a melancholy motion; they regarded one another with looks of the deepest dejection, each holding his right hand, motionless, on his heart. At their feet were inscribed the events of their several reigns, their power, their pride, and their crimes; Soliman Raad, Soliman Daki, and Soliman, called Gian Ben Gian, who, after having chained up the dives in the dark caverns of Kaf, became so presumptuous as to doubt of the Supreme Power. All these maintained great state, though not to be compared with the eminence of Soliman Ben Daoud.

This king, so renowned for his wisdom, was on the loftiest elevation, and placed immediately under the dome. He appeared to possess more animation than the rest. Though, from time to time, he laboured with profound sighs; and, like his companions, kept his right hand on his heart, yet his countenance was more composed, and he seemed to be listening to the sullen roar of a cataract visible in part through one of the grated portals. This was the only sound that intruded on the silence of these doleful mansions. A range of brazen cases, surrounded the elevation. 'Remove the covers from these cabalistic depositories,' said the Giaour to Vathek, 'and avail thyself of the talismans which will break asunder all these gates of bronze, and not only render thee master of the treasures contained within them, but also of the spirits by which they are guarded.'

The Caliph, whom this ominious preliminary had entirely disconcerted, approached the vase with faltering footsteps; and was ready to sink with terror when he heard the groans of Soliman. As he proceeded, a voice from the livid lips of the prophet articulated these words: 'In my lifetime I filled a magnificent throne; having, on my right hand, twelve thousand seats of gold, where the patriarchs and the prophets heard my doctrines: on my left, the sages and doctors, upon as many thrones of silver, were present at all my decisions. Whilst I thus administered justice to innumerable multitudes, the birds of the air, hovering over me, served as a canopy against the rays of the sun. My people flourished; and my palace rose to the clouds. I erected a temple to the Most High, which was the wonder of the universe; but I basely suffered myself to be seduced by the love of women, and a curiosity that could not be restrained by sublunary things. I listened to the counsels of Aherman and the daughter of Pharaoh; and adored fire and the hosts of Heaven. I forsook the holy city, and commanded the Genii to rear the stupendous palace of Istakhar, and the terrace of the watch-towers; each of which was consecrated to a star. There, for a while, I enjoyed myself in the zenith of glory and pleasure. Not only men but supernatural beings were subject also to my will. I began to think, as these unhappy monarchs around had already thought, that the vengeance of Heaven was asleep; when, at once, the thunder burst my structures asunder, and precipitated me hither: where, however, I do not remain, like the other inhabitants, totally destitute of hope; for an angel of light hath revealed that in consideration of the piety of my early youth my woes shall come to an end, when this cataract shall for ever cease to flow. Till then I am in torments, ineffable torments! an unrelenting fire preys on my heart.'

Having uttered this exclamation, Soliman raised his hands towards heaven, in token of supplication; and the Caliph discerned through his bosom, which was transparent as crystal, his heart enveloped in flames. At a sight so full of horror, Nouronihar fell back, like one petrified, into the arms of Vathek, who cried out with a convulsive sob, 'O Giaour! whither hast thou brought us! Allow us to depart, and I will relinquish all thou hast promised. O Mahomet! remains there no more mercy?' – 'None! none!' replied the malicious dive. 'Know, miserable Prince! thou art now in the abode of vengeance and despair. Thy heart, also, will be kindled like those of the other votaries of Eblis. A few days are allotted thee previous to this fatal period: employ them as thou wilt; recline on these heaps of gold; command the infernal potentates; range, at thy pleasure, through these immense subterranean domains: no barrier shall be shut against thee. As for me, I have fulfilled my mission: I now leave thee to thyself.' At these words he vanished.

The Caliph and Nouronihar remained in the most abject affliction. Their tears were unable to flow, and scarcely could they support themselves. At length, taking each other despondingly by the hand, they went faltering from this fatal hall, indifferent which way they turned their steps. Every portal opened at their approach. The dives fell prostrate before them. Every reservoir of riches was disclosed to their view; but they no longer felt the incentives of curiosity, of pride, or avarice. With like apathy they heard the chorus of Genii, and saw the stately banquets prepared to regale them. They went wandering on, from chamber to chamber, hall to hall, and gallery to gallery; all without bounds or limit; all distinguishable by the same lowering gloom; all adorned with the same awful grandeur; all traversed by persons in search of repose and consolation, but who sought them in vain; for every one carried within him a heart tormented in flames. Shunned by these various sufferers, who seemed by their looks to be upbraiding the partners of their guilt, they withdrew from them to wait, in direful suspense, the moment which should render them to each other the like objects of terror.

'What?' exclaimed Nouronihar; 'will the time come when I shall snatch my hand from thine?' – 'Ah!' said Vathek, 'and shall my eyes ever cease to drink from thine long draughts of enjoyment? Shall the moments of our reciprocal ecstasies be reflected on with horror? It was not thou that broughtest me hither; the principles by which Carathis perverted my youth have been the sole cause of my perdition! it is but right she should have her share of it.' Having given vent to these painful expressions, he called to an afrit, who was stirring up one of the braziers, and bade him fetch the Princess Carathis from the palace of Samarah.

After issuing these orders, the Caliph and Nouronihar continued walking amidst the silent crowd, till they heard voices at the end of the gallery. Presuming them to proceed from some unhappy beings, who, like themselves, were awaiting their final doom, they followed the sound, and found it to come from a small square chamber, where they discovered, sitting on sofas, four young men of goodly figure, and a lovely female, who were holding a melancholy conversation by the glimmering of a lonely lamp. Each had a gloomy and forlorn air; and two of them were embracing each other with great tenderness. On seeing the Caliph and the daughter of Fakreddin enter, they arose, saluted, and made room for them. Then he who appeared the most considerable of the group, addressed himself thus to Vathek: 'Strangers! who doubtless are in the same state of suspense with ourselves, as you do not yet bear your hand on your heart, if you come hither to pass the interval allotted, previous to the infliction of our common punishment, condescend to relate the adventures that have brought you to this fatal place; and we, in return, will acquaint you with ours, which deserve but too well to be heard. To trace back our crimes to their source, though we are not permitted to repent, is the only employment suited to wretches like us!'

The Caliph and Nouronihar assented to the proposal; and Vathek began, not without tears and lamentations, a sincere recital of every circumstance that had passed. When the afflicting narrative was closed, the young man entered on his own. Each person proceeded in order; and, when the third prince had reached the midst of his adventures, a sudden noise interrupted him, which caused the vault to tremble and to open.

Immediately a cloud descended, which, gradually dissipating, discovered Carathis on the back of an afrit, who grievously complained of his burden. She, instantly springing to the ground, advanced towards her son, and said, 'What dost thou here, in this little square chamber? As the dives are become subject to thy beck, I expected to have found thee on the throne of the pre-Adamite kings.'

'Execrable woman!' answered the Caliph; 'cursed be the day thou gavest me birth! Go, follow this afrit; let him conduct thee to the hall of the prophet Soliman: there thou wilt learn to what these palaces are destined, and how much I ought to abhor the impious knowledge thou hast taught me.'

'Has the height of power, to which thou art arrived, turned thy brain?' answered Carathis; 'but I ask no more than permission to show my respect for Soliman the prophet. It is, however, proper thou shouldst know that (as the afrit has informed me neither of us shall return to Samarah) I requested his permission to arrange my affairs, and he politely consented. Availing myself, therefore, of the few moments allowed me, I set fire to the tower, and consumed in it the mutes, negresses, and serpents, which have rendered me so much good service; nor should I have been less kind to Morakanabad, had he not prevented me, by deserting at last to thy brother. As for Bababalouk, who had the folly to return to Samarah, to provide husbands for thy wives, I undoubtedly would have put him to the torture; but being in a hurry, I only hung him, after having decoyed him in a snare, with thy wives, whom I buried alive by the help of my negresses, who thus spent their last moments greatly to their satisfaction. With respect to Dilara, who ever stood high in my favour, she hath evinced the greatness of her mind, by fixing herself near, in the service of one of the Magi; and, I think, will soon be one of our society.'

Vathek, too much cast down to express the indignation excited by such a discourse, ordered the afrit to remove Carathis from his presence, and continued immersed in thoughts which his companions durst not disturb.

Carathis, however, eagerly entered the dome of Soliman, and without regarding in the least the groans of the prophet, undauntedly removed the covers of the vases and violently seized on the talismans. Then, with a voice more loud than had hitherto been heard within these mansions, she compelled the dives to disclose to her the most secret treasures, the most profound stores, which the afrit himself had not seen. She passed, by rapid descents, known only to Eblis and his most favoured potentates; and thus penetrated the very entrails of the earth, where breathes the sansar, or the icy wind of death. Nothing appalled her dauntless soul. She perceived, however, in all the inmates who bore their hands on their heart, a little singularity not much to her taste.

As she was emerging from one of the abysses, Eblis stood forth to her view; but notwithstanding he displayed the full effulgence of his infernal majesty, she preserved her countenance unaltered, and even paid her compliments with considerable firmness.

This superb monarch thus answered: 'Princess, whose knowledge and whose crimes have merited a conspicuous rank in my empire, thou dost well to avail thyself of the leisure that remains; for the flames and torments, which are ready to seize on thy heart, will not fail to provide thee soon with full employment.' He said, and was lost in the curtains of his tabernacle.

Carathis paused for a moment with surprise; but, resolved to follow the advice of Eblis, she assembled all the choirs of Genii, and all the dives, to pay her homage. Thus marched she, in triumph, through a vapour of perfumes, amidst the acclamations of all the malignant spirits, with most of whom she had formed a previous acquaintance. She even attempted to dethrone one of the Solimans, for the purpose of usurping his place; when a voice, proceeding from the abyss of death, proclaimed, 'All is accomplished!' Instantaneously the haughty forehead of the intrepid princess became corrugated with agony; she uttered a tremendous yell, and fixed, no more to be withdrawn, her right hand upon her heart, which was become a receptacle of eternal fire.

In this delirium, forgetting all ambitious projects, and her thirst for that knowledge which should ever be hidden from mortals, she overturned the offerings of the Genii; and, having execrated the hour she was begotten and the womb that had borne her, glanced off in a rapid whirl that rendered her invisible, and continued to revolve without intermission.

Almost at the same instant, the same voice announced to the Caliph, Nouronihar, the four princes, and the princess, the awful and irrevocable decree. Their hearts immediately took fire, and they, at once, lost the most precious gift of heaven – HOPE. These unhappy beings recoiled, with looks of the most furious distraction. Vathek beheld in the eyes of Nouronihar nothing but rage and vengeance; nor could she discern aught in his but aversion and despair. The two princes who were friends, and, till that moment, had preserved their attachment, shrunk back, gnashing their teeth with mutual and unchangeable hatred. Kalilah and his sister made reciprocal gestures of imprecation; all testified their horror for each other by the most ghastly convulsions, and screams that could not be smothered. All severally plunged themselves into the accursed multitude, there to wander in an eternity of unabating anguish.

Such was, and such should be, the punishment of unrestrained passions and atrocious deeds! Such shall be the chastisement of that blind curiosity, which would transgress those bounds the wisdom of the Creator has prescribed to human knowledge; and such the dreadful disappointment of that restless ambition, which, aiming at discoveries reserved for beings of a supernatural order, perceives not, through its infatuated pride, that the condition of man upon earth is to be – humble and ignorant.

Thus the Caliph Vathek, who, for the sake of empty

pomp and forbidden power, had sullied himself with a thousand crimes, became a prey to grief without end, and remorse without mitigation; whilst the humble, the despised Gulchenrouz passed whole ages in undisturbed tranquillity, and in the pure happiness of childhood.

**Facsimile of the title page of the first edition of *Frankenstein***

# FRANKENSTEIN;

OR,

# THE MODERN PROMETHEUS.

IN THREE VOLUMES.

Did I request thee, Maker, from my clay
To mould me man? Did I solicit thee
From darkness to promote me?——

PARADISE LOST.

VOL. I.

London:
*PRINTED FOR*
LACKINGTON, HUGHES, HARDING, MAVOR, & JONES,
FINSBURY SQUARE.

1818.

# AUTHOR'S INTRODUCTION TO THE STANDARD NOVELS EDITION

THE publishers of the Standard Novels, in selecting *Frankenstein* for one of their series, expressed a wish that I should furnish them with some account of the origin of the story. I am the more willing to comply, because I shall thus give a general answer to the question, so very frequently asked me, 'How I, then a young girl, came to think of and to dilate upon so very hideous an idea?' It is true that I am very averse to bringing myself forward in print; but as my account will only appear as an appendage to a former production, and as it will be confined to such topics as have connexion with my authorship alone, I can scarcely accuse myself of a personal intrusion.

It is not singular that, as the daughter of two persons of distinguished literary celebrity, I should very early in life have thought of writing. As a child I scribbled; and my favourite pastime during the hours given me for recreation was to 'write stories'. Still, I had a dearer pleasure than this, which was the formation of castles in the air – the indulging in waking dreams – the following up trains of thought, which had for their subject the formation of a succession of imaginary incidents. My dreams were at once more fantastic and agreeable than my writings. In the latter I was a close imitator – rather doing as others had done than putting down the suggestions of my own mind. What I wrote was intended at least for one other eye – my childhood's companion and friend; but my dreams were all my own; I accounted for them to nobody; they were my refuge when annoyed – my dearest pleasure when free.

I lived principally in the country as a girl, and passed a

considerable time in Scotland. I made occasional visits to the more picturesque parts; but my habitual residence was on the blank and dreary northern shores of the Tay, near Dundee. Blank and dreary on retrospection I call them; they were not so to me then. They were the aerie of freedom, and the pleasant region where unheeded I could commune with the creatures of my fancy. I wrote then – but in a most commonplace style. It was beneath the trees of the grounds belonging to our house, or on the bleak sides of the woodless mountains near, that my true compositions, the airy flights of my imagination, were born and fostered. I did not make myself the heroine of my tales. Life appeared to me too common-place an affair as regarded myself. I could not figure to myself that romantic woes or wonderful events would ever be my lot; but I was not confined to my own identity, and I could people the hours with creations far more interesting to me at that age than my own sensations.

After this my life became busier, and reality stood in place of fiction. My husband, however, was from the first very anxious that I should prove myself worthy of my parentage and enrol myself on the page of fame. He was forever inciting me to obtain literary reputation, which even on my own part I cared for then, though since I have become infinitely indifferent to it. At this time he desired that I should write, not so much with the idea that I could produce any thing worthy of notice, but that he might himself judge how far I possessed the promise of better things hereafter. Still I did nothing. Travelling, and the cares of a family, occupied my time; and study, in the way of reading or improving my ideas in communication with his far more cultivated mind, was all of literary employment that engaged my attention.

In the summer of 1816 we visited Switzerland and became the neighbours of Lord Byron. At first we spent our pleasant hours on the lake or wandering on its shores; and Lord Byron, who was writing the third canto of *Childe*

*Harold*, was the only one among us who put his thoughts upon paper. These, as he brought them successively to us, clothed in all the light and harmony of poetry, seemed to stamp as divine the glories of heaven and earth, whose influences we partook with him.

But it proved a wet, ungenial summer, and incessant rain often confined us for days to the house. Some volumes of ghost stories translated from the German into French fell into our hands. There was the *History of the Inconstant Lover*, who, when he thought to clasp the bride to whom he had pledged his vows, found himself in the arms of the pale ghost of her whom he had deserted. There was the tale of the sinful founder of his race whose miserable doom it was to bestow the kiss of death on all the younger sons of his fated house, just when they reached the age of promise. His gigantic, shadowy form, clothed like the ghost in *Hamlet*, in complete armour, but with the beaver up, was seen at midnight, by the moon's fitful beams, to advance slowly along the gloomy avenue. The shape was lost beneath the shadow of the castle walls; but soon a gate swung back, a step was heard, the door of the chamber opened, and he advanced to the couch of the blooming youths, cradled in healthy sleep. Eternal sorrow sat upon his face as he bent down and kissed the forehead of the boys, who from that hour withered like flowers snapt upon the stalk. I have not seen these stories since then, but their incidents are as fresh in my mind as if I had read them yesterday.

'We will each write a ghost story,' said Lord Byron, and his proposition was acceded to. There were four of us. The noble author began a tale, a fragment of which he printed at the end of his poem of Mazeppa. Shelley, more apt to embody ideas and sentiments in the radiance of brilliant imagery and in the music of the most melodious verse that adorns our language than to invent the machinery of a story, commenced one founded on the experiences of his early life. Poor Polidori had some terrible idea about a skull-headed lady who was so punished for peeping through a key-hole – what to see I forget – something very shocking and wrong of course; but when she was reduced to a worse condition than the renowned Tom of Coventry, he did not know what to do with her and was obliged to dispatch her to the tomb of the Capulets, the only place for which she was fitted. The illustrious poets also, annoyed by the platitude of prose, speedily relinquished their uncongenial task.

I busied myself *to think of a story* – a story to rival those which had excited us to this task. One which would speak to the mysterious fears of our nature and awaken thrilling horror – one to make the reader dread to look round, to curdle the blood, and quicken the beatings of the heart. If I did not accomplish these things, my ghost story would be unworthy of its name. I thought and pondered – vainly. I felt that blank incapability of invention which is the greatest misery of authorship, when dull Nothing replies to our anxious invocations. 'Have you thought of a story?' I was asked each morning, and each morning I was forced to reply with a mortifying negative.

Every thing must have a beginning, to speak in Sanchean phrase; and that beginning must be linked to something that went before. The Hindus give the world an elephant to support it, but they make the elephant stand upon a tortoise. Invention, it must be humbly admitted, does not consist in creating out of void, but out of chaos; the materials must, in the first place, be afforded: it can give form to dark, shapeless substances, but cannot bring into being the substance itself. In all matters of discovery and invention, even of those that appertain to the imagination, we are continually reminded of the story of Columbus and his egg. Invention consists in the capacity of seizing on the capabilities of a subject; and in the power of moulding and fashioning ideas suggested to it.

Many and long were the conversations between Lord Byron and Shelley, to which I was a devout but nearly silent listener. During one of these, various philosophical doctrines were discussed, and among others the nature of the principle of life, and whether there was any probability of its ever being discovered and communicated. They talked of the experiments of Dr Darwin (I speak not of what the doctor really did, or said that he did, but, as more to my purpose, of what was then spoken of as having been done by him), who preserved a piece of vermicelli in a glass case till by some extraordinary means it began to move with voluntary motion. Not thus, after all, would life be given. Perhaps a corpse would be reanimated; galvanism had given token of such things: perhaps the component parts of a creature might be manufactured, brought together, and endued with vital warmth.

Night waned upon this talk, and even the witching hour had gone by before we retired to rest. When I placed my head on my pillow, I did not sleep, nor could I be said to think. My imagination, unbidden, possessed and guided me, gifting the successive images that arose in my mind with a vividness far beyond the usual bounds of reverie. I saw – with shut eyes, but acute mental vision – I saw the pale student of unhallowed arts kneeling beside the thing he had put together. I saw the hideous phantasm of a man stretched out, and then, on the working of some powerful engine, show signs of life, and stir with an uneasy, half-vital motion. Frightful must it be; for supremely frightful would be the effect of any human endeavour to mock the stupendous mechanism of the Creator of the world. His success would terrify the artist; he would rush away from his odious handiwork, horror-stricken. He would hope that, left to itself, the slight spark of life which he had communicated would fade; that this thing which had received such imperfect animation would subside into dead matter, and he might sleep in the belief that the silence of the grave would quench forever the transient existence of the hideous corpse which he had looked upon as the cradle of life. He sleeps; but he is awakened; he opens his eyes; behold, the horrid thing stands at his bedside, opening his curtains and looking on him with yellow, watery, but speculative eyes.

I opened mine in terror. The idea so possessed my mind that a thrill of fear ran though me, and I wished to exchange the ghastly image of my fancy for the realities around. I see them still: the very room, the dark parquet, the closed shutters with the moonlight struggling through, and the sense I had that the glassy lake and white high Alps were beyond. I could not so easily get rid of my hideous phantom; still it haunted me. I must try to think of something else. I recurred to my ghost story – my tiresome, unlucky ghost story! Oh! If I could only contrive one which would frighten my reader as I myself had been frightened that night!

Swift as light and as cheering was the idea that broke in upon me. 'I have found it! What terrified me will terrify others; and I need only describe the spectre which had haunted my midnight pillow.' On the morrow I announced that I had *thought of a story*. I began that day with the words, 'It was on a dreary night of November,' making only a transcript of the grim terrors of my waking dream.

At first I thought but of a few pages – of a short tale, but Shelley urged me to develope the idea at greater length. I certainly did not owe the suggestion of one incident, nor scarcely of one train of feeling, to my husband, and yet but for his incitement it would never have taken the form in which it was presented to the world. From this declaration I must except the preface. As far as I can recollect, it was entirely written by him

And now, once again, I bid my hideous progeny go forth and prosper. I have an affection for it, for it was the offspring of happy days, when death and grief were but words which found no true echo in my heart. Its several pages speak of many a walk, many a drive, and many a conversation, when I was not alone; and my companion was one who, in this world, I shall never see more. But this is for myself; my readers have nothing to do with these associations.

I will add but one word as to the alterations I have made. They are principally those of style. I have changed no portion of the story nor introduced any new ideas or circumstances. I have mended the language where it was so bald as to interfere with the interest of the narrative; and these changes occur almost exclusively in the beginning of the first volume. Throughout they are entirely confined to such parts as are mere adjuncts to the story, leaving the core and substance of it untouched.

M. W. S.

London, 15 October 1831

# PREFACE

THE event on which this fiction is founded has been supposed, by Dr Darwin[1] and some of the physiological writers of Germany, as not of impossible occurrence. I shall not be supposed as according the remotest degree of serious faith to such an imagination; yet, in assuming it as the basis of a work of fancy, I have not considered myself as merely weaving a series of supernatural terrors. The event on which the interest of the story depends is exempt from the disadvantages of a mere tale of spectres or enchantment. It was recommended by the novelty of the situations which it developes, and however impossible as a physical fact, affords a point of view to the imagination for the delineating of human passions more comprehensive and commanding than any which the ordinary relations of existing events can yield.

I have thus endeavoured to preserve the truth of the elementary principles of human nature, while I have not scrupled to innovate upon their combinations. The *Iliad*, the tragic poetry of Greece, Shakespeare in the *Tempest* and *Midsummer Night's Dream*, and most especially Milton in *Paradise Lost* conform to this rule; and the most humble novelist, who seeks to confer or receive amusement from his labours, may, without presumption, apply to prose fictions a licence, or rather a rule, from the adoption of which so many exquisite combinations of human feeling have resulted in the highest specimens of poetry.

The circumstance on which my story rests was suggested in casual conversation. It was commenced partly as a source of amusement, and partly as an expedient for exercising any untried resources of mind. Other motives were mingled with these as the work proceeded. I am by no means indifferent to the manner in which whatever moral tendencies exist in the sentiments or characters it contains shall affect the reader; yet my chief concern in this respect has been limited to the avoiding the enervating effects of the novels of the present day, and to the exhibition of the amiableness of domestic affection, and the excellence of universal virtue. The opinions which naturally spring from the character and situation of the hero are by no means to be conceived as existing always in my own conviction; nor is any inference justly to be drawn from the following pages as prejudicing any philosophical doctrine of whatever kind.

It is a subject also of additional interest to the author that this story was begun in the majestic region where the scene is principally laid and in society which cannot cease to be regretted. I passed the summer of 1816 in the environs of Geneva. The season was cold and rainy, and in the evenings we crowded around a blazing wood fire and occasionally amused ourselves with some German stories of ghosts which happened to fall into our hands. These tales excited in us a playful desire of imitation. Two other friends (a tale from the pen of one of whom would be far more acceptable to the public than anything I can ever hope to produce) and myself agreed to write each a story founded on some supernatural occurrence.

The weather, however, suddenly became serene; and my two friends left me on a journey among the Alps and lost, in the magnificent scenes which they present, all memory of their ghostly visions. The following tale is the only one which has been completed.

Marlow, September 1817

# LETTER 1

*To Mrs Saville, England*

St Petersburgh, Dec. 11th 17—

YOU will rejoice to hear that no disaster has accompanied the commencement of an enterprize which you have regarded with such evil forebodings. I arrived here yesterday; and my first task is to assure my dear sister of my welfare and increasing confidence in the success of my undertaking.

I am already far north of London; and as I walk in the streets of Petersburgh, I feel a cold northern breeze play upon my cheeks, which braces my nerves and fills me with delight. Do you understand this feeling? This breeze, which has travelled from the regions towards which I am advancing, gives me a foretaste of those icy climes. Inspirited by this wind of promise, my daydreams become more fervent and vivid. I try in vain to be persuaded that the pole is the seat of frost and desolation; it ever presents itself to my imagination as the region of beauty and delight. There, Margaret, the sun is forever visible, its broad disk just skirting the horizon and diffusing a perpetual splendour. There – for with your leave, my sister, I will put some trust in preceding navigators – there snow and frost are banished; and, sailing over a calm sea, we may be wafted to a land surpassing in wonders and in beauty every region hitherto discovered on the habitable globe. Its productions and features may be without example, as the phaenomena of the heavenly bodies undoubtedly are in those undiscovered solitudes. What may not be expected in a country of eternal light? I may there discover the wondrous power which attracts the needle and may regulate a thousand celestial observations that require only this voyage to render their seeming eccentricities consistent forever. I shall satiate my ardent curiosity with the sight of a part of the world never before visited, and may tread a land never before imprinted by the foot of man. These are my enticements, and they are sufficient to conquer all fear of danger or death and to induce me to commence this laborious voyage with the joy a child feels when he embarks in a little boat, with his holiday mates, on an expedition of discovery up his native river. But supposing all these conjectures to be false, you cannot contest the inestimable benefit which I shall confer on all mankind to the last generation, by discovering a passage near the pole to those countries, to reach which at present so many months are requisite; or by ascertaining the secret of the magnet, which, if at all possible, can only be effected by an undertaking such as mine.

These reflections have dispelled the agitation with which I began my letter, and I feel my heart glow with an enthusiasm which elevates me to heaven; for nothing contributes so much to tranquillize the mind as a steady purpose – a point on which the soul may fix its intellectual eye. This expedition has been the favourite dream of my early years. I have read with ardour the accounts of the various voyages which have been made in the prospect of arriving at the North Pacific Ocean through the seas which surround the pole. You may remember that a history of all the voyages made for purposes of discovery composed the whole of our good Uncle Thomas's library. My education was neglected, yet I was passionately fond of reading. These volumes were my study day and night, and my familiarity with them increased that regret which I had felt, as a child, on learning that my father's dying injunction had forbidden my uncle to allow me to embark in a seafaring life.

These visions faded when I perused, for the first time, those poets whose effusions entranced my soul and lifted it to heaven. I also became a poet and for one year lived in a Paradise of my own creation; I imagined that I also might obtain a niche in the temple where the names of Homer and Shakespeare are consecrated. You are well acquainted with my failure and how heavily I bore the disappointment. But just at that time I inherited the fortune of my cousin, and my thoughts were turned into the channel of their earlier bent.

Six years have passed since I resolved on my present undertaking. I can, even now, remember the hour from which I dedicated myself to this great enterprize. I commenced by inuring my body to hardship. I accompanied the whale-fishers on several expeditions to the North Sea; I voluntarily endured cold, famine, thirst, and want of sleep; I often worked harder than the common sailors during the day, and devoted my nights to the study of mathematics, the theory of medicine, and those branches of physical science from which a naval adventurer might derive the greatest practical advantage. Twice I actually hired myself as an under-mate in a Greenland whaler, and acquitted myself to admiration. I must own I felt a little proud when my captain offered me the second dignity in the vessel and intreated me to remain with the greatest earnestness; so valuable did he consider my services.

And now, dear Margaret, do I not deserve to accomplish some great purpose? My life might have been passed in ease and luxury; but I preferred glory to every enticement that wealth placed in my path. Oh, that some encouraging voice would answer in the affirmative! My courage and my resolution is firm; but my hopes fluctuate, and my spirits are often depressed. I am about to proceed on a long and difficult voyage, the emergencies of which will demand all my fortitude: I am required not only to raise the spirits of others, but sometimes to sustain my own, when theirs are failing.

This is the most favourable period for travelling in Russia. They fly quickly over the snow in their sledges;

the motion is pleasant, and, in my opinion, far more agreeable than that of an English stagecoach. The cold is not excessive, if you are wrapped in furs – a dress which I have already adopted, for there is a great difference between walking the deck and remaining seated motionless for hours, when no exercise prevents the blood from actually freezing in your veins. I have no ambition to lose my life on the post-road between St Petersburgh and Archangel.

I shall depart for the latter town in a fortnight or three weeks; and my intention is to hire a ship there, which can easily be done by paying the insurance for the owner, and to engage as many sailors as I think necessary among those who are accustomed to the whale-fishing. I do not intend to sail until the month of June; and when shall I return? Ah, dear sister, how can I answer this question? If I succeed, many, many months, perhaps years, will pass before you and I may meet. If I fail, you will see me again soon, or never.

Farewell, my dear, excellent Margaret. Heaven shower down blessings on you, and save me, that I may again and again testify my gratitude for all your love and kindness.

Your affectionate brother,

R. Walton

## LETTER 2

*To Mrs Saville, England*

Archangel, 28th March, 17—

How slowly the time passes here, encompassed as I am by frost and snow! Yet a second step is taken towards my enterprize. I have hired a vessel and am occupied in collecting my sailors; those whom I have already engaged appear to be men on whom I can depend and are certainly possessed of dauntless courage.

But I have one want which I have never yet been able to satisfy; and the absence of the object of which I now feel as a most severe evil. I have no friend, Margaret: when I am glowing with the enthusiasm of success, there will be none to participate in my joy; if I am assailed by disappointment, no one will endeavour to sustain me in dejection. I shall commit my thoughts to paper, it is true; but that is a poor medium for the communication of feeling. I desire the company of a man who could sympathize with me, whose eyes would reply to mine. You may deem me romantic, my dear sister, but I bitterly feel the want of a friend. I have no one near me, gentle yet courageous, possessed of a cultivated as well as of a capacious mind, whose tastes are like my own, to approve or amend my plans. How would such a friend repair the faults of your poor brother! I am too ardent in execution and too impatient of difficulties. But it is a still greater evil to me that I am self-educated: for the first fourteen years of my life I ran wild on a common and read nothing but our Uncle Thomas's books of voyages. At that age I became acquainted with the celebrated poets of our own country; but it was only when it had ceased to be in my power to derive its most important benefits from such a conviction, that I perceived the necessity of becoming acquainted with more languages than that of my native country. Now I am twenty-eight and am in reality more illiterate than many schoolboys of fifteen. It is true that I have thought more and that my daydreams are more extended and magnificent, but they want (as the painters call it) *keeping*; and I greatly need a friend who would have sense enough not to despise me as romantic, and affection enough for me to endeavour to regulate my mind.

Well, these are useless complaints; I shall certainly find no friend on the wide ocean, nor even here in Archangel, among merchants and seamen. Yet some feelings, unallied to the dross of human nature, beat even in these rugged bosoms. My lieutenant, for instance, is a man of wonderful courage and enterprize; he is madly desirous of glory: or rather, to word my phrase more characteristically, of advancement in his profession. He is an Englishman, and in the midst of national and professional prejudices, unsoftened by cultivation, retains some of the noblest endowments of humanity. I first became acquainted with him on board a whale vessel: finding that he was unemployed in this city, I easily engaged him to assist in my enterprize.

The master is a person of an excellent disposition, and is remarkable in the ship for his gentleness and the mildness of his discipline. This circumstance, added to his well-known integrity and dauntless courage, made me very desirous to engage him. A youth passed in solitude, my best years spent under your gentle and feminine fosterage, has so refined the groundwork of my character that I cannot overcome an intense distaste to the usual brutality exercised on board ship: I have never believed it to be necessary, and when I heard of a mariner equally noted for his kindliness of heart and the respect and obedience paid to him by his crew, I felt myself peculiarly fortunate in being able to secure his services. I heard of him first in rather a romantic manner, from a lady who owes to him the happiness of her life. This, briefly, is his story. Some years ago he loved a young Russian lady of moderate fortune, and having amassed a considerable sum in prize-money, the father of the girl consented to the match. He saw his mistress once before the destined ceremony; but she was bathed in tears, and, throwing herself at his feet, intreated him to spare her, confessing at the same time that she loved another, but that he was poor, and that her father would never consent to the union. My generous friend reassured the suppliant, and on being informed of the name of her lover, instantly abandoned his pursuit. He had already bought a farm with his money, on which he had designed to pass the remainder of his life; but he bestowed the whole on his rival, together with the remains of his prize-money to purchase stock, and then himself solicited the young woman's father to consent to her marriage with her lover. But the old man decidedly refused, thinking himself bound in honour to my friend, who, when he found the father inexorable, quitted his country, nor returned until he heard that his former mistress was married according to her inclinations. 'What a noble fellow!' you will exclaim. He is so; but then he is wholly uneducated: he is as silent as a Turk, and a kind of ignorant carelessness attends him, which, while it renders his conduct the more astonishing, detracts from the interest and sympathy which otherwise he would command.

Yet do not suppose, because I complain a little, or because I can conceive a consolation for my toils which I may never know, that I am wavering in my resolutions. Those are as fixed as fate, and my voyage is only now delayed until the weather shall permit my embarkation. The winter has been dreadfully severe, but the spring promises well, and it is considered as a remarkably early season, so that perhaps I may sail sooner than I expected. I shall do nothing rashly: you know me sufficiently to confide in my prudence and considerateness whenever the safety of others is committed to my care.

I cannot describe to you my sensations on the near prospect of my undertaking. It is impossible to communicate to you a conception of the trembling sensation, half pleasurable and half fearful, with which I am preparing to depart. I am going to unexplored regions, to 'the land of mist and snow,' but I shall kill no albatross; therefore do not be alarmed for my safety or if I should come back to you as worn and woeful as the 'Ancient Mariner.' You will smile at my allusion, but I will disclose a secret. I have often attributed my attachment to, my passionate enthusiasm for, the dangerous mysteries of ocean to that production of the most imaginative of modern poets. There is something at work in my soul which I do not understand. I am practically industrious – painstaking, a workman to execute with perseverance and labour – but besides this, there is a love for the marvellous, a belief in the marvellous, intertwined in all my projects, which hurries me out of the common pathways of men, even to the wild sea and unvisited regions I am about to explore.

But to return to dearer considerations. Shall I meet you again, after having traversed immense seas, and returned by the most southern cape of Africa or America? I dare not expect such success, yet I cannot bear to look on the reverse of the picture. Continue for the present to write to me by every opportunity: I may receive your letters on some occasions when I need them most to support my spirits. I love you very tenderly. Remember me with affection, should you never hear from me again.

Your affectionate brother,
Robert Walton

## LETTER 3

*To Mrs Saville, England*

July 7th, 17—

My dear Sister,

I write a few lines in haste to say that I am safe – and well advanced on my voyage. This letter will reach England by a merchantman now on its homeward voyage from Archangel; more fortunate than I, who may not see my native land, perhaps, for many years. I am, however, in good spirits: my men are bold and apparently firm of purpose, nor do the floating sheets of ice that continually pass us, indicating the dangers of the region towards which we are advancing, appear to dismay them. We have already reached a very high latitude; but it is the height of summer, and although not so warm as in England, the southern gales, which blow us speedily towards those shores which I so ardently desire to attain, breathe a degree of renovating warmth which I had not expected.

No incidents have hitherto befallen us that would make a figure in a letter. One or two stiff gales and the springing of a leak are accidents which experienced navigators scarcely remember to record, and I shall be well content if nothing worse happen to us during our voyage.

Adieu, my dear Margaret. Be assured that for my own sake, as well as yours, I will not rashly encounter danger. I will be cool, persevering, and prudent.

But success *shall* crown my endeavours. Wherefore not? Thus far I have gone, tracing a secure way over the pathless seas, the very stars themselves being witnesses and testimonies of my triumph. Why not still proceed over the untamed yet obedient element? What can stop the determined heart and resolved will of man?

My swelling heart involuntarily pours itself out thus. But I must finish. Heaven bless my beloved sister!

R. W.

## LETTER 4

*To Mrs Saville, England*

August 5th, 17—

So strange an accident has happened to us that I cannot forbear recording it, although it is very probable that you will see me before these papers can come into your possession.

Last Monday (July 31st) we were nearly surrounded by ice, which closed in the ship on all sides, scarcely leaving her the sea-room in which she floated. Our situation was somewhat dangerous, especially as we were compassed round by a very thick fog. We accordingly lay to, hoping that some change would take place in the atmosphere and weather.

About two o'clock the mist cleared away, and we beheld, stretched out in every direction, vast and irregular plains of ice, which seemed to have no end. Some of my comrades groaned, and my own mind began to grow watchful with anxious thoughts, when a strange sight suddenly attracted our attention and diverted our solicitude from our own situation. We perceived a low carriage, fixed on a sledge and drawn by dogs, pass on towards the north, at the distance of half a mile; a being which had the shape of a man, but apparently of gigantic stature, sat in the sledge and guided the dogs. We watched the rapid progress of the traveller with our telescopes until he was lost among the distant inequalities of the ice.

This appearance excited our unqualified wonder. We were, as we believed, many hundred miles from any land; but this apparition seemed to denote that it was not, in reality, so distant as we had supposed. Shut in, however, by ice, it was impossible to follow his track, which we had observed with the greatest attention.

About two hours after this occurrence we heard the ground sea, and before night the ice broke and freed our ship. We, however, lay to until the morning, fearing to encounter in the dark those large loose masses which float about after the breaking up of the ice. I profited of this time to rest for a few hours.

In the morning, however, as soon as it was light, I went upon deck and found all the sailors busy on one side of the vessel, apparently talking to some one in the sea. It was, in fact, a sledge, like that we had seen before, which had drifted towards us in the night on a large fragment of ice. Only one dog remained alive; but there was a human being within it whom the sailors were persuading to enter the vessel. He was not, as the other traveller seemed to be, a savage inhabitant of some undiscovered island, but a European. When I appeared on deck the master said, 'Here is our captain, and he will not allow you to perish on the open sea.'

On perceiving me, the stranger addressed me in English, although with a foreign accent. 'Before I come on board your vessel,' said he, 'will you have the kindness to inform me whither you are bound?'

You may conceive my astonishment on hearing such a question addressed to me from a man on the brink of destruction and to whom I should have supposed that my vessel would have been a resource which he would not have exchanged for the most precious wealth the earth can afford. I replied, however, that we were on a voyage of discovery towards the northern pole.

Upon hearing this he appeared satisfied and consented to come on board. Good God! Margaret, if you had seen the man who thus capitulated for his safety, your surprize would have been boundless. His limbs were nearly frozen, and his body dreadfully emaciated by fatigue and suffering. I never saw a man in so wretched a condition. We attempted to carry him into the cabin, but as soon as he had quitted the fresh air, he fainted. We accordingly brought him back to the deck and restored him to animation by rubbing him with brandy and forcing him to swallow a small quantity. As soon as he showed signs of life we wrapped him up in blankets and placed him near the chimney of the kitchen stove. By slow degrees he recovered and ate a little soup, which restored him wonderfully.

Two days passed in this manner before he was able to speak, and I often feared that his sufferings had deprived him of understanding. When he had in some measure recovered, I removed him to my own cabin and attended on him as much as my duty would permit. I never saw a more interesting creature: his eyes have generally an expression of wildness, and even madness, but there are moments when, if any one performs an act of kindness towards him or does him any the most trifling service, his whole countenance is lighted up, as it were, with a beam of benevolence and sweetness that I never saw equalled. But he is generally melancholy and despairing, and sometimes he gnashes his teeth, as if impatient of the weight of woes that oppresses him.

When my guest was a little recovered I had great trouble to keep off the men, who wished to ask him a thousand questions; but I would not allow him to be tormented by their idle curiosity, in a state of body and mind whose restoration evidently depended upon entire repose. Once, however, the lieutenant asked why he had come so far upon the ice in so strange a vehicle?

His countenance instantly assumed an aspect of the deepest gloom, and he replied, 'To seek one who fled from me.'

'And did the man whom you pursued travel in the same fashion?'

'Yes.'

'Then I fancy we have seen him, for the day before we

picked you up we saw some dogs drawing a sledge, with a man in it, across the ice.'

This aroused the stranger's attention, and he asked a multitude of questions concerning the route which the daemon, as he called him, had pursued. Soon after, when he was alone with me, he said, 'I have, doubtless, excited your curiosity, as well as that of these good people; but you are too considerate to make enquiries.'

'Certainly; it would indeed be very impertinent and inhuman in me to trouble you with any inquisitiveness of mine.'

'And yet you rescued me from a strange and perilous situation; you have benevolently restored me to life.'

Soon after this he enquired if I thought that the breaking up of the ice had destroyed the other sledge? I replied that I could not answer with any degree of certainty, for the ice had not broken until near midnight, and the traveller might have arrived at a place of safety before that time; but of this I could not judge.

From this time a new spirit of life animated the decaying frame of the stranger. He manifested the greatest eagerness to be upon deck to watch for the sledge which had before appeared; but I have persuaded him to remain in the cabin, for he is far too weak to sustain the rawness of the atmosphere. I have promised that some one should watch for him and give him instant notice if any new object should appear in sight.

Such is my journal of what relates to this strange occurrence up to the present day. The stranger has gradually improved in health but is very silent and appears uneasy when anyone except myself enters his cabin. Yet his manners are so conciliating and gentle that the sailors are all interested in him, although they have had very little communication with him. For my own part, I begin to love him as a brother, and his constant and deep grief fills me with sympathy and compassion. He must have been a noble creature in his better days, being even now in wreck so attractive and amiable.

I said in one of my letters, my dear Margaret, that I should find no friend on the wide ocean; yet I have found a man who, before his spirit had been broken by misery, I should have been happy to have possessed as the brother of my heart.

I shall continue my journal concerning the stranger at intervals, should I have any fresh incidents to record.

August 13th, 17—

My affection for my guest increases every day. He excites at once my admiration and my pity to an astonishing degree. How can I see so noble a creature destroyed by misery without feeling the most poignant grief? He is so gentle, yet so wise; his mind is so cultivated, and when he speaks, although his words are culled with the choicest art, yet they flow with rapidity and unparalleled eloquence.

He is now much recovered from his illness and is continually on the deck, apparently watching for the sledge that preceded his own. Yet, although unhappy, he is not so utterly occupied by his own misery but that he interests himself deeply in the projects of others. He has frequently conversed with me on mine, which I have communicated to him without disguise. He entered attentively into all my arguments in favour of my eventual success and into every minute detail of the measures I had taken to secure it. I was easily led by the sympathy which he evinced to use the language of my heart, to give utterance to the burning ardour of my soul, and to say, with all the fervour that warmed me, how gladly I would sacrifice my fortune, my existence, my every hope, to the furtherance of my enterprize. One man's life or death were but a small price to pay for the acquirement of the knowledge which I sought, for the dominion I should acquire and transmit over the elemental foes of our race. As I spoke, a dark gloom spread over my listener's countenance. At first I perceived that he tried to suppress his emotion; he placed his hands before his eyes, and my voice quivered and failed me as I beheld tears trickle fast from between his fingers; a groan burst from his heaving breast. I paused; at length he spoke, in broken accents: 'Unhappy man! Do you share my madness? Have you drunk also of the intoxicating draught? Hear me; let me reveal my tale, and you will dash the cup from your lips!'

Such words, you may imagine, strongly excited my curiosity; but the paroxysm of grief that had seized the stranger overcame his weakened powers, and many hours of repose and tranquil conversation were necessary to restore his composure.

Having conquered the violence of his feelings, he appeared to despise himself for being the slave of passion; and quelling the dark tyranny of despair, he led me again to converse concerning myself personally. He asked me the history of my earlier years. The tale was quickly told: but it awakened various trains of reflection. I spoke of my desire of finding a friend, of my thirst for a more intimate sympathy with a fellow mind than had ever fallen to my lot, and expressed my conviction that a man could boast of little happiness who did not enjoy this blessing.

'I agree with you,' replied the stranger; 'we are unfashioned creatures, but half made up, if one wiser, better, dearer than ourselves – such a friend ought to be – do not lend his aid to perfectionate our weak and faulty natures. I once had a friend, the most noble of human creatures, and am entitled, therefore, to judge respecting friendship. You have hope, and the world before you, and have no cause for despair. But I – I have lost every thing and cannot begin life anew.'

As he said this his countenance became expressive of a calm, settled grief that touched me to the heart. But he was silent and presently retired to his cabin.

Even broken in spirit as he is, no one can feel more deeply

than he does the beauties of nature. The starry sky, the sea, and every sight afforded by these wonderful regions, seems still to have the power of elevating his soul from earth. Such a man has a double existence: he may suffer misery and be overwhelmed by disappointments, yet when he has retired into himself, he will be like a celestial spirit that has a halo around him, within whose circle no grief or folly ventures.

Will you smile at the enthusiasm I express concerning this divine wanderer? You would not if you saw him. You have been tutored and refined by books and retirement from the world, and you are therefore somewhat fastidious; but this only renders you the more fit to appreciate the extraordinary merits of this wonderful man. Sometimes I have endeavoured to discover what quality it is which he possesses that elevates him so immeasurably above any other person I ever knew. I believe it to be an intuitive discernment, a quick but never-failing power of judgment, a penetration into the causes of things, unequalled for clearness and precision; add to this a facility of expression and a voice whose varied intonations are soul-subduing music.

August 19, 17—

Yesterday the stranger said to me, 'You may easily perceive, Captain Walton, that I have suffered great and unparalleled misfortunes. I had determined at one time that the memory of these evils should die with me, but you have won me to alter my determination. You seek for knowledge and wisdom, as I once did; and I ardently hope that the gratification of your wishes may not be a serpent to sting you, as mine has been. I do not know that the relation of my disasters will be useful to you; yet, when I reflect that you are pursuing the same course, exposing yourself to the same dangers which have rendered me what I am, I imagine that you may deduce an apt moral from my tale; one that may direct you if you succeed in your undertaking and console you in case of failure. Prepare to hear of occurrences which are usually deemed marvellous. Were we among the tamer scenes of nature I might fear to encounter your unbelief, perhaps your ridicule; but many things will appear possible in these wild and mysterious regions which would provoke the laughter of those unacquainted with the ever-varied powers of nature; nor can I doubt but that my tale conveys in its series internal evidence of the truth of the events of which it is composed.'

You may easily imagine that I was much gratified by the offered communication, yet I could not endure that he should renew his grief by a recital of his misfortunes. I felt the greatest eagerness to hear the promised narrative, partly from curiosity and partly from a strong desire to ameliorate his fate if it were in my power. I expressed these feelings in my answer.

'I thank you,' he replied, 'for your sympathy, but it is useless; my fate is nearly fulfilled. I wait but for one event, and then I shall repose in peace. I understand your feeling,' continued he, perceiving that I wished to interrupt him; 'but you are mistaken, my friend, if thus you will allow me to name you; nothing can alter my destiny; listen to my history, and you will perceive how irrevocably it is determined.'

He then told me that he would commence his narrative the next day when I should be at leisure. This promise drew from me the warmest thanks. I have resolved every night, when I am not imperatively occupied by my duties, to record, as nearly as possible in his own words, what he has related during the day. If I should be engaged, I will at least make notes. This manuscript will doubtless afford you the greatest pleasure; but to me, who know him and who hear it from his own lips – with what interest and sympathy shall I read it in some future day! Even now, as I commence my task, his full-toned voice swells in my ears; his lustrous eyes dwell on me with all their melancholy sweetness; I see his thin hand raised in animation, while the lineaments of his face are irradiated by the soul within. Strange and harrowing must be his story, frightful the storm which embraced the gallant vessel on its course and wrecked it – thus!

# CHAPTER 1

I AM by birth a Genevese, and my family is one of the most distinguished of that republic. My ancestors had been for many years counsellors and syndics, and my father had filled several public situations with honour and reputation. He was respected by all who knew him for his integrity and indefatigable attention to public business. He passed his younger days perpetually occupied by the affairs of his country; a variety of circumstances had prevented his marrying early, nor was it until the decline of life that he became a husband and the father of a family.

As the circumstances of his marriage illustrate his character, I cannot refrain from relating them. One of his most intimate friends was a merchant who, from a flourishing state, fell, through numerous mischances, into poverty. This man, whose name was Beaufort, was of a proud and unbending disposition and could not bear to live in poverty and oblivion in the same country where he had formerly been distinguished for his rank and magnificence. Having paid his debts, therefore, in the most honourable manner, he retreated with his daughter to the town of Lucerne, where he lived unknown and in wretchedness. My father loved Beaufort with the truest friendship and was deeply grieved by his retreat in these unfortunate circumstances. He bitterly deplored the false pride which led his friend to a conduct so little worthy of the affection that united them. He lost no time in endeavouring to seek him out, with the hope of persuading him to begin the world again through his credit and assistance.

Beaufort had taken effectual measures to conceal himself, and it was ten months before my father discovered his abode. Overjoyed at this discovery, he hastened to the house, which was situated in a mean street near the Reuss. But when he entered, misery and despair alone welcomed him. Beaufort had saved but a very small sum of money from the wreck of his fortunes, but it was sufficient to provide him with sustenance for some months, and in the mean time he hoped to procure some respectable employment in a merchant's house. The interval was, consequently, spent in inaction; his grief only became more deep and rankling when he had leisure for reflection, and at length it took so fast hold of his mind that at the end of three months he lay on a bed of sickness, incapable of any exertion.

His daughter attended him with the greatest tenderness, but she saw with despair that their little fund was rapidly decreasing and that there was no other prospect of support. But Caroline Beaufort possessed a mind of an uncommon mould, and her courage rose to support her in her adversity. She procured plain work; she plaited straw; and by various means contrived to earn a pittance scarcely sufficient to support life.

Several months passed in this manner. Her father grew worse; her time was more entirely occupied in attending him; her means of subsistence decreased; and in the tenth month her father died in her arms, leaving her an orphan and a beggar. This last blow overcame her, and she knelt by Beaufort's coffin, weeping bitterly, when my father entered the chamber. He came like a protecting spirit to the poor girl, who committed herself to his care; and after the interment of his friend he conducted her to Geneva and placed her under the protection of a relation. Two years after this event Caroline became his wife.

There was a considerable difference between the ages of my parents, but this circumstance seemed to unite them only closer in bonds of devoted affection. There was a sense of justice in my father's upright mind which rendered it necessary that he should approve highly to love strongly. Perhaps during former years he had suffered from the late-discovered unworthiness of one beloved and so was disposed to set a greater value on tried worth. There was a show of gratitude and worship in his attachment to my mother, differing wholly from the doating fondness of age, for it was inspired by reverence for her virtues and a desire to be the means of, in some degree, recompensing her for the sorrows she had endured, but which gave inexpressible grace to his behaviour to her. Every thing was made to yield to her wishes and her convenience. He strove to shelter her, as a fair exotic is sheltered by the gardener, from every rougher wind, and to surround her with all that could tend to excite pleasurable emotion in her soft and benevolent mind. Her health, and even the tranquillity of her hitherto constant spirit, had been shaken by what she had gone through. During the two years that had elapsed previous to their marriage my father had gradually relinquished all his public functions; and immediately after their union they sought the pleasant climate of Italy, and the change of scene and interest attendant on a tour through that land of wonders, as a restorative for her weakened frame.

From Italy they visited Germany and France. I, their eldest child, was born at Naples, and as an infant accompanied them in their rambles. I remained for several years their only child. Much as they were attached to each other, they seemed to draw inexhaustible stores of affection from a very mine of love to bestow them upon me. My mother's tender caresses and my father's smile of benevolent pleasure while regarding me are my first recollections. I was their plaything and their idol, and something better – their child, the innocent and helpless creature bestowed on them by heaven, whom to bring up to good, and whose future lot it was in their hands to direct to happiness or misery, according as they fulfilled their duties towards me. With this deep consciousness of what they owed towards the being to which they had given life, added to the active spirit of tenderness that animated both, it may be imagined that while during every hour of my infant life I received a lesson of patience, of charity, and of self-control, I was so guided by a silken cord that all seemed but one train of enjoyment to me.

For a long time I was their only care. My mother had much desired to have a daughter, but I continued their single offspring. When I was about five years old, while making an excursion beyond the frontiers of Italy, they passed a week on the shores of the Lake of Como. Their benevolent disposition often made them enter the cottages of the poor. This, to my mother, was more than a duty; it was a necessity, a passion – remembering what she had suffered, and how she had been relieved – for her to act in her turn the guardian angel to the afflicted. During one of their walks a poor cot in the foldings of a vale attracted their notice as being singularly disconsolate, while the number of half-clothed children gathered about it spoke of penury in its worst shape. One day, when my father had gone by himself to Milan, my mother, accompanied by me, visited this abode. She found a peasant and his wife, hard working, bent down by care and labour, distributing a scanty meal to five hungry babes. Among these there was one which attracted my mother far above all the rest. She appeared of a different stock. The four others were dark-eyed, hardy little vagrants; this child was thin and very fair. Her hair was the brightest living gold, and despite the poverty of her clothing, seemed to set a crown of distinction on her head. Her brow was clear and ample, her blue eyes cloudless, and her lips and the moulding of her face so expressive of sensibility and sweetness that none could behold her without looking on her as of a distinct species, a being heaven-sent, and bearing a celestial stamp in all her features.

The peasant woman, perceiving that my mother fixed eyes of wonder and admiration on this lovely girl, eagerly communicated her history. She was not her child, but the daughter of a Milanese nobleman. Her mother was a German and had died on giving her birth. The infant had been placed with these good people to nurse: they were better off then. They had not been long married, and their eldest child was but just born. The father of their charge was one of those Italians nursed in the memory of the antique glory of Italy – one among the *schiavi ognor frementi,*[1] who exerted himself to obtain the liberty of his country. He became the victim of its weakness. Whether he had died or still lingered in the dungeons of Austria was not known. His property was confiscated; his child became an orphan and a beggar. She continued with her foster parents and bloomed in their rude abode, fairer than a garden rose among dark-leaved brambles.

When my father returned from Milan, he found playing with me in the hall of our villa a child fairer than pictured cherub – a creature who seemed to shed radiance from her looks and whose form and motions were lighter than the chamois of the hills. The apparition was soon explained. With his permission my mother prevailed on her rustic guardians to yield their charge to her. They were fond of the sweet orphan. Her presence had seemed a blessing to them, but it would be unfair to her to keep her in poverty and want when Providence afforded her such powerful protection. They consulted their village priest, and the result was that Elizabeth Lavenza became the inmate of my parents' house – my more than sister – the beautiful and adored companion of all my occupations and my pleasures.

Everyone loved Elizabeth. The passionate and almost reverential attachment with which all regarded her became, while I shared it, my pride and my delight. On the evening previous to her being brought to my home, my mother had said playfully, 'I have a pretty present for my Victor – tomorrow he shall have it.' And when, on the morrow, she presented Elizabeth to me as her promised gift, I, with childish seriousness, interpreted her words literally and looked upon Elizabeth as mine – mine to protect, love, and cherish. All praises bestowed on her I received as made to a possession of my own. We called each other familiarly by the name of cousin. No word, no expression could body forth the kind of relation in which she stood to me – my more than sister, since till death she was to be mine only.

# CHAPTER 2

WE were brought up together; there was not quite a year difference in our ages. I need not say that we were strangers to any species of disunion or dispute. Harmony was the soul of our companionship, and the diversity and contrast that subsisted in our characters drew us nearer together. Elizabeth was of a calmer and more concentrated disposition; but, with all my ardour, I was capable of a more intense application and was more deeply smitten with the thirst for knowledge. She busied herself with following the aerial creations of the poets; and in the majestic and wondrous scenes which surrounded our Swiss home – the sublime shapes of the mountains, the changes of the seasons, tempest and calm, the silence of winter, and the life and turbulence of our Alpine summers – she found ample scope for admiration and delight. While my companion contemplated with a serious and satisfied spirit the magnificent appearances of things, I delighted in investigating their causes. The world was to me a secret which I desired to divine. Curiosity, earnest research to learn the hidden laws of nature, gladness akin to rapture, as they were unfolded to me, are among the earliest sensations I can remember.

On the birth of a second son, my junior by seven years, my parents gave up entirely their wandering life and fixed themselves in their native country. We possessed a house in Geneva, and a *campagne*[1] on Belrive, the eastern shore of the lake, at the distance of rather more than a league from the city. We resided principally in the latter, and the lives of my parents were passed in considerable seclusion. It was my temper to avoid a crowd and to attach myself fervently to a few. I was indifferent, therefore, to my schoolfellows in general; but I united myself in the bonds of the closest friendship to one among them. Henry Clerval was the son of a merchant of Geneva. He was a boy of singular talent and fancy. He loved enterprize, hardship, and even danger for its own sake. He was deeply read in books of chivalry and romance. He composed heroic songs and began to write many a tale of enchantment and knightly adventure. He tried to make us act plays and to enter into masquerades, in which the characters were drawn from the heroes of Roncesvalles, of the Round Table of King Arthur, and the chivalrous train who shed their blood to redeem the holy sepulchre from the hands of the infidels.[2]

No human being could have passed a happier childhood than myself. My parents were possessed by the very spirit of kindness and indulgence. We felt that they were not the tyrants to rule our lot according to their caprice, but the agents and creators of all the many delights which we enjoyed. When I mingled with other families I distinctly discerned how peculiarly fortunate my lot was, and gratitude assisted the development of filial love.

My temper was sometimes violent, and my passions vehement; but by some law in my temperature they were turned not towards childish pursuits but to an eager desire to learn, and not to learn all things indiscriminately. I confess that neither the structure of languages, nor the code of governments, nor the politics of various states possessed attractions for me. It was the secrets of heaven and earth that I desired to learn; and whether it was the outward substance of things or the inner spirit of nature and the mysterious soul of man that occupied me, still my enquiries were directed to the metaphysical, or in its highest sense, the physical secrets of the world.

Meanwhile Clerval occupied himself, so to speak, with the moral relations of things. The busy stage of life, the virtues of heroes, and the actions of men were his theme; and his hope and his dream was to become one among those whose names are recorded in story as the gallant and adventurous benefactors of our species. The saintly soul of Elizabeth shone like a shrine-dedicated lamp in our peaceful home. Her sympathy was ours; her smile, her soft voice, the sweet glance of her celestial eyes, were ever there to bless and animate us. She was the living spirit of love to soften and attract; I might have become sullen in my study, rough through the ardour of my nature, but that she was there to subdue me to a semblance of her own gentleness. And Clerval – could aught ill entrench on the noble spirit of Clerval? Yet he might not have been so perfectly humane, so thoughtful in his generosity, so full of kindness and tenderness amidst his passion for adventurous exploit, had she not unfolded to him the real loveliness of beneficence and made the doing good the end and aim of his soaring ambition.

I feel exquisite pleasure in dwelling on the recollections of childhood, before misfortune had tainted my mind and changed its bright visions of extensive usefulness into gloomy and narrow reflections upon self. Besides, in drawing the picture of my early days, I also record those events which led, by insensible steps, to my after tale of misery, for when I would account to myself for the birth of that passion which afterwards ruled my destiny I find it arise, like a mountain river, from ignoble and almost forgotten sources; but, swelling as it proceeded, it became the torrent which, in its course, has swept away all my hopes and joys.

Natural philosophy is the genius that has regulated my fate; I desire, therefore, in this narration, to state those facts which led to my predilection for that science. When I was thirteen years of age we all went on a party of pleasure to the baths near Thonon; the inclemency of the weather obliged us to remain a day confined to the inn. In this house I chanced to find a volume of the works of Cornelius Agrippa.[3] I opened it with apathy; the theory which he attempts to demonstrate and the wonderful facts which he relates soon changed this feeling into enthusiasm.

A new light seemed to dawn upon my mind, and, bounding with joy, I communicated my discovery to my father. My father looked carelessly at the title page of my book and said, 'Ah! Cornelius Agrippa! My dear Victor, do not waste your time upon this; it is sad trash.'

If, instead of this remark, my father had taken the pains to explain to me that the principles of Agrippa had been entirely exploded and that a modern system of science had been introduced which possessed much greater powers than the ancient, because the powers of the latter were chimerical, while those of the former were real and practical; under such circumstances I should certainly have thrown Agrippa aside and have contented my imagination, warmed as it was, by returning with greater ardour to my former studies. It is even possible that the train of my ideas would never have received the fatal impulse that led to my ruin. But the cursory glance my father had taken of my volume by no means assured me that he was acquainted with its contents; and I continued to read with the greatest avidity.

When I returned home my first care was to procure the whole works of this author, and afterwards of Paracelsus and Albertus Magnus.[4] I read and studied the wild fancies of these writers with delight; they appeared to me treasures known to few besides myself. I have described myself as always having been imbued with a fervent longing to penetrate the secrets of nature. In spite of the intense labour and wonderful discoveries of modern philosophers, I always came from my studies discontented and unsatisfied. Sir Isaac Newton is said to have avowed that he felt like a child picking up shells beside the great and unexplored ocean of truth. Those of his successors in each branch of natural philosophy with whom I was acquainted appeared even to my boy's apprehensions as tyros engaged in the same pursuit.

The untaught peasant beheld the elements around him and was acquainted with their practical uses. The most learned philosopher knew little more. He had partially unveiled the face of Nature, but her immortal lineaments were still a wonder and a mystery. He might dissect, anatomize, and give names; but, not to speak of a final cause, causes in their secondary and tertiary grades were utterly unknown to him. I had gazed upon the fortifications and impediments that seemed to keep human beings from entering the citadel of nature, and rashly and ignorantly I had repined.

But here were books, and here were men who had penetrated deeper and knew more. I took their word for all that they averred, and I became their disciple. It may appear strange that such should arise in the eighteenth century; but while I followed the routine of education in the schools of Geneva, I was, to a great degree, self-taught with regard to my favourite studies. My father was not scientific, and I was left to struggle with a child's blindness, added to a student's thirst for knowledge. Under the guidance of my new preceptors I entered with the greatest diligence into the search of the philosopher's stone and the elixir of life; but the latter soon obtained my undivided attention. Wealth was an inferior object, but what glory would attend the discovery if I could banish disease from the human frame and render man invulnerable to any but a violent death!

Nor were these my only visions. The raising of ghosts or devils was a promise liberally accorded by my favourite authors, the fulfilment of which I most eagerly sought; and if my incantations were always unsuccessful, I attributed the failure rather to my own inexperience and mistake than to a want of skill or fidelity in my instructors. And thus for a time I was occupied by exploded systems, mingling, like an unadept, a thousand contradictory theories and floundering desperately in a very slough of multifarious knowledge, guided by an ardent imagination and childish reasoning, till an accident again changed the current of my ideas.

When I was about fifteen years old we had retired to our house near Belrive, when we witnessed a most violent and terrible thunderstorm. It advanced from behind the mountains of Jura, and the thunder burst at once with frightful loudness from various quarters of the heavens. I remained, while the storm lasted, watching its progress with curiosity and delight. As I stood at the door, on a sudden I beheld a stream of fire issue from an old and beautiful oak which stood about twenty yards from our house; and so soon as the dazzling light vanished, the oak had disappeared, and nothing remained but a blasted stump. When we visited it the next morning, we found the tree shattered in a singular manner. It was not splintered by the shock, but entirely reduced to thin ribbons of wood. I never beheld anything so utterly destroyed.

Before this I was not unacquainted with the more obvious laws of electricity. On this occasion a man of great research in natural philosophy was with us, and excited by this catastrophe, he entered on the explanation of a theory which he had formed on the subject of electricity and galvanism, which was at once new and astonishing to me. All that he said threw greatly into the shade Cornelius Agrippa, Albertus Magnus, and Paracelsus, the lords of my imagination; but by some fatality the overthrow of these men disinclined me to pursue my accustomed studies. It seemed to me as if nothing would or could ever be known. All that had so long engaged my attention suddenly grew despicable. By one of those caprices of the mind which we are perhaps most subject to in early youth, I at once gave up my former occupations, set down natural history and all its progeny as a deformed and abortive creation, and entertained the greatest disdain for a would-be science which could never even step within the threshold of real knowledge. In this mood of mind I betook myself to the mathematics and the branches of study appertaining to that science as being built upon secure foundations, and so worthy of my consideration.

Thus strangely are our souls constructed, and by such slight ligaments are we bound to prosperity or ruin. When I look back, it seems to me as if this almost miraculous change of inclination and will was the immediate suggestion of the guardian angel of my life – the last effort made by the spirit of preservation to avert the storm that was even then hanging in the stars and ready to envelope me. Her victory was announced by an unusual tranquillity and gladness of soul which followed the relinquishing of my ancient and latterly tormenting studies. It was thus that I was to be taught to associate evil with their prosecution, happiness with their disregard.

It was a strong effort of the spirit of good, but it was ineffectual. Destiny was too potent, and her immutable laws had decreed my utter and terrible destruction.

## CHAPTER 3

WHEN I had attained the age of seventeen my parents resolved that I should become a student at the university of Ingolstadt. I had hitherto attended the schools of Geneva, but my father thought it necessary for the completion of my education that I should be made acquainted with other customs than those of my native country. My departure was therefore fixed at an early date, but before the day resolved upon could arrive, the first misfortune of my life occurred – an omen, as it were, of my future misery.

Elizabeth had caught the scarlet fever; her illness was severe, and she was in the greatest danger. During her illness many arguments had been urged to persuade my mother to refrain from attending upon her. She had at first yielded to our intreaties, but when she heard that the life of her favourite was menaced, she could no longer control her anxiety. She attended her sickbed; her watchful attentions triumphed over the malignity of the distemper – Elizabeth was saved, but the consequences of this imprudence were fatal to her preserver. On the third day my mother sickened; her fever was accompanied by the most alarming symptoms, and the looks of her medical attendants prognosticated the worst event. On her deathbed the fortitude and benignity of this best of women did not desert her. She joined the hands of Elizabeth and myself. 'My children,' she said, 'my firmest hopes of future happiness were placed on the prospect of your union. This expectation will now be the consolation of your father. Elizabeth, my love, you must supply my place to my younger children. Alas! I regret that I am taken from you; and, happy and beloved as I have been, is it not hard to quit you all? But these are not thoughts befitting me; I will endeavour to resign myself cheerfully to death and will indulge a hope of meeting you in another world.'

She died calmly, and her countenance expressed affection even in death. I need not describe the feelings of those whose dearest ties are rent by that most irreparable evil, the void that presents itself to the soul, and the despair that is exhibited on the countenance. It is so long before the mind can persuade itself that she whom we saw every day and whose very existence appeared a part of our own, can have departed forever – that the brightness of a beloved eye can have been extinguished and the sound of a voice so familiar and dear to the ear can be hushed, never more to be heard. These are the reflections of the first days; but when the lapse of time proves the reality of the evil, then the actual bitterness of grief commences. Yet from whom has not that rude hand rent away some dear connexion? And why should I describe a sorrow which all have felt, and must feel? The time at length arrives when grief is rather an indulgence than a necessity; and the smile that plays upon the lips, although it may be deemed a sacrilege, is not banished. My mother was dead, but we had still duties which we ought to perform; we must continue our course with the rest and learn to think ourselves fortunate whilst one remains whom the spoiler has not seized.

My departure for Ingolstadt, which had been deferred by these events, was now again determined upon. I obtained from my father a respite of some weeks. It appeared to me sacrilege so soon to leave the repose, akin to death, of the house of mourning and to rush into the thick of life. I was new to sorrow, but it did not the less alarm me. I was unwilling to quit the sight of those that remained to me, and above all, I desired to see my sweet Elizabeth in some degree consoled.

She indeed veiled her grief and strove to act the comforter to us all. She looked steadily on life and assumed its duties with courage and zeal. She devoted herself to those whom she had been taught to call her uncle and cousins. Never was she so enchanting as at this time, when she recalled the sunshine of her smiles and spent them upon us. She forgot even her own regret in her endeavours to make us forget.

The day of my departure at length arrived. Clerval spent the last evening with us. He had endeavoured to persuade his father to permit him to accompany me and to become my fellow student, but in vain. His father was a narrow-minded trader and saw idleness and ruin in the aspirations and ambition of his son. Henry deeply felt the misfortune of being debarred from a liberal education. He said little, but when he spoke I read in his kindling eye and in his animated glance a restrained but firm resolve not to be chained to the miserable details of commerce.

We sat late. We could not tear ourselves away from each other nor persuade ourselves to say the word 'Farewell!' It was said, and we retired under the pretence of seeking repose, each fancying that the other was deceived; but when at morning's dawn I descended to the carriage which was to convey me away, they were all there – my father again to bless me, Clerval to press my hand once more, my Elizabeth to renew her intreaties that I would write often and to bestow the last feminine attentions on her playmate and friend.

I threw myself into the chaise that was to convey me away and indulged in the most melancholy reflections. I, who had ever been surrounded by amiable companions, continually engaged in endeavoring to bestow mutual pleasure – I was now alone. In the university whither I was going I must form my own friends and be my own protector. My life had hitherto been remarkably secluded and domestic, and this had given me invincible repugnance to new countenances. I loved my brothers, Elizabeth, and Clerval; these were 'old familiar faces,' but I believed myself totally unfitted for the company of strangers. Such were my reflections as I commenced my journey; but as I proceeded, my spirits and hopes rose. I ardently desired the acquisition of knowledge. I had often, when at home, thought it hard to remain during my youth cooped up in one place and had longed to enter the world and take my station among other human beings. Now my desires were complied with, and it would, indeed, have been folly to repent.

I had sufficient leisure for these and many other reflections during my journey to Ingolstadt, which was long and fatiguing. At length the high white steeple of the town met my eyes. I alighted and was conducted to my solitary apartment to spend the evening as I pleased.

The next morning I delivered my letters of introduction and paid a visit to some of the principal professors. Chance – or rather the evil influence, the Angel of Destruction, which asserted omnipotent sway over me from the moment I turned my reluctant steps from my father's door – led me first to M. Krempe, professor of natural philosophy. He was an uncouth man, but deeply imbued in the secrets of his science. He asked me several questions concerning my progress in the different branches of science appertaining to natural philosophy. I replied carelessly, and partly in contempt, mentioned the names of my alchemists as the principal authors I had studied. The professor stared. 'Have you,' he said, 'really spent your time in studying such nonsense?'

I replied in the affirmative. 'Every minute,' continued M. Krempe with warmth, 'every instant that you have wasted on those books is utterly and entirely lost. You have burdened your memory with exploded systems and useless names. Good God! In what desert land have you lived, where no one was kind enough to inform you that these fancies which you have so greedily imbibed are a thousand years old and as musty as they are ancient? I little expected, in this enlightened and scientific age, to find a disciple of Albertus Magnus and Paracelsus. My dear sir, you must begin your studies entirely anew.'

So saying, he stepped aside and wrote down a list of several books treating of natural philosophy which he desired me to procure, and dismissed me after mentioning that in the beginning of the following week he intended to commence a course of lectures upon natural philosophy in its general relations, and that M. Waldman, a fellow professor, would lecture upon chemistry the alternate days that he omitted.

I returned home not disappointed, for I have said that I had long considered those authors useless whom the professor reprobated; but I returned not at all the more inclined to recur to these studies in any shape. M. Krempe was a little squat man with a gruff voice and a repulsive countenance; the teacher, therefore, did not prepossess me in favour of his pursuits. In rather a too philosophical and connected a strain, perhaps, I have given an account of the conclusions I had come to concerning them in my early years. As a child I had not been content with the results promised by the modern professors of natural science. With a confusion of ideas only to be accounted for by my extreme youth and my want of a guide on such matters, I had retrod the steps of knowledge along the paths of time and exchanged the discoveries of recent enquirers for the dreams of forgotten alchemists. Besides, I had a contempt for the uses of modern natural philosophy. It was very different when the masters of the science sought immortality and power; such views, although futile, were grand; but now the scene was changed. The ambition of the enquirer seemed to limit itself to the annihilation of those visions on which my interest in science was chiefly founded. I was required to exchange chimeras of boundless grandeur for realities of little worth.

Such were my reflections during the first two or three days of my residence at Ingolstadt, which were chiefly spent in becoming acquainted with the localities and the principal residents in my new abode. But as the ensuing week commenced, I thought of the information which M.

Krempe had given me concerning the lectures. And although I could not consent to go and hear that little conceited fellow deliver sentences out of a pulpit, I recollected what he had said of M. Waldman, whom I had never seen, as he had hitherto been out of town.

Partly from curiosity and partly from idleness, I went into the lecturing room, which M. Waldman entered shortly after. This professor was very unlike his colleague. He appeared about fifty years of age, but with an aspect expressive of the greatest benevolence; a few grey hairs covered his temples, but those at the back of his head were nearly black. His person was short but remarkably erect; and his voice the sweetest I had ever heard. He began his lecture by a recapitulation of the history of chemistry and the various improvements made by different men of learning, pronouncing with fervour the names of the most distinguished discoverers. He then took a cursory view of the present state of the science and explained many of its elementary terms. After having made a few preparatory experiments, he concluded with a panegyric upon modern chemistry, the terms of which I shall never forget: –

'The ancient teachers of this science,' said he, 'promised impossibilities and performed nothing. The modern masters promise very little; they know that metals cannot be transmuted and that the elixir of life is a chimera. But these philosophers, whose hands seem only made to dabble in dirt, and their eyes to pore over the microscope or crucible, have indeed performed miracles. They penetrate into the recesses of nature and show how she works in her hiding-places. They ascend into the heavens; they have discovered how the blood circulates, and the nature of the air we breathe. They have acquired new and almost unlimited powers; they can command the thunders of heaven, mimic the earthquake, and even mock the invisible world with its own shadows.'

Such were the professor's words – rather let me say such the words of the fate – enounced to destroy me. As he went on I felt as if my soul were grappling with a palpable enemy; one by one the various keys were touched which formed the mechanism of my being; chord after chord was sounded, and soon my mind was filled with one thought, one conception, one purpose. So much has been done, exclaimed the soul of Frankenstein – more, far more, will I achieve; treading in the steps already marked, I will pioneer a new way, explore unknown powers, and unfold to the world the deepest mysteries of creation.

I closed not my eyes that night. My internal being was in a state of insurrection and turmoil; I felt that order would thence arise, but I had no power to produce it. By degrees, after the morning's dawn, sleep came. I awoke, and my yesternight's thoughts were as a dream. There only remained a resolution to return to my ancient studies and to devote myself to a science for which I believed myself to possess a natural talent. On the same day I paid M. Waldman a visit. His manners in private were even more mild and attractive than in public, for there was a certain dignity in his mien during his lecture which in his own house was replaced by the greatest affability and kindness. I gave him pretty nearly the same account of my former pursuits as I had given to his fellow professor. He heard with attention the little narration concerning my studies and smiled at the names of Cornelius Agrippa and Paracelsus, but without the contempt that M. Krempe had exhibited. He said that 'these were men to whose indefatigable zeal modern philosophers were indebted for most of the foundations of their knowledge. They had left to us, as an easier task, to give new names and arrange in connected classifications the facts which they in a great degree had been the instruments of bringing to light. The labours of men of genius, however erroneously directed, scarcely ever fail in ultimately turning to the solid advantage of mankind.' I listened to his statement, which was delivered without any presumption or affectation, and then added that his lecture had removed my prejudices against modern chemists; I expressed myself in measured terms, with the modesty and deference due from a youth to his instructor, without letting escape (inexperience in life would have made me ashamed) any of the enthusiasm which stimulated my intended labours. I requested his advice concerning the books I ought to procure.

'I am happy,' said M. Waldman, 'to have gained a disciple; and if your application equals your ability, I have no doubt of your success. Chemistry is that branch of natural philosophy in which the greatest improvements have been and may be made; it is on that account that I have made it my peculiar study; but at the same time, I have not neglected the other branches of science. A man would make but a very sorry chemist if he attended to that department of human knowledge alone. If your wish is to become really a man of science and not merely a petty experimentalist, I should advise you to apply to every branch of natural philosophy, including mathematics.'

He then took me into his laboratory and explained to me the uses of his various machines, instructing me as to what I ought to procure and promising me the use of his own when I should have advanced far enough in the science not to derange their mechanism. He also gave me the list of books which I had requested, and I took my leave.

Thus ended a day memorable to me; it decided my future destiny.

# CHAPTER 4

FROM this day natural philosophy, and particularly chemistry, in the most comprehensive sense of the term, became nearly my sole occupation. I read with ardour those works, so full of genius and discrimination, which modern enquirers have written on these subjects. I attended the lectures and cultivated the acquaintance of the men of science of the university, and I found even in M. Krempe a great deal of sound sense and real information, combined, it is true, with a repulsive physiognomy and manners, but not on that account the less valuable. In M. Waldman I found a true friend. His gentleness was never tinged by dogmatism, and his instructions were given with an air of frankness and good nature that banished every idea of pedantry. In a thousand ways he smoothed for me the path of knowledge and made the most abstruse enquiries clear and facile to my apprehension. My application was at first fluctuating and uncertain; it gained strength as I proceeded and soon became so ardent and eager that the stars often disappeared in the light of morning whilst I was yet engaged in my laboratory.

As I applied so closely, it may be easily conceived that my progress was rapid. My ardour was indeed the astonishment of the students, and my proficiency that of the masters. Professor Krempe often asked me, with a sly smile, how Cornelius Agrippa went on? whilst M. Waldman expressed the most heartfelt exultation in my progress. Two years passed in this manner, during which I paid no visit to Geneva, but was engaged, heart and soul, in the pursuit of some discoveries which I hoped to make. None but those who have experienced them can conceive of the enticements of science. In other studies you go as far as others have gone before you, and there is nothing more to know; but in a scientific pursuit there is continual food for discovery and wonder. A mind of moderate capacity which closely pursues one study must infallibly arrive at great proficiency in that study; and I, who continually sought the attainment of one object of pursuit and was solely wrapped up in this, improved so rapidly that at the end of two years I made some discoveries in the improvement of some chemical instruments, which procured me great esteem and admiration at the university. When I had arrived at this point and had become as well acquainted with the theory and practice of natural philosophy as depended on the lessons of any of the professors at Ingolstadt, my residence there being no longer conducive to my improvements, I thought of returning to my friends and my native town, when an incident happened that protracted my stay.

One of the phaenomena which had peculiarly attracted my attention was the structure of the human frame, and, indeed, any animal endued with life. Whence, I often asked myself, did the principle of life proceed? It was a bold question, and one which has ever been considered as a mystery; yet with how many things are we upon the brink of becoming acquainted, if cowardice or carelessness did not restrain our enquiries. I revolved these circumstances in my mind and determined thenceforth to apply myself more particularly to those branches of natural philosophy which relate to physiology. Unless I had been animated by an almost supernatural enthusiasm, my application to this study would have been irksome and almost intolerable. To examine the causes of life, we must first have recourse to death. I became acquainted with the science of anatomy, but this was not sufficient; I must also observe the natural decay and corruption of the human body. In my education my father had taken the greatest precautions that my mind should be impressed with no supernatural horrors. I do not ever remember to have trembled at a tale of superstition or to have feared the apparition of a spirit. Darkness had no effect upon my fancy, and a churchyard was to me merely the receptacle of bodies deprived of life, which, from being the seat of beauty and strength, had become food for the worm. Now I was led to examine the cause and progress of this decay and forced to spend days and nights in vaults and charnel-houses. My attention was fixed upon every object the most insupportable to the delicacy of the human feelings. I saw how the fine form of man was degraded and wasted; I beheld the corruption of death succeed to the blooming cheek of life; I saw how the worm inherited the wonders of the eye and brain. I paused, examining and analysing all the minutiae of causation, as exemplified in the change from life to death, and death to life, until from the midst of this darkness a sudden light broke in upon me – a light so brilliant and wondrous, yet so simple, that while I became dizzy with the immensity of the prospect which it illustrated, I was surprized that among so many men of genius who had directed their enquiries towards the same science, that I alone should be reserved to discover so astonishing a secret.

Remember, I am not recording the vision of a madman. The sun does not more certainly shine in the heavens than that which I now affirm is true. Some miracle might have produced it, yet the stages of the discovery were distinct and probable. After days and nights of incredible labour and fatigue, I succeeded in discovering the cause of generation and life; nay, more, I became myself capable of bestowing animation upon lifeless matter.

The astonishment which I had at first experienced on this discovery soon gave place to delight and rapture. After so much time spent in painful labour, to arrive at once at the summit of my desires was the most gratifying consummation of my toils. But this discovery was so great and overwhelming that all the steps by which I had been progressively led to it were obliterated, and I beheld only the result. What had been the study and desire of the wisest men since the creation of the world was now within my grasp. Not that, like a magic scene, it all opened upon me at once: the information I had obtained was of a nature rather to direct my endeavours so soon as I should point them towards the object of my search than to exhibit that object already accomplished. I was like the Arabian who had been buried with the dead and found a passage to life, aided only by one glimmering and seemingly ineffectual light.

I see by your eagerness and the wonder and hope which your eyes express, my friend, that you expect to be informed of the secret with which I am acquainted; that cannot be; listen patiently until the end of my story, and you will easily perceive why I am reserved upon that subject. I will not lead you on, unguarded and ardent as I then was, to your destruction and infallible misery. Learn from me, if not by my precepts, at least by my example, how dangerous is the acquirement of knowledge and how much happier that man is who believes his native town to be the world, than he who aspires to become greater than his nature will allow.[1]

When I found so astonishing a power placed within my hands, I hesitated a long time concerning the manner in which I should employ it. Although I possessed the capacity of bestowing animation, yet to prepare a frame for the reception of it, with all its intricacies of fibres, muscles, and veins, still remained a work of inconceivable difficulty and labour. I doubted at first whether I should attempt the creation of a being like myself, or one of simpler organization; but my imagination was too much exalted by my first success to permit me to doubt of my ability to give life to an animal as complex and wonderful as man. The materials at present within my command hardly appeared adequate to so arduous an undertaking, but I doubted not that I should ultimately succeed. I prepared myself for a multitude of reverses; my operations might be incessantly baffled, and at last my work be imperfect: yet when I considered the improvement which every day takes place in science and mechanics, I was encouraged to hope my present attempts would at least lay the foundations of future success. Nor could I consider the magnitude and complexity of my plan as any argument of its impracticability. It was with these feelings that I began the creation of a human being. As the minuteness of the parts formed a great hindrance to my speed, I resolved, contrary to my first intention, to make the being of a gigantic stature; that is to say, about eight feet in height, and proportionably large. After having formed this determination and having spent some months in successfully collecting and arranging my materials, I began.

No one can conceive the variety of feelings which bore me onwards, like a hurricane, in the first enthusiasm of success. Life and death appeared to me ideal bounds, which I should first break through, and pour a torrent of light into our dark world. A new species would bless me as its creator and source; many happy and excellent natures would owe their being to me. No father could claim the gratitude of his child so completely as I should deserve theirs. Pursuing these reflections, I thought that if I could bestow animation upon lifeless matter, I might in process of time (although I now found it impossible) renew life where death had apparently devoted the body to corruption.

These thoughts supported my spirits, while I pursued my undertaking with unremitting ardour. My cheek had grown pale with study, and my person had become emaciated with confinement. Sometimes, on the very brink of certainty, I failed; yet still I clung to the hope which the next day or the next hour might realize. One secret which I alone possessed was the hope to which I had dedicated myself; and the moon gazed on my midnight labours, while, with unrelaxed and breathless eagerness, I pursued nature to her hiding-places. Who shall conceive the horrors of my secret toil as I dabbled among the unhallowed damps of the grave or tortured the living animal to animate the lifeless clay? My limbs now tremble, and my eyes swim with the remembrance; but then a resistless and almost frantic impulse urged me forward; I seemed to have lost all soul or sensation but for this one pursuit. It was indeed but a passing trance, that only made me feel with renewed acuteness so soon as, the unnatural stimulus ceasing to operate, I had returned to my old habits. I collected bones from charnel-houses and disturbed, with profane fingers, the tremendous secrets of the human frame. In a solitary chamber, or rather cell, at the top of the house, and separated from all the other apartments by a gallery and staircase, I kept my workshop of filthy creation: my eye-balls were starting from their sockets in attending to the details of my employment. The dissecting room and the slaughter-house furnished many of my materials; and often did my human nature turn with loathing from my occupation, whilst, still urged on by an eagerness which perpetually increased, I brought my work near to a conclusion.

The summer months passed while I was thus engaged, heart and soul, in one pursuit. It was a most beautiful season; never did the fields bestow a more plentiful harvest or the vines yield a more luxuriant vintage: but my eyes were insensible to the charms of nature. And the same feelings which made me neglect the scenes around me caused me also to forget those friends who were so many miles absent, and whom I had not seen for so long a time. I knew my silence disquieted them, and I well remembered the words of my father: 'I know that while you are pleased with yourself you will think of us with affection, and we shall hear regularly from you. You must pardon me if I regard any interruption in your correspondence as a proof that your other duties are equally neglected.'

I knew well therefore what would be my father's feelings, but I could not tear my thoughts from my employment, loathsome in itself, but which had taken an irresistible hold of my imagination. I wished, as it were, to procrastinate all that related to my feelings of affection until the great object, which swallowed up every habit of my nature, should be completed.

I then thought that my father would be unjust if he ascribed my neglect to vice or faultiness on my part, but I am now convinced that he was justified in conceiving that I should not be altogether free from blame. A human being in perfection ought always to preserve a calm and peaceful mind and never to allow passion or a transitory desire to disturb his tranquillity. I do not think that the pursuit of knowledge is an exception to this rule. If the study to which you apply yourself has a tendency to weaken your affections and to destroy your taste for those simple pleasures in which no alloy can possibly mix, then that study is certainly unlawful, that is to say, not befitting the human mind. If this rule were always observed; if no man allowed any pursuit whatsoever to interfere with the tranquillity of his domestic affections, Greece had not been enslaved, Caesar would have spared his country, America would have been discovered more gradually, and the empires of Mexico and Peru had not been destroyed.

But I forget that I am moralizing in the most interesting part of my tale, and your looks remind me to proceed.

My father made no reproach in his letters and only took notice of my silence by enquiring into my occupations more particularly than before. Winter, spring, and summer passed away during my labours; but I did not watch the blossom or the expanding leaves – sights which before always yielded me supreme delight – so deeply was I engrossed in my occupation. The leaves of that year had withered before my work drew near to a close, and now every day showed me more plainly how well I had succeeded. But my enthusiasm was checked by my anxiety, and I appeared rather like one doomed by slavery to toil in the mines, or any other unwholesome trade than an artist occupied by his favourite employment. Every night I was oppressed by a slow fever, and I became nervous to a most painful degree; the fall of a leaf startled me, and I shunned my fellow creatures as if I had been guilty of a crime. Sometimes I grew alarmed at the wreck I perceived that I had become; the energy of my purpose alone sustained me: my labours would soon end, and I believed that exercise and amusement would then drive away incipient disease; and I promised myself both of these when my creation should be complete.

# CHAPTER 5

It was on a dreary night of November that I beheld the accomplishment of my toils. With an anxiety that almost amounted to agony, I collected the instruments of life around me, that I might infuse a spark of being into the lifeless thing that lay at my feet. It was already one in the morning; the rain pattered dismally against the panes, and my candle was nearly burnt out, when, by the glimmer of the half-extinguished light, I saw the dull yellow eye of the creature open; it breathed hard, and a convulsive motion agitated its limbs.

How can I describe my emotions at this catastrophe, or how delineate the wretch whom with such infinite pains and care I had endeavoured to form? His limbs were in proportion, and I had selected his features as beautiful. Beautiful! Great God! His yellow skin scarcely covered the work of muscles and arteries beneath; his hair was of a lustrous black, and flowing; his teeth of a pearly whiteness; but these luxuriances only formed a more horrid contrast with his watery eyes, that seemed almost of the same colour as the dun-white sockets in which they were set, his shrivelled complexion and straight black lips.

The different accidents of life are not so changeable as the feelings of human nature. I had worked hard for nearly two years, for the sole purpose of infusing life into an inanimate body. For this I had deprived myself of rest and health. I had desired it with an ardour that far exceeded moderation; but now that I had finished, the beauty of the dream vanished, and breathless horror and disgust filled my heart. Unable to endure the aspect of the being I had created, I rushed out of the room and continued a long time traversing my bedchamber, unable to compose my mind to sleep. At length lassitude succeeded to the tumult I had before endured, and I threw myself on the bed in my clothes, endeavouring to seek a few moments of forgetfulness. But it was in vain; I slept, indeed, but I was disturbed by the wildest dreams. I thought I saw Elizabeth, in the bloom of health, walking in the streets of Ingolstadt. Delighted and surprized, I embraced her, but as I imprinted the first kiss on her lips, they became livid with the hue of death; her features appeared to change, and I thought that I held the corpse of my dead mother in my arms; a shroud enveloped her form, and I saw the grave-worms crawling in the folds of the flannel. I started from my sleep with horror; a cold dew covered my forehead, my teeth chattered, and every limb became convulsed; when, by the dim and yellow light of the moon, as it forced its way through the window shutters, I beheld the wretch – the miserable monster whom I had created. He held up the curtain of the bed; and his eyes, if eyes they may be called, were fixed on me. His jaws opened, and he muttered some inarticulate sounds, while a grin wrinkled his cheeks. He might have spoken, but I did not hear; one hand was stretched out, seemingly to detain me, but I escaped and rushed downstairs. I took refuge in the courtyard belonging to the house which I inhabited, where I remained during the rest of the night, walking up and down in the greatest agitation, listening attentively, catching and fearing each sound as if it were to announce the approach of the daemoniacal corpse to which I had so miserably given life.

Oh! No mortal could support the horror of that countenance. A mummy again endued with animation could not be so hideous as that wretch. I had gazed on him while unfinished; he was ugly then, but when those muscles and joints were rendered capable of motion, it became a thing such as even Dante could not have conceived.

I passed the night wretchedly. Sometimes my pulse beat so quickly and hardly that I felt the palpitation of every artery; at others, I nearly sank to the ground through languor and extreme weakness. Mingled with this horror, I felt the bitterness of disappointment; dreams that had been my food and pleasant rest for so long a space were now become a hell to me; and the change was so rapid, the overthrow so complete!

Morning, dismal and wet, at length dawned and discovered[1] to my sleepless and aching eyes the church of Ingolstadt, its white steeple and clock, which indicated the sixth hour. The porter opened the gates of the court, which had that night been my asylum, and I issued into the streets, pacing them with quick steps, as if I sought to avoid the wretch whom I feared every turning of the street would present to my view. I did not dare return to the apartment which I inhabited, but felt impelled to hurry on, although drenched by the rain which poured from a black and comfortless sky.

I continued walking in this manner for some time, endeavouring by bodily exercise to ease the load that weighed upon my mind. I traversed the streets without any clear conception of where I was or what I was doing. My heart palpitated in the sickness of fear, and I hurried on with irregular steps, not daring to look about me:

> Like one, that on a lonesome road
>   Doth walk in fear and dread,
> And having once turned round walks on,
>   And turns no more his head;
> Because he knows, a frightful fiend
>   Doth close behind him tread.[2]

Continuing thus, I came at length opposite to the inn at which the various diligences and carriages usually stopped. Here I paused, I knew not why; but I remained some minutes with my eyes fixed on a coach that was coming towards me from the other end of the street. As it drew nearer I observed that it was the Swiss diligence; it stopped just where I was standing, and on the door being opened, I perceived Henry Clerval, who, on seeing me, instantly sprung out. 'My dear Frankenstein,' exclaimed he, 'how glad I am to see you! How fortunate that you should be here at the very moment of my alighting!'

Nothing could equal my delight on seeing Clerval; his presence brought back to my thoughts my father, Elizabeth, and all those scenes of home so dear to my recollection. I grasped his hand, and in a moment forgot my horror and misfortune; I felt suddenly, and for the first time during many months, calm and serene joy. I welcomed my friend, therefore, in the most cordial manner, and we walked towards my college. Clerval continued talking for some time about our mutual friends and his own good fortune in being permitted to come to Ingolstadt. 'You may easily believe,' said he, 'how great was the difficulty to persuade my father that all necessary knowledge was not comprised in the noble art of bookkeeping; and, indeed, I believe I left him incredulous to the last, for his constant answer to my unwearied intreaties was the same as that to the Dutch schoolmaster in *The Vicar of Wakefield*: "I have ten thousand florins a year without Greek, I eat heartily without Greek."[3] But his affection for me at length overcame his dislike of learning, and he has permitted me to undertake a voyage of discovery to the land of knowledge.'

'It gives me the greatest delight to see you; but tell me how you left my father, brothers, and Elizabeth.'

'Very well, and very happy, only a little uneasy that they hear from you so seldom. By the bye, I mean to lecture you a little upon their account myself. But, my dear Frankenstein,' continued he, stopping short and gazing full in my face, 'I did not before remark how very ill you appear; so thin and pale; you look as if you had been watching for several nights.'

'You have guessed right; I have lately been so deeply engaged in one occupation that I have not allowed myself sufficient rest, as you see; but I hope, I sincerely hope, that all these employments are now at an end and that I am at length free.'

I trembled excessively; I could not endure to think of, and far less to allude to, the occurrences of the preceding night. I walked with a quick pace, and we soon arrived at my college. I then reflected, and the thought made me shiver, that the creature whom I had left in my apartment might still be there, alive and walking about. I dreaded to behold this monster, but I feared still more that Henry should see him. Intreating him, therefore, to remain a few minutes at the bottom of the stairs, I darted up towards my own room. My hand was already on the lock of the door before I recollected myself. I then paused, and a cold shivering came over me. I threw the door forcibly open, as children are accustomed to do when they expect a spectre to stand in waiting for them on the other side; but nothing appeared. I stepped fearfully in: the apartment was empty, and my bedroom was also freed from its hideous guest. I could hardly believe that so great a good fortune could have befallen me, but when I became assured that my enemy had indeed fled, I clapped my hands for joy and ran down to Clerval.

We ascended into my room, and the servant presently brought breakfast; but I was unable to contain myself. It was not joy only that possessed me; I felt my flesh tingle with excess of sensitiveness, and my pulse beat rapidly. I was unable to remain for a single instant in the same place; I jumped over the chairs, clapped my hands, and laughed aloud. Clerval at first attributed my unusual spirits to joy on his arrival, but when he observed me more attentively, he saw a wildness in my eyes for which he could not account, and my loud, unrestrained, heartless laughter frightened and astonished him.

'My dear Victor,' cried he, 'what, for God's sake, is the matter? Do not laugh in that manner. How ill you are! What is the cause of all this?'

'Do not ask me,' cried I, putting my hands before my

eyes, for I thought I saw the dreaded spectre glide into the room; '*he* can tell. Oh, save me! Save me!' I imagined that the monster seized me; I struggled furiously and fell down in a fit.

Poor Clerval! What must have been his feelings? A meeting, which he anticipated with such joy, so strangely turned to bitterness. But I was not the witness of his grief, for I was lifeless and did not recover my senses for a long, long time.

This was the commencement of a nervous fever which confined me for several months. During all that time Henry was my only nurse. I afterwards learned that, knowing my father's advanced age and unfitness for so long a journey, and how wretched my sickness would make Elizabeth, he spared them this grief by concealing the extent of my disorder. He knew that I could not have a more kind and attentive nurse than himself; and, firm in the hope he felt of my recovery, he did not doubt that, instead of doing harm, he performed the kindest action that he could towards them.

But I was in reality very ill, and surely nothing but the unbounded and unremitting attentions of my friend could have restored me to life. The form of the monster on whom I had bestowed existence was forever before my eyes, and I raved incessantly concerning him. Doubtless my words surprised Henry; he at first believed them to be the wanderings of my disturbed imagination, but the pertinacity with which I continually recurred to the same subject persuaded him that my disorder indeed owed its origin to some uncommon and terrible event.

By very slow degrees, and with frequent relapses that alarmed and grieved my friend, I recovered. I remember the first time I became capable of observing outward objects with any kind of pleasure, I perceived that the fallen leaves had disappeared and that the young buds were shooting forth from the trees that shaded my window. It was a divine spring, and the season contributed greatly to my convalescence. I felt also sentiments of joy and affection revive in my bosom; my gloom disappeared, and in a short time I became as cheerful as before I was attacked by the fatal passion.

'Dearest Clerval,' exclaimed I, 'how kind, how very good you are to me. This whole winter, instead of being spent in study, as you promised yourself, has been consumed in my sick room. How shall I ever repay you? I feel the greatest remorse for the disappointment of which I have been the occasion, but you will forgive me.'

'You will repay me entirely if you do not discompose yourself, but get well as fast as you can; and since you appear in such good spirits, I may speak to you on one subject, may I not?'

I trembled. One subject! What could it be? Could he allude to an object on whom I dared not even think?

'Compose yourself,' said Clerval, who observed my change of colour, 'I will not mention it if it agitates you; but your father and cousin would be very happy if they received a letter from you in your own handwriting. They hardly know how ill you have been and are uneasy at your long silence.'

'Is that all, my dear Henry? How could you suppose that my first thought would not fly towards those dear, dear friends whom I love and who are so deserving of my love?'

'If this is your present temper, my friend, you will perhaps be glad to see a letter that has been lying here some days for you; it is from your cousin, I believe.'

# CHAPTER 6

CLERVAL then put the following letter into my hands. It was from my own Elizabeth:

'My dearest Cousin,

'You have been ill, very ill, and even the constant letters of dear kind Henry are not sufficient to reassure me on your account. You are forbidden to write – to hold a pen; yet one word from you, dear Victor, is necessary to calm our apprehensions. For a long time I have thought that each post would bring this line, and my persuasions have restrained my uncle from undertaking a journey to Ingolstadt. I have prevented his encountering the inconveniences and perhaps dangers of so long a journey, yet how often have I regretted not being able to perform it myself! I figure to myself that the task of attending on your sickbed has devolved on some mercenary old nurse, who could never guess your wishes nor minister to them with the care and affection of your poor cousin. Yet that is over now: Clerval writes that indeed you are getting better. I eagerly hope that you will confirm this intelligence soon in your own handwriting.

'Get well – and return to us. You will find a happy, cheerful home and friends who love you dearly. Your father's health is vigorous, and he asks but to see you, but to be assured that you are well; and not a care will ever cloud his benevolent countenance. How pleased you would be to remark the improvement of our Ernest! He is now sixteen and full of activity and spirit. He is desirous to be a true Swiss and to enter into foreign service, but we cannot part with him, at least until his elder brother return to us. My uncle is not pleased with the idea of a military career in a distant country, but Ernest never had your powers of application. He looks upon study as an odious fetter; his time is spent in the open air, climbing the hills or rowing on the lake. I fear that he will become an idler unless we yield the point and permit him to enter on the profession which he has selected.

'Little alteration, except the growth of our dear children, has taken place since you left us. The blue lake and snow-clad mountains – they never change; and I think our placid home and our contented hearts are regulated by the same immutable laws. My trifling occupations take up my time and amuse me, and I am rewarded for any exertions by seeing none but happy, kind faces around me. Since you left us, but one change has taken place in our little household. Do you remember on what occasion Justine Moritz entered our family? Probably you do not; I will relate her history, therefore, in a few words. Madame Moritz, her mother, was a widow with four children, of whom Justine was the third. This girl had always been the favourite of her father, but through a strange perversity, her mother could not endure her, and after the death of M. Moritz, treated her very ill. My aunt observed this, and when Justine was twelve years of age, prevailed on her mother to allow her to live at our house. The republican institutions of our country have produced simpler and happier manners than those which prevail in the great monarchies that surround it. Hence there is less distinction between the several classes of its inhabitants; and the lower orders, being neither so poor nor so despised, their manners are more refined and moral. A servant in Geneva does not mean the same thing as a servant in France and England. Justine, thus received in our family, learned the duties of a servant, a condition which, in our fortunate country, does not include the idea of ignorance and a sacrifice of the dignity of a human being.

'Justine, you may remember, was a great favourite of yours; and I recollect you once remarked that if you were in an ill humour, one glance from Justine could dissipate it, for the same reason that Ariosto gives concerning the beauty of Angelica 1 – she looked so frank-hearted and happy. My aunt conceived a great attachment for her, by which she was induced to give her an education superior to that which she had at first intended. This benefit was fully repaid; Justine was the most grateful little creature in the world: I do not mean that she made any professions; I never heard one pass her lips, but you could see by her eyes that she almost adored her protectress. Although her disposition was gay and in many respects inconsiderate, yet she paid the greatest attention to every gesture of my aunt. She thought her the model of all excellence and endeavoured to imitate her phraseology and manners, so that even now she often reminds me of her.

'When my dearest aunt died every one was too much occupied in their own grief to notice poor Justine, who had attended her illness with the most anxious affection. Poor Justine was very ill, but other trials were reserved for her.

'One by one, her brothers and sister died; and her mother, with the exception of her neglected daughter, was left childless. The conscience of the woman was troubled; she began to think that the deaths of her favourites was a judgment from heaven to chastise her partiality. She was a Roman Catholic, and I believe her confessor confirmed the idea which she had conceived. Accordingly, a few months after your departure for Ingolstadt, Justine was called home by her repentant mother. Poor girl! She wept when she quitted our house; she was much altered since the death of my aunt; grief had given softness and a winning mildness to her manners which had before been remarkable for vivacity. Nor was her residence at her mother's house of a nature to restore her gaiety. The poor woman was very vacillating in her repentance. She sometimes begged Justine to forgive her unkindness but much oftener accused her of having caused the deaths of her brothers and sister. Perpetual fretting at length threw Madame Moritz into a decline, which at first increased her irritability, but she is now at peace forever. She died on the first approach of cold weather, at the beginning of this last winter. Justine has returned to us, and I assure you I love her tenderly. She is very clever and gentle and extremely pretty; as I mentioned before, her mien and her expressions continually remind me of my dear aunt.

'I must say also a few words to you, my dear cousin, of little darling William. I wish you could see him; he is very tall of his age, with sweet laughing blue eyes, dark eyelashes, and curling hair. When he smiles, two little dimples appear on each cheek, which are rosy with health. He has already had one or two little *wives*, but Louisa Biron is his favourite, a pretty little girl of five years of age.

'Now, dear Victor, I dare say you wish to be indulged in a little gossip concerning the good people of Geneva. The pretty Miss Mansfield has already received the congratulatory visits on her approaching marriage with a young Englishman, John Melbourne, Esq. Her ugly sister, Manon, married M. Duvillard, the rich banker, last autumn. Your favourite schoolfellow, Louis Manoir, has suffered misfortunes since the departure of Clerval from Geneva. But he has already recovered his spirits and is reported to be on the point of marrying a very lively, pretty Frenchwoman, Madame Tavernier. She is a widow, and much older than Manoir, but she is very much admired and a favourite with every body.

'I have written myself into better spirits, dear cousin; but my anxiety returns upon me as I conclude. Write, dearest Victor – one line – one word will be a blessing to us. Ten thousand thanks to Henry for his kindness, his affection, and his many letters; we are sincerely grateful. Adieu! My cousin, take care of yourself, and, I intreat you, write!

'Elizabeth Lavenza

'Geneva, March 18th, 17—'

'Dear, dear Elizabeth!' I exclaimed when I had read her letter. 'I will write instantly and relieve them from the anxiety they must feel.' I wrote, and this exertion greatly fatigued me; but my convalescence had commenced, and proceeded regularly. In another fortnight I was able to leave my chamber.

One of my first duties on my recovery was to introduce Clerval to the several professors of the university. In doing this, I underwent a kind of rough usage, ill befitting the wounds that my mind had sustained. Ever since the fatal night, the end of my labours, and the beginning of my misfortunes, I had conceived a violently antipathy even to the name of natural philosophy. When I was otherwise quite restored to health, the sight of a chemical instrument would renew all the agony of my nervous symptoms. Henry saw this and had removed all my apparatus from my view. He had also changed my apartment, for he perceived that I had acquired a dislike for the room which had previously been my laboratory. But these cares of Clerval were made of no avail when I visited the professors. M. Waldman inflicted torture when he praised, with kindness and warmth, the astonishing progress I had made in the sciences. He soon perceived that I disliked the subject, but not guessing the real cause, he attributed my feelings to modesty and changed the subject from my improvement to the science itself, with a desire, as I evidently saw, of drawing me out. What could I do? He meant to please, and he tormented me. I felt as if he had placed carefully, one by one, in my view those instruments which were to be afterwards used in putting me to a slow and cruel death. I writhed under his words yet dared not exhibit the pain I felt. Clerval, whose eyes and feelings were always quick in discerning the sensations of others, declined the subject, alleging, in excuse, his total ignorance; and the conversation took a more general turn. I thanked my friend from my heart, but I did not speak. I saw plainly that he was surprized, but he never attempted to draw my secret from me; and although I loved him with a mixture of affection and reverence that knew no bounds, yet I could never persuade myself to confide to him that event which was so often present to my recollection but which I feared the detail to another would only impress more deeply.

M. Krempe was not equally docile; and in my condition at that time, of almost insupportable sensitiveness, his harsh, blunt encomiums gave me even more pain than the benevolent approbation of M. Waldman. 'D—n the fellow!' cried he. 'Why, M. Clerval, I assure you he has outstripped us all. Aye, stare if you please; but it is nevertheless true. A youngster who, but a few years ago, believed in Cornelius Agrippa as firmly as in the Gospel, has now set himself at the head of the university; and if he is not soon pulled down, we shall all be out of countenance. Ay, ay,' continued he, observing my face expressive of suffering, 'M. Frankenstein is modest, an excellent quality in a young man. Young men should be diffident of themselves, you know, M. Clerval; I was myself when young, but that wears out in a very short time.'

M. Krempe had now commenced a eulogy on himself,

which happily turned the conversation from a subject that was so annoying to me.

Clerval had never sympathized in my tastes for natural science, and his literary pursuits differed wholly from those which had occupied me. He came to the university with the design of making himself complete master of the Oriental languages, as thus he should open a field for the plan of life he had marked out for himself. Resolved to pursue no inglorious career, he turned his eyes towards the East as affording scope for his spirit of enterprize. The Persian, Arabic, and Sanskrit languages engaged his attention, and I was easily induced to enter on the same studies. Idleness had ever been irksome to me, and now that I wished to fly from reflection and hated my former studies, I felt great relief in being the fellow pupil with my friend, and found not only instruction but consolation in the works of the Orientalists. I did not, like him, attempt a critical knowledge of their dialects, for I did not contemplate making any other use of them than temporary amusement. I read merely to understand their meaning, and they well repaid my labours. Their melancholy is soothing, and their joy elevating, to a degree I never experienced in studying the authors of any other country. When you read their writings, life appears to consist in a warm sun and a garden of roses, in the smiles and frowns of a fair enemy, and the fire that consumes your own heart. How different from the manly and heroical poetry of Greece and Rome!

Summer passed away in these occupations, and my return to Geneva was fixed for the latter end of autumn; but being delayed by several accidents, winter and snow arrived, the roads were deemed impassable, and my journey was retarded until the ensuing spring. I felt this delay very bitterly, for I longed to see my native town and my beloved friends. My return had only been delayed so long from an unwillingness to leave Clerval in a strange place before he had become acquainted with any of its inhabitants. The winter, however, was spent cheerfully, and although the spring was uncommonly late, when it came its beauty compensated for its dilatoriness.

The month of May had already commenced, and I expected the letter daily which was to fix the date of my departure, when Henry proposed a pedestrian tour in the environs of Ingolstadt, that I might bid a personal farewell to the country I had so long inhabited. I acceded with pleasure to this proposition: I was fond of exercise, and Clerval had always been my favourite companion in the rambles of this nature that I had taken among the scenes of my native country.

We passed a fortnight in these perambulations; my health and spirits had long been restored, and they gained additional strength from the salubrious air I breathed, the natural incidents of our progress, and the conversation of my friend. Study had before secluded me from the intercourse of my fellow creatures and rendered me unsocial, but Clerval called forth the better feelings of my heart; he again taught me to love the aspect of nature and the cheerful faces of children. Excellent friend! How sincerely did you love me and endeavour to elevate my mind until it was on a level with your own! A selfish pursuit had cramped and narrowed me until your gentleness and affection warmed and opened my senses; I became the same happy creature who, a few years ago, loved and beloved by all, had no sorrow or care. When happy, inanimate nature had the power of bestowing on me the most delightful sensations. A serene sky and verdant fields filled me with ecstasy. The present season was indeed divine; the flowers of spring bloomed in the hedges, while those of summer were already in bud. I was undisturbed by thoughts which during the preceding year had pressed upon me, notwithstanding my endeavours to throw them off, with an invincible burden.

Henry rejoiced in my gaiety and sincerely sympathized in my feelings; he exerted himself to amuse me, while he expressed the sensations that filled his soul. The resources of his mind on this occasion were truly astonishing; his conversation was full of imagination, and very often, in imitation of the Persian and Arabic writers, he invented tales of wonderful fancy and passion. At other times he repeated my favourite poems or drew me out into arguments, which he supported with great ingenuity.

We returned to our college on a Sunday afternoon; the peasants were dancing, and everyone we met appeared gay and happy. My own spirits were high, and I bounded along with feelings of unbridled joy and hilarity.

# CHAPTER 7

On my return, I found the following letter from my father:

'My dear Victor,

'You have probably waited impatiently for a letter to fix the date of your return to us, and I was at first tempted to write only a few lines, merely mentioning the day on which I should expect you. But that would be a cruel kindness, and I dare not do it. What would be your surprize, my son, when you expect a happy and glad welcome, to behold, on the contrary, tears and wretchedness? And how, Victor, can I relate our misfortune? Absence cannot have rendered you callous to our joys and griefs; and how shall I inflict pain on my long-absent son? I wish to prepare you for the woeful news, but I know it is impossible; even now your eye skims over the page to seek the words which are to convey to you the horrible tidings.

'William is dead! That sweet child, whose smiles delighted and warmed my heart, who was so gentle, yet so gay! Victor, he is murdered!

'I will not attempt to console you, but will simply relate the circumstances of the transaction.

'Last Thursday (May 7th) I, my niece, and your two brothers went to walk in Plainpalais. The evening was warm and serene, and we prolonged our walk farther than usual. It was already dusk before we thought of returning, and then we discovered that William and Ernest, who had gone on before, were not to be found. We accordingly rested on a seat until they should return. Presently Ernest came and enquired if we had seen his brother; he said that he had been playing with him, that William had run away to hide himself, and that he vainly sought for him, and afterwards waited for him a long time, but he did not return.

'This account rather alarmed us, and we continued to search for him until night fell, when Elizabeth conjectured that he might have returned to the house. He was not there. We returned again, with torches, for I could not rest when I thought that my sweet boy had lost himself and was exposed to all the damps and dews of night; Elizabeth also suffered extreme anguish. About five in the morning I discovered my lovely boy, whom the night before I had seen blooming and active in health, stretched on the grass livid and motionless; the print of the murderer's finger was on his neck.

'He was conveyed home, and the anguish that was visible in my countenance betrayed the secret to Elizabeth. She was very earnest to see the corpse. At first I attempted to prevent her, but she persisted, and entering the room where it lay, hastily examined the neck of the victim, and clasping her hands, exclaimed, "Oh, God! I have murdered my darling child!"

'She fainted, and was restored with extreme difficulty. When she again lived, it was only to weep and sigh. She told me that that same evening William had teased her to let him wear a very valuable miniature that she possessed of your mother. This picture is gone and was doubtless the temptation which urged the murderer to the deed. We have no trace of him at present, although our exertions to discover him are unremitted; but they will not restore my beloved William!

'Come, dearest Victor; you alone can console Elizabeth. She weeps continually and accuses herself unjustly as the cause of his death; her words pierce my heart. We are all unhappy, but will not that be an additional motive for you, my son, to return and be our comforter? Your dear mother! Alas, Victor! I now say, thank God she did not live to witness the cruel, miserable death of her youngest darling!

'Come, Victor; not brooding thoughts of vengeance against the assassin, but with feelings of peace and gentleness, that will heal, instead of festering, the wounds of our minds. Enter the house of mourning, my friend, but with kindness and affection for those who love you, and not with hatred for your enemies.

'Your affectionate and afflicted father,

'Alphonse Frankenstein

'Geneva, May 12th, 17—'

Clerval, who had watched my countenance as I read this letter, was surprized to observe the despair that succeeded to the joy I at first expressed on receiving news from my friends. I threw the letter on the table and covered my face with my hands.

'My dear Frankenstein,' exclaimed Henry when he perceived me weep with bitterness, 'are you always to be unhappy? My dear friend, what has happened?'

I motioned to him to take up the letter, while I walked up and down the room in the extremest agitation. Tears also gushed from the eyes of Clerval as he read the account of my misfortune.

'I can offer you no consolation, my friend,' said he; 'your disaster is irreparable. What do you intend to do?'

'To go instantly to Geneva; come with me, Henry, to order the horses.'

During our walk Clerval endeavoured to say a few words of consolation; he could only express his heartfelt sympathy. 'Poor William!' said he. 'Dear lovely child, he now sleeps with his angel mother! Who that had seen him bright and joyous in his young beauty but must weep over his untimely loss! To die so miserably; to feel the murderer's grasp! How much more a murderer, that could destroy such radiant innocence! Poor little fellow! One only consolation have we; his friends mourn and weep, but he is at rest. The pang is over, his sufferings are at an end forever. A sod covers his gentle form, and he knows no pain. He can no longer be a subject for pity; we must reserve that for his miserable survivors.'

Clerval spoke thus as we hurried through the streets; the words impressed themselves on my mind, and I remembered them afterwards in solitude. But now, as soon as the horses arrived, I hurried into a cabriolet and bade farewell to my friend.

My journey was very melancholy. At first I wished to hurry on, for I longed to console and sympathize with my loved and sorrowing friends; but when I drew near my native town, I slackened my progress. I could hardly sustain the multitude of feelings that crowded into my mind. I passed through scenes familiar to my youth but which I had not seen for nearly six years. How altered every thing might be during that time! One sudden and desolating change had taken place; but a thousand little circumstances might have by degrees worked other alterations, which, although they were done more tranquilly, might not be the less decisive. Fear overcame me; I dared not advance, dreading a thousand nameless evils that made me tremble, although I was unable to define them.

I remained two days at Lausanne in this painful state of mind. I contemplated the lake; the waters were placid, all around was calm, and the snowy mountains, 'the palaces of nature', were not changed. By degrees the calm and heavenly scene restored me, and I continued my journey towards Geneva.

The road ran by the side of the lake, which became narrower as I approached my native town. I discovered more distinctly the black sides of Jura and the bright summit of Mont Blanc. I wept like a child. 'Dear mountains! My own beautiful lake! How do you welcome your wanderer? Your summits are clear; the sky and lake are blue and placid. Is this to prognosticate peace or to mock at my unhappiness?'

I fear, my friend, that I shall render myself tedious by dwelling on these preliminary circumstances, but they were days of comparative happiness, and I think of them with pleasure. My country, my beloved country! Who but a native can tell the delight I took in again beholding thy streams, thy mountains, and more than all, thy lovely lake!

Yet, as I drew nearer home, grief and fear again overcame me. Night also closed around, and when I could hardly see the dark mountains, I felt still more gloomily. The picture appeared a vast and dim scene of evil, and I foresaw obscurely that I was destined to become the most wretched of human beings. Alas! I prophesied truly, and failed only in one single circumstance, that in all the misery I imagined and dreaded, I did not conceive the hundredth part of the anguish I was destined to endure.

It was completely dark when I arrived in the environs of Geneva; the gates of the town were already shut, and I was obliged to pass the night at Secheron, a village at the distance of half a league from the city. The sky was serene, and as I was unable to rest, I resolved to visit the spot where my poor William had been murdered. As I could not pass through the town, I was obliged to cross the lake in a boat to arrive at Plainpalais. During this short voyage I saw the lightnings playing on the summit of Mont Blanc in the most beautiful figures. The storm appeared to approach rapidly; and, on landing, I ascended a low hill, that I might observe its progress. It advanced; the heavens were clouded, and I soon felt the rain coming slowly in large drops, but its violence quickly increased.

I quitted my seat and walked on, although the darkness and storm increased every minute and the thunder burst with a terrific crash over my head. It was echoed from Salêve, the Juras, and the Alps of Savoy; vivid flashes of lightning dazzled my eyes, illuminating the lake, making it appear like a vast sheet of fire; then for an instant every thing seemed of a pitchy darkness, until the eye recovered itself from the preceding flash. The storm, as is often the case in Switzerland, appeared at once in various parts of the heavens. The most violent storm hung exactly north of the town, over that part of the lake which lies between the promontory of Belrive and the village of Copêt. Another storm enlightened Jura with faint flashes, and another darkened and sometimes disclosed the Môle, a peaked mountain to the east of the lake.

While I watched the tempest, so beautiful yet terrific, I wandered on with a hasty step. This noble war in the sky elevated my spirits; I clasped my hands and exclaimed aloud, 'William, dear angel! This is thy funeral, this thy dirge!' As I said these words, I perceived in the gloom a figure which stole from behind a clump of trees near me; I stood fixed, gazing intently; I could not be mistaken. A flash of lightning illuminated the object and discovered its shape plainly to me; its gigantic stature, and the deformity of its aspect, more hideous than belongs to humanity, instantly informed me that it was the wretch, the filthy daemon to whom I had given life. What did he there? Could he be (I shuddered at the conception) the murderer of my brother? No sooner did that idea cross my imagination than I became convinced of its truth; my teeth chattered, and I was forced to lean against a tree for support. The figure passed me quickly, and I lost it in the gloom. Nothing in human shape could have destroyed that fair child. *He* was the murderer! I could not doubt it. The mere presence of the idea was an irresistible proof of the fact. I thought of pursuing the devil, but it would have been in vain, for another flash discovered him to me hanging among the rocks of the nearly perpendicular ascent of Mount Salêve, a hill that bounds Plainpalais on the south. He soon reached the summit and disappeared.

I remained motionless. The thunder ceased, but the rain still continued, and the scene was enveloped in an impenetrable darkness. I revolved in my mind the events which I had until now sought to forget: the whole train of my progress towards the creation, the appearance of the work of my own hands alive at my bedside, its departure. Two years had now nearly elapsed since the night on which he first received life, and was this his first crime? Alas! I had turned loose into the world a depraved wretch whose delight was in carnage and misery; had he not murdered my brother?

No one can conceive the anguish I suffered during the remainder of the night, which I spent, cold and wet, in the open air. But I did not feel the inconvenience of the weather; my imagination was busy in scenes of evil and despair. I considered the being whom I had cast among mankind and endowed with the will and power to effect purposes of horror, such as the deed which he had now done, nearly in the light of my own vampire, my own spirit let loose from the grave and forced to destroy all that was dear to me.[1]

Day dawned, and I directed my steps towards the town. The gates were open, and I hastened to my father's house. My first thought was to discover what I knew of the murderer and cause instant pursuit to be made. But I paused when I reflected on the story that I had to tell. A being whom I myself had formed, and endued with life, had met me at midnight among the precipices of an inaccessible mountain. I remembered also the nervous fever with which I had been seized just at the time that I dated my creation, and which would give an air of delirium to a tale otherwise so utterly improbable. I well knew that if any other had communicated such a relation to me, I should have looked upon it as the ravings of insanity. Besides, the strange nature of the animal would elude all pursuit, even if I were so far credited as to persuade my relatives to commence it. And then of what use would be pursuit? Who could arrest a creature capable of scaling the overhanging sides of Mount Salêve? These reflections determined me, and I resolved to remain silent.

It was about five in the morning when I entered my father's house. I told the servants not to disturb the family and went into the library to attend their usual hour of rising.

Six years had elapsed, passed as a dream but for one indelible trace, and I stood in the same place where I had last embraced my father before my departure for Ingolstadt. Beloved and venerable parent! He still remained to me. I gazed on the picture of my mother which stood over the mantelpiece. It was a historical subject, painted at my father's desire, and represented Caroline Beaufort in an agony of despair, kneeling by the coffin of her dead father. Her garb was rustic and her cheek pale, but there was an air of dignity and beauty that hardly permitted the sentiment of pity. Below this picture was a miniature of William, and my tears flowed when I looked upon it. While I was thus engaged, Ernest entered; he had heard me arrive and hastened to welcome me. He expressed a sorrowful delight to see me. 'Welcome, my dearest Victor,' said he. 'Ah! I wish you had come three months ago, and then you would have found us all joyous and delighted. You come to us now to share a misery which nothing can alleviate; yet your presence will, I hope, revive our father, who seems sinking under his misfortune; and your persuasions will induce poor Elizabeth to cease her vain and tormenting self-accusations. Poor William! He was our darling and our pride!'

Tears, unrestrained, fell from my brother's eyes; a sense of mortal agony crept over my frame. Before, I had only imagined the wretchedness of my desolated home; the reality came on me as a new and a not less terrible disaster. I tried to calm Ernest; I enquired more minutely concerning my father and her I named my cousin.

'She most of all,' said Ernest, 'requires consolation; she accused herself of having caused the death of my brother, and that made her very wretched. But since the murderer has been discovered—'

'The murderer discovered! Good God! How can that be? Who could attempt to pursue him? It is impossible; one might as well try to overtake the winds or confine a mountain stream with a straw. I saw him too; he was free last night!'

'I do not know what you mean,' replied my brother in accents of wonder, 'but to us the discovery we have made completes our misery. No one would believe it at first; and even now Elizabeth will not be convinced, notwithstanding all the evidence. Indeed, who would credit that Justine Moritz, who was so amiable and fond of all the family, could suddenly become capable of so frightful, so appalling a crime?'

'Justine Moritz! Poor, poor girl, is she the accused? But

it is wrongfully; every one knows that; no one believes it, surely, Ernest?'

'No one did at first, but several circumstances came out that have almost forced conviction upon us; and her own behaviour has been so confused as to add to the evidence of facts a weight that, I fear, leaves no hope for doubt. But she will be tried today, and you will then hear all.'

He related that, the morning on which the murder of poor William had been discovered, Justine had been taken ill and confined to her bed for several days. During this interval one of the servants, happening to examine the apparel she had worn on the night of the murder, had discovered in her pocket the picture of my mother, which had been judged to be the temptation of the murderer. The servant instantly showed it to one of the others, who, without saying a word to any of the family, went to a magistrate; and, upon their deposition, Justine was apprehended. On being charged with the fact, the poor girl confirmed the suspicion in a great measure by her extreme confusion of manner.

This was a strange tale, but it did not shake my faith, and I replied earnestly, 'You are all mistaken; I know the murderer. Justine, poor, good Justine, is innocent.'

At that instant my father entered. I saw unhappiness deeply impressed on his countenance, but he endeavoured to welcome me cheerfully, and after we had exchanged our mournful greeting, would have introduced some other topic than that of our disaster, had not Ernest exclaimed, 'Good God, Papa! Victor says that he knows who was the murderer of poor William.'

'We do also, unfortunately,' replied my father; 'for indeed I had rather have been forever ignorant than have discovered so much depravity and ingratitude in one I valued so highly.'

'My dear father, you are mistaken; Justine is innocent.'

'If she is, God forbid that she should suffer as guilty. She is to be tried today, and I hope, I sincerely hope, that she will be acquitted.'

This speech calmed me. I was firmly convinced in my own mind that Justine, and indeed every human being, was guiltless of this murder. I had no fear, therefore, that any circumstantial evidence could be brought forward strong enough to convict her. My tale was not one to announce publicly; its astounding horror would be looked upon as madness by the vulgar. Did any one indeed exist, except I, the creator, who would believe, unless his senses convinced him, in the existence of the living monument of presumption and rash ignorance which I had let loose upon the world?

We were soon joined by Elizabeth. Time had altered her since I last beheld her; it had endowed her with loveliness surpassing the beauty of her childish years. There was the same candour, the same vivacity, but it was allied to an expression more full of sensibility and intellect. She welcomed me with the greatest affection. 'Your arrival, my dear cousin,' said she, 'fills me with hope. You perhaps will find some means to justify my poor guiltless Justine. Alas! Who is safe, if she be convicted of crime? I rely on her innocence as certainly as I do upon my own. Our misfortune is doubly hard to us; we have not only lost that lovely darling boy, but this poor girl, whom I sincerely love, is to be torn away by even a worse fate. If she is condemned, I never shall know joy more. But she will not, I am sure she will not; and then I shall be happy again, even after the sad death of my little William.'

'She is innocent, my Elizabeth,' said I, 'and that shall be proved; fear nothing, but let your spirits be cheered by the assurance of her acquittal.'

'How kind and generous you are! Every one else believes in her guilt, and that made me wretched, for I knew that it was impossible; and to see every one else prejudiced in so deadly a manner rendered me hopeless and despairing.' She wept.

'Dearest niece,' said my father, 'dry your tears. If she is, as you believe, innocent, rely on the justice of our laws, and the activity with which I shall prevent the slightest shadow of partiality.'

# CHAPTER 8

WE passed a few sad hours until eleven o'clock, when the trial was to commence. My father and the rest of the family being obliged to attend as witnesses, I accompanied them to the court. During the whole of this wretched mockery of justice I suffered living torture. It was to be decided whether the result of my curiosity and lawless devices would cause the death of two of my fellow beings: one a smiling babe full of innocence and joy, the other far more dreadfully murdered, with every aggravation of infamy that could make the murder memorable in horror. Justine also was a girl of merit and possessed qualities which promised to render her life happy; now all was to be obliterated in an ignominious grave, and I the cause! A thousand times rather would I have confessed myself guilty of the crime ascribed to Justine, but I was absent when it was committed, and such a declaration would have been considered as the ravings of a madman and would not have exculpated her who suffered through me.

The appearance of Justine was calm. She was dressed in mourning, and her countenance, always engaging, was rendered, by the solemnity of her feelings, exquisitely beautiful. Yet she appeared confident in innocence and did not tremble, although gazed on and execrated by thousands, for all the kindness which her beauty might otherwise have excited was obliterated in the minds of the spectators by the imagination of the enormity she was supposed to have committed. She was tranquil, yet her tranquillity was evidently constrained; and as her confusion had before been adduced as a proof of her guilt, she worked up her mind to an appearance of courage. When she entered the court she threw her eyes round it and quickly discovered where we were seated. A tear seemed to dim her eye when she saw us, but she quickly recovered herself, and a look of sorrowful affection seemed to attest her utter guiltlessness.

The trial began, and after the advocate against her had stated the charge, several witnesses were called. Several strange facts combined against her, which might have staggered any one who had not such proof of her innocence as I had. She had been out the whole of the night on which the murder had been committed and towards morning had been perceived by a market-woman not far from the spot where the body of the murdered child had been afterwards found. The woman asked her what she did there, but she looked very strangely and only returned a confused and unintelligible answer. She returned to the house about eight o'clock, and when one enquired where she had passed the night, she replied that she had been looking for the child and demanded earnestly if any thing had been heard concerning him. When shown the body, she fell into violent hysterics and kept her bed for several days. The picture was then produced which the servant had found in her pocket; and when Elizabeth, in a faltering voice, proved that it was the same which, an hour before the child had been missed, she had placed round his neck, a murmur of horror and indignation filled the court.

Justine was called on for her defence. As the trial had proceeded, her countenance had altered. Surprize, horror, and misery were strongly expressed. Sometimes she struggled with her tears, but when she was desired to plead, she collected her powers and spoke in an audible although variable voice.

'God knows,' she said, 'how entirely I am innocent. But I do not pretend that my protestations should acquit me; I rest my innocence on a plain and simple explanation of the facts which have been adduced against me, and I hope the character I have always borne will incline my judges to a favourable interpretation where any circumstance appears doubtful or suspicious.'

She then related that, by the permission of Elizabeth, she had passed the evening of the night on which the murder had been committed at the house of an aunt at Chêne, a village situated at about a league from Geneva. On her return, at about nine o'clock, she met a man who asked her if she had seen any thing of the child who was lost. She was alarmed by this account and passed several hours in looking for him, when the gates of Geneva were shut, and she was forced to remain several hours of the night in a barn belonging to a cottage, being unwilling to call up the inhabitants, to whom she was well known. Most of the night she spent here watching; towards morning she believed that she slept for a few minutes; some steps disturbed her, and she awoke. It was dawn, and she quitted her asylum, that she might again endeavour to find my brother. If she had gone near the spot where his body lay, it was without her knowledge. That she had been bewildered when questioned by the market-woman was not surprising, since she had passed a sleepless night and the fate of poor William was yet uncertain. Concerning the picture she could give no account.

'I know,' continued the happy victim, 'how heavily and fatally this one circumstance weighs against me, but I have no power of explaining it; and when I have expressed my utter ignorance, I am only left to conjecture concerning the probabilities by which it might have been placed in my pocket. But here also I am checked. I believe that I have no enemy on earth, and none surely would have been so wicked as to destroy me wantonly. Did the murderer place it there? I know of no opportunity afforded him for so doing; or, if I had, why should he have stolen the jewel, to part with it again so soon?

'I commit my cause to the justice of my judges, yet I see no room for hope. I beg permission to have a few witnesses examined concerning my character, and if their testimony shall not overweigh my supposed guilt, I must be condemned, although I would pledge my salvation on my innocence.'

Several witnesses were called who had known her for many years, and they spoke well of her; but fear and hatred of the crime of which they supposed her guilty rendered them timorous and unwilling to come forward. Elizabeth saw even this last resource, her excellent dispositions and irreproachable conduct, about to fail the accused, when, although violently agitated, she desired permission to address the court.

'I am,' said she, 'the cousin of the unhappy child who was murdered, or rather his sister, for I was educated by and have lived with his parents ever since and even long before his birth. It may therefore be judged indecent in me to come forward on this occasion, but when I see a fellow creature about to perish through the cowardice of her pretended friends, I wish to be allowed to speak, that I may say what I know of her character. I am well acquainted with the accused. I have lived in the same house with her, at one time for five and at another for nearly two years. During all that period she appeared to me the most amiable and benevolent of human creatures. She nursed Madame Frankenstein, my aunt, in her last illness, with the greatest affection and care and afterwards attended her own mother during a tedious illness, in a manner that excited the admiration of all who knew her, after which she again lived in my uncle's house, where she was beloved by all the family. She was warmly attached to the child who is now dead and acted towards him like a most affectionate mother. For my own part, I do not hesitate to say that, notwithstanding all the evidence produced against her, I believe and rely on her perfect innocence. She had no temptation for such an action; as to the bauble on which the chief proof rests, if she had earnestly desired it, I should have willingly given it to her, so much do I esteem and value her.'

A murmur of approbation followed Elizabeth's simple and powerful appeal, but it was excited by her generous interference, and not in favour of poor Justine, on whom the public indignation was turned with renewed violence, charging her with the blackest ingratitude. She herself wept as Elizabeth spoke, but she did not answer. My own agitation and anguish was extreme during the whole trial. I believed in her innocence; I knew it. Could the daemon who had (I did not for a minute doubt) murdered my brother also in his hellish sport have betrayed the innocent to death and ignominy? I could not sustain the horror of my situation, and when I perceived that the popular voice and the countenances of the judges had already condemned my unhappy victim, I rushed out of the court in agony. The tortures of the accused did not equal mine; she was sustained by innocence, but the fangs of remorse tore my bosom and would not forgo their hold.

I passed a night of unmingled wretchedness. In the morning I went to the court; my lips and throat were parched. I dared not ask the fatal question, but I was known, and the officer guessed the cause of my visit. The ballots had been thrown; they were all black, and Justine was condemned.

I cannot pretend to describe what I then felt. I had before experienced sensations of horror, and I have endeavoured to bestow upon them adequate expressions, but words cannot convey an idea of the heart-sickening despair that I then endured. The person to whom I addressed myself added that Justine had already confessed her guilt. 'That evidence,' he observed, 'was hardly required in so glaring a case, but I am glad of it; and, indeed, none of our judges like to condemn a criminal upon circumstantial evidence, be it ever so decisive.'

This was strange and unexpected intelligence; what could it mean? Had my eyes deceived me? And was I really as mad as the whole world would believe me to be if I disclosed the object of my suspicions? I hastened to return home, and Elizabeth eagerly demanded the result.

'My cousin,' replied I, 'it is decided as you may have expected; all judges had rather that ten innocent should suffer than that one guilty should escape. But she has confessed.'

This was a dire blow to poor Elizabeth, who had relied with firmness upon Justine's innocence. 'Alas!' said she. 'How shall I ever again believe in human goodness? Justine, whom I loved and esteemed as my sister, how could she put on those smiles of innocence only to betray? Her mild eyes seemed incapable of any severity or guile, and yet she has committed a murder.'

Soon after we heard that the poor victim had expressed a desire to see my cousin. My father wished her not to go but said that he left it to her own judgment and feelings to decide. 'Yes,' said Elizabeth, 'I will go, although she is guilty; and you, Victor, shall accompany me; I cannot go alone.' The idea of this visit was torture to me, yet I could not refuse.

We entered the gloomy prison chamber and beheld Justine sitting on some straw at the farther end; her hands were manacled, and her head rested on her knees. She rose on seeing us enter, and when we were left alone with her, she threw herself at the feet of Elizabeth, weeping bitterly. My cousin wept also.

'Oh, Justine!' said she. 'Why did you rob me of my last consolation? I relied on your innocence, and although I was then very wretched, I was not so miserable as I am now.'

'And do you also believe that I am so very, very wicked? Do you also join with my enemies to crush me, to condemn me as a murderer?' Her voice was suffocated with sobs.

'Rise, my poor girl,' said Elizabeth; 'why do you kneel, if you are innocent? I am not one of your enemies; I believed you guiltless, notwithstanding every evidence, until I heard that you had yourself declared your guilt. That report, you say, is false; and be assured, dear Justine, that nothing can shake my confidence in you for a moment, but your own confession.'

'I did confess, but I confessed a lie. I confessed, that I might obtain absolution; but now that falsehood lies heavier at my heart than all my other sins. The God of heaven forgive me! Ever since I was condemned, my confessor has besieged me; he threatened and menaced, until I almost began to think that I was the monster that he said I was. He threatened excommunication and hell fire in my last moments if I continued obdurate. Dear lady, I had none to support me; all looked on me as a wretch doomed to ignominy and perdition. What could I do? In an evil hour I subscribed to a lie; and now only am I truly miserable.'

She paused, weeping, and then continued, 'I thought with horror, my sweet lady, that you should believe your Justine, whom your blessed aunt had so highly honoured and whom you loved, was a creature capable of a crime which none but the devil himself could have perpetrated. Dear William! Dearest blessed child! I soon shall see you again in heaven, where we shall all be happy; and that consoles me, going as I am to suffer ignominy and death.'

'Oh, Justine! Forgive me for having for one moment distrusted you. Why did you confess? But do not mourn, dear girl. Do not fear. I will proclaim, I will prove your innocence. I will melt the stony hearts of your enemies by my tears and prayers. You shall not die! You, my play-fellow, my companion, my sister, perish on the scaffold! No! No! I never could survive so horrible a misfortune.'

Justine shook her head mournfully. 'I do not fear to die,' she said; 'that pang is past. God raises my weakness and gives me courage to endure the worst. I leave a sad and bitter world; and if you remember me and think of me as of one unjustly condemned, I am resigned to the fate awaiting me. Learn from me, dear lady, to submit in patience to the will of heaven!'

During this conversation I had retired to a corner of the prison room, where I could conceal the horrid anguish that possessed me. Despair! Who dared talk of that? The poor victim, who on the morrow was to pass the awful boundary between life and death, felt not, as I did, such deep and bitter agony. I gnashed my teeth and ground them together, uttering a groan that came from my inmost soul. Justine started. When she saw who it was, she approached me and said, 'Dear sir, you are very kind to visit me; you, I hope, do not believe that I am guilty?'

I could not answer. 'No, Justine,' said Elizabeth; 'he is more convinced of your innocence than I was, for even when he heard that you had confessed, he did not credit it.'

'I truly thank him. In these last moments I feel the sincerest gratitude towards those who think of me with kindness. How sweet is the affection of others to such a wretch as I am! It removes more than half my misfortune, and I feel as if I could die in peace, now that my innocence is acknowledged by you, dear lady, and your cousin.'

Thus the poor sufferer tried to comfort others and herself. She indeed gained the resignation she desired. But I, the true murderer, felt the never-dying worm alive in my bosom, which allowed of no hope or consolation. Elizabeth also wept and was unhappy, but hers also was the misery of innocence, which, like a cloud that passes over the fair moon, for a while hides but cannot tarnish its brightness. Anguish and despair had penetrated into the core of my heart; I bore a hell within me which nothing could extinguish. We stayed several hours with Justinc, and it was with great difficulty that Elizabeth could tear herself away. 'I wish,' cried she, 'that I were to die with you; I cannot live in this world of misery.'

Justine assumed an air of cheerfulness, while she with difficulty repressed her bitter tears. She embraced Elizabeth and said, in a voice of half-suppressed emotion, 'Farewell, sweet lady, dearest Elizabeth, my beloved and only friend; may heaven, in its bounty, bless and preserve you; may this be the last misfortune that you will ever suffer! Live, and be happy, and make others so.'

And on the morrow Justine died. Elizabeth's heart-rending eloquence failed to move the judges from their settled conviction in the criminality of the saintly sufferer. My passionate and indignant appeals were lost upon them. And when I received their cold answers and heard the harsh, unfeeling reasoning of these men, my purposed avowal died away on my lips. Thus I might proclaim myself a madman, but not revoke the sentence passed upon my wretched victim. She perished on the scaffold as a murderess!

From the tortures of my own heart, I turned to contemplate the deep and voiceless grief of my Elizabeth. This also was my doing! And my father's woe, and the desolation of that late so smiling home – all was the work of my thrice-accursed hands! Ye weep, unhappy ones, but these are not your last tears! Again shall you raise the funeral wail, and the sound of your lamentations shall again and again be heard! Frankenstein, your son, your kinsman, your early, much-loved friend; he who would spend each vital drop of blood for your sakes – who has no thought nor sense of joy except as it is mirrored also in your dear countenances – who would fill the air with blessings and spend his life in serving you – he bids you weep – to shed countless tears; happy beyond his hopes, if thus inexorable fate be satisfied, and if the destruction pause before the peace of the grave have succeeded to your sad torments!

Thus spoke my prophetic soul, as, torn by remorse, horror, and despair, I beheld those I loved spend vain sorrow upon the graves of William and Justine, the first hapless victims to my unhallowed arts.

## CHAPTER 9

NOTHING is more painful to the human mind than, after the feelings have been worked up by a quick succession of events, the dead calmness of inaction and certainty which follows and deprives the soul both of hope and fear. Justine died, she rested, and I was alive. The blood flowed freely in my veins, but a weight of despair and remorse pressed on my heart which nothing could remove. Sleep fled from my eyes; I wandered like an evil spirit, for I had committed deeds of mischief beyond description horrible, and more, much more (I persuaded myself) was yet behind. Yet my heart overflowed with kindness and the love of virtue. I had begun life with benevolent intentions and thirsted for the moment when I should put them in practice and make myself useful to my fellow beings. Now all was blasted; instead of that serenity of conscience which allowed me to look back upon the past with self-satisfaction, and from thence to gather promise of new hopes, I was seized by remorse and the sense of guilt, which hurried me away to a hell of intense tortures such as no language can describe.

This state of mind preyed upon my health, which had perhaps never entirely recovered from the first shock it had sustained. I shunned the face of man; all sound of joy or complacency was torture to me; solitude was my only consolation – deep, dark, deathlike solitude.

My father observed with pain the alteration perceptible in my disposition and habits and endeavoured by arguments deduced from the feelings of his serene conscience and guiltless life to inspire me with fortitude, and awaken in me the courage to dispel the dark cloud which brooded over me. 'Do you think, Victor,' said he, 'that I do not suffer also? No one could love a child more than I loved your brother' – tears came into his eyes as he spoke – 'but is it not a duty to the survivors that we should refrain from augmenting their unhappiness by an appearance of immoderate grief? It is also a duty owed to yourself, for excessive sorrow prevents improvement or enjoyment, or even the discharge of daily usefulness, without which no man is fit for society.'

This advice, although good, was totally inapplicable to my case; I should have been the first to hide my grief and console my friends if remorse had not mingled its bitterness, and terror its alarm, with my other sensations. Now I could only answer my father with a look of despair and endeavour to hide myself from his view.

About this time we retired to our house at Belrive. This change was particularly agreeable to me. The shutting of the gates regularly at ten o'clock and the impossibility of remaining on the lake after that hour had rendered our residence within the walls of Geneva very irksome to me. I was now free. Often, after the rest of the family had retired for the night, I took the boat and passed many hours upon the water. Sometimes, with my sails set, I was carried by the wind; and sometimes, afer rowing into the middle of the lake, I left the boat to pursue its own course and gave way to my own miserable reflections. I was often tempted, when all was at peace around me, and I the only unquiet thing that wandered restless in a scene so beautiful and heavenly – if I except some bat, or the frogs, whose harsh and interrupted croaking was heard only when I approached the shore – often, I say, I was tempted to plunge into the silent lake, that the waters might close over me and my calamities forever. But I was restrained, when I thought of the heroic and suffering Elizabeth, whom I tenderly loved, and whose existence was bound up in mine. I thought also of my father and surviving brother; should I by my base desertion leave them exposed and unprotected to the malice of the fiend whom I had let loose among them?

At these moments I wept bitterly and wished that peace would revisit my mind only that I might afford them consolation and happiness. But that could not be. Remorse extinguished every hope. I had been the author of unalterable evils, and I lived in daily fear lest the monster whom I had created should perpetrate some new wickedness. I had an obscure feeling that all was not over and that he would still commit some signal crime, which by its enormity should almost efface the recollection of the past. There was always scope for fear so long as anything I loved remained behind. My abhorrence of this fiend cannot be conceived. When I thought of him I gnashed my teeth, my eyes became inflamed, and I ardently wished to extinguish that life which I had so thoughtlessly bestowed. When I reflected on his crimes and malice, my hatred and revenge burst all bounds of moderation. I would have made a pilgrimage to the highest peak of the Andes, could I, when there, have precipitated him to their base. I wished to see him again, that I might wreak the utmost extent of abhorrence on his head and avenge the deaths of William and Justine.

Our house was the house of mourning. My father's health was deeply shaken by the horror of the recent events. Elizabeth was sad and desponding; she no longer took delight in her ordinary occupations; all pleasure seemed to her sacrilege toward the dead; eternal woe and tears she then thought was the just tribute she should pay to innocence so blasted and destroyed. She was no longer that happy creature who in earlier youth wandered with me on the banks of the lake and talked with ecstasy of our future prospects. The first of these sorrows which are sent to wean us from the earth had visited her, and its dimming influence quenched her dearest smiles.

'When I reflect, my dear cousin,' said she, 'on the miserable death of Justine Moritz, I no longer see the world and its works as they before appeared to me. Before, I looked upon the accounts of vice and injustice that I read in books or heard from others as tales of ancient days or imaginary evils; at least they were remote and more familiar to reason than to the imagination; but now misery has come home, and men appear to me as monsters thirsting for each other's blood. Yet I am certainly unjust. Every body believed that poor girl to be guilty, and if she could have committed the crime for which she suffered, assuredly she would have been the most depraved of human creatures. For the sake of a few jewels, to have murdered the son of her benefactor and friend, a child whom she had nursed from its birth, and appeared to love as if it had been her own! I could not consent to the death of any human being, but certainly I should have thought such a creature unfit to remain in the society of men. But she was innocent. I know, I feel, she was innocent; you are of the same opinion, and that confirms me. Alas! Victor, when falsehood can look so like the truth, who can assure themselves of certain happiness? I feel as if I were walking on the edge of a precipice, towards which thousands are crowding and endeavouring to plunge me into the abyss. William and Justine were assassinated, and the murderer escapes; he walks about the world free, and perhaps respected. But even if I were condemned to suffer on the scaffold for the same crimes, I would not change places with such a wretch.'

I listened to this discourse with the extremest agony. I, not in deed, but in effect, was the true murderer. Elizabeth read my anguish in my countenance, and kindly taking my hand, said, 'My dearest friend, you must calm yourself. These events have affected me, God knows how deeply; but I am not so wretched as you are. There is an expression of despair, and sometimes of revenge, in your countenance that makes me tremble. Dear Victor, banish these dark passions. Remember the friends around you, who centre all their hopes in you. Have we lost the power of rendering you happy? Ah! While we love, while we are true to each other, here in this land of peace and beauty, your native country, we may reap every tranquil blessing – what can disturb our peace?'

And could not such words from her whom I fondly prized before every other gift of fortune suffice to chase away the fiend that lurked in my heart? Even as she spoke I drew near to her, as if in terror, lest at that very moment the destroyer had been near to rob me of her.

Thus not the tenderness of friendship, nor the beauty of earth, nor of heaven, could redeem my soul from woe; the very accents of love were ineffectual. I was encompassed by a cloud which no beneficial influence could penetrate. The wounded deer dragging its fainting limbs to some untrodden brake, there to gaze upon the arrow which had pierced it, and to die – was but a type of me.

Sometimes I could cope with the sullen despair that overwhelmed me, but sometimes the whirlwind passions of my soul drove me to seek, by bodily exercise and by change of place, some relief from my intolerable sensations. It was during an access of this kind that I suddenly left my home, and bending my steps towards the near Alpine valleys, sought in the magnificence, the eternity of such scenes, to forget myself and my ephemeral, because human, sorrows. My wanderings were directed towards the valley of Chamounix. I had visited it frequently during my boyhood. Six years had passed since then: *I* was a wreck – but nought had changed in those savage and enduring scenes.

I performed the first part of my journey on horseback. I afterwards hired a mule, as the more sure-footed and least liable to receive injury on these rugged roads. The weather was fine; it was about the middle of the month of August, nearly two months after the death of Justine; that miserable epoch from which I dated all my woe. The weight upon my spirit was sensibly lightened as I plunged yet deeper in the ravine of Arve. The immense mountains and precipices that overhung me on every side, the sound of the river raging among the rocks, and the dashing of the waterfalls around, spoke of a power mighty as Omnipotence – and I ceased to fear or to bend before any being less almighty than that which had created and ruled the elements, here displayed in their most terrific guise. Still, as I ascended higher, the valley assumed a more magnificent and astonishing character. Ruined castles hanging on the precipices of piny mountains, the impetuous Arve, and cottages every here and there peeping forth from among the trees formed a scene of singular beauty. But it was augmented and rendered sublime by the mighty Alps, whose white and shining pyramids and domes towered above all, as belonging to another earth, the habitations of another race of beings.

I passed the bridge of Pélissier, where the ravine, which the river forms, opened before me, and I began to ascend the mountain that overhangs it. Soon after I entered the valley of Chamounix. This valley is more wonderful and sublime, but not so beautiful and picturesque as that of Servox, through which I had just passed. The high and snowy mountains were its immediate boundaries, but I saw no more ruined castles and fertile fields. Immense glaciers approached the road; I heard the rumbling thunder of the falling avalanche and marked the smoke of its passage. Mont Blanc, the supreme and magnificent Mont Blanc, raised itself from the surrounding *aiguilles*,[1] and its tremendous dome overlooked the valley.

A tingling long-lost sense of pleasure often came across me during this journey. Some turn in the road, some new object suddenly perceived and recognized, reminded me of days gone by, and were associated with the light-hearted gaiety of boyhood. The very winds whispered in soothing accents, and maternal Nature bade me weep no more. Then again the kindly influence ceased to act – I found myself fettered again to grief and indulging in all the misery of reflection. Then I spurred on my animal, striving so to forget the world, my fears, and more than all, myself – or, in a more desperate fashion, I alighted and threw myself on the grass, weighed down by horror and despair.

At length I arrived at the village of Chamounix. Exhaustion succeeded to the extreme fatigue both of body and of mind which I had endured. For a short space of time I remained at the window watching the pallid lightnings that played above Mont Blanc and listening to the rushing of the Arve, which pursued its noisy way beneath. The same lulling sounds acted as a lullaby to my too keen sensations; when I placed my head upon my pillow, sleep crept over me; I felt it as it came and blessed the giver of oblivion.

## CHAPTER 10

I SPENT the following day roaming through the valley. I stood beside the sources of the Arveiron, which take their rise in a glacier, that with slow pace is advancing down from the summit of the hills to barricade the valley. The abrupt sides of vast mountains were before me; the icy wall of the glacier overhung me; a few shattered pines were scattered around; and the solemn silence of this glorious presence-chamber of imperial nature was broken only by the brawling waves or the fall of some vast fragment, the thunder sound of the avalanche or the cracking, reverberated along the mountains, of the accumulated ice, which, through the silent working of immutable laws, was ever and anon rent and torn, as if it had been but a plaything in their hands. These sublime and magnificent scenes afforded me the greatest consolation that I was capable of receiving. They elevated me from all littleness of feeling, and although they did not remove my grief, they subdued and tranquillized it. In some degree, also, they diverted my mind from the thoughts over which it had brooded for the last month. I retired to rest at night; my slumbers, as it were, waited on and ministered to by the assemblance of grand shapes which I had contemplated during the day. They congregated round me; the unstained snowy mountain-top, the glittering pinnacle, the pine woods, and ragged bare ravine, the eagle, soaring amidst the clouds – they all gathered round me and bade me be at peace.

Where had they fled when the next morning I awoke? All of soul-inspiriting fled with sleep, and dark melancholy clouded every thought. The rain was pouring in torrents, and thick mists hid the summits of the mountains, so that I even saw not the faces of those mighty friends. Still I would penetrate their misty veil and seek them in their cloudy retreats. What were rain and storm to me? My mule was brought to the door, and I resolved to ascend to the summit of Montanvert. I remembered the effect that the view of the tremendous and ever-moving glacier had produced upon my mind when I first saw it. It had then filled me with a sublime ecstasy that gave wings to the soul and allowed it to soar from the obscure world to light and joy. The sight of the awful and majestic in nature had indeed always the effect of solemnizing my mind and causing me to forget the passing cares of life. I determined to go without a guide, for I was well acquainted with the path, and the presence of another would destroy the solitary grandeur of the scene.

The ascent is precipitous, but the path is cut into continual and short windings, which enable you to surmount the perpendicularity of the mountain. It is a scene terrifically desolate. In a thousand spots the traces of the winter avalanche may be perceived, where trees lie broken and strewed on the ground, some entirely destroyed, others bent, leaning upon the jutting rocks of the mountain or transversely upon other trees. The path, as you ascend higher, is intersected by ravines of snow, down which stones continually roll from above; one of them is particularly dangerous, as the slightest sound, such as even speaking in a loud voice, produces a concussion of air sufficient to draw destruction upon the head of the speaker. The pines are not tall or luxuriant, but they are sombre and add an air of severity to the scene. I looked on the valley beneath; vast mists were rising from the rivers which ran through it and curling in thick wreaths around the opposite mountains, whose summits were hid in the uniform clouds, while rain poured from the dark sky and added to the melancholy impression I received from the objects around me. Alas! Why does man boast of sensibilities superior to those apparent in the brute; it only renders them more necessary beings.[1] If our impulses were confined to hunger, thirst, and desire, we might be nearly free; but now we are moved by every wind that blows and a chance word or scene that that word may convey to us.

> We rest; a dream has power to poison sleep.
>   We rise; one wand'ring thought pollutes the day.
> We feel, conceive, or reason; laugh or weep,
>   Embrace fond woe, or cast our cares away;
> It is the same: for, be it joy or sorrow,
>   The path of its departure still is free.
> Man's yesterday may ne'er be like his morrow;
>   Nought may endure but mutability![2]

It was nearly noon when I arrived at the top of the ascent. For some time I sat upon the rock that overlooks the sea of ice. A mist covered both that and the surrounding mountains. Presently a breeze dissipated the cloud, and I descended upon the glacier. The surface is very uneven, rising like the waves of a troubled sea, descending low, and interspersed by rifts that sink deep. The field of ice is almost a league in width, but I spent nearly two hours in crossing it. The opposite mountain is a bare perpendicular rock. From the side where I now stood Montanvert was exactly opposite, at the distance of a league; and above it rose Mont Blanc, in awful majesty. I remained in a recess of the rock, gazing on this wonderful and stupendous scene. The sea, or rather the vast river of ice, wound among its dependent mountains, whose aerial summits hung over its recesses. Their icy and glittering peaks shone in the sunlight over the clouds. My heart, which was before sorrowful, now swelled with something like joy; I exclaimed – 'Wandering spirits, if indeed ye wander, and do not rest in your narrow beds, allow me this faint happiness, or take me, as your companion, away from the joys of life.'

As I said this I suddenly beheld the figure of a man, at some distance, advancing towards me with superhuman speed. He bounded over the crevices in the ice, among which I had walked with caution; his stature, also, as he approached, seemed to exceed that of man. I was troubled; a mist came over my eyes, and I felt a faintness seize me; but I was quickly restored by the cold gale of the mountains. I perceived, as the shape came nearer (sight tremendous and abhorred!) that it was the wretch whom I had created. I trembled with rage and horror, resolving to wait his approach and then close with him in mortal combat. He approached; his countenance bespoke bitter anguish, combined with disdain and malignity, while its unearthly ugliness rendered it almost too horrible for human eyes. But I scarcely observed this; rage and hatred had at first deprived me of utterance, and I recovered only to overwhelm him with words expressive of furious detestation and contempt.

'Devil,' I exclaimed, 'do you dare approach me? And do not you fear the fierce vengeance of my arm wreaked on your miserable head? Begone, vile insect! Or rather, stay, that I may trample you to dust! And, oh! That I could, with the extinction of your miserable existence, restore those victims whom you have so diabolically murdered!'

'I expected this reception,' said the daemon. 'All men hate the wretched; how, then, must I be hated, who am miserable beyond all living things! Yet you, my creator, detest and spurn me, thy creature, to whom thou art bound by ties only dissoluble by the annihilation of one of us. You purpose to kill me. How dare you sport thus with life? Do your duty towards me, and I will do mine towards you and the rest of mankind. If you will comply with my conditions, I will leave them and you at peace; but if you refuse, I will glut the maw of death, until it be satiated with the blood of your remaining friends.'

'Abhorred monster! Fiend that thou art! The tortures of hell are too mild a vengeance for thy crimes. Wretched devil! You reproach me with your creation; come on, then, that I may extinguish the spark which I so negligently bestowed.'

My rage was without bounds; I sprang on him, impelled by all the feelings which can arm one being against the existence of another.

He easily eluded me and said – 'Be calm! I intreat you to hear me before you give vent to your hatred on my devoted head. Have I not suffered enough, that you seek to increase my misery? Life, although it may only be an accumulation of anguish, is dear to me, and I will defend it. Remember, thou hast made me more powerful than thyself; my height is superior to thine, my joints more supple. But I will not be tempted to set myself in opposition to thee. I am thy creature, and I will be even mild and docile to my natural lord and king if thou wilt also perform thy part, the which thou owest me. Oh, Frankenstein, be not equitable to every other and trample upon me alone, to whom thy justice, and even thy clemency and affection, is most due. Remember that I am thy creature; I ought to be thy Adam, but I am rather the fallen angel, whom thou drivest from joy for no misdeed. Everywhere I see bliss, from which I alone am irrevocably excluded. I was benevolent and good; misery made me a fiend. Make me happy, and I shall again be virtuous.'

'Begone! I will not hear you. There can be no community between you and me; we are enemies. Begone, or let us try our strength in a fight, in which one must fall.'

'How can I move thee? Will no intreaties cause thee to turn a favourable eye upon thy creature, who implores thy goodness and compassion? Believe me, Frankenstein, I was benevolent; my soul glowed with love and humanity; but am I not alone, miserably alone? You, my creator, abhor me; what hope can I gather from your fellow creatures, who owe me nothing? They spurn and hate me. The desert mountains and dreary glaciers are my refuge. I have wandered here many days; the caves of ice, which I only do not fear, are a dwelling to me, and the only one which man does not grudge. These bleak skies I hail, for they are kinder to me than your fellow beings. If the multitude of mankind knew of my existence, they would do as you do, and arm themselves for my destruction. Shall I not then hate them who abhor me? I will keep no terms with my enemies. I am miserable, and they shall share my wretchedness. Yet it is in your power to recompense me, and deliver them from an evil which it only remains for you to make so great, that not only you and your family, but thousands of others, shall be swallowed up in the whirlwinds of its rage. Let your compassion be moved, and do not disdain me. Listen to my tale; when you have heard that, abandon or commiserate me, as you shall judge that I deserve. But hear me. The guilty are allowed, by human laws, bloody as they are, to speak in their own defence before they are condemned. Listen to me, Frankenstein. You accuse me of murder, and yet you would, with a satisfied conscience, destroy your own creature. Oh, praise the eternal justice of man! Yet I ask you not to spare me; listen to me, and then, if you can, and if you will, destroy the work of your hands.'

'Why do you call to my remembrance,' I rejoined, 'circumstances of which I shudder to reflect, that I have been the miserable origin and author? Cursed be the day, abhorred devil, in which you first saw light! Cursed (although I curse myself) be the hands that formed you! You have made me wretched beyond expression. You have left me no power to consider whether I am just to you or not. Begone! Relieve me from the sight of your detested form.'

'Thus I relieve thee, my creator,' he said, and placed his hated hands before my eyes, which I flung from me with violence; 'thus I take from thee a sight which you abhor. Still thou canst listen to me and grant me thy compassion. By the virtues that I once possessed, I demand this from you. Hear my tale; it is long and strange, and the temperature of this place is not fitting to your fine sensations; come to the hut upon the mountain. The sun is yet high in the heavens; before it descends to hide itself behind yon snowy precipices and illuminate another world, you will have heard my story and can decide. On you it rests, whether I quit forever the neighbourhood of man and lead a harmless life, or become the scourge of your fellow creatures and the author of your own speedy ruin.'

As he said this he led the way across the ice; I followed. My heart was full, and I did not answer him, but as I proceeded, I weighed the various arguments that he had used and determined at least to listen to his tale. I was partly urged by curiosity, and compassion confirmed my resolution. I had hitherto supposed him to be the murderer of my brother, and I eagerly sought a confirmation or denial of this opinion. For the first time, also, I felt what the duties of a creator towards his creature were, and that I ought to render him happy before I complained of his wickedness. These motives urged me to comply with his demand. We crossed the ice, therefore, and ascended the opposite rock. The air was cold, and the rain again began to descend; we entered the hut, the fiend with an air of exultation, I with a heavy heart and depressed spirits. But I consented to listen, and seating myself by the fire which my odious companion had lighted, he thus began his tale.

## CHAPTER 11

'It is with considerable difficulty that I remember the original era of my being; all the events of that period appear confused and indistinct. A strange multiplicity of sensations seized me, and I saw, felt, heard, and smelt at the same time; and it was, indeed, a long time before I learned to distinguish between the operations of my various senses. By degrees, I remember, a stronger light pressed upon my nerves, so that I was obliged to shut my eyes. Darkness then came over me and troubled me, but hardly had I felt this when, by opening my eyes, as I now suppose, the light poured in upon me again. I walked and, I believe, descended, but I presently found a great alteration in my sensations. Before, dark and opaque bodies had surrounded me, impervious to my touch or sight; but I now found that I could wander on at liberty, with no obstacles which I could not either surmount or avoid. The light became more and more oppressive to me, and the heat wearying me as I walked, I sought a place where I could receive shade. This was the forest near Ingolstadt; and here I lay by the side of a brook resting from my fatigue, until I felt tormented by hunger and thirst. This roused me from my nearly dormant state, and I ate some berries which I found hanging on the trees or lying on the ground. I slaked my thirst at the brook, and then lying down, was overcome by sleep.

'It was dark when I awoke; I felt cold also, and half frightened, as it were, instinctively, finding myself so desolate. Before I had quitted your apartment, on a sensation of cold, I had covered myself with some clothes, but these were insufficient to secure me from the dews of night. I was a poor, helpless, miserable wretch; I knew, and could distinguish, nothing; but feeling pain invade me on all sides, I sat down and wept.

'Soon a gentle light stole over the heavens and gave me a sensation of pleasure. I started up and beheld a radiant form rise from among the trees. I gazed with a kind of wonder. It moved slowly, but it enlightened my path, and I again went out in search of berries. I was still cold when under one of the trees I found a huge cloak, with which I covered myself, and sat down upon the ground. No distinct ideas occupied my mind; all was confused. I felt light, and hunger, and thirst, and darkness; innumerable sounds rang in my ears, and on all sides various scents saluted me; the only object that I could distinguish was the bright moon, and I fixed my eyes on that with pleasure.

'Several changes of day and night passed, and the orb of night had greatly lessened, when I began to distinguish my sensations from each other. I gradually saw plainly the clear stream that supplied me with drink and the trees that shaded me with their foliage. I was delighted when I first discovered that a pleasant sound, which often saluted my ears, proceeded from the throats of the little winged animals who had often intercepted the light from my eyes. I began also to observe, with greater accuracy, the forms that surrounded me, and to perceive the boundaries of the radiant roof of light which canopied me. Sometimes I tried to imitate the pleasant songs of the birds but was unable. Sometimes I wished to express my sensations in my own mode, but the uncouth and inarticulate sounds which broke from me frightened me into silence again.

'The moon had disappeared from the night, and again, with a lessened form, showed itself, while I still remained in the forest. My sensations had by this time become distinct, and my mind received every day additional ideas. My eyes became accustomed to the light and to perceive objects in their right forms; I distinguished the insect from the herb, and by degrees, one herb from another. I found that the sparrow uttered none but harsh notes, whilst those of the blackbird and thrush were sweet and enticing.

'One day, when I was oppressed by cold, I found a fire which had been left by some wandering beggars, and was overcome with delight at the warmth I experienced from it. In my joy I thrust my hand into the live embers, but quickly drew it out again with a cry of pain. How strange, I thought, that the same cause should produce such opposite effects! I examined the materials of the fire, and to my joy found it to be composed of wood. I quickly collected some branches, but they were wet and would not burn. I was pained at this and sat still watching the operation of the fire. The wet wood which I had placed near the heat dried and itself became inflamed. I reflected on this, and by touching the various branches, I discovered the cause and busied myself in collecting a great quantity of wood, that I might dry it and have a plentiful supply of fire. When night came on and brought sleep with it, I was in the greatest fear lest my fire should be extinguished. I covered it carefully with dry wood and leaves and placed wet branches upon it; and then, spreading my cloak, I lay on the ground and sank into sleep.

'It was morning when I awoke, and my first care was to visit the fire. I uncovered it, and a gentle breeze quickly fanned it into a flame. I observed this also and contrived a fan of branches, which roused the embers when they were nearly extinguished. When night came again I found, with pleasure, that the fire gave light as well as heat and that the discovery of this element was useful to me in my food, for I found some of the offals that the travellers had left had been roasted, and tasted much more savoury than the berries I gathered from the trees. I tried, therefore, to dress my food in the same manner, placing it on the live embers. I found that the berries were spoiled by this operation, and the nuts and roots much improved.

'Food, however, became scarce, and I often spent the

whole day searching in vain for a few acorns to assuage the pangs of hunger. When I found this, I resolved to quit the place that I had hitherto inhabited, to seek for one where the few wants I experienced would be more easily satisfied. In this emigration I exceedingly lamented the loss of the fire which I had obtained through accident and knew not how to reproduce it. I gave several hours to the serious consideration of this difficulty, but I was obliged to relinquish all attempts to supply it, and wrapping myself up in my cloak, I struck across the wood towards the setting sun. I passed three days in these rambles and at length discovered the open country. A great fall of snow had taken place the night before, and the fields were of one uniform white; the appearance was disconsolate, and I found my feet chilled by the cold damp substance that covered the ground.

'It was about seven in the morning, and I longed to obtain food and shelter; at length I perceived a small hut, on a rising ground, which had doubtless been built for the convenience of some shepherd. This was a new sight to me, and I examined the structure with great curiosity. Finding the door open, I entered. An old man sat in it, near a fire, over which he was preparing his breakfast. He turned on hearing a noise, and perceiving me, shrieked loudly, and quitting the hut, ran across the fields with a speed of which his debilitated form hardly appeared capable. His appearance, different from any I had ever before seen, and his flight, somewhat surprised me. But I was enchanted by the appearance of the hut; here the snow and rain could not penetrate; the ground was dry; and it presented to me then as exquisite and divine a retreat as Pandaemonium appeared to the daemons of hell after their sufferings in the lake of fire. I greedily devoured the remnants of the shepherd's breakfast, which consisted of bread, cheese, milk, and wine; the latter, however, I did not like. Then, overcome by fatigue, I lay down among some straw and fell asleep.

'It was noon when I awoke, and allured by the warmth of the sun, which shone brightly on the white ground, I determined to recommence my travels; and, depositing the remains of the peasant's breakfast in a wallet I found, I proceeded across the fields for several hours, until at sunset I arrived at a village. How miraculous did this appear! The huts, the neater cottages, and stately houses engaged my admiration by turns. The vegetables in the gardens, the milk and cheese that I saw placed at the windows of some of the cottages, allured my appetite. One of the best of these I entered, but I had hardly placed my foot within the door before the children shrieked, and one of the women fainted. The whole village was roused; some fled, some attacked me, until, grievously bruised by stones and many other kinds of missile weapons, I escaped to the open country and fearfully took refuge in a low hovel, quite bare, and making a wretched appearance after the palaces I had beheld in the village. This hovel, however, joined a cottage of a neat and pleasant appearance, but after my late dearly bought experience, I dared not enter it. My place of refuge was constructed of wood, but so low that I could with difficulty sit upright in it. No wood, however, was placed on the earth which formed the floor, but it was dry; and although the wind entered it by innumerable chinks, I found it an agreeable asylum from the snow and rain.

'Here, then, I retreated and lay down happy to have found a shelter, however miserable, from the inclemency of the season, and still more from the barbarity of man.

'As soon as morning dawned I crept from my kennel, that I might view the adjacent cottage and discover if I could remain in the habitation I had found. It was situated against the back of the cottage and surrounded on the sides which were exposed by a pig sty and a clear pool of water. One part was open, and by that I had crept in; but now I covered every crevice by which I might be perceived with stones and wood, yet in such a manner that I might move them on occasion to pass out; all the light I enjoyed came through the sty, and that was sufficient for me.

'Having thus arranged my dwelling and carpeted it with clean straw, I retired, for I saw the figure of a man at a distance, and I remembered too well my treatment the night before to trust myself in his power. I had first, however, provided for my sustenance for that day by a loaf of coarse bread, which I purloined, and a cup with which I could drink, more conveniently than from my hand, of the pure water which flowed by my retreat. The floor was a little raised, so that it was kept perfectly dry, and by its vicinity to the chimney of the cottage it was tolerably warm.

'Being thus provided, I resolved to reside in this hovel until something should occur which might alter my determination. It was indeed a paradise compared to the bleak forest, my former residence, the rain-dropping branches, and dank earth. I ate my breakfast with pleasure and was about to remove a plank to procure myself a little water when I heard a step, and looking through a small chink, I beheld a young creature, with a pail on her head, passing before my hovel. The girl was young and of gentle demeanour, unlike what I have since found cottagers and farmhouse servants to be. Yet she was meanly dressed, a coarse blue petticoat and a linen jacket being her only garb; her fair hair was plaited but not adorned: she looked patient yet sad. I lost sight of her, and in about a quarter of an hour she returned bearing the pail, which was now partly filled with milk. As she walked along, seemingly incommoded by the burden, a young man met her, whose countenance expressed a deeper despondence. Uttering a few sounds with an air of melancholy, he took the pail from her head and bore it to the cottage himself. She followed, and they disappeared. Presently I saw the young man again, with some tools in his hand, cross the field behind the cottage; and the girl was also busied, sometimes in the house and sometimes in the yard.

'On examining my dwelling, I found that one of the windows of the cottage had formerly occupied a part of it, but the panes had been filled up with wood. In one of these which was a small and almost imperceptible chink through which the eye could just penetrate. Through this crevice a small room was visible, whitewashed and clean but very bare of furniture. In one corner, near a small fire, sat an old man, leaning his head on his hands in a disconsolate attitude. The young girl was occupied in arranging the cottage; but presently she took something out of a drawer, which employed her hands, and she sat down beside the old man, who, taking up an instrument, began to play and to produce sounds sweeter than the voice of the thrush or the nightingale. It was a lovely sight, even to me, poor wretch! who had never beheld aught beautiful before. The silver hair and benevolent countenance of the aged cottager won my reverence, while the gentle manners of the girl enticed my love. He played a sweet mournful air which I perceived drew tears from the eyes of his amiable companion, of which the old man took no notice, until she sobbed audibly; he then pronounced a few sounds, and the fair creature, leaving her work, knelt at his feet. He raised her and smiled with such kindness and affection that I felt sensations of a peculiar and overpowering nature; they were a mixture of pain and pleasure, such as I had never before experienced, either from hunger or cold, warmth or food; and I withdrew from the window, unable to bear these emotions.

'Soon after this the young man returned, bearing on his shoulders a load of wood. The girl met him at the door, helped to relieve him of his burden, and taking some of the fuel into the cottage, placed it on the fire; then she and the youth went apart into a nook of the cottage, and he showed her a large loaf and a piece of cheese. She seemed pleased and went into the garden for some roots and plants, which she placed in water, and then upon the fire. She afterwards continued her work, whilst the young man went into the garden and appeared busily employed in digging and pulling up roots. After he had been employed thus about an hour, the young woman joined him and they entered the cottage together.

'The old man had, in the mean time, been pensive, but on the appearance of his companions he assumed a more cheerful air, and they sat down to eat. The meal was quickly dispatched. The young woman was again occupied in arranging the cottage, the old man walked before the cottage in the sun for a few minutes, leaning on the arm of the youth. Nothing could exceed in beauty the contrast between these two excellent creatures. One was old, with silver hairs and a countenance beaming with benevolence and love; the younger was slight and graceful in his figure, and his features were moulded with the finest symmetry, yet his eyes and attitude expressed the utmost sadness and despondency. The old man returned to the cottage, and the youth, with tools different from those he had used in the morning, directed his steps across the fields.

'Night quickly shut in, but to my extreme wonder, I found that the cottagers had a means of prolonging light by the use of tapers, and was delighted to find that the setting of the sun did not put an end to the pleasure I experienced in watching my human neighbours. In the evening the young girl and her companion were employed in various occupations which I did not understand; and the old man again took up the instrument which produced the divine sounds that had enchanted me in the morning. So soon as he had finished, the youth began, not to play, but to utter sounds that were monotonous, and neither resembling the harmony of the old man's instrument nor the songs of the birds; I since found that he read aloud, but at that time I knew nothing of the science of words or letters.

'The family, after having been thus occupied for a short time, extinguished their lights and retired, as I conjectured, to rest.'

## CHAPTER 12

'I LAY on my straw, but I could not sleep. I thought of the occurrences of the day. What chiefly struck me was the gentle manners of these people, and I longed to join them, but dared not. I remembered too well the treatment I had suffered the night before from the barbarous villagers, and resolved, whatever course of conduct I might hereafter think it right to pursue, that for the present I would remain quietly in my hovel, watching and endeavouring to discover the motives which influenced their actions.

'The cottagers arose the next morning before the sun. The young woman arranged the cottage and prepared the food, and the youth departed after the first meal.

'This day was passed in the same routine as that which preceded it. The young man was constantly employed out of doors, and the girl in various laborious occupations within. The old man, whom I soon perceived to be blind, employed his leisure hours on his instrument or in contemplation. Nothing could exceed the love and respect which the younger cottagers exhibited towards their venerable companion. They performed towards him every little office of affection and duty with gentleness, and he rewarded them by his benevolent smiles.

'They were not entirely happy. The young man and his companion often went apart and appeared to weep. I saw no cause for their unhappiness, but I was deeply affected by it. If such lovely creatures were miserable, it was less strange that I, an imperfect and solitary being, should be wretched. Yet why were these gentle beings unhappy? They possessed a delightful house (for such it was in my eyes) and every luxury; they had a fire to warm them when chill and delicious viands when hungry; they were dressed in excellent clothes; and, still more, they enjoyed one another's company and speech, interchanging each day looks of affection and kindness. What did their tears imply? Did they really express pain? I was at first unable to solve these questions, but perpetual attention and time explained to me many appearances which were at first enigmatic.

'A considerable period elapsed before I discovered one of the causes of the uneasiness of this amiable family: it was poverty, and they suffered that evil in a very distressing degree. Their nourishment consisted entirely of the vegetables of their garden and the milk of one cow, which gave very little during the winter, when its masters could scarcely procure food to support it. They often, I believe, suffered the pangs of hunger very poignantly, especially the two younger cottagers, for several times they placed food before the old man when they reserved none for themselves.

'This trait of kindness moved me sensibly. I had been accustomed, during the night, to steal a part of their store for my own consumption, but when I found that in doing this I inflicted pain on the cottagers, I abstained and satisfied myself with berries, nuts, and roots which I gathered from a neighbouring wood.

'I discovered also another means through which I was enabled to assist their labours. I found that the youth spent a great part of each day in collecting wood for the family fire, and during the night I often took his tools, the use of which I quickly discovered, and brought home firing sufficient for the consumption of several days.

'I remember, the first time that I did this, the young woman, when she opened the door in the morning, appeared greatly astonished on seeing a great pile of wood on the outside. She uttered some words in a loud voice, and the youth joined her, who also expressed surprize. I observed, with pleasure, that he did not go to the forest that day, but spent it in repairing the cottage and cultivating the garden.

'By degrees I made a discovery of still greater moment. I found that these people possessed a method of communicating their experience and feelings to one another by articulate sounds. I perceived that the words they spoke sometimes produced pleasure or pain, smiles or sadness, in the minds and countenances of the hearers. This was indeed a godlike science, and I ardently desired to become acquainted with it. But I was baffled in every attempt I made for this purpose. Their pronunciation was quick, and the words they uttered, not having any apparent connection with visible objects, I was unable to discover any clue by which I could unravel the mystery of their reference. By great application, however, and after having remained during the space of several revolutions of the moon in my hovel, I discovered the names that were given to some of the most familiar objects of discourse; I learned and applied the words, "fire," "milk," "bread," and "wood." I learned also the names of the cottagers themselves. The youth and his companion had each of them several names, but the old man had only one, which was "father." The girl was called "sister" or "Agatha," and the youth "Felix," "brother," or "son." I cannot describe the delight I felt when I learned the ideas appropriated to each of these sounds and was able to pronounce them. I distinguished several other words without being able as yet to understand or apply them, such as "good," "dearest," "unhappy."

'I spent the winter in this manner. The gentle manners and beauty of the cottagers greatly endeared them to me; when they were unhappy, I felt depressed; when they rejoiced, I sympathized in their joys. I saw few human beings besides them, and if any other happened to enter the cottage, their harsh manners and rude gait only enhanced to me the superior accomplishments of my friends. The old man, I could perceive, often endeavoured to encourage his children, as sometimes I found that he called them, to cast off their melancholy. He would talk in a cheerful accent, with an expression of goodness that bestowed pleasure even upon me. Agatha listened with respect, her eyes sometimes filled with tears, which she endeavoured to wipe away unperceived; but I generally found that her countenance and tone were more cheerful after having listened to the exhortations of her father. It was not thus with Felix. He was always the saddest of the group, and even to my unpractised senses, he appeared to have suffered more deeply than his friends. But if his countenance was more sorrowful, his voice was more cheerful than that of his sister, especially when he addressed the old man.

'I could mention innumerable instances which, although slight, marked the dispositions of these amiable cottagers. In the midst of poverty and want, Felix carried with pleasure to his sister the first little white flower that peeped out from beneath the snowy ground. Early in the morning, before she had risen, he cleared away the snow that obstructed her path to the milk-house, drew water from the well, and brought the wood from the out-house, where, to his perpetual astonishment, he found his store always replenished by an invisible hand. In the day, I believe, he worked sometimes for a neighbouring farmer, because he often went forth and did not return until dinner, yet brought no wood with him. At other times he worked in the garden, but as there was little to do in the frosty season, he read to the old man and Agatha.

'This reading had puzzled me extremely at first, but by degrees I discovered that he uttered many of the same sounds when he read as when he talked. I conjectured, therefore, that he found on the paper signs for speech which he understood, and I ardently longed to comprehend these also; but how was that possible when I did not even understand the sounds for which they stood as signs? I improved, however, sensibly in this science, but not sufficiently to follow up any kind of conversation, although I applied my whole mind to the endeavour: for I easily perceived that, although I eagerly longed to discover myself[1] to the cottagers, I ought not to make the attempt until I had first become master of their language, which knowledge might enable me to make them overlook the deformity of my figure; for with this also the contrast perpetually presented to my eyes had made me acquainted.

'I had admired the perfect forms of my cottagers – their grace, beauty, and delicate complexions; but how was I terrified when I viewed myself in a transparent pool! At first I started back, unable to believe that it was indeed I who was reflected in the mirror; and when I became fully convinced that I was in reality the monster that I am, I was filled with the bitterest sensations of despondence and mortification. Alas! I did not yet entirely know the fatal effects of this miserable deformity.

'As the sun became warmer and the light of day longer, the snow vanished, and I beheld the bare trees and the black earth. From this time Felix was more employed, and the heart-moving indications of impending famine disappeared. Their food, as I afterwards found, was coarse, but it was wholesome; and they procured a sufficiency of it. Several new kinds of plants sprang up in the garden, which they dressed; and these signs of comfort increased daily as the season advanced.

'The old man, leaning on his son, walked each day at noon, when it did not rain, as I found it was called when the heavens poured forth its waters. This frequently took place, but a high wind quickly dried the earth, and the season became far more pleasant than it had been.

'My mode of life in my hovel was uniform. During the morning I attended the motions of the cottagers, and when they were dispersed in various occupations, I slept; the remainder of the day was spent in observing my friends. When they had retired to rest, if there was any moon or the night was star-light, I went into the woods and collected my own food and fuel for the cottage. When I returned, as often as it was necessary, I cleared their path from the snow and performed those offices that I had seen done by Felix. I afterwards found that these labours, performed by an invisible hand, greatly astonished them; and once or twice I heard them, on these occasions, utter the words "good spirit," "wonderful," but I did not then understand the signification of these terms.

'My thoughts now became more active, and I longed to discover the motives and feelings of these lovely creatures; I was inquisitive to know why Felix appeared so miserable and Agatha so sad. I thought (foolish wretch!) that it might be in my power to restore happiness to these deserving people. When I slept or was absent, the forms of the venerable blind father, the gentle Agatha, and the excellent Felix flitted before me. I looked upon them as superior beings who would be the arbiters of my future destiny. I formed in my imagination a thousand pictures of presenting myself to them, and their reception of me. I imagined that they would be disgusted, until, by my gentle demeanour and conciliating words, I should first win their favour and afterwards their love.

'These thoughts exhilarated me and led me to apply with fresh ardour to the acquiring the art of language. My organs were indeed harsh, but supple; and although my voice was very unlike the soft music of their tones, yet I pronounced such words as I understood with tolerable ease. It was as the ass and the lap-dog; yet surely the gentle ass whose intentions were affectionate, although his manners were rude, deserved better treatment than blows and execration.

'The pleasant showers and genial warmth of spring greatly altered the aspect of the earth. Men, who before this change seemed to have been hid in caves, dispersed themselves and were employed in various arts of cultivation. The birds sang in more cheerful notes, and the leaves began to bud forth on the trees. Happy, happy earth! Fit habitation for gods, which, so short a time before, was bleak, damp, and unwholesome. My spirits were elevated by the enchanting appearance of nature; the past was blotted from my memory, the present was tranquil, and the future gilded by bright rays of hope and anticipations of joy.'

## CHAPTER 13

'I NOW hasten to the more moving part of my story. I shall relate events that impressed me with feelings which, from what I had been, have made me what I am.

'Spring advanced rapidly; the weather became fine and the skies cloudless. It surprized me that what before was desert and gloomy should now bloom with the most beautiful flowers and verdure. My senses were gratified and refreshed by a thousand scents of delight and a thousand sights of beauty.

'It was on one of these days, when my cottagers periodically rested from labour – the old man played on his guitar, and the children listened to him – that I observed the countenance of Felix was melancholy beyond expression; he sighed frequently, and once his father paused in his music, and I conjectured by his manner that he enquired the cause of his son's sorrow. Felix replied in a cheerful accent, and the old man was recommencing his music when some one tapped at the door.

'It was a lady on horseback, accompanied by a countryman as a guide. The lady was dressed in a dark suit and covered with a thick black veil. Agatha asked a question, to which the stranger only replied by pronouncing, in a sweet accent, the name of Felix. Her voice was musical but unlike that of either of my friends. On hearing this word, Felix came up hastily to the lady, who, when she saw him, threw up her veil, and I beheld a countenance of angelic beauty and expression. Her hair of a shining raven black, and curiously braided; her eyes were dark, but gentle, although animated; her features of a regular proportion, and her complexion wondrously fair, each cheek tinged with a lovely pink.

'Felix seemed ravished with delight when he saw her, every trait of sorrow vanished from his face, and it instantly expressed a degree of ecstatic joy, of which I could hardly have believed it capable; his eyes sparkled, as his cheek flushed with pleasure; and at that moment I thought him as beautiful as the stranger. She appeared affected by different feelings; wiping a few tears from her lovely eyes, she held out her hand to Felix, who kissed it rapturously and called her, as well as I could distinguish, his sweet Arabian. She did not appear to understand him, but smiled. He assisted her to dismount. and dismissing her guide, conducted her into the cottage. Some conversation took place between him and his father, and the young stranger knelt at the old man's feet and would have kissed his hand, but he raised her and embraced her affectionately.

'I soon perceived that although the stranger uttered aticulate sounds and appeared to have a language of her own, she was neither understood by, nor herself understood, the cottagers. They made many signs which I did not comprehend, but I saw that her presence diffused gladness through the cottage, dispelling their sorrow as the sun dissipates the morning mists. Felix seemed peculiarly happy and with smiles of delight welcomed his Arabian. Agatha, the ever-gentle Agatha, kissed the hands of the lovely stranger, and pointing to her brother, made signs which appeared to me to mean that he had been sorrowful until she came. Some hours passed thus, while they, by their countenances, expressed joy, the cause of which I did not comprehend. Presently I found, by the frequent recurrence of some sound which the stranger repeated after them, that she was endeavouring to learn their language; and the idea instantly occurred to me that I should make use of the same instructions to the same end. The stranger learned about twenty words at the first lesson, most of them, indeed, were those which I had before understood, but I profited by the others.

'As night came on Agatha and the Arabian retired early. When they separated Felix kissed the hand of the stranger and said, "Good night, sweet Safie." He sat up much longer, conversing with his father, and by the frequent repetition of her name, I conjectured that their lovely guest was the subject of their conversation. I ardently desired to understand them, and bent every faculty towards that purpose, but found it utterly impossible.

'The next morning Felix went out to his work, and after the usual occupations of Agatha were finished, the Arabian sat at the feet of the old man, and taking his guitar, played some airs so entrancingly beautiful that they at once drew tears of sorrow and delight from my eyes. She sang, and her voice flowed in a rich cadence, swelling or dying away like a nightingale of the woods.

'When she had finished, she gave the guitar to Agatha, who at first declined it. She played a simple air, and her voice accompanied it in sweet accents, but unlike the wondrous strain of the stranger. The old man appeared enraptured and said some words which Agatha endeavoured to explain to Safie, and by which he appeared to wish to express that she bestowed on him the greatest delight by her music.

'The days now passed as peaceably as before, with the sole alteration that joy had taken place of sadness in the countenances of my friends. Safie was always gay and happy; she and I improved rapidly in the knowledge of language, so that in two months I began to comprehend most of the words uttered by my protectors.

'In the meanwhile also the black ground was covered with herbage, and the green banks interspersed with innumerable flowers, sweet to the scent and the eyes, stars of pale radiance among the moonlight woods; the sun became warmer, the nights clear and balmy; and my nocturnal rambles were an extreme pleasure to me, although they were considerably shortened by the late setting and early rising of the sun, for I never ventured abroad during daylight, fearful of meeting with the same treatment I had formerly endured in the first village which I entered.

'My days were spent in close attention, that I might more speedily master the language; and I may boast that I improved more rapidly than the Arabian, who understood very little and conversed in broken accents, whilst I comprehended and could imitate almost every word that was spoken.

'While I improved in speech, I also learned the science of letters as it was taught to the stranger, and this opened before me a wide field for wonder and delight.

'The book from which Felix instructed Safie was Volney's *Ruins of Empires*.[1] I should not have understood the purport of this book had not Felix, in reading it, given very minute explanations. He had chosen this work, he said, because the declamatory style was framed in imitation of the Eastern authors. Through this work I obtained a cursory knowledge of history and a view of the several empires at present existing in the world; it gave me an insight into the manners, governments, and religions of the different nations of the earth. I heard of the slothful Asiatics, of the stupendous genius and mental activity of the Grecians, of the wars and wonderful virtue of the early Romans – of their subsequent degenerating – of the decline of that mighty empire, of chivalry, Christianity, and kings. I heard of the discovery of the American hemisphere and wept with Safie over the hapless fate of its original inhabitants.

'These wonderful narrations inspired me with strange feelings. Was man, indeed, at once so powerful, so virtuous, and magnificent, yet so vicious and base? He appeared at one time a mere scion of the evil principle and at another as all that can be conceived as noble and godlike. To be a great and virtuous man appeared the highest honour that can befall a sensitive being; to be base and vicious, as many on record have been, appeared the lowest degradation, a condition more abject than that of the blind mole or harmless worm. For a long time I could not conceive how one man could go forth to murder his fellow, or even why there were laws and governments; but when I heard details of vice and bloodshed, my wonder ceased and I turned away with disgust and loathing.

'Every conversation of the cottagers now opened new wonders to me. While I listened to the instructions which Felix bestowed upon the Arabian, the strange system of human society was explained to me. I heard of the division of property, of immense wealth and squalid poverty; of rank, descent, and noble blood.

'The words induced me to turn towards myself. I learned that the possessions most esteemed by your fellow creatures were high and unsullied descent united with riches. A man might be respected with only one of these advantages, but without either he was considered, except in very rare instances, as a vagabond and a slave, doomed to waste his powers for the profits of the chosen few! And what was I? Of my creation and creator I was absolutely ignorant, but I knew that I possessed no money, no friends, no kind of property, I was, besides, endued with a figure hideously deformed and loathsome; I was not even of the same nature as man. I was more agile than they and could subsist upon coarser diet; I bore the extremes of heat and cold with less injury to my frame; my stature far exceeded theirs. When I looked around I saw and heard of none like me. Was I, then, a monster, a blot upon the earth, from which all men fled and whom all men disowned?

'I cannot describe to you the agony that these reflections inflicted upon me; I tried to dispel them, but sorrow only increased with knowledge. Oh, that I had forever remained in my native wood, nor known nor felt beyond the sensations of hunger, thirst, and heat!

'Of what a strange nature is knowledge! It clings to the mind, when it has once seized on it, like a lichen on the rock. I wished sometimes to shake off all thought and feeling, but I learned that there was but one means to overcome the sensation of pain, and that was death – a state which I feared yet did not understand. I admired virtue and good feelings and loved the gentle manners and amiable qualities of my cottagers, but I was shut out from intercourse with them, except through means which I obtained by stealth, when I was unseen and unknown, and which rather increased than satisfied the desire I had of becoming one among my fellows. The gentle words of Agatha and the animated smiles of the charming Arabian were not for me. The mild exhortations of the old man and the lively conversation of the loved Felix were not for me. Miserable, unhappy wretch!

'Other lessons were impressed upon me even more deeply. I heard of the difference of sexes, and the birth and growth of children; how the father doated on the smiles of the infant, and the lively sallies of the older child; how all the life and cares of the mother were wrapped up in the precious charge; how the mind of youth expanded and gained knowledge; of brother, sister, and all the various relationships which bind one human being to another in mutual bonds.

'But where were my friends and relations? No father had watched my infant days, no mother had blessed me with smiles and caresses; or if they had, all my past life was now a blot, a blind vacancy in which I distinguished nothing. From my earliest remembrance I had been as I then was in height and proportion. I had never yet seen a being resembling me or who claimed any intercourse with me. What was I? The question again recurred, to be answered only with groans.

'I will soon explain to what these feelings tended, but allow me now to return to the cottagers, whose story excited in me such various feelings of indignation, delight, and wonder, but which all terminated in additional love and reverence for my protectors (for so I loved, in an innocent, half-painful self-deceit, to call them).'

## CHAPTER 14

'SOME time elapsed before I learned the history of my friends. It was one which could not fail to impress itself deeply on my mind, unfolding as it did a number of circumstances, each interesting and wonderful to one so utterly inexperienced as I was.

'The name of the old man was De Lacey. He was descended from a good family in France, where he had lived for many years in affluence, respected by his superiors and beloved by his equals. His son was bred in the service of his country, and Agatha had ranked with ladies of the highest distinction. A few months before my arrival they had lived in a large and luxurious city called Paris, surrounded by friends and possessed of every enjoyment which virtue, refinement of intellect, or taste, accompanied by a moderate fortune, could afford.

'The father of Safie had been the cause of their ruin. He was a Turkish merchant and had inhabited Paris for many years, when, for some reason which I could not learn, he became obnoxious to the government. He was seized and cast into prison the very day that Safie arrived from Constantinople to join him. He was tried and condemned to death. The injustice of his sentence was very flagrant; all Paris was indignant; and it was judged that his religion and wealth rather than the crime alleged against him had been the cause of his condemnation.

'Felix had accidentally been present at the trial; his horror and indignation were uncontrollable when he heard the decision of the court. He made, at that moment, a solemn vow to deliver him and then looked around for the means. After many fruitless attempts to gain admittance to the prison, he found a strongly grated window in an unguarded part of the building, which lighted the dungeon of the unfortunate Muhammadan, who, loaded with chains, waited in despair the execution of the barbarous sentence. Felix visited the grate at night and made known to the prisoner his intentions in his favour. The Turk, amazed and delighted, endeavoured to kindle the zeal of his deliverer by promises of reward and wealth. Felix rejected his offers with contempt, yet when he saw the lovely Safie, who was allowed to visit her father and who, by her gestures, expressed her lively gratitude, the youth could not help owning to his own mind that the captive possessed a treasure which would fully reward his toil and hazard.

'The Turk quickly perceived the impression that his daughter had made on the heart of Felix and endeavoured to secure him more entirely in his interests by the promise of her hand in marriage so soon as he should be conveyed to a place of safety. Felix was too delicate to accept this offer, yet he looked forward to the probability of the event as to the consummation of his happiness.

'During the ensuing days, while the preparations were going forward for the escape of the merchant, the zeal of Felix was warmed by several letters that he received from this lovely girl, who found means to express her thoughts in the language of her lover by the aid of an old man, a servant of her father who understood French. She thanked him in the most ardent terms for his intended services towards her parent, and at the same time she gently deplored her own fate.

'I have copies of these letters; for I found means, during my residence in the hovel, to procure the implements of writing; and the letters were often in the hands of Felix or Agatha. Before I depart I will give them to you; they will prove the truth of my tale; but at present, as the sun is already far declined, I shall only have time to repeat the substance of them to you.

'Safie related that her mother was a Christian Arab,

seized and made a slave by the Turks; recommended by her beauty, she had won the heart of the father of Safie, who married her. The young girl spoke in high and enthusiastic terms of her mother, who, born in freedom, spurned the bondage to which she was now reduced. She instructed her daughter in the tenets of her religion and taught her to aspire to higher powers of intellect and an independence of spirit forbidden to the female followers of Muhammad. This lady died, but her lessons were indelibly impressed on the mind of Safie, who sickened at the prospect of again returning to Asia and being immured within the walls of a harem, allowed only to occupy herself with infantile amusements, ill-suited to the temper of her soul, now accustomed to grand ideas and a noble emulation for virtue. The prospect of marrying a Christian and remaining in a country where women were allowed to take a rank in society was enchanting to her.

'The day for the execution of the Turk was fixed, but on the night previous to it he quitted his prison and before morning was distant many leagues from Paris. Felix had procured passports in the name of his father, sister, and himself. He had previously communicated his plan to the former, who aided the deceit by quitting his house, under the pretence of a journey and concealing himself, with his daughter, in an obscure part of Paris.

'Felix conducted the fugitives through France to Lyons and across Mont Cenis to Leghorn, where the merchant had decided to wait a favourable opportunity of passing into some part of the Turkish dominions.

'Safie resolved to remain with her father until the moment of his departure, before which time the Turk renewed his promise that she should be united to his deliverer; and Felix remained with them in expectation of that event; and in the mean time he enjoyed the society of the Arabian, who exhibited towards him the simplest and tenderest affection. They conversed with one another through the means of an interpreter, and sometimes with the interpretation of looks; and Safie sang to him the divine airs of her native country.

'The Turk allowed this intimacy to take place and encouraged the hopes of the youthful lovers, while in his heart he had formed far other plans. He loathed the idea that his daughter should be united to a Christian, but he feared the resentment of Felix if he should appear lukewarm, for he knew that he was still in the power of his deliverer if he should choose to betray him to the Italian state which they inhabited. He revolved a thousand plans by which he should be enabled to prolong the deceit until it might be no longer necessary, and secretly to take his daughter with him when he departed. His plans were facilitated by the news which arrived from Paris.

'The government of France were greatly enraged at the escape of their victim and spared no pains to detect and punish his deliverer. The plot of Felix was quickly discovered, and De Lacey and Agatha were thrown into prison. The news reached Felix and roused him from his dream of pleasure. His blind and aged father and his gentle sister lay in a noisome dungeon while he enjoyed the free air and the society of her whom he loved. This idea was torture to him. He quickly arranged with the Turk that if the latter should find a favourable opportunity for escape before Felix could return to Italy, Safie should remain as a boarder at a convent at Leghorn; and then, quitting the lovely Arabian, he hastened to Paris and delivered himself up to the vengeance of the law, hoping to free De Lacey and Agatha by this proceeding.

'He did not succeed. They remained confined for five months before the trial took place, the result of which deprived them of their fortune and condemned them to a perpetual exile from their native country.

'They found a miserable asylum in the cottage in Germany, where I discovered them. Felix soon learned that the treacherous Turk, for whom he and his family endured such unheard-of oppression, on discovering that his deliverer was thus reduced to poverty and ruin, became a traitor to good feeling and honour and had quitted Italy with his daughter, insultingly sending Felix a pittance of money to aid him, as he said, in some plan of future maintenance.

'Such were the events that preyed on the heart of Felix and rendered him, when I first saw him, the most miserable of his family. He could have endured poverty, and while this distress had been the meed of his virtue, he gloried in it; but the ingratitude of the Turk and the loss of his beloved Safie were misfortunes more bitter and irreparable. The arrival of the Arabian now infused new life into his soul.

'When the news reached Leghorn that Felix was deprived of his wealth and rank, the merchant commanded his daughter to think no more of her lover, but to prepare to return to her native country. The generous nature of Safie was outraged by this command; she attempted to expostulate with her father, but he left her angrily, reiterating his tyrannical mandate.

'A few days after, the Turk entered his daughter's apartment and told her hastily that he had reason to believe that his residence at Leghorn had been divulged and that he should speedily be delivered up to the French government; he had consequently hired a vessel to convey him to Constantinople, for which city he should sail in a few hours. He intended to leave his daughter under the care of a confidential servant, to follow at her leisure with the greater part of his property, which had not yet arrived at Leghorn.

'When alone, Safie resolved in her own mind the plan of conduct that it would become her to pursue in this emergency. A residence in Turkey was abhorrent to her; her religion and her feelings were alike averse to it. By some papers of her father which fell into her hands she heard of the exile of her lover and learnt the name of the spot where he then resided. She hesitated some time, but at length she formed her determination. Taking with her some jewels that belonged to her and a sum of money, she quitted Italy with an attendant, a native of Leghorn, but who understood the common language of Turkey, and departed for Germany.

'She arrived in safety at a town about twenty leagues from the cottage of De Lacey, when her attendant fell dangerously ill. Safie nursed her with the most devoted affection, but the poor girl died, and the Arabian was left alone, unacquainted with the language of the country and utterly ignorant of the customs of the world. She fell, however, into good hands. The Italian had mentioned the name of the spot for which they were bound, and after her death the woman of the house in which they had lived took care that Safie should arrive in safety at the cottage of her lover.'

## CHAPTER 15

'Such was the history of my beloved cottagers. It impressed me deeply. I learned, from the views of social life which it developed, to admire their virtues and to deprecate the vices of mankind.

'As yet I looked upon crime as a distant evil; benevolence and generosity were ever present before me, inciting within me a desire to become an actor in the busy scene where so many admirable qualities were called forth and displayed. But in giving an account of the progress of my intellect, I must not omit a circumstance which occurred in the beginning of the month of August of the same year.

'One night during my accustomed visit to the neighbouring wood where I collected my own food and brought home firing for my protectors, I found on the ground a leathern portmanteau containing several articles of dress and some books. I eagerly seized the prize and returned with it to my hovel. Fortunately the books were written in the language, the elements of which I had acquired at the cottage; they consisted of *Paradise Lost*, a volume of Plutarch's *Lives*, and the *Sorrows of Werter*.[1] The possession of these treasures gave me extreme delight; I now continually studied and exercised my mind upon these histories, whilst my friends were employed in their ordinary occupations.

'I can hardly describe to you the effect of these books. They produced in me an infinity of new images and feelings, that sometimes raised me to ecstasy, but more frequently sunk me into the lowest dejection. In the *Sorrows of Werter*, besides the interest of its simple and affecting story, so many opinions are canvassed and so many lights thrown upon what had hitherto been to me obscure subjects that I found in it a never-ending source of speculation and astonishment. The gentle and domestic manners it described, combined with lofty sentiments and feelings, which had for their object something out of self, accorded well with my experience among my protectors and with the wants which were forever alive in my own bosom. But I thought Werter himself a more divine being than I had ever beheld or imagined; his character contained no pretension, but it sank deep. The disquisitions upon death and suicide were calculated to fill me with wonder. I did not pretend to enter into the merits of the case, yet I inclined towards the opinions of the hero, whose extinction I wept, without precisely understanding it.

'As I read, however, I applied much personally to my own feelings and condition. I found myself similar yet at the same time strangely unlike to the beings concerning whom I read and to whose conversation I was a listener. I sympathized with and partly understood them, but I was unformed in mind; I was dependent on none and related to none. "The path of my departure was free," and there was none to lament my annihilation. My person was hideous and my stature gigantic. What did this mean? Who was I? What was I? Whence did I come? What was my destination? These questions continually recurred, but I was unable to solve them.

'The volume of Plutarch's *Lives* which I possessed contained the histories of the first founders of the ancient republics. This book had a far different effect upon me from the *Sorrows of Werter*. I learned from Werter's imaginations despondency and gloom, but Plutarch taught me high thoughts; he elevated me above the wretched sphere of my own reflections, to admire and love the heroes of past ages. Many things I read surpassed my understanding and experience. I had a very confused knowledge of kingdoms, wide extents of country, mighty rivers, and boundless seas. But I was perfectly unacquainted with towns and large assemblages of men. The cottage of my protectors had been the only school in which I had studied human nature, but this book developed new and mightier scenes of action. I read of men concerned in public affairs, governing or massacring their species. I felt the greatest ardour for virtue rise within me, and abhorrence for vice, as far as I understood the signification of those terms, relative as they were, as I applied them, to pleasure and pain alone. Induced by these feelings, I was of course led to admire peaceable lawgivers, Numa, Solon, and Lycurgus, in preference to Romulus and Theseus. The patriarchal lives of my protectors caused these impressions to take a firm hold on my mind; perhaps, if my first introduction to humanity had been made by a young soldier, burning for glory and slaughter, I should have been imbued with different sensations.

'But *Paradise Lost* excited different and far deeper emotions. I read it, as I had read the other volumes which had fallen into my hands, as a true history. It moved every feeling of wonder and awe that the picture of an omnipotent God warring with his creatures was capable of exciting. I often referred the several situations, as their similarity struck me, to my own. Like Adam, I was apparently united by no link to any other being in existence; but his state was far different from mine in every other respect. He had come forth from the hands of God a perfect creature, happy and prosperous, guarded by the especial care of his Creator; he was allowed to converse with and acquire knowledge from beings of a superior nature, but I was wretched, helpless, and alone. Many times I considered Satan as the fitter emblem of my condition, for often, like him, when I viewed the bliss of my protectors, the bitter gall of envy rose within me.

'Another circumstance strengthened and confirmed these feelings. Soon after my arrival in the hovel I discovered some papers in the pocket of the dress which I had taken from your laboratory. At first I had neglected them, but now that I was able to decipher the characters in which they were written, I began to study them with diligence. It was your journal of the four months that preceded my creation. You minutely described in these papers every step you took in the progress of your work; this history was mingled with accounts of domestic occurrences. You doubtless recollect these papers. Here they are. Every thing is related in them which bears reference to my accursed origin; the whole detail of that series of disgusting circumstances which produced it is set in view; the minutest description of my odious and loathsome person is given, in language which painted your own horrors and rendered mine indelible. I sickened as I read. "Hateful day when I received life!" I exclaimed in agony. "Accursed creator! Why did you form a monster so hideous that even *you* turned from me in disgust? God, in pity, made man beautiful and alluring, after his own image; but my form is a filthy type of yours, more horrid even from the very resemblance. Satan had had his companions, fellow devils, to admire and encourage him, but I am solitary and abhorred."

'These were the reflections of my hours of despondency and solitude; but when I contemplated the virtues of the cottagers, their amiable and benevolent dispositions, I persuaded myself that when they should become acquainted with my admiration of their virtues they would compassionate me and overlook my personal deformity. Could they turn from their door one, however monstrous, who solicited their compassion and friendship? I resolved, at least, not to despair, but in every way to fit myself for an interview with them which would decide my fate. I postponed this attempt for some months longer, for the importance attached to its success inspired me with a dread lest I should fail. Besides, I found that my understanding improved so much with every day's experience that I was unwilling to commence this undertaking until a few more months should have added to my sagacity.

'Several changes, in the mean time, took place in the

cottage. The presence of Safie diffused happiness among its inhabitants, and I also found that a greater degree of plenty reigned there. Felix and Agatha spent more time in amusement and conversation, and were assisted in their labours by servants. They did not appear rich, but they were contented and happy; their feelings were serene and peaceful, while mine became every day more tumultuous. Increase of knowledge only discovered to me more clearly what a wretched outcast I was. I cherished hope, it is true, but it vanished when I beheld my person reflected in water or my shadow in the moonshine, even as that frail image and that inconstant shade.

'I endeavoured to crush these fears and to fortify myself for the trial which in a few months I resolved to undergo; and sometimes I allowed my thoughts, unchecked by reason, to ramble in the fields of Paradise, and dared to fancy amiable and lovely creatures sympathizing with my feelings and cheering my gloom; their angelic countenances breathed smiles of consolation. But it was all a dream; no Eve soothed my sorrows nor shared my thoughts; I was alone. I remembered Adam's supplication to his Creator.[2] But where was mine? He had abandoned me, and in the bitterness of my heart I cursed him.

'Autumn passed thus. I saw, with surprize and grief, the leaves decay and fall, and nature again assume the barren and bleak appearance it had worn when I first beheld the woods and the lovely moon. Yet I did not heed the bleakness of the weather; I was better fitted by my conformation for the endurance of cold than heat. But my chief delights were the sight of the flowers, the birds, and all the gay apparel of summer; when those deserted me, I turned with more attention towards the cottagers. Their happiness was not decreased by the absence of summer. They loved and sympathized with one another; and their joys, depending on each other, were not interrupted by the casualties that took place around them. The more I saw of them, the greater became my desire to claim their protection and kindness; my heart yearned to be known and loved by these amiable creatures; to see their sweet looks directed towards me with affection was the utmost limit of my ambition. I dared not think that they would turn them from me with disdain and horror. The poor that stopped at their door were never driven away. I asked, it is true, for greater treasures than a little food or rest: I required kindness and sympathy; but I did not believe myself unworthy of it.

'The winter advanced, and an entire revolution of the seasons had taken place since I awoke into life. My attention at this time was solely directed towards my plan of introducing myself into the cottage of my protectors. I revolved many projects, but that on which I finally fixed was to enter the dwelling when the blind old man should be alone. I had sagacity enough to discover that the unnatural hideousness of my person was the chief object of horror with those who had formerly beheld me. My voice, although harsh, had nothing terrible in it; I thought, therefore, that if in the absence of his children I could gain the good will and mediation of the old De Lacey, I might by his means be tolerated by my younger protectors.

'One day, when the sun shone on the red leaves that strewed the ground and diffused cheerfulness, although it denied warmth, Safie, Agatha, and Felix departed on a long country walk, and the old man, at his own desire, was left alone in the cottage. When his children had departed, he took up his guitar and played several mournful but sweet airs, more sweet and mournful than I had ever heard him play before. At first his countenance was illuminated with pleasure, but as he continued, thoughtfulness and sadness succeeded; at length, laying aside the instrument, he sat absorbed in reflection.

'My heart beat quick; this was the hour and moment of trial, which would decide my hopes or realize my fears. The servants were gone to a neighbouring fair. All was silent in and around the cottage; it was an excellent opportunity; yet, when I proceeded to execute my plan, my limbs failed me and I sank to the ground. Again I rose, and exerting all the firmness of which I was master, removed the planks which I had placed before my hovel to conceal my retreat. The fresh air revived me, and with renewed determination I approached the door of their cottage.

'I knocked. "Who is there?" said the old man – "Come in."

'I entered. "Pardon this intrusion," said I; "I am a traveller in want of a little rest; you would greatly oblige me if you would allow me to remain a few minutes before the fire."

'"Enter," said De Lacey, "and I will try in what manner I can to relieve your wants; but, unfortunately, my children are from home, and as I am blind, I am afraid I shall find it difficult to procure food for you."

'"Do not trouble yourself, my kind host; I have food; it is warmth and rest only that I need."

'I sat down, and a silence ensued. I knew that every minute was precious to me, yet I remained irresolute in what manner to commence the interview, when the old man addressed me. "By your language, stranger, I suppose you are my countryman; are you French?"

'"No; but I was educated by a French family and understand that language only. I am now going to claim the protection of some friends, whom I sincerely love, and of whose favour I have some hopes."

'"Are they Germans?"

'"No, they are French. But let us change the subject. I am an unfortunate and deserted creature; I look around and I have no relation or friend upon earth. These amiable people to whom I go have never seen me and know little of me. I am full of fears, for if I fail there, I am an outcast in the world forever."

'"Do not despair. To be friendless is indeed to be unfortunate, but the hearts of men, when unprejudiced by any obvious self-interest, are full of brotherly love and charity. Rely, therefore, on your hopes; and if these friends are good and amiable, do not despair."

'"They are kind – they are the most excellent creatures in the world; but, unfortunately, they are prejudiced against me. I have good dispositions; my life has been hitherto harmless and in some degree beneficial; but a fatal prejudice clouds their eyes, and where they ought to see a feeling and kind friend, they behold only a detestable monster."

'"That is indeed unfortunate; but if you are really blameless, cannot you undeceive them?"

'"I am about to undertake that task; and it is on that account that I feel so many overwhelming terrors. I tenderly love these friends; I have, unknown to them, been for many months in the habits of daily kindness towards them; but they believe that I wish to injure them, and it is that prejudice which I wish to overcome."

'"Where do these friends reside?"

'"Near this spot."

'The old man paused and then continued, "If you will unreservedly confide to me the particulars of your tale, I perhaps may be of use in undeceiving them. I am blind and cannot judge of your countenance, but there is something in your words which persuades me that you are sincere. I am poor and an exile, but it will afford me true pleasure to be in any way serviceable to a human creature."

'"Excellent man! I thank you and accept your generous offer. You raise me from the dust by this kindness; and I trust that, by your aid, I shall not be driven from the society and sympathy of your fellow creatures."

'"Heaven forbid! Even if you were really criminal, for that can only drive you to desperation, and not instigate you to virtue. I also am unfortunate; I and my family have been condemned, although innocent; judge, therefore, if I do not feel for your misfortunes."

'"How can I thank you, my best and only benefactor? From your lips first have I heard the voice of kindness directed towards me; I shall be forever grateful; and your present humanity assures me of success with those friends whom I am on the point of meeting."

'"May I know the names and residence of those friends?"

'I paused. This, I thought, was the moment of decision, which was to rob me of or bestow happiness on me forever. I struggled vainly for firmness sufficient to answer him, but the effort destroyed all my remaining strength; I sank on the chair and sobbed aloud. At that moment I heard the steps of my younger protectors. I had not a moment to lose, but seizing the hand of the old man, I cried, "Now is the time! Save and protect me! You and your family are the friends whom I seek. Do not you desert me in the hour of trial!"

'"Great God!" exclaimed the old man. "Who are you?"

'At that instant the cottage door was opened, and Felix, Safie, and Agatha entered. Who can describe their horror and consternation on beholding me? Agatha fainted, and Safie, unable to attend to her friend, rushed out of the cottage. Felix darted forward, and with supernatural force tore me from his father, to whose knees I clung; in a transport of fury, he dashed me to the ground and struck me violently with a stick. I could have torn him limb from limb, as the lion rends the antelope. But my heart sank within me as with bitter sickness, and I refrained. I saw him on the point of repeating his blow, when, overcome by pain and anguish, I quitted the cottage, and in the general tumult escaped unperceived to my hovel.'

## CHAPTER 16

'CURSED, cursed creator! Why did I live? Why, in that instant, did I not extinguish the spark of existence which you had so wantonly bestowed? I know not; despair had not yet taken possession of me; my feelings were those of rage and revenge. I could with pleasure have destroyed the cottage and its inhabitants and have glutted myself with their shrieks and misery.

'When night came I quitted my retreat and wandered in the wood; and now, no longer restrained by the fear of discovery, I gave vent to my anguish in fearful howlings. I was like a wild beast that had broken the toils, destroying the objects that obstructed me and ranging through the wood with a staglike swiftness. Oh! What a miserable night I passed! The cold stars shone in mockery, and the bare trees waved their branches above me; now and then the sweet voice of a bird burst forth amidst the univeral stillness. All, save I, were at rest or in enjoyment; I, like the arch-fiend, bore a hell within me, and finding myself unsympathized with, wished to tear up the trees, spread havoc and destruction around me, and then to have sat down and enjoyed the ruin.

'But this was a luxury of sensation that could not endure; I became fatigued with excess of bodily exertion and sank on the damp grass in the sick impotence of despair. There was none among the myriads of men that existed who would pity or assist me; and should I feel kindness towards my enemies? No; from that moment I declared ever-lasting war against the species, and more than all, against him who had formed me and sent me forth to this insupportable misery.

'The sun rose; I heard the voices of men and knew that

it was impossible to return to my retreat during that day. Accordingly I hid myself in some thick underwood, determining to devote the ensuing hours to reflection on my situation.

'The pleasant sunshine and the pure air of day restored me to some degree of tranquillity; and when I considered what had passed at the cottage, I could not help believing that I had been too hasty in my conclusions. I had certainly acted imprudently. It was apparent that my conversation had interested the father in my behalf, and I was a fool in having exposed my person to the horror of his children. I ought to have familiarized the old De Lacey to me, and by degrees to have discovered myself to the rest of his family, when they should have been prepared for my approach. But I did not believe my errors to be irretrievable, and after much consideration I resolved to return to the cottage, seek the old man, and by my representations win him to my party.

'These thoughts calmed me, and in the afternoon I sank into a profound sleep; but the fever of my blood did not allow me to be visited by peaceful dreams. The horrible scene of the preceding day was forever acting before my eyes; the females were flying and the enraged Felix tearing me from his father's feet. I awoke exhausted, and finding that it was already night, I crept forth from my hiding-place, and went in search of food.

'When my hunger was appeased, I directed my steps towards the well-known path that conducted to the cottage. All there was at peace. I crept into my hovel and remained in silent expectation of the accustomed hour when the family arose. That hour passed, the sun mounted high in the heavens, but the cottagers did not appear. I trembled violently, apprehending some dreadful misfortune. The inside of the cottage was dark, and I heard no motion; I cannot describe the agony of this suspense.

'Presently two countrymen passed by, but pausing near the cottage, they entered into conversation, using violent gesticulations; but I did not understand what they said, as they spoke the language of the country, which differed from that of my protectors. Soon after, however, Felix approached with another man; I was surprized, as I knew that he had not quitted the cottage that morning, and waited anxiously to discover from his discourse the meaning of these unusual appearances.

'"Do you consider," said his companion to him, "that you will be obliged to pay three months' rent and to lose the produce of your garden? I do not wish to take any unfair advantage, and I beg therefore that you will take some days to consider of your determination."

'"It is utterly useless," replied Felix; "we can never again inhabit your cottage. The life of my father is in the greatest danger, owing to the dreadful circumstance that I have related. My wife and my sister will never recover from their horror. I intreat you not to reason with me any more. Take possession of your tenement and let me fly from this place."

'Felix trembled violently as he said this. He and his companion entered the cottage, in which they remained for a few minutes, and then departed. I never saw any of the family of De Lacey more.

'I continued for the remainder of the day in my hovel in a state of utter and stupid despair. My protectors had departed and had broken the only link that held me to the world. For the first time the feelings of revenge and hatred filled my bosom, and I did not strive to control them, but allowing myself to be borne away by the stream, I bent my mind towards injury and death. When I thought of my friends, of the mild voice of De Lacey, the gentle eyes of Agatha, and the exquisite beauty of the Arabian, these thoughts vanished and a gush of tears somewhat soothed me. But again when I reflected that they had spurned and deserted me, anger returned, a rage of anger, and unable to injure anything human, I turned my fury towards inanimate objects. As night advanced I placed a variety of combustibles around the cottage, and after having destroyed every vestige of cultivation in the garden, I waited with forced impatience until the moon had sunk to commence my operations.

'As the night advanced, a fierce wind arose from the woods and quickly dispersed the clouds that had loitered in the heavens; the blast tore along like a mighty avalanche and produced a kind of insanity in my spirits that burst all bounds of reason and reflection. I lighted the dry branch of a tree and danced with fury around the devoted cottage, my eyes still fixed on the western horizon, the edge of which the moon nearly touched. A part of its orb was at length hid, and I waved my brand; it sank, and with a loud scream I fired the straw, and heath, and bushes, which I had collected. The wind fanned the fire, and the cottage was quickly enveloped by the flames, which clung to it and licked it with their forked and destroying tongues.

'As soon as I was convinced that no assistance could save any part of the habitation, I quitted the scene and sought for refuge in the woods.

'And now, with the world before me, whither should I bend my steps? I resolved to fly far from the scene of my misfortunes; but to me, hated and despised, every country must be equally horrible. At length the thought of you crossed my mind. I learned from your papers that you were my father, my creator; and to whom could I apply with more fitness than to him who had given me life? Among the lessons that Felix had bestowed upon Safie, geography had not been omitted; I had learned from these the relative situations of the different countries of the earth. You had mentioned Geneva as the name of your native town, and towards this place I resolved to proceed.

'But how was I to direct myself? I knew that I must travel in a southwesterly direction to reach my destination, but the sun was my only guide. I did not know the names of the towns that I was to pass through, nor could I ask information from a single human being; but I did not despair. From you only could I hope for succour, although towards you I felt no sentiment but that of hatred. Unfeeling, heartless creator! You had endowed me with perceptions and passions and then cast me abroad an object for the scorn and horror of mankind. But on you only had I any claim for pity and redress, and from you I determined to seek that justice which I vainly attempted to gain from any other being that wore the human form.

'My travels were long and the sufferings I endured intense. It was late in autumn when I quitted the district where I had so long resided. I travelled only at night, fearful of encountering the visage of a human being. Nature decayed around me, and the sun became heatless; rain and snow poured around me; mighty rivers were frozen; the surface of the earth was hard and chill, and bare, and I found no shelter. Oh, earth! How often did I imprecate curses on the cause of my being! The mildness of my nature had fled, and all within me was turned to gall and bitterness. The nearer I approached to your habitation, the more deeply did I feel the spirit of revenge enkindled in my heart. Snow fell, and the waters were hardened, but I rested not. A few incidents now and then directed me, and I possessed a map of the country; but I often wandered wide from my path. The agony of my feelings allowed me no respite; no incident occurred from which my rage and misery could not extract its food; but a circumstance that happened when I arrived on the confines of Switzerland, when the sun had recovered its warmth and the earth again began to look green, confirmed in an especial manner the bitterness and horror of my feelings.

'I generally rested during the day and travelled only when I was secured by night from the view of man. One morning, however, finding that my path lay through a deep wood, I ventured to continue my journey after the sun had risen; the day, which was one of the first of spring, cheered even me by the loveliness of its sunshine and the balminess of the air. I felt emotions of gentleness and pleasure, that had long appeared dead, revive within me. Half surprised by the novelty of these sensations, I allowed myself to be borne away by them, and forgetting my solitude and deformity, dared to be happy. Soft tears again bedewed my cheeks, and I even raised my humid eyes with thankfulness towards the blessed sun, which bestowed such joy upon me.

'I continued to wind among the paths of the wood, until I came to its boundary which was skirted by a deep and rapid river, into which many of the trees bent their branches, now budding with the fresh spring. Here I paused, not exactly knowing what path to pursue, when I heard the sound of voices, that induced me to conceal myself under the shade of a cypress. I was scarcely hid when a young girl came running towards the spot where I was concealed, laughing, as if she ran from some one in sport. She continued her course along the precipitous sides of the river, when suddenly her foot slipped, and she fell into the rapid stream. I rushed from my hiding-place and with extreme labour from the force of the current, saved her and dragged her to shore. She was senseless, and I endeavoured by every means in my power to restore animation, when I was suddenly interrupted by the approach of a rustic, who was probably the person from whom she had playfully fled. On seeing me, he darted towards me, and tearing the girl from my arms, hastened towards the deeper parts of the wood. I followed speedily, I hardly knew why; but when the man saw me draw near, he aimed a gun, which he carried, at my body, and fired. I sank to the ground, and my injurer, with increased swiftness, escaped into the wood.

'This was then the reward of my benevolence! I had saved a human being from destruction, and as a recompense I now writhed under the miserable pain of a wound which shattered the flesh and bone. The feelings of kindness and gentleness which I had entertained but a few moments before gave place to hellish rage and gnashing of teeth. Inflamed by pain, I vowed eternal hatred and vengeance to all mankind. But the agony of my wound overcame me; my pulses paused, and I fainted.

'For some weeks I led a miserable life in the woods, endeavouring to cure the wound which I had received. The ball had entered my shoulder, and I knew not whether it had remained there or passed through; at any rate I had no means of extracting it. My sufferings were augmented also by the oppressive sense of the injustice and ingratitude of their infliction. My daily vows rose for revenge – a deep and deadly revenge, such as would alone compensate for the outrages and anguish I had endured.

'After some weeks my wound healed, and I continued my journey. The labours I endured were no longer to be alleviated by the bright sun or gentle breezes of spring; all joy was but a mockery which insulted my desolate state and made me feel more painfully that I was not made for the enjoyment of pleasure.

'But my toils now drew near a close, and in two months from this time I reached the environs of Geneva.

'It was evening when I arrived, and I retired to a hiding place among the fields that surround it to meditate in what manner I should apply to you. I was oppressed by fatigue and hunger and far too unhappy to enjoy the gentle breezes of evening or the prospect of the sun setting behind the stupendous mountains of Jura.

'At this time a slight sleep relieved me from the pain of reflection, which was disturbed by the approach of a beautiful child, who came running into the recess I had chosen, with all the sportiveness of infancy. Suddenly, as I gazed on him, an idea seized me that this little creature was unprejudiced and had lived too short a time to have imbibed a horror of deformity. If, therefore, I could seize him and educate him as my companion and friend, I should not be so desolate in this peopled earth.

'Urged by this impulse, I seized on the boy as he passed and drew him towards me. As soon as he beheld my form, he placed his hands before his eyes and uttered a shrill scream; I drew his hand forcibly from his face and said, "Child, what is the meaning of this? I do not intend to hurt you; listen to me."

'He struggled violently. "Let me go," he cried; "monster! Ugly wretch! You wish to eat me and tear me to pieces. You are an ogre. Let me go, or I will tell my papa."

'"Boy, you will never see your father again; you must come with me."

'"Hideous monster! Let me go. My papa is a syndic – he is M. Frankenstein – he will punish you. You dare not keep me."

'"Frankenstein! You belong then to my enemy – to him towards whom I have sworn eternal revenge; you shall be my first victim."

'The child still struggled and loaded me with epithets which carried despair to my heart; I grasped his throat to silence him, and in a moment he lay dead at my feet.

'I gazed on my victim, and my heart swelled with exultation and hellish triumph; clapping my hands, I exclaimed, "I too can create desolation; my enemy is not invulnerable; this death will carry despair to him, and a thousand other miseries shall torment and destroy him."

'As I fixed my eyes on the child, I saw something glittering on his breast. I took it; it was a portrait of a most lovely woman. In spite of my malignity, it softened and attracted me. For a few moments I gazed with delight on her dark eyes, fringed by deep lashes, and her lovely lips; but presently my rage returned; I remembered that I was forever deprived of the delights that such beautiful creatures could bestow and that she whose resemblance I contemplated would, in regarding me, have changed that air of divine benignity to one expressive of disgust and affright.

'Can you wonder that such thoughts transported me with rage? I only wonder that at that moment, instead of venting my sensations in exclamations and agony, I did not rush among mankind and perish in the attempt to destroy them.

'While I was overcome by these feelings, I left the spot where I had committed the murder, and seeking a more secluded hiding-place, I entered a barn which had appeared to me to be empty. A woman was sleeping on some straw; she was young, not indeed so beautiful as her whose portrait I held, but of an agreeable aspect and blooming in the loveliness of youth and health. Here, I thought, is one of those whose joy-imparting smiles are bestowed on all but me. And then I bent over her and whispered, "Awake, fairest, thy lover is near – he who would give his life but to obtain one look of affection from thine eyes; my beloved, awake!"

'The sleeper stirred; a thrill of terror ran through me. Should she indeed awake, and see me, and curse me, and denounce the murderer? Thus would she assuredly act if her darkened eyes opened and she beheld me. The thought was madness; it stirred the fiend within me – not I, but she, shall suffer; the murder I have committed because I am forever robbed of all that she could give me, she shall atone. The crime had its source in her; be hers the punishment! Thanks to the lessons of Felix and the sanguinary laws of man, I had learned now to work mischief. I bent over her and placed the portrait securely in one of the folds of her dress. She moved again, and I fled.

'For some days I haunted the spot where these scenes had taken place, sometimes wishing to see you, sometimes resolved to quit the world and its miseries forever. At length I wandered towards these mountains, and have ranged through their immense recesses, consumed by a burning passion which you alone can gratify. We may not part until you have promised to comply with my requisition. I am alone and miserable; man will not associate with me; but one as deformed and horrible as myself would not deny herself to me. My companion must be of the same species and have the same defects. This being you must create.'

## CHAPTER 17

THE being finished speaking and fixed his looks upon me in the expectation of a reply. But I was bewildered, perplexed, and unable to arrange my ideas sufficiently to understand the full extent of his proposition. He continued, 'You must create a female for me with whom I can live in the interchange of those sympathies necessary for my being. This you alone can do, and I demand it of you as a right which you must not refuse to concede.'

The latter part of his tale had kindled anew in me the anger that had died away while he narrated his peaceful life among the cottagers, and as he said this I could no longer suppress the rage that burned within me.

'I do refuse it,' I replied; 'and no torture shall ever extort a consent from me. You may render me the most miserable of men, but you shall never make me base in my own eyes. Shall I create another like yourself, whose joint wickedness might desolate the world? Begone! I have answered you; you may torture me, but I will never consent.'

'You are in the wrong,' replied the fiend; 'and instead of threatening, I am content to reason with you. I am malicious because I am miserable. Am I not shunned and hated by all mankind? You, my creator, would tear me to pieces and triumph; remember that, and tell me why I should pity man more than he pities me? You would not call it murder if you could precipitate me into one of those ice-rifts and destroy my frame, the work of your own hands. Shall I respect man when he condemns me? Let him live with me in the interchange of kindness, and instead of injury I would bestow every benefit upon him with tears of gratitude at his acceptance. But that cannot be; the human senses are insurmountable barriers to our union. Yet mine shall not be the submission of abject slavery. I will revenge my injuries; if I cannot inspire love, I will cause fear, and chiefly towards you my arch-enemy, because my creator, do I swear inextinguishable hatred. Have a care; I will work at your destruction, nor finish until I desolate your heart, so that you shall curse the hour of your birth.'

A fiendish rage animated him as he said this; his face was wrinkled into contortions too horrible for human eyes to behold; but presently he calmed himself and proceeded, 'I intended to reason. This passion is detrimental to me, for you do not reflect that *you* are the cause of its excess. If any being felt emotions of benevolence towards me, I should return them a hundred and a hundredfold; for that one creature's sake I would make peace with the whole kind! But I now indulge in dreams of bliss that cannot be realized. What I ask of you is reasonable and moderate; I demand a creature of another sex, but as hideous as myself; the gratification is small, but it is all that I can receive, and it shall content me. It is true, we shall be monsters, cut off from all the world; but on that account we shall be more attached to one another. Our lives will not be happy, but they will be harmless and free from the misery I now feel. Oh! My creator, make me happy; let me feel gratitude towards you for one benefit! Let me see that I excite the sympathy of some existing thing; do not deny me my request!'

I was moved. I shuddered when I thought of the possible consequences of my consent, but I felt that there was some justice in his argument. His tale and the feelings he now expressed proved him to be a creature of fine sensations, and did I not as his maker owe him all the portion of happiness that it was in my power to bestow? He saw my change of feeling and continued, 'If you consent, neither you nor any other human being shall ever see us again; I will go to the vast wilds of South America. My food is not that of man; I do not destroy the lamb and the kid to glut my appetite; acorns and berries afford me sufficient nourishment. My companion will be of the same nature as myself and will be content with the same fare. We shall make our bed of dried leaves; the sun will shine on us as on man and will ripen our food. The picture I present to you is peaceful and human, and you must feel that you could deny it only in the wantonness of power and cruelty. Pitiless as you have been towards me, I now see compassion in your eyes; let me seize the favourable moment and persuade you to promise what I so ardently desire.'

'You propose,' replied I, 'to fly from the habitations of man, to dwell in those wilds where the beasts of the field will be your only companions. How can you, who long for the love and sympathy of man, persevere in this exile? You will return and again seek their kindness, and you will meet with their detestation; your evil passions will be renewed, and you will then have a companion to aid you in the task of destruction. This may not be; cease to argue the point, for I cannot consent.'

'How inconstant are your feelings! But a moment ago you were moved by my representations, and why do you again harden yourself to my complaints? I swear to you, by the earth which I inhabit, and by you that made me, that with the companion you bestow I will quit the neighbourhood of man and dwell, as it may chance, in the most savage of places. My evil passions will have fled, for I shall meet with sympathy! My life will flow quietly away, and in my dying moments I shall not curse my maker.'

His words had a strange effect upon me. I compassionated him and sometimes felt a wish to console him, but when I looked upon him, when I saw the filthy mass that moved and talked, my heart sickened and my feelings were altered to those of horror and hatred. I tried to stifle these sensations; I thought that as I could not sympathize with him, I had no right to withhold from him the small portion of happiness which was yet in my power to bestow.

'You swear,' I said, 'to be harmless; but have you not already shown a degree of malice that should reasonably make me distrust you? May not even this be a feint that will increase your triumph by affording a wider scope for your revenge?'

'How is this? I must not be trifled with, and I demand an answer. If I have no ties and no affections, hatred and vice must be my portion; the love of another will destroy the cause of my crimes, and I shall become a thing of whose existence every one will be ignorant. My vices are the children of a forced solitude that I abhor, and my virtues will necessarily arise when I live in communion with an equal. I shall feel the affections of a sensitive being and become linked to the chain of existence and events from which I am now excluded.'

I paused some time to reflect on all he had related and the various arguments which he had employed. I thought of the promise of virtues which he had displayed on the opening of his existence and the subsequent blight of all kindly feeling by the loathing and scorn which his protectors had manifested towards him. His power and threats were not omitted in my calculations; a creature who could exist in the ice caves of the glaciers and hide himself from pursuit among the ridges of inaccessible precipices was a being possessing faculties it would be vain to cope with. After a long pause of reflection I concluded that the justice due both to him and my fellow creatures demanded of me that I should comply with his request. Turning to him, therefore, I said, 'I consent to your demand, on your solemn oath to quit Europe forever, and every other place in the neighbourhood of man, as soon as I shall deliver into your hands a female who will accompany you in your exile.'

'I swear,' he cried, 'by the sun, and by the blue sky of heaven, and by the fire of love that burns my heart, that if you grant my prayer, while they exist you shall never behold me again. Depart to your home and commence your labours; I shall watch their progress with unutterable anxiety; and fear not but that when you are ready I shall appear.'

Saying this, he suddenly quitted me, fearful, perhaps, of any change in my sentiments. I saw him descend the mountain with greater speed than the flight of an eagle, and quickly lost among the undulations of the sea of ice.

His tale had occupied the whole day, and the sun was upon the verge of the horizon when he departed. I knew that I ought to hasten my descent towards the valley, as I should soon be encompassed in darkness; but my heart was heavy, and my steps slow. The labour of winding among the little paths of the mountain and fixing my feet firmly as I advanced, perplexed me, occupied as I was by the emotions which the occurrences of the day had produced. Night was far advanced when I came to the half-way resting-place and seated myself beside the fountain. The stars shone at intervals as the clouds passed from over them; the dark pines rose before me, and every here and there a broken tree lay on the ground; it was a scene of wonderful solemnity and stirred strange thoughts within me. I wept bitterly, and clasping my hands in agony, I exclaimed, 'Oh! Stars and clouds and winds, ye are all about to mock me; if ye really pity me, crush sensation and memory; let me become as nought; but if not, depart, depart, and leave me in darkness.'

These were wild and miserable thoughts, but I cannot describe to you how the eternal twinkling of the stars weighed upon me and how I listened to every blast of wind as if it were a dull ugly siroc on its way to consume me.

Morning dawned before I arrived at the village of Chamounix; I took no rest, but returned immediately to Geneva. Even in my own heart I could give no expression to my sensations – they weighed on me with a mountain's weight and their excess destroyed my agony beneath them. Thus I returned home, and entering the house, presented myself to the family. My haggard and wild appearance awoke intense alarm, but I answered no question, scarcely did I speak. I felt as if I were placed under a ban – as if I had no right to claim their sympathies – as if never more might I enjoy companionship with them. Yet even thus I loved them to adoration; and to save them, I resolved to dedicate myself to my most abhorred task. The prospect of such an occupation made every other circumstance of existence pass before me like a dream, and that thought only had to me the reality of life.

# CHAPTER 18

DAY after day, week after week, passed away on my return to Geneva; and I could not collect the courage to recommence my work. I feared the vengeance of the disappointed fiend, yet I was unable to overcome my repugnance to the task which was enjoined me. I found that I could not compose a female without again devoting several months to profound study and laborious disquisition. I had heard of some discoveries having been made by an English philosopher, the knowledge of which was material to my success, and I sometimes thought of obtaining my father's consent to visit England for this purpose; but I clung to every pretence of delay and shrank from taking the first step in an undertaking whose immediate necessity began to appear less absolute to me. A change indeed had taken place in me; my health, which had hitherto declined, was now much restored; and my spirits, when unchecked by the memory of my unhappy promise, rose proportionably. My father saw this change with pleasure, and he turned his thoughts towards the best method of eradicating the remains of my melancholy, which every now and then would return by fits, and with a devouring blackness overcast the approaching sunshine. At these moments I took refuge in the most perfect solitude. I passed whole days on the lake alone in a little boat, watching the clouds and listening to the rippling of the waves, silent and listless. But the fresh air and bright sun seldom failed to restore me to some degree of composure, and on my return I met the salutations of my friends with a readier smile and a more cheerful heart.

It was after my return from one of these rambles that my father, calling me aside, thus addressed me, 'I am happy to remark, my dear son, that you have resumed your former pleasures and seem to be returning to yourself. And yet you are still unhappy and still avoid our society. For some time I was lost in conjecture as to the cause of this, but yesterday an idea struck me, and if it is well founded, I conjure you to avow it. Reserve on such a point would be not only useless, but draw down treble misery on us all.'

I trembled violently at his exordium, and my father continued, 'I confess, my son, that I have always looked forward to your marriage with our dear Elizabeth as the tie of our domestic comfort and the stay of my declining years. You were attached to each other from your earliest infancy; you studied together, and appeared, in dispositions and tastes, entirely suited to one another. But so blind is the experience of man that what I conceived to be the best assistants to my plan may have entirely destroyed it. You, perhaps, regard her as your sister, without any wish that she might become your wife. Nay, you may have met with another whom you may love; and considering yourself as bound in honour to Elizabeth, this struggle may occasion the poignant misery which you appear to feel.'

'My dear father, reassure yourself. I love my cousin tenderly and sincerely. I never saw any woman who excited, as Elizabeth does, my warmest admiration and affection. My future hopes and prospects are entirely bound up in the expectation of our union.'

'The expression of your sentiments of this subject, my dear Victor, gives me more pleasure than I have for some time experienced. If you feel thus, we shall assuredly be happy, however present events may cast a gloom over us. But it is this gloom which appears to have taken so strong a hold of your mind, that I wish to dissipate. Tell me, therefore, whether you object to an immediate solemnization of the marriage. We have been unfortunate, and recent events have drawn us from that everyday tranquillity befitting my years and infirmities. You are younger; yet

I do not suppose, possessed as you are of a competent fortune, that an early marriage would at all interfere with any future plans of honour and utility that you may have formed. Do not suppose, however, that I wish to dictate happiness to you or that a delay on your part would cause me any serious uneasiness. Interpret my words with candour and answer me, I conjure you, with confidence and sincerity.'

I listened to my father in silence and remained for some time incapable of offering any reply. I revolved rapidly in my mind a multitude of thoughts and endeavoured to arrive at some conclusion. Alas! To me the idea of an immediate union with my Elizabeth was one of horror and dismay. I was bound by a solemn promise which I had not yet fulfilled and dared not break, or if I did, what manifold miseries might not impend over me and my devoted family! Could I enter into a festival with this deadly weight yet hanging round my neck and bowing me to the ground? I must perform my engagement and let the monster depart with his mate before I allowed myself to enjoy the delight of a union from which I expected peace.

I remembered also the necessity imposed upon me of either journeying to England or entering into a long correspondence with those philosophers of that country whose knowledge and discoveries were of indispensable use to me in my present undertaking. The latter method of obtaining the desired intelligence was dilatory and unsatisfactory; besides, I had an insurmountable aversion to the idea of engaging myself in my loathsome task in my father's house while in habits of familiar intercourse with those I loved. I knew that a thousand fearful accidents might occur, the slightest of which would disclose a tale to thrill all connected with me with horror. I was aware also that I should often lose all self-command, all capacity of hiding the harrowing sensations that would possess me during the progress of my unearthly occupation. I must absent myself from all I loved while thus employed. Once commenced, it would quickly be achieved, and I might be restored to my family in peace and happiness. My promise fulfilled, the monster would depart forever. Or (so my fond fancy imaged) some accident might meanwhile occur to destroy him and put an end to my slavery forever.

These feelings dictated my answer to my father. I expressed a wish to visit England, but concealing the true reasons of this request, I clothed my desires under a guise which excited no suspicion, while I urged my desire with an earnestness that easily induced my father to comply. After so long a period of an absorbing melancholy that resembled madness in its intensity and effects, he was glad to find that I was capable of taking pleasure in the idea of such a journey, and he hoped that change of scene and varied amusement would, before my return, have restored me entirely to myself.

The duration of my absence was left to my own choice; a few months, or at most a year, was the period contemplated. One paternal kind precaution he had taken to ensure my having a companion. Without previously communicating with me, he had, in concert with Elizabeth, arranged that Clerval should join me at Strasbourg. This interfered with the solitude I coveted for the prosecution of my task; yet at the commencement of my journey the presence of my friend could in no way be an impediment, and truly I rejoiced that thus I should be saved many hours of lonely, maddening reflection. Nay, Henry might stand between me and the intrusion of my foe. If I were alone, would he not at times force his abhorred presence on me to remind me of my task or to contemplate its progress?

To England, therefore, I was bound, and it was understood that my union with Elizabeth should take place immediately on my return. My father's age rendered him extremely averse to delay. For myself, there was one reward I promised myself from my detested toils – one consolation for my unparalleled sufferings; it was the prospect of that day when, enfranchised from my miserable slavery, I might claim Elizabeth and forget the past in my union with her.

I now made arrangements for my journey, but one feeling haunted me which filled me with fear and agitation. During my absence I should leave my friends unconscious of the existence of their enemy and unprotected from his attacks, exasperated as he might be by my departure. But he had promised to follow me wherever I might go, and would he not accompany me to England? This imagination was dreadful in itself, but soothing inasmuch as it supposed the safety of my friends. I was agonized with the idea of the possibility that the reverse of this might happen. But through the whole period during which I was the slave of my creature I allowed myself to be governed by the impulses of the moment; and my present sensations strongly intimated that the fiend would follow me and exempt my family from the danger of his machinations.

It was in the latter end of September that I again quitted my native country. My journey had been my own suggestion, and Elizabeth therefore acquiesced, but she was filled with disquiet at the idea of my suffering, away from her, the inroads of misery and grief. It had been her care which provided me a companion in Clerval – and yet a man is blind to a thousand minute circumstances which call forth a woman's sedulous attention. She longed to bid me hasten my return; a thousand conflicting emotions rendered her mute as she bade me a tearful, silent farewell.

I threw myself into the carriage that was to convey me away, hardly knowing whither I was going, and careless of what was passing around. I remembered only, and it was with a bitter anguish that I reflected on it, to order that my chemical instruments should be packed to go with me. Filled with dreary imaginations, I passed through many beautiful and majestic scenes, but my eyes were fixed and unobserving. I could only think of the bourne of my travels and the work which was to occupy me whilst they endured.

After some days spent in listless indolence, during which I traversed many leagues, I arrived at Strasbourg, where I waited two days for Clerval. He came. Alas, how great was the contrast between us! He was alive to every new scene, joyful when he saw the beauties of the setting sun, and more happy when he beheld it rise and recommence a new day. He pointed out to me the shifting colours of the landscape and the appearances of the sky. 'This is what it is to live,' he cried; 'now I enjoy existence! But you, my dear Frankenstein, wherefore are you desponding and sorrowful?' In truth, I was occupied by gloomy thoughts and neither saw the descent of the evening star nor the golden sunrise reflected in the Rhine. And you, my friend, would be far more amused with the journal of Clerval, who observed the scenery with an eye of feeling and delight, than in listening to my reflections. I, a miserable wretch, haunted by a curse that shut up every avenue to enjoyment.

We had agreed to descend the Rhine in a boat from Strasbourg to Rotterdam, whence we might take shipping for London. During this voyage we passed many willowy islands and saw several beautiful towns. We stayed a day at Mannheim, and on the fifth from our departure from Strasbourg, arrived at Mainz. The course of the Rhine below Mainz becomes much more picturesque. The river descends rapidly and winds between hills, not high, but steep, and of beautiful forms. We saw many ruined castles standing on the edges of precipices, surrounded by black woods, high and inaccessible. This part of the Rhine, indeed, presents a singularly variegated landscape. In one spot you view rugged hills, ruined castles overlooking tremendous precipices, with the dark Rhine rushing beneath; and on the sudden turn of a promontory, flourishing vineyards with green sloping banks and a meandering river and populous towns occupy the scene.

We travelled at the time of the vintage and heard the song of the labourers as we glided down the stream. Even I, depressed in mind, and my spirits continually agitated by gloomy feelings, even I was pleased. I lay at the bottom of the boat, and as I gazed on the cloudless blue sky, I seemed to drink in a tranquillity to which I had long been a stranger. And if these were my sensations, who can describe those of Henry? He felt as if he had been transported to fairy-land and enjoyed a happiness seldom tasted by man. 'I have seen,' he said, 'the most beautiful scenes of my own country; I have visited the lakes of Lucerne and Uri, where the snowy mountains descend almost perpendicularly to the water, casting black and impenetrable shades, which would cause a gloomy and mournful appearance were it not for the most verdant islands that relieve the eye by their gay appearance; I have seen this lake agitated by a tempest, when the wind tore up whirlwinds of water and gave you an idea of what the water-spout must be on the great ocean; and the waves dash with fury the base of the mountain, where the priest and his mistress were overwhelmed by an avalanche and where their dying voices are still said to be heard amid the pauses of the nightly wind; I have seen the mountains of La Valais, and the Pays de Vaud; but this country, Victor, pleases me more than all those wonders. The mountains of Switzerland are more majestic and strange, but there is a charm in the banks of this divine river that I never before saw equalled. Look at that castle which overhangs yon precipice; and that also on the island, almost concealed amongst the foliage of those lovely trees; and now that group of labourers coming from among their vines; and that village half hid in the recess of the mountain. Oh, surely the spirit that inhabits and guards this place has a soul more in harmony with man than those who pile the glacier or retire to the inaccessible peaks of the mountains of our own country.'

Clerval! Beloved friend! Even now it delights me to record your words and to dwell on the praise of which you are so eminently deserving. He was a being formed in the "very poetry of nature." His wild and enthusiastic imagination was chastened by the sensibility of his heart. His soul overflowed with ardent affections, and his friendship was of that devoted and wondrous nature that the world-minded teach us to look for only in the imagination. But even human sympathies were not sufficient to satisfy his eager mind. The scenery of external nature, which others regard only with admiration, he loved with ardour:

> The sounding cataract
> Haunted him like a passion: the tall rock,
> The mountain, and the deep and gloomy wood,
> Their colours and their forms, were then to him
> An appetite; a feeling, and a love,
> That had no need of a remoter charm,
> By thought supplied, or any interest
> Unborrow'd from the eye.[1]

And where does he now exist? Is this gentle and lovely being lost forever? Has this mind, so replete with ideas, imaginations fanciful and magnificent, which formed a world, whose existence depended on the life of its creator – has this mind perished? Does it now only exist in my memory? No, it is not thus; your form so divinely wrought, and beaming with beauty, has decayed, but your spirit still visits and consoles your unhappy friend.

Pardon this gush of sorrow; these ineffectual words are but a slight tribute to the unexampled worth of Henry, but they soothe my heart, overflowing with the anguish which his remembrance creates. I will proceed with my tale.

Beyond Cologne we descended to the plains of Holland; and we resolved to post the remainder of our way, for the wind was contrary and the stream of the river was too gentle to aid us.

Our journey here lost the interest arising from beautiful scenery, but we arrived in a few days at Rotterdam, whence we proceeded by sea to England. It was on a clear morning, in the latter days of December, that I first saw the white cliffs of Britain. The banks of the Thames presented a new scene; they were flat but fertile, and almost every town was marked by the remembrance of some story. We saw Tilbury Fort and remembered the Spanish Armada; Gravesend, Woolwich, and Greenwich – places which I had heard of even in my country.

At length we saw the numerous steeples of London, St Paul's towering above all, and the Tower famed in English history.

# CHAPTER 19

LONDON was our present point of rest; we determined to remain several months in this wonderful and celebrated city. Clerval desired the intercourse of the men of genius and talent who flourished at this time, but this was with me a secondary object; I was principally occupied with the means of obtaining the information necessary for the completion of my promise and quickly availed myself of the letters of introduction that I had brought with me, addressed to the most distinguished natural philosopher.

If this journey had taken place during my days of study and happiness, it would have afforded me inexpressible pleasure. But a blight had come over my existence, and I only visited these people for the sake of the information they might give me on the subject in which my interest was so terribly profound. Company was irksome to me; when alone, I could fill my mind with the sights of heaven and earth; the voice of Henry soothed me, and I could thus cheat myself into a transitory peace. But busy, uninteresting, joyous faces brought back despair to my heart. I saw an insurmountable barrier placed between me and my fellow men; this barrier was sealed with the blood of William and Justine, and to reflect on the events connected with those names filled my soul with anguish.

But in Clerval I saw the image of my former self; he was inquisitive and anxious to gain experience and instruction. The difference of manners which he observed was to him an inexhaustible source of instruction and amusement. He was also pursuing an object he had long had in view. His design was to visit India, in the belief that he had in his knowledge of its various languages, and in the views he had taken of its society, the means of materially assisting the progress of European colonization and trade. In Britain only could he further the execution of his plan. He was forever busy, and the only check to his enjoyments was my sorrowful and dejected mind. I tried to conceal this as much as possible, that I might not debar him from the pleasures natural to one who was entering on a new scene of life, undisturbed by any care or bitter recollection. I often refused to accompany him, alleging another engagement, that I might remain alone. I now also began to collect the materials necessary for my new creation, and this was to me like the torture of single drops of water continually falling on the head. Every thought that was devoted to it was an extreme anguish, and every word that I spoke in allusion to it caused my lips to quiver, and my heart to palpitate.

After passing some months in London, we received a letter from a person in Scotland who had formerly been our visitor at Geneva. He mentioned the beauties of his native country and asked us if those were not sufficient allurements to induce us to prolong our journey as far north as Perth, where he resided. Clerval eagerly desired to accept this invitation, and I, although I abhorred society, wished to view again mountains and streams and all the wondrous works with which Nature adorns her chosen dwelling-places.

We had arrived in England at the beginning of October, and it was now February. We accordingly determined to commence our journey towards the north at the expiration of another month. In this expedition we did not intend to follow the great road to Edinburgh, but to visit Windsor, Oxford, Matlock, and the Cumberland lakes, resolving to arrive at the completion of this tour about the end of July. I packed up my chemical instruments and the materials I had collected, resolving to finish my labours in some obscure nook in the northern highlands of Scotland.

We quitted London on the 27th of March and remained a few days at Windsor, rambling in its beautiful forest.

This was a new scene to us mountaineers; the majestic oaks, the quantity of game, and the herds of stately deer were all novelties to us.

From thence we proceeded to Oxford. As we entered this city our minds were filled with the remembrance of the events that had been transacted there more than a century and a half before. It was here that Charles I had collected his forces. This city had remained faithful to him, after the whole nation had forsaken his cause to join the standard of Parliament and liberty. The memory of that unfortunate king and his companions, the amiable Falkland, the insolent Goring, his queen, and son, gave a peculiar interest to every part of the city which they might be supposed to have inhabited. The spirit of elder days found a dwelling here, and we delighted to trace its footsteps. If these feelings had not found an imaginary gratification, the appearance of the city had yet in itself sufficient beauty to obtain our admiration. The colleges are ancient and picturesque; the streets are almost magnificent; and the lovely Isis, which flows beside it through meadows of exquisite verdure, is spread forth into a placid expanse of waters, which reflects its majestic assemblage of towers, and spires, and domes, embosomed among aged trees.

I enjoyed this scene, and yet my enjoyment was embittered both by the memory of the past and the anticipation of the future. I was formed for peaceful happiness. During my youthful days discontent never visited my mind, and if I was ever overcome by *ennui*, the sight of what is beautiful in nature or the study of what is excellent and sublime in the productions of man could always interest my heart and communicate elasticity to my spirits. But I am a blasted tree; the bolt has entered my soul; and I felt then that I should survive to exhibit what I shall soon cease to be – a miserable spectacle of wrecked humanity, pitiable to others and intolerable to myself.

We passed a considerable period at Oxford, rambling among its environs and endeavouring to identify every spot which might relate to the most animating epoch of English history. Our little voyages of discovery were often prolonged by the successive objects that presented themselves. We visited the tomb of the illustrious Hampden and the field on which that patriot fell. For a moment my soul was elevated from its debasing and miserable fears to contemplate the divine ideas of liberty and self-sacrifice of which these sights were the monuments and the remembrancers. For an instant I dared to shake off my chains and look around me with a free and lofty spirit, but the iron had eaten into my flesh, and I sank again, trembling and hopeless, into my miserable self.

We left Oxford with regret and proceeded to Matlock, which was our next place of rest. The country in the neighbourhood of this village resembled, to a greater degree, the scenery of Switzerland; but every thing is on a lower scale, and the green hills want the crown of distant white Alps which always attend on the piny mountains of my native country. We visited the wondrous cave and the little cabinets of natural history, where the curiosities are disposed in the same manner as in the collections at Servox and Chamounix. The latter name made me tremble when pronounced by Henry, and I hastened to quit Matlock, with which that terrible scene was thus associated.

From Derby, still journeying northwards, we passed two months in Cumberland and Westmorland. I could now almost fancy myself among the Swiss mountains. The little patches of snow which yet lingered on the northern sides of the mountains, the lakes, and the dashing of the rocky streams were all familiar and dear sights to me. Here also we made some acquaintances, who almost contrived to cheat me into happiness. The delight of Clerval was proportionably greater than mine; his mind expanded in the company of men of talent, and he found in his own nature greater capacities and resources than he could have imagined himself to have possessed while he associated with his inferiors. 'I could pass my life here,' said he to me;

'and among these mountains I should scarcely regret Switzerland and the Rhine.'

But he found that a traveller's life is one that includes much pain amidst its enjoyments. His feelings are forever on the stretch; and when he begins to sink into repose, he finds himself obliged to quit that on which he rests in pleasure for something new, which again engages his attention, and which also he forsakes for other novelties.

We had scarcely visited the various lakes of Cumberland and Westmorland and conceived an affection for some of the inhabitants when the period of our appointment with our Scotch friend approached, and we left them to travel on. For my own part I was not sorry. I had now neglected my promise for some time, and I feared the effects of the daemon's disappointment. He might remain in Switzerland and wreak his vengeance on my relatives. This idea pursued me and tormented me at every moment from which I might otherwise have snatched repose and peace. I waited for my letters with feverish impatience; if they were delayed I was miserable and overcome by a thousand fears; and when they arrived and I saw the superscription of Elizabeth or my father, I hardly dared to read and ascertain my fate. Sometimes I thought that the fiend followed me and might expedite my remissness by murdering my companion. When these thoughts possessed me, I would not quit Henry for a moment, but followed him as his shadow, to protect him from the fancied rage of his destroyer. I felt as if I had committed some great crime, the consciousness of which haunted me. I was guiltless, but I had indeed drawn down a horrible curse upon my head, as mortal as that of crime.

I visited Edinburgh with languid eyes and mind; and yet that city might have interested the most unfortunate being. Clerval did not like it so well as Oxford, for the antiquity of the latter city was more pleasing to him. But the beauty and regularity of the new town of Edinburgh, its romantic castle and its environs, the most delightful in the world, Arthur's Seat, St Bernard's Well, and the Pentland Hills compensated him for the change and filled him with cheerfulness and admiration. But I was impatient to arrive at the termination of my journey.

We left Edinburgh in a week, passing through Coupar, St Andrew's, and along the banks of the Tay, to Perth, where our friend expected us. But I was in no mood to laugh and talk with strangers or enter into their feelings of plans with the good humour expected from a guest; and accordingly I told Clerval that I wished to make the tour of Scotland alone. 'Do you,' said I, 'enjoy yourself, and let this be our rendezvous. I may be absent a month or two; but do not interfere with my motions, I intreat you; leave me to peace and solitude for a short time; and when I return, I hope it will be with a lighter heart, more congenial to your own temper.'

Henry wished to dissuade me, but seeing me bent on this plan, ceased to remonstrate. He intreated me to write often. 'I had rather be with you,' he said, 'in your solitary rambles, than with these Scotch people, whom I do not know; hasten, then, my dear friend, to return, that I may again feel myself somewhat at home, which I cannot do in your absence.'

Having parted from my friend, I determined to visit some remote spot of Scotland and finish my work in solitude. I did not doubt but that the monster followed me and would discover himself to me when I should have finished, that he might receive his companion.

With this resolution I traversed the northern highlands and fixed on one of the remotest of the Orkneys as the scene of my labours. It was a place fitted for such a work, being hardly more than a rock whose high sides were continually beaten upon by the waves. The soil was barren, scarcely affording pasture for a few miserable cows, and oatmeal for its inhabitants, which consisted of five persons, whose gaunt and scraggy limbs gave tokens of their miserable fare. Vegetables and bread, when they indulged in such luxuries, and even fresh water, was to be procured from the mainland, which was about five miles distant.

On the whole island there were but three miserable huts, and one of these was vacant when I arrived. This I hired. It contained but two rooms, and these exhibited all the squalidness of the most miserable penury. The thatch had fallen in, the walls were unplastered, and the door was off its hinges. I ordered it to be repaired, bought some furniture, and took possession, an incident which would doubtless have occasioned some surprise had not all the senses of the cottagers been benumbed by want and squalid poverty. As it was, I lived ungazed at and unmolested, hardly thanked for the pittance of food and clothes which I gave, so much does suffering blunt even the coarsest sensations of men.

In this retreat I devoted the morning to labour; but in the evening, when the weather permitted, I walked on the stony beach of the sea to listen to the waves as they roared and dashed at my feet. It was a monotonous yet ever-changing scene. I thought of Switzerland; it was far different from this desolate and appalling landscape. Its hills are covered with vines, and its cottages are scattered thickly in the plains. Its fair lakes reflect a blue and gentle sky, and when troubled by the winds, their tumult is but as the play of a lively infant when compared to the roarings of the giant ocean.

In this manner I distributed my occupations when I first arrived, but as I proceeded in my labour, it became every day more horrible and irksome to me. Sometimes I could not prevail on myself to enter my laboratory for several days, and at other times I toiled day and night in order to complete my work. It was, indeed, a filthy process in which I was engaged. During my first experiment, a kind of enthusiastic frenzy had blinded me to the horror of my employment; my mind was intently fixed on the consummation of my labour, and my eyes were shut to the horror of my proceedings. But now I went to it in cold blood, and my heart often sickened at the work of my hands.

Thus situated, employed in the most detestable occupation, immersed in a solitude where nothing could for an instant call my attention from the actual scene in which I was engaged, my spirits became unequal; I grew restless and nervous. Every moment I feared to meet my persecutor. Sometimes I sat with my eyes fixed on the ground, fearing to raise them lest they should encounter the object which I so much dreaded to behold. I feared to wander from the sight of my fellow creatures lest when alone he should come to claim his companion.

In the mean time I worked on, and my labour was already considerably advanced. I looked towards its completion with a tremulous and eager hope, which I dared not trust myself to question but which was intermixed with obscure forebodings of evil that made my heart sicken in my bosom.

# CHAPTER 20

I SAT one evening in my laboratory; the sun had set, and the moon was just rising from the sea; I had not sufficient light for my employment, and I remained idle, in a pause of consideration of whether I should leave my labour for the night or hasten its conclusion by an unremitting attention to it. As I sat, a train of reflection occurred to me which led me to consider the effects of what I was now doing. Three years before, I was engaged in the same manner and had created a fiend whose unparalleled barbarity had desolated my heart and filled it forever with the bitterest remorse. I was now about to form another being of whose dispositions I was alike ignorant; she might become ten thousand times more malignant than her mate and delight, for its own sake, in murder and wretchedness. He had sworn to quit the neighbourhood of man and hide himself in deserts, but she had not; and she, who in all probability was to become a thinking and reasoning animal, might refuse to comply with a compact made before her creation. They might even hate each other; the creature who already lived loathed his own deformity, and might he not conceive a greater abhorrence for it when it came before his eyes in the female form? She also might turn with disgust from him to the superior beauty of man; she might quit him, and he be again alone, exasperated by the fresh provocation of being deserted by one of his own species.

Even if they were to leave Europe and inhabit the deserts of the new world, yet one of the first results of those sympathies for which the daemon thirsted would be children, and a race of evils would be propagated upon the earth who might make the very existence of the species of man a condition precarious and full of terror. Had I right, for my own benefit, to inflict this curse upon everlasting generations? I had before been moved by the sophisms of the being I had created; I had been struck senseless by his fiendish threats; but now, for the first time, the wickedness of my promise burst upon me; I shuddered to think that future ages might curse me as their pest, whose selfishness had not hesitated to buy its own peace at the price, perhaps, of the existence of the whole human race.

I trembled and my heart failed within me, when, on looking up, I saw by the light of the moon the daemon at the casement. A ghastly grin wrinkled his lips as he gazed on me, where I sat fulfilling the task which he had allotted to me. Yes, he had followed me in my travels; he had loitered in forests, hid himself in caves, or taken refuge in wide and desert heaths; and he now came to mark my progress and claim the fulfilment of my promise.

As I looked on him, his countenance expressed the utmost extent of malice and treachery. I thought with a sensation of madness on my promise of creating another like to him, and trembling with passion, tore to pieces the thing on which I was engaged. The wretch saw me destroy the creature on whose future existence he depended for happiness, and with a howl of devilish despair and revenge, withdrew.

I left the room, and locking the door, made a solemn vow in my own heart never to resume my labours; and then, with trembling steps, I sought my own apartment. I was alone; none were near me to dissipate the gloom and relieve me from the sickening oppression of the most terrible reveries.

Several hours passed, and I remained near my window gazing on the sea; it was almost motionless, for the winds were hushed, and all nature reposed under the eye of the quiet moon. A few fishing vessels alone specked the water, and now and then the gentle breeze wafted the sound of voices as the fishermen called to one another. I felt the silence, although I was hardly conscious of its extreme profundity, until my ear was suddenly arrested by the paddling of oars near the shore, and a person landed close to my house.

In a few minutes after, I heard the creaking of my door, as if some one endeavoured to open it softly. I trembled from head to foot; I felt a presentiment of who it was and wished to rouse one of the peasants who dwelt in a cottage not far from mine; but I was overcome by the sensation of helplessness, so often felt in frightful dreams, when you in vain endeavour to fly from an impending danger, and was rooted to the spot.

Presently I heard the sound of footsteps along the passage; the door opened, and the wretch whom I dreaded appeared. Shutting the door, he approached me and said in a smothered voice, 'You have destroyed the work which you began; what is it that you intend? Do you dare to break your promise? I have endured toil and misery; I left Switzerland with you; I crept along the shores of the Rhine, among its willow islands and over the summits of its hills. I have dwelt many months in the heaths of England and among the deserts of Scotland. I have endured incalculable fatigue, and cold, and hunger; do you dare destroy my hopes?'

'Begone! I do break my promise; never will I create another like yourself, equal in deformity and wickedness.'

'Slave, I before reasoned with you, but you have proved yourself unworthy of my condescension. Remember that I have power; you believe yourself miserable, but I can make you so wretched that the light of day will be hateful to you. You are my creator, but I am your master; obey!'

'The hour of my irresolution is past, and the period of your power is arrived. Your threats cannot move me to do an act of wickedness; but they confirm me in a determination of not creating you a companion in vice. Shall I, in cool blood, set loose upon the earth a daemon whose delight is in death and wretchedness? Begone! I am firm, and your words will only exasperate my rage.'

The monster saw my determination in my face and gnashed his teeth in the impotence of anger. 'Shall each man,' cried he, 'find a wife for his bosom, and each beast have his mate, and I be alone? I had feelings of affection, and they were requited by detestation and scorn. Man! You may hate, but beware! Your hours will pass in dread and misery, and soon the bolt will fall which must ravish from you your happiness forever. Are you to be happy while I grovel in the intensity of my wretchedness? You can blast my other passions, but revenge remains – revenge, henceforth dearer than light or food! I may die, but first you, my tyrant and tormentor, shall curse the sun that gazes on your misery. Beware, for I am fearless and therefore powerful. I will watch with the wiliness of a snake, that I may sting with its venom. Man, you shall repent of the injuries you inflict.'

'Devil, cease; and do not poison the air with these sounds of malice. I have declared my resolution to you, and I am no coward to bend beneath words. Leave me; I am inexorable.'

'It is well. I go; but remember, I shall be with you on your wedding-night.'

I started forward and exclaimed, 'Villain! Before you sign my death-warrant, be sure that you are yourself safe.'

I would have seized him, but he eluded me and quitted the house with precipitation. In a few moments I saw him in his boat, which shot across the waters with an arrowy swiftness and was soon lost amidst the waves.

All was again silent, but his words rang in my ears. I burned with rage to pursue the murderer of my peace and precipitate him into the ocean. I walked up and down my room hastily and perturbed, while my imagination conjured up a thousand images to torment and sting me. Why had I not followed him and closed with him in mortal strife? But I had suffered him to depart, and he had directed his course towards the mainland. I shuddered to think who might be the next victim sacrificed to his insatiate revenge. And then I thought again of his words – '*I will be with you on your wedding-night.*' That, then, was the period fixed for the fulfilment of my destiny. In that hour I should die and at once satisfy and extinguish his malice. The prospect did not move me to fear; yet when I thought of my beloved Elizabeth, of her tears and endless sorrow, when she should find her lover so barbarously snatched from her, tears, the first I had shed for many months, streamed from my eyes, and I resolved not to fall before my enemy without a bitter struggle.

The night passed away, and the sun rose from the ocean; my feelings became calmer, if it may be called calmness when the violence of rage sinks into the depths of despair. I left the house, the horrid scene of the last night's contention, and walked on the beach of the sea, which I almost regarded as an insuperable barrier between me and my fellow creatures; nay, a wish that such should prove the fact stole across me. I desired that I might pass my life on that barren rock, wearily, it is true, but uninterrupted by any sudden shock of misery. If I returned, it was to be sacrificed or to see those whom I most loved die under the grasp of a daemon whom I had myself created.

I walked about the isle like a restless spectre, separated from all it loved and miserable in the separation. When it became noon, and the sun rose higher, I lay down on the grass and was overpowered by a deep sleep. I had been awake the whole of the preceding night, my nerves were agitated, and my eyes inflamed by watching and misery. The sleep into which I now sank refreshed me; and when I awoke, I again felt as if I belonged to a race of human beings like myself, and I began to reflect upon what had passed with greater composure; yet still the words of the fiend rang in my ears like a death-knell; they appeared like a dream, yet distinct and oppressive as a reality.

The sun had far descended, and I still sat on the shore, satisfying my appetite, which had become ravenous, with an oaten cake, when I saw a fishing-boat land close to me, and one of the men brought me a packet; it contained letters from Geneva, and one from Clerval intreating me to join him. He said that he was wearing away his time fruitlessly where he was, that letters from the friends he had formed in London desired his return to complete the negotiation they had entered into for his Indian enterprize. He could not any longer delay his departure; but as his journey to London might be followed, even sooner than he now conjectured, by his longer voyage, he intreated me to bestow as much of my society on him as I could spare. He besought me, therefore, to leave my solitary isle and to meet him at Perth, that we might proceed southwards together. This letter in a degree recalled me to life, and I determined to quit my island at the expiration of two days.

Yet, before I departed, there was a task to perform, on which I shuddered to reflect; I must pack up my chemical instruments, and for that purpose I must enter the room which had been the scene of my odious work, and I must handle those utensils the sight of which was sickening to me. The next morning, at daybreak, I summoned sufficient courage and unlocked the door of my laboratory. The remains of the half-finished creature, whom I had destroyed, lay scattered on the floor, and I almost felt as if I had mangled the living flesh of a human being. I paused to collect myself and then entered the chamber. With trembling hand I conveyed the instruments out of the room, but I reflected that I ought not to leave the relics of my work to excite the horror and suspicion of the peasants; and I accordingly put them into a basket, with a great quantity of stones, and laying them up, determined to throw them into the sea that very night; and in the mean time I sat upon the beach, employed in cleaning and arranging my chemical apparatus.

Nothing could be more complete than the alteration that

had taken place in my feelings since the night of the appearance of the daemon. I had before regarded my promise with a gloomy despair as a thing that, with whatever consequences, must be fulfilled; but I now felt as if a film had been taken from before my eyes and that I for the first time saw clearly. The idea of renewing my labours did not for one instant occur to me; the threat I had heard weighed on my thoughts, but I did not reflect that a voluntary act of mine could avert it. I had resolved in my own mind that to create another like the fiend I had first made would be an act of the basest and most atrocious selfishness, and I banished from my mind every thought that could lead to a different conclusion.

Between two and three in the morning the moon rose; and I then, putting my basket aboard a little skiff, sailed out about four miles from the shore. The scene was perfectly solitary; a few boats were returning towards land, but I sailed away from them. I felt as if I was about the commission of a dreadful crime and avoided with shuddering anxiety any encounter with my fellow creatures. At one time the moon, which had before been clear, was suddenly overspread by a thick cloud, and I took advantage of the moment of darkness and cast my basket into the sea; I listened to the gurgling sound as it sank and then sailed away from the spot. The sky became clouded, but the air was pure, although chilled by the northeast breeze that was then rising. But it refreshed me and filled me with such agreeable sensations that I resolved to prolong my stay on the water, and fixing the rudder in a direct position, stretched myself at the bottom of the boat. Clouds hid the moon, everything was obscure, and I heard only the sound of the boat as its keel cut through the waves; the murmur lulled me, and in a short time I slept soundly.

I do not know how long I remained in this situation, but when I awoke I found that the sun had already mounted considerably. The wind was high, and the waves continually threatened the safety of my little skiff. I found that the wind was northeast and must have driven me far from the coast from which I had embarked. I endeavoured to change my course but quickly found that if I again made the attempt the boat would be instantly filled with water.

Thus situated, my only resource was to drive before the wind. I confess that I felt a few sensations of terror. I had no compass with me and was so slenderly acquainted with the geography of this part of the world that the sun was of little benefit to me. I might be driven into the wide Atlantic and feel all the tortures of starvation or be swallowed up in the immeasurable waters that roared and buffeted around me. I had already been out many hours and felt the torment of a burning thirst, a prelude to my other sufferings. I looked on the heavens, which were covered by clouds that flew before the wind, only to be replaced by others; I looked upon the sea; it was to be my grave. 'Fiend,' I exclaimed, 'your task is already fulfilled!' I thought of Elizabeth, of my father, and of Clerval – all left behind, on whom the monster might satisfy his sanguinary and merciless passions. This idea plunged me into a reverie so despairing and frightful that even now, when the scene is on the point of closing before me forever, I shudder to reflect on it.

Some hours passed thus; but by degrees, as the sun declined towards the horizon, the wind died away into a gentle breeze and the sea became free from breakers. But these gave place to a heavy swell; I felt sick and hardly able to hold the rudder, when suddenly I saw a line of high land towards the south.

Almost spent, as I was, by fatigue and the dreadful suspense I endured for several hours, this sudden certainty of life rushed like a flood of warm joy to my heart, and tears gushed from my eyes.

How mutable are our feelings, and how strange is that clinging love we have of life even in the excess of misery! I constructed another sail with a part of my dress and eagerly steered my course towards the land. It had a wild and rocky appearance, but as I approached nearer I easily perceived the traces of cultivation. I saw vessels near the shore and found myself suddenly transported back to the neighbourhood of civilized man. I carefully traced the windings of the land and hailed a steeple which I at length saw issuing from behind a small promontory. As I was in a state of extreme debility, I resolved to sail directly towards the town, as a place where I could most easily procure nourishment. Fortunately I had money with me. As I turned the promontory I perceived a small neat town and a good harbour, which I entered, my heart bounding with joy at my unexpected escape.

As I was occupied in fixing the boat and arranging the sails, several people crowded towards the spot. They seemed much surprized at my appearance, but instead of offering me any assistance, whispered together with gestures that at any other time might have produced in me a slight sensation of alarm. As it was, I merely remarked that they spoke English, and I therefore addressed them in that language. 'My good friends,' said I, 'will you be so kind as to tell me the name of this town and inform me where I am?'

'You will know that soon enough,' replied a man with a hoarse voice. 'Maybe you are come to a place that will not prove much to your taste, but you will not be consulted as to your quarters, I promise you.'

I was exceedingly surprized on receiving so rude an answer from a stranger, and I was also disconcerted on perceiving the frowning and angry countenances of his companions. 'Why do you answer me so roughly?' I replied. 'Surely it is not the custom of Englishmen to receive strangers so inhospitably.'

'I do not know,' said the man, 'what the custom of the English may be, but it is the custom of the Irish to hate villains.'

While this strange dialogue continued, I perceived the crowd rapidly increase. Their faces expressed a mixture of curiosity and anger, which annoyed and in some degree alarmed me. I enquired the way to the inn, but no one replied. I then moved forward, and a murmuring sound arose from the crowd as they followed and surrounded me, when an ill-looking man approaching tapped me on the shoulder and said, 'Come, sir, you must follow me to Mr Kirwin's to give an account of yourself.'

'Who is Mr Kirwin? Why am I to give an account of myself? Is not this a free country?'

'Ay, sir, free enough for honest folks. Mr Kirwin is a magistrate, and you are to give an account of the death of a gentleman who was found murdered here last night.'

This answer startled me, but I presently recovered myself. I was innocent; that could easily be proved; accordingly I followed my conductor in silence and was led to one of the best houses in the town. I was ready to sink from fatigue and hunger, but being surrounded by a crowd, I thought it politic to rouse all my strength, that no physical debility might be construed into apprehension or conscious guilt. Little did I then expect the calamity that was in a few moments to overwhelm me and extinguish in horror and despair all fear of ignominy or death.

I must pause here, for it requires all my fortitude to recall the memory of the frightful events which I am about to relate, in proper detail, to my recollection.

# CHAPTER 21

I WAS soon introduced into the presence of the magistrate, an old benevolent man with calm and mild manners. He looked upon me, however, with some degree of severity, and then, turning towards my conductors, he asked who appeared as witnesses on this occasion.

About half a dozen men came forward; and, one being selected by the magistrate, he deposed that he had been out fishing the night before with his son and brother-in-law, Daniel Nugent, when, about ten o'clock, they observed a strong northerly blast rising, and they accordingly put in for port. It was a very dark night, as the moon had not yet risen; they did not land at the harbour, but, as they had been accustomed, at a creek about two miles below. He walked on first, carrying a part of the fishing tackle, and his companions followed him at some distance. As he was proceeding along the sands, he struck his foot against something and fell at his length on the ground. His companions came up to assist him, and by the light of their lantern they found that he had fallen on the body of a man, who was to all appearance dead. Their first supposition was that it was the corpse of some person who had been drowned and was thrown on shore by the waves, but on examination they found that the clothes were not wet and even that the body was not then cold. They instantly carried it to the cottage of an old woman near the spot and endeavoured, but in vain, to restore it to life. It appeared to be a handsome young man, about five and twenty years of age. He had apparently been strangled, for there was no sign of any violence except the black mark of fingers on his neck.

The first part of this deposition did not in the least interest me, but when the mark of the fingers was mentioned I remembered the murder of my brother and felt myself extremely agitated; my limbs trembled, and a mist came over my eyes, which obliged me to lean on a chair for support. The magistrate observed me with a keen eye and of course drew an unfavourable augury from my manner.

The son confirmed his father's account, but when Daniel Nugent was called he swore positively that just before the fall of his companion, he saw a boat, with a single man in it, at a short distance from the shore; and as far as he could judge by the light of a few stars, it was the same boat in which I had just landed.

A woman deposed that she lived near the beach and was standing at the door of her cottage, waiting for the return of the fishermen, about an hour before she heard of the discovery of the body, when she saw a boat with only one man in it push off from that part of the shore where the corpse was afterwards found.

Another woman confirmed the account of the fishermen having brought the body into her house; it was not cold. They put it into a bed and rubbed it, and Daniel went to the town for an apothecary, but life was quite gone.

Several other men were examined concerning my landing, and they agreed that, with the strong north wind that had arisen during the night, it was very probable that I had beaten about for many hours and had been obliged to return nearly to the same spot from which I had departed. Besides, they observed that it appeared that I had brought the body from another place, and it was likely that as I did not appear to know the shore, I might have put into the harbour ignorant of the distance of the town of — from the place where I had deposited the corpse.

Mr Kirwin, on hearing this evidence, desired that I should be taken into the room where the body lay for interment, that it might be observed what effect the sight of it would produce upon me. This idea was probably suggested by the extreme agitation I had exhibited when the mode of the murder had been described. I was accordingly conducted, by the magistrate and several other persons, to the inn. I could not help being struck by the strange coincidences that had taken place during this eventful night; but, knowing that I had been conversing with several persons in the island I had inhabited about the time that the body had been found, I was perfectly tranquil as to the consequences of the affair.

I entered the room where the corpse lay and was led up to the coffin. How can I describe my sensations of beholding it? I feel yet parched with horror, nor can I reflect on that terrible moment without shuddering and agony. The examination, the presence of the magistrate and witnesses, passed like a dream from my memory when I saw the lifeless form of Henry Clerval stretched before me. I gasped for breath, and throwing myself on the body, I exclaimed, 'Have my murderous machinations deprived you also, my dearest Henry, of life? Two I have already destroyed; other victims await their destiny; but you, Clerval, my friend, my benefactor —'

The human frame could no longer support the agonies that I endured, and I was carried out of the room in strong convulsions.

A fever succeeded to this. I lay for two months on the point of death; my ravings, as I afterwards heard, were frightful; I called myself the murderer of William, of Justine, and of Clerval. Sometimes I intreated my attendants to assist me in the destruction of the fiend by whom I was tormented; and at others I felt the fingers of the monster already grasping my neck, and screamed aloud with agony and terror. Fortunately, as I spoke my native language, Mr Kirwin alone understood me; but my gestures and bitter cries were sufficient to affright the other witnesses.

Why did I not die? More miserable than man ever was before, why did I not sink into forgetfulness and rest? Death snatches away many blooming children, the only hopes of their doating parents; how many brides and youthful lovers have been one day in the bloom of health and hope, and the next a prey for worms and the decay of the tomb! Of what materials was I made that I could thus resist so many shocks, which, like the turning of the wheel, continually renewed the torture?

But I was doomed to live and in two months found myself as awaking from a dream, in a prison, stretched on a wretched bed, surrounded by jailers, turnkeys, bolts, and all the miserable apparatus of a dungeon. It was morning, I remember, when I thus awoke to understanding; I had forgotten the particulars of what had happened and only felt as if some great misfortune had suddenly overwhelmed me; but when I looked around and saw the barred windows and the squalidness of the room in which I was, all flashed across my memory and I groaned bitterly.

This sound disturbed an old woman who was sleeping in a chair beside me. She was a hired nurse, the wife of one of the turnkeys, and her countenance expressed all those bad qualities which often characterize that class. The lines of her face were hard and rude, like that of persons accustomed to see without sympathizing in sights of misery. Her tone expressed her entire indifference; she addressed me in English, and the voice struck me as one that I had heard during my sufferings. 'Are you better now, sir?' said she.

I replied in the same language, with a feeble voice, 'I believe I am; but if it be all true, if indeed I did not dream, I am sorry that I am still alive to feel this misery and horror.'

'For that matter,' replied the old woman, 'if you mean about the gentleman you murdered, I believe that it were better for you if you were dead, for I fancy it will go hard with you! However, that's none of my business; I am sent to nurse you and get you well; I do my duty with a safe conscience; it were well if everybody did the same.'

I turned with loathing from the woman who could utter

so unfeeling a speech to a person just saved, on the very edge of death; but I felt languid and unable to reflect on all that had passed. The whole series of my life appeared to me as a dream; I sometimes doubted if indeed it were all true, for it never presented itself to my mind with the force of reality.

As the images that floated before me became more distinct, I grew feverish; a darkness pressed around me; no one was near me who soothed me with the gentle voice of love; no dear hand supported me. The physician came and prescribed medicines, and the old woman prepared them for me; but utter carelessness was visible in the first, and the expression of brutality was strongly marked in the visage of the second. Who could be interested in the fate of a murderer but the hangman who would gain his fee?

These were my first reflections, but I soon learned that Mr Kirwin had shown me extreme kindness. He had caused the best room in the prison to be prepared for me (wretched indeed was the best); and it was he who had provided a physician and a nurse. It is true, he seldom came to see me, for although he ardently desired to relieve the sufferings of every human creature, he did not wish to be present at the agonies and miserable ravings of a murderer. He came, therefore, sometimes to see that I was not neglected, but his visits were short and with long intervals.

One day, while I was gradually recovering, I was seated in a chair, my eyes half open and my cheeks livid like those in death. I was overcome by gloom and misery and often reflected I had better seek death than desire to remain in a world which to me was replete with wretchedness. At one time I considered whether I should not declare myself guilty and suffer the penalty of the law, less innocent than poor Justine had been. Such were my thoughts when the door of my apartment was opened and Mr Kirwin entered. His countenance expressed sympathy and compassion; he drew a chair close to mine and addressed me in French,

'I fear that this place is very shocking to you; can I do any thing to make you more comfortable?'

'I thank you, but all that you mention is nothing to me; on the whole earth there is no comfort which I am capable of receiving.'

'I know that the sympathy of a stranger can be but of little relief to one borne down as you are by so strange a misfortune. But you will, I hope, soon quit this melancholy abode, for doubtless evidence can easily be brought to free you from the criminal charge.'

'That is my least concern; I am, by a course of strange events, become the most miserable of mortals. Persecuted and tortured as I am and have been, can death be any evil to me?'

'Nothing indeed could be more unfortunate and agonizing than the strange chances that have lately occurred. You were thrown, by some surprising accident, on this shore, renowned for its hospitality; seized immediately, and charged with murder. The first sight that was presented to your eyes was the body of your friend, murdered in so unaccountable a manner and placed, as it were, by some fiend across your path.'

As Mr Kirwin said this, notwithstanding the agitation I endured on this retrospect of my sufferings, I also felt considerable surprise at the knowledge he seemed to possess concerning me. I suppose some astonishment was exhibited in my countenance, for Mr Kirwin hastened to say, 'Immediately upon your being taken ill, all the papers that were on your person were brought me, and I examined them that I might discover some trace by which I could send to your relations an account of your misfortune and illness. I found several letters, and, among others, one which I discovered from its commencement to be from your father. I instantly wrote to Geneva; nearly two months have elapsed since the departure of my letter. But you are ill; even now you tremble; you are unfit for agitation of any kind.'

'This suspense is a thousand times worse than the most horrible event; tell me what new scene of death has been acted, and whose murder I am now to lament?'

'Your family is perfectly well,' said Mr Kirwin with gentleness; 'and some one, a friend, is come to visit you.'

I know not by what chain of thought the idea presented itself, but it instantly darted into my mind that the murderer had come to mock at my misery and taunt me with the death of Clerval, as a new incitement for me to comply with his hellish desires. I put my hand before my eyes, and cried out in agony, 'Oh! Take him away! I cannot see him; for God's sake, do not let him enter!'

Mr Kirwin regarded me with a troubled countenance. He could not help regarding my exclamation as a presumption of my guilt and said in rather a severe tone, 'I should have thought, young man, that the presence of your father would have been welcome instead of inspiring such violent repugnance.'

'My father!' cried I, while every feature and every muscle was relaxed from anguish to pleasure. 'Is my father indeed come? How kind, how very kind! But where is he, why does he not hasten to me?'

My change of manner surprized and pleased the magistrate; perhaps he thought that my former exclamation was a momentary return of delirium, and now he instantly resumed his former benevolence. He rose and quitted the room with my nurse, and in a moment my father entered it.

Nothing, at this moment, could have given me greater pleasure than the arrival of my father. I stretched out my hand to him and cried, 'Are you, then, safe – and Elizabeth – and Ernest?'

My father calmed me with assurances of their welfare and endeavoured, by dwelling on these subjects so interesting to my heart, to raise my desponding spirits; but he soon felt that a prison cannot be the abode of cheerfulness. 'What a place is this that you inhabit, my son!' said he, looking mournfully at the barred windows and wretched appearance of the room. 'You travelled to seek happiness, but a fatality seems to pursue you. And poor Clerval —'

The name of my unfortunate and murdered friend was an agitation too great to be endured in my weak state; I shed tears.

'Alas! Yes, my father,' replied I; 'some destiny of the most horrible kind hangs over me, and I must live to fulfil it, or surely I should have died on the coffin of Henry.'

We were not allowed to converse for any length of time, for the precarious state of my health rendered every precaution necessary that could ensure tranquillity. Mr Kirwin came in and insisted that my strength should not be exhausted by too much exertion. But the appearance of my father was to me like that of my good angel, and I gradually recovered my health.

As my sickness quitted me, I was absorbed by a gloomy and black melancholy that nothing could dissipate. The image of Clerval was forever before me, ghastly and murdered. More than once the agitation into which these reflections threw me made my friends dread a dangerous relapse. Alas! Why did they preserve so miserable and detested a life? It was surely that I might fulfil my destiny, which is now drawing to a close. Soon, oh, very soon, will death extinguish these throbbings and relieve me from the mighty weight of anguish that bears me to the dust; and, in executing the award of justice, I shall also sink to rest. Then the appearance of death was distant, although the wish was ever present to my thoughts; and I often sat for hours motionless and speechless, wishing for some mighty revolution that might bury me and my destroyer in its ruins.

The season of the assizes approached. I had already been three months in prison, and although I was still weak and in continual danger of a relapse, I was obliged to travel nearly a hundred miles to the country town where the court was held. Mr Kirwin charged himself with every care of collecting witnesses and arranging my defence. I was spared the disgrace of appearing publicly as a criminal, as the case was not brought before the court that decides on life and death. The grand jury rejected the bill, on its being proved that I was on the Orkney Islands at the hour the body of my friend was found; and a fortnight after my removal I was liberated from prison.

My father was enraptured on finding me freed from the vexations of a criminal charge, that I was again allowed to breathe the fresh atmosphere and permitted to return to my native country. I did not participate in these feelings, for to me the walls of a dungeon or a palace were alike hateful. The cup of life was poisoned forever, and although the sun shone upon me, as upon the happy and gay of heart, I saw around me nothing but a dense and frightful darkness, penetrated by no light but the glimmer of two eyes that glared upon me. Sometimes they were the expressive eyes of Henry, languishing in death, the dark orbs nearly covered by the lids and the long black lashes that fringed them; sometimes it was the watery, clouded eyes of the monster, as I first saw them in my chamber at Ingolstadt.

My father tried to awaken in me the feelings of affection. He talked of Geneva, which I should soon visit, of Elizabeth and Ernest; but these words only drew deep groans from me. Sometimes, indeed, I felt a wish for happiness and thought with melancholy delight of my beloved cousin or longed, with a devouring *maladie du pays*,[1] to see once more the blue lake and rapid Rhone, that had been so dear to me in early childhood; but my general state of feeling was a torpor in which a prison was as welcome a residence as the divinest scene in nature; and these fits were seldom interrupted but by paroxysms of anguish and despair. At these moments I often endeavoured to put an end to the existence I loathed, and it required unceasing attendance and vigilance to restrain me from committing some dreadful act of violence.

Yet one duty remained to me, the recollection of which

finally triumphed over my selfish despair. It was necessary that I should return without delay to Geneva, there to watch over the lives of those I so fondly loved and to lie in wait for the murderer, that if any chance led me to the place of his concealment, or if he dared again to blast me by his presence, I might, with unfailing aim, put an end to the existence of the monstrous image which I had endued with the mockery of a soul still more monstrous. My father still desired to delay our departure, fearful that I could not sustain the fatigues of a journey, for I was a shattered wreck – the shadow of a human being. My strength was gone. I was a mere skeleton, and fever night and day preyed upon my wasted frame.

Still, as I urged our leaving Ireland with such inquietude and impatience, my father thought it best to yield. We took our passage on board a vessel bound for Havre-de-Grâce and sailed with a fair wind from the Irish shores. It was midnight. I lay on the deck looking at the stars and listening to the dashing of the waves. I hailed the darkness that shut Ireland from my sight, and my pulse beat with a feverish joy when I reflected that I should soon see Geneva. The past appeared to me in the light of a frightful dream; yet the vessel in which I was, the wind that blew me from the detested shore of Ireland, and the sea which surrounded me, told me too forcibly that I was deceived by no vision and that Clerval, my friend and dearest companion, had fallen a victim to me and the monster of my creation. I repassed, in my memory, my whole life – my quiet happiness while residing with my family in Geneva, the death of my mother, and my departure for Ingolstadt. I remembered, shuddering, the mad enthusiasm that hurried me on to the creation of my hideous enemy, and I called to mind the night in which he first lived. I was unable to pursue the train of thought; a thousand feelings pressed upon me, and I wept bitterly.

Ever since my recovery from the fever I had been in the custom of taking every night a small quantity of laudanum, for it was by means of this drug only that I was enabled to gain the rest necessary for the preservation of life. Oppressed by the recollection of my various misfortunes, I now swallowed double my usual quantity and soon slept profoundly. But sleep did not afford me respite from thought and misery; my dreams presented a thousand objects that scared me. Towards morning I was possessed by a kind of nightmare; I felt the fiend's grasp in my neck and could not free myself from it; groans and cries rang in my ears. My father, who was watching over me, perceiving my restlessness, awoke me; the dashing waves were around, the cloudy sky above, the fiend was not here: a sense of security, a feeling that a truce was established between the present hour and the irresistible, disastrous future imparted to me a kind of calm forgetfulness, of which the human mind is by its structure peculiarly susceptible.

## CHAPTER 22

THE voyage came to an end. We landed, and proceeded to Paris. I soon found that I had overtaxed my strength and that I must repose before I could continue my journey. My father's care and attentions were indefatigable, but he did not know the origin of my sufferings and sought erroneous methods to remedy the incurable ill. He wished me to seek amusement in society. I abhorred the face of man. Oh, not abhorred! They were my brethren, my fellow beings, and I felt attracted even to the most repulsive among them, as to creatures of an angelic nature and celestial mechanism. But I felt that I had no right to share their intercourse. I had unchained an enemy among them whose joy it was to shed their blood and to revel in their groans. How they would, each and all, abhor me and hunt me from the world did they know my unhallowed acts and the crimes which had their source in me!

My father yielded at length to my desire to avoid society and strove by various arguments to banish my despair. Sometimes he thought that I felt deeply the degradation of being obliged to answer a charge of murder, and he endeavoured to prove to me the futility of pride.

'Alas! My father,' said I, 'how little do you know me. Human beings, their feelings and passions, would indeed be degraded if such a wretch as I felt pride. Justine, poor unhappy Justine, was as innocent as I, and she suffered the same charge; she died for it; and I am the cause of this – I murdered her. William, Justine, and Henry – they all died by my hands.'

My father had often, during my imprisonment, heard me make the same assertion; when I thus accused myself, he sometimes seemed to desire an explanation, and at others he appeared to consider it as the offspring of delirium, and that, during my illness, some idea of this kind had presented itself to my imagination, the remembrance of which I preserved in my convalescence. I avoided explanation and maintained a continual silence concerning the wretch I had created. I had a persuasion that I should be supposed mad, and this in itself would forever have chained my tongue. But, besides, I could not bring myself to disclose a secret which would fill my hearer with consternation and make fear and unnatural horror the inmates of his breast. I checked, therefore, my impatient thirst for sympathy and was silent when I would have given the world to have confided the fatal secret. Yet, still, words like those I have recorded would burst uncontrollably from me. I could offer no explanation of them, but their truth in part relieved the burden of my mysterious woe.

Upon this occasion my father said, with an expression of unbounded wonder, 'My dearest Victor, what infatuation is this? My dear son, I intreat you never to make such an assertion again.'

'I am not mad,' I cried energetically; 'the sun and the heavens, who have viewed my operations, can bear witness of my truth. I am the assassin of those most innocent victims; they died by my machinations. A thousand times would I have shed my own blood, drop by drop, to have saved their lives; but I could not, my father, indeed I could not sacrifice the whole human race.'

The conclusion of this speech convinced my father that my ideas were deranged, and he instantly changed the subject of our conversation and endeavoured to alter the course of my thoughts. He wished as much as possible to obliterate the memory of the scenes that had taken place in Ireland and never alluded to them or suffered me to speak of my misfortunes.

As time passed away I became more calm; misery had her dwelling in my heart, but I no longer talked in the same incoherent manner of my own crimes; sufficient for me was the consciousness of them. By the utmost self-violence I curbed the imperious voice of wretchedness, which sometimes desired to declare itself to the whole world, and my manners were calmer and more composed than they had ever been since my journey to the sea of ice.

A few days before we left Paris on our way to Switzerland, I received the following letter from Elizabeth:

'My dear Friend,

'It gave me the greatest pleasure to receive a letter from my uncle dated at Paris; you are no longer at a formidable distance, and I may hope to see you in less than a fortnight. My poor cousin, how much you must have suffered! I expect to see you looking even more ill than when you quitted Geneva. This winter has been passed most miserably, tortured as I have been by anxious suspense; yet I hope to see peace in your countenance and to find that your heart is not totally void of comfort and tranquillity.

'Yet I fear that the same feelings now exist that made you so miserable a year ago, even perhaps augmented by time. I would not disturb you at this period, when so many misfortunes weigh upon you, but a conversation that I had with my uncle previous to his departure renders some explanation necessary before we meet.

'Explanation! You may possibly say, What can Elizabeth have to explain? If you really say this, my questions are answered and all my doubts satisfied. But you are distant from me, and it is possible that you may dread and yet be pleased with this explanation; and in a probability of this being the case, I dare not any longer postpone writing what, during your absence, I have often wished to express to you but have never had the courage to begin.

'You well know, Victor, that our union had been the favourite plan of your parents ever since our infancy. We were told this when young, and taught to look forward to it as an event that would certainly take place. We were affectionate playfellows during childhood, and, I believe, dear and valued friends to one another as we grew older. But as brother and sister often entertain a lively affection towards each other without desiring a more intimate union, may not such also be our case? Tell me, dearest Victor. Answer me, I conjure you, by our mutual happiness, with simple truth – Do you not love another?

'You have travelled; you have spent several years of your life at Ingolstadt; and I confess to you, my friend, that when I saw you last autumn so unhappy, flying to solitude from the society of every creature, I could not help supposing that you might regret our connexion and believe yourself bound in honour to fulfil the wishes of your parents, although they opposed themselves to your inclinations. But this is false reasoning. I confess to you, my friend, that I love you and that in my airy dreams of futurity you have been my constant friend and companion. But it is your happiness I desire as well as my own when I declare to you that our marriage would render me eternally miserable unless it were the dictate of your own free choice. Even now I weep to think that, borne down as you are by the cruellest misfortunes, you may stifle, by the word "honour," all hope of that love and happiness which would alone restore you to yourself. I, who have so disinterested an affection for you, may increase your miseries tenfold by being an obstacle to your wishes. Ah! Victor, be assured that your cousin and playmate has too sincere a love for you not to be made miserable by this supposition. Be happy, my friend; and if you obey me in this one request, remain satisfied that nothing on earth will have the power to interrupt my tranquillity.

'Do not let this letter disturb you; do not answer tomorrow, or the next day, or even until you come, if it will give you pain. My uncle will send me news of your health, and if I see but one smile on your lips when we meet, occasioned by this or any other exertion of mine, I shall need no other happiness.

'Elizabeth Lavenza

'Geneva, May 18th, 17—'

This letter revived in my memory what I had before forgotten, the threat of the fiend – '*I will be with you on your wedding-night!*' Such was my sentence, and on that night would the daemon employ every art to destroy me and tear me from the glimpse of happiness which promised partly to console my sufferings. On that night he had determined to consummate his crimes by my death. Well, be it so; a deadly struggle would then assuredly take place, in which if he were victorious I should be at peace and his power over me be at an end. If he were vanquished, I should be a free man. Alas! What freedom? Such as the peasant enjoys when his family have been massacred before his eyes, his cottage burnt, his lands laid waste, and he is turned adrift, homeless, penniless, and alone, but free. Such would be my liberty except that in my Elizabeth I possessed a treasure, alas, balanced by those horrors of remorse and guilt which would pursue me until death.

Sweet and beloved Elizabeth! I read and reread her letter, and some softened feelings stole into my heart and dared to whisper paradisiacal dreams of love and joy; but the apple was already eaten, and the angel's arm bared to drive me from all hope. Yet I would die to make her happy. If the monster executed his threat, death was inevitable; yet, again, I considered whether my marriage would hasten my fate. My destruction might indeed arrive a few months sooner, but if my torturer should suspect that I postponed it, influenced by his menaces, he would surely find other and perhaps more dreadful means of revenge. He had vowed *to be with me on my wedding-night*, yet he did not consider that threat as binding him to peace in the mean time, for as if to show me that he was not yet satiated with blood, he had murdered Clerval immediately after the enunciation of his threats. I resolved, therefore, that if my immediate union with my cousin would conduce either to hers or my father's happiness, my adversary's designs against my life should not retard it a single hour.

In this state of mind I wrote to Elizabeth. My letter was calm and affectionate. 'I fear, my beloved girl,' I said, 'little happiness remains for us on earth; yet all that I may one day enjoy is centred in you. Chase away your idle fears; to you alone do I consecrate my life and my endeavours for contentment. I have one secret, Elizabeth, a dreadful one; when revealed to you, it will chill your frame with horror, and then, far from being surprised at my misery, you will only wonder that I survive what I have endured. I will confide this tale of misery and terror to you the day after our marriage shall take place, for, my sweet cousin, there must be perfect confidence between us. But until then, I conjure you, do not mention or allude to it. This I most earnestly intreat, and I know you will comply.'

In about a week after the arrival of Elizabeth's letter we returned to Geneva. The sweet girl welcomed me with warm affection, yet tears were in her eyes as she beheld my emaciated frame and feverish cheeks. I saw a change in her also. She was thinner and had lost much of that heavenly vivacity that had before charmed me; but her gentleness and soft looks of compassion made her a more fit companion for one blasted and miserable as I was.

The tranquillity which I now enjoyed did not endure. Memory brought madness with it, and when I thought of what had passed, a real insanity possessed me; sometimes I was furious and burnt with rage, sometimes low and despondent. I neither spoke nor looked at any one, but sat motionless, bewildered by the multitude of miseries that overcame me.

Elizabeth alone had the power to draw me from these fits; her gentle voice would soothe me when transported by passion and inspire me with human feelings when sunk in torpor. She wept with me and for me. When reason returned, she would remonstrate and endeavour to inspire me with resignation. Ah! It is well for the unfortunate to be resigned, but for the guilty there is no peace. The agonies of remorse poison the luxury there is otherwise sometimes found in indulging the excess of grief.

Soon after my arrival my father spoke of my immediate marriage with Elizabeth. I remained silent.

'Have you, then, some other attachment?'

'None on earth. I love Elizabeth and look forward to our union with delight. Let the day therefore be fixed; and on it I will consecrate myself, in life or death, to the happiness of my cousin.'

'My dear Victor, do not speak thus. Heavy misfortunes have befallen us, but let us only cling closer to what remains and transfer our love for those whom we have lost to those who yet live. Our circle will be small but bound close by the ties of affection and mutual misfortune. And when time shall have softened your despair, new and dear objects of care will be born to replace those of whom we have been so cruelly deprived.'

Such were the lessons of my father. But to me the remembrance of the threat returned; nor can you wonder that, omnipotent as the fiend had yet been in his deeds of blood, I should almost regard him as invincible, and that when he had pronounced the words '*I shall be with you on your wedding-night*,' I should regard the threatened fate as unavoidable. But death was no evil to me if the loss of Elizabeth were balanced with it, and I therefore, with a contented and even cheerful countenance, agreed with my father that if my cousin would consent, the ceremony should take place in ten days, and thus put, as I imagined, the seal to my fate.

Great God! If for one instant I had thought what might be the hellish intention of my fiendish adversary, I would rather have banished myself forever from my native country and wandered a friendless outcast over the earth than have consented to this miserable marriage. But, as if possessed of magic powers, the monster had blinded me to his real intentions; and when I thought that I had prepared only my own death, I hastened that of a far dearer victim.

As the period fixed for our marriage drew nearer, whether from cowardice or a prophetic feeling, I felt my heart sink within me. But I concealed my feelings by an appearance of hilarity that brought smiles and joy to the countenance of my father, but hardly deceived the ever-watchful and nicer eye of Elizabeth. She looked forward to our union with placid contentment, not unmingled with a little fear, which past misfortunes had impressed, that what now appeared certain and tangible happiness might soon dissipate into an airy dream and leave no trace but deep and everlasting regret.

Preparations were made for the event, congratulatory visits were received, and all wore a smiling appearance. I shut up, as well as I could, in my own heart the anxiety that preyed there and entered with seeming earnestness into the plans of my father, although they might only serve as the decorations of my tragedy. Through my father's exertions a part of the inheritance of Elizabeth had been restored to her by the Austrian government. A small possession on the shores of Como belonged to her. It was agreed that, immediately after our union, we should proceed to Villa Lavenza and spent our first days of happiness beside the beautiful lake near which it stood.

In the mean time I took every precaution to defend my person in case the fiend should openly attack me. I carried pistols and a dagger constantly about me and was ever on the watch to prevent artifice, and by these means gained a greater degree of tranquillity. Indeed, as the period approached, the threat appeared more as a delusion, not to be regarded as worthy to disturb my peace, while the happiness I hoped for in my marriage wore a greater appearance of certainty as the day fixed for its solemnization drew nearer and I heard it continually spoken of as an occurrence which no accident could possibly prevent.

Elizabeth seemed happy; my tranquil demeanour contributed greatly to calm her mind. But on the day that was to fulfil my wishes and my destiny, she was melancholy, and a presentiment of evil pervaded her; and perhaps also she thought of the dreadful secret which I had promised to reveal to her on the following day. My father was in the mean time overjoyed and in the bustle of preparation only recognized in the melancholy of his niece the diffidence of a bride.

After the ceremony was performed a large party assembled at my father's, but it was agreed that Elizabeth and

I should commence our journey by water, sleeping that night at Evian and continuing our voyage on the following day. The day was fair, the wind favourable; all smiled on our nuptial embarkation.

Those were the last moments of my life during which I enjoyed the feeling of happiness. We passed rapidly along; the sun was hot, but we were sheltered from its rays by a kind of canopy while we enjoyed the beauty of the scene, sometimes on one side of the lake, where we saw Mont Salêve, the pleasant banks of Montalègre, and at a distance, surmounting all, the beautiful Mont Blanc and the assemblage of snowy mountains that in vain endeavour to emulate her; sometimes coasting the opposite banks, we saw the mighty Jura opposing its dark side to the ambition that would quit its native country, and an almost insurmountable barrier to the invader who should wish to enslave it.

I took the hand of Elizabeth. 'You are sorrowful, my love. Ah! If you know what I have suffered and what I may yet endure, you would endeavour to let me taste the quiet and freedom from despair that this one day at least permits me to enjoy.'

'Be happy, my dear Victor,' replied Elizabeth; 'there is, I hope, nothing to distress you; and be assured that if a lively joy is not painted in my face, my heart is contented. Something whispers to me not to depend too much on the prospect that is opened before us, but I will not listen to such a sinister voice. Observe how fast we move along and how the clouds, which sometimes obscure and sometimes rise above the dome of Mont Blanc, render this scene of beauty still more interesting. Look also at the innumerable fish that are swimming in the clear waters, where we can distinguish every pebble that lies at the bottom. What a divine day! How happy and serene all nature appears!'

Thus Elizabeth endeavoured to divert her thoughts and mine from all reflection upon melancholy subjects. But her temper was fluctuating; joy for a few instants shone in her eyes, but it continually gave place to distraction and reverie.

The sun sank lower in the heavens; we passed the river Drance and observed its path through the chasms of the higher and the glens of the lower hills. The Alps here come closer to the lake, and we approached the amphitheatre of mountains which forms its eastern boundary. The spire of Evian shone under the woods that surrounded it and the range of mountain above mountain by which it was overhung.

The wind, which had hitherto carried us along with amazing rapidity, sank at sunset to a light breeze; the soft air just ruffled the water and caused a pleasant motion among the trees as we approached the shore, from which it wafted the most delightful scent of flowers and hay. The sun sank beneath the horizon as we landed, and as I touched the shore I felt those cares and fears revive which soon were to clasp me and cling to me forever.

# CHAPTER 23

IT was eight o'clock when we landed; we walked for a short time on the shore, enjoying the transitory light, and then retired to the inn and contemplated the lovely scene of waters, woods, and mountains, obscured in darkness, yet still displaying their black outlines.

The wind, which had fallen in the south, now rose with great violence in the west. The moon had reached her summit in the heavens and was beginning to descend; the clouds swept across it swifter than the flight of the vulture and dimmed her rays, while the lake reflected the scene of the busy heavens, rendered still busier by the restless waves that were beginning to rise. Suddenly a heavy storm of rain descended.

I had been calm during the day, but so soon as night obscured the shapes of objects, a thousand fears arose in my mind. I was anxious and watchful, while my right hand grasped a pistol which was hidden in my bosom; every sound terrified me, but I resolved that I would sell my life dearly and not shrink from the conflict until my own life or that of my adversary was extinguished.

Elizabeth observed my agitation for some time in timid and fearful silence, but there was something in my glance which communicated terror to her, and trembling, she asked, 'What is it that agitates you, my dear Victor? What is it you fear?'

'Oh! Peace, peace, my love,' replied I; 'this night, and all will be safe; but this night is dreadful, very dreadful.'

I passed an hour in this state of mind, when suddenly I reflected how fearful the combat which I momentarily expected would be to my wife, and I earnestly intreated her to retire, resolving not to join her until I had obtained some knowledge as to the situation of my enemy.

She left me, and I continued some time walking up and down the passages of the house and inspecting every corner that might afford a retreat to my adversary. But I discovered no trace of him and was beginning to conjecture that some fortunate chance had intervened to prevent the execution of his menaces when suddenly I heard a shrill and dreadful scream. It came from the room into which Elizabeth had retired. As I heard it, the whole truth rushed into my mind, my arms dropped, the motion of every muscle and fibre was suspended; I could feel the blood trickling in my veins and tingling in the extremities of my limbs. This state lasted but for an instant; the scream was repeated, and I rushed into the room.

Great God! Why did I not then expire! Why am I here to relate the destruction of the best hope and the purest creature of earth? She was there, lifeless and inanimate, thrown across the bed, her head hanging down and her pale and distorted features half covered by her hair. Every where I turn I see the same figure – her bloodless arms and relaxed form flung by the murderer on its bridal bier. Could I behold this and live? Alas! Life is obstinate and clings closest where it is most hated. For a moment only did I lose recollection; I fell senseless on the ground.

When I recovered I found myself surrounded by the people of the inn; their countenances expressed a breathless terror, but the horror of others appeared only as a mockery, a shadow of the feelings that oppressed me. I escaped fom them to the room where lay the body of Elizabeth, my love, my wife, so lately living, so dear, so worthy. She had been moved from the posture in which I had first beheld her, and now, as she lay, her head upon her arm and a handkerchief thrown across her face and neck, I might have supposed her asleep. I rushed towards her and embraced her with ardour, but the deadly languor and coldness of the limbs told me that what I now held in my arms had ceased to be the Elizabeth whom I had loved and cherished. The murderous mark of the fiend's grasp was on her neck, and the breath had ceased to issue from her lips.

While I still hung over her in the agony of despair, I happened to look up. The windows of the room had before been darkened, and I felt a kind of panic on seeing the pale yellow light of the moon illuminate the chamber. The shutters had been thrown back, and with a sensation of horror not to be described, I saw at the open window a figure the most hideous and abhorred. A grin was on the face of the monster; he seemed to jeer, as with his fiendish finger he pointed towards the corpse of my wife. I rushed towards the window, and drawing a pistol from my bosom, fired; but he eluded me, leaped from his station, and running with the swiftness of lightning, plunged into the lake.

The report of the pistol brought a crowd into the room. I pointed to the spot where he had disappeared, and we followed the track with boats; nets were cast, but in vain. After passing several hours, we returned hopeless, most of my companions believing it to have been a form conjured up by my fancy. After having landed, they proceeded to search the country, parties going in different directions among the woods and vines.

I attempted to accompany them and proceeded a short distance from the house, but my head whirled round, my steps were like those of a drunken man, I fell at last in a state of utter exhaustion; a film covered my eyes, and my skin was parched with the heat of fever. In this state I was carried back and placed on a bed, hardly conscious of what had happened; my eyes wandered round the room as if to seek something that I had lost.

After an interval I arose, and as if by instinct, crawled into the room where the corpse of my beloved lay. There were women weeping around; I hung over it and joined my sad tears to theirs; all this time no distinct idea presented itself to my mind, but my thoughts rambled to various subjects, reflecting confusedly on my misfortunes and their cause. I was bewildered, in a cloud of wonder and horror. The death of William, the execution of Justine, the murder of Clerval, and lastly of my wife; even at that moment I knew not that my only remaining friends were safe from the malignity of the fiend; my father even now might be writhing under his grasp, and Ernest might be dead at his feet. This idea made me shudder and recalled me to action. I started up and resolved to return to Geneva with all possible speed.

There were no horses to be procured, and I must return by the lake; but the wind was unfavourable, and the rain fell in torrents. However, it was hardly morning, and I might reasonably hope to arrive by night. I hired men to row and took an oar myself, for I had always experienced relief from mental torment in bodily exercise. But the overflowing misery I now felt, and the excess of agitation that I endured, rendered me incapable of any exertion. I threw down the oar, and leaning my head upon my hands, gave way to every gloomy idea that arose. If I looked up, I saw scenes which were familiar to me in my happier time and which I had contemplated but the day before in the company of her who was now but a shadow and a recollection. Tears streamed from my eyes. The rain had ceased for a moment, and I saw the fish play in the waters as they had done a few hours before; they had then been observed by Elizabeth. Nothing is so painful to the human mind as a great and sudden change. The sun might shine or the clouds might lower: but nothing could appear to me as it had done the day before. A fiend had snatched from me every hope of future happiness; no creature had ever been so miserable as I was; so frightful an event is single in the history of man.

But why should I dwell upon the incidents that followed this last overwhelming event? Mine has been a tale of horrors; I have reached their acme, and what I must now relate can but be tedious to you. Know that, one by one, my friends were snatched away; I was left desolate. My own strength is exhausted, and I must tell, in a few words, what remains of my hideous narration.

I arrived at Geneva. My father and Ernest yet lived, but the former sunk under the tidings that I bore. I see him now, excellent and venerable old man! His eyes wandered in vacancy, for they had lost their charm and their delight – his Elizabeth, his more than daughter, whom he doated on with all that affection which a man feels, who in the decline of life, having few affections, clings more earnestly to those that remain. Cursed, cursed be the fiend that brought misery on his grey hairs and doomed him to waste in wretchedness! He could not live under the horrors that were accumulated around him; the springs of existence suddenly gave way; he was unable to rise from his bed, and in a few days he died in my arms.

What then became of me? I know not; I lost sensation, and chains and darkness were the only objects that pressed upon me. Sometimes, indeed, I dreamt that I wandered in flowery meadows and pleasant vales with the friends of my youth, but I awoke and found myself in a dungeon. Melancholy followed, but by degrees I gained a clear conception of my miseries and situation and was then released from my prison. For they had called me mad, and during many months, as I understood, a solitary cell had been my habitation.

Liberty, however, had been a useless gift to me, had I not, as I awakened to reason, at the same time awakened to revenge. As the memory of past misfortunes pressed upon me, I began to reflect on their cause – the monster whom I had created, the miserable daemon whom I had sent abroad into the world for my destruction. I was possessed by a maddening rage when I thought of him, and desired and ardently prayed that I might have him within my grasp to wreak a great and signal revenge on his cursed head.

Nor did my hate long confine itself to useless wishes; I began to reflect on the best means of securing him; and for this purpose, about a month after my release, I repaired to a criminal judge in the town and told him that I had an accusation to make, that I knew the destroyer of my family, and that I required him to exert his whole authority for the apprehension of the murderer.

The magistrate listened to me with attention and kindness. 'Be assured, sir,' said he, 'no pains or exertions on my part shall be spared to discover the villain.'

'I thank you,' replied I; 'listen, therefore, to the deposition that I have to make. It is indeed a tale so strange that I should fear you would not credit it were there not something in truth which, however wonderful, forces conviction. The story is too connected to be mistaken for a dream, and I have no motive for falsehood.' My manner as I thus addressed him was impressive but calm; I had formed in my own heart a resolution to pursue my destroyer to death, and this purpose quieted my agony and for an interval reconciled me to life. I now related my history briefly but with firmness and precision, marking the dates with accuracy and never deviating into invective or exclamation.

The magistrate appeared at first perfectly incredulous, but as I continued he became more attentive and interested; I saw him sometimes shudder with horror; at others a lively surprise, unmingled with disbelief, was painted on his countenance.

When I had concluded my narration I said, 'This is the being whom I accuse and for whose seizure and punishment I call upon you to exert your whole power. It is your duty as a magistrate, and I believe and hope that your feelings as a man will not revolt from the execution of those functions on this occasion.'

This address caused a considerable change in the physiognomy of my own auditor. He had heard my story with that half kind of belief that is given to a tale of spirits and supernatural events; but when he was called upon to act officially in consequence, the whole tide of his incredulity returned. He, however, answered mildly, 'I would willingly afford you every aid in your pursuit, but the creature of whom you speak appears to have powers which would put all my exertions to defiance. Who can follow an animal which can traverse the sea of ice and inhabit caves and dens where no man would venture to intrude? Besides, some months have elapsed since the commission of his crimes, and no one can conjecture to what place he has wandered or what region he may now inhabit.'

'I do not doubt that he hovers near the spot which I inhabit, and if he has indeed taken refuge in the Alps, he may be hunted like the chamois and destroyed as a beast of prey. But I perceive your thoughts; you do not credit my narrative and do not intend to pursue my enemy with the punishment which is his desert.'

As I spoke, rage sparkled in my eyes; the magistrate was intimidated. 'You are mistaken,' said he. 'I will exert myself, and if it is in my power to seize the monster, be assured that he shall suffer punishment proportionate to his crimes. But I fear, from what you have yourself described to be his properties, that this will prove impracticable; and thus, while every proper measure is pursued, you should make up your mind to disappointment.'

'That cannot be; but all that I can say will be of little avail. My revenge is of no moment to you; yet, while I allow it to be a vice, I confess that it is the devouring and only passion of my soul. My rage is unspeakable when I reflect that the murderer, whom I have turned loose upon society, still exists. You refuse my just demand; I have but one resource, and I devote myself, either in my life or death, to his destruction.'

I trembled with excess of agitation as I said this; there was a frenzy in my manner, and something, I doubt not, of that haughty fierceness which the martyrs of old are said to have possessed. But to a Genevan magistrate, whose mind was occupied by far other ideas than those of devotion and heroism, this elevation of mind had much the appearance of madness. He endeavoured to soothe me as a nurse does a child and reverted to my tale as the effects of delirium.

'Man,' I cried, 'how ignorant art thou in thy pride of wisdom! Cease; you know not what it is you say.'

I broke from the house angry and disturbed and retired to meditate on some other mode of action.

## CHAPTER 24

My present situation was one in which all voluntary thought was swallowed up and lost. I was hurried away by fury; revenge alone endowed me with strength and composure; it moulded my feelings and allowed me to be calculating and calm at periods when otherwise delirium or death would have been my portion.

My first resolution was to quit Geneva forever; my country, which, when I was happy and beloved, was dear to me, now, in my adversity, became hateful. I provided myself with a sum of money, together with a few jewels which had belonged to my mother, and departed.

And now my wanderings began which are to cease but with life. I have traversed a vast portion of the earth and have endured all the hardships which travellers in deserts and barbarous countries are wont to meet. How I have lived I hardly know; many times have I stretched my failing limbs upon the sandy plain and prayed for death. But revenge kept me alive; I dared not die and leave my adversary in being.

When I quitted Geneva my first labour was to gain some clue by which I might trace the steps of my fiendish enemy. But my plan was unsettled, and I wandered many hours round the confines of the town, uncertain what path I should pursue. As night approached I found myself at the entrance of the cemetery where William, Elizabeth, and my father reposed. I entered it and approached the tomb which marked their graves. Every thing was silent except the leaves of the trees, which were gently agitated by the wind; the night was nearly dark, and the scene would have been solemn and affecting even to an uninterested observer. The spirits of the departed seemed to flit around and to cast a shadow, which was felt but not seen, around the head of the mourner.

The deep grief which this scene had at first excited quickly gave way to rage and despair. They were dead, and I lived; their murderer also lived, and to destroy him I must drag out my weary existence. I knelt on the grass and kissed the earth and with quivering lips exclaimed, 'By the sacred earth on which I kneel, by the shades that wander near me, by the deep and eternal grief that I feel, I swear; and by thee, O Night, and the spirits that preside over thee, to pursue the daemon who caused this misery, until he or I shall perish in mortal conflict. For this purpose I will preserve my life; to execute this dear revenge will I again behold the sun and tread the green herbage of earth, which otherwise should vanish from my eyes forever. And I call on you, spirits of the dead, and on you, wandering ministers of vengeance, to aid and conduct me in my work. Let the cursed and hellish monster drink deep of agony; let him feel the despair that now torments me.'

I had begun my adjuration with solemnity and an awe which almost assured me that the shades of my murdered friends heard and approved my devotion, but the furies possessed me as I concluded, and rage choked my utterance.

I was answered through the stillness of night by a loud and fiendish laugh. It rang on my ears long and heavily; the mountains re-echoed it, and I felt as if all hell surrounded me with mockery and laughter. Surely in that moment I should have been possessed by frenzy and have destroyed my miserable existence but that my vow was heard and that I was reserved for vengeance. The laughter died away, when a well-known and abhorred voice, apparently close to my ear, addressed me in an audible whisper, 'I am satisfied, miserable wretch! You have determined to live, and I am satisfied.'

I darted towards the spot from which the sound proceeded, but the devil eluded my grasp. Suddenly the broad disk of the moon arose and shone full upon his ghastly and distorted shape as he fled with more than mortal speed.

I pursued him; and for many months this has been my task. Guided by a slight clue, I followed the windings of the Rhone, but vainly. The blue Mediterranean appeared, and by a strange chance, I saw the fiend enter by night and hide himself in a vessel bound for the Black Sea. I took my passage in the same ship, but he escaped, I know not how.

Amidst the wilds of Tartary and Russia, although he still evaded me, I have ever followed in his track. Sometimes the peasants, scared by this horrid apparition, informed me of his path; sometimes he himself, who feared that if I lost all trace of him I should despair and die, left some mark to guide me. The snows descended on my head, and I saw the print of his huge step on the white plain. To you first entering on life, to whom care is new and agony unknown, how can you understand what I have felt and still feel? Cold, want, and fatigue were the least pains which I was destined to endure; I was cursed by some devil and carried about with me my eternal hell; yet still a spirit of good followed and directed my steps and, when I most murmured, would suddenly extricate me from seemingly insurmountable difficulties. Sometimes, when nature, overcome by hunger, sunk under the exhaustion, a repast was prepared for me in the desert that restored and inspirited me. The fare was, indeed, coarse, such as the peasants of the country ate, but I will not doubt that it was set there by the spirits that I had invoked to aid me. Often, when all was dry, the heavens cloudless, and I was parched by thirst, a slight cloud would bedim the sky, shed the few drops that revived me, and vanish.

I followed, when I could, the courses of the rivers; but the daemon generally avoided these, as it was here that the population of the country chiefly collected. In other places human beings were seldom seen, and I generally subsisted on the wild animals that crossed my path. I had money with me and gained the friendship of the villagers by distributing it; or I brought with me some food that I had killed, which, after taking a small part, I always presented to those who had provided me with fire and utensils for cooking.

My life, as it passed thus, was indeed hateful to me, and it was during sleep alone that I could taste joy. O blessed sleep! Often, when most miserable, I sank to repose, and my dreams lulled me even to rapture. The spirits that guarded me had provided these moments, or rather hours, of happiness that I might retain strength to fulfil my pilgrimage. Deprived of this respite, I should have sunk under my hardships. During the day I was sustained and inspirited by the hope of night: for in sleep I saw my friends, my wife, and my beloved country; again I saw the benevolent countenance of my father, heard the silver tones of my Elizabeth's voice, and beheld Clerval enjoying health and youth. Often, when wearied by a toilsome march, I persuaded myself that I was dreaming until night should come and that I should then enjoy reality in the arms of my dearest friends. What agonizing fondness did I feel for them! How did I cling to their dear forms, as sometimes they haunted even my waking hours, and persuade myself that they still lived! At such moments vengeance, that burned within me, died in my heart, and I pursued my path towards the destruction of the daemon more as a task enjoined by heaven, as the mechanical impulse of some power of which I was unconscious, than as the ardent desire of my soul.

What his feelings were whom I pursued I cannot know. Sometimes, indeed, he left marks in writing on the barks of the trees or cut in stone that guided me and instigated my fury. 'My reign is not yet over' – these words were legible in one of these inscriptions – 'you live, and my power is complete. Follow me; I seek the everlasting ices of the north, where you will feel the misery of cold and frost, to which I am impassive. You will find near this place, if you follow not too tardily, a dead hare; eat and be refreshed. Come on, my enemy; we have yet to wrestle for our lives, but many hard and miserable hours must you endure until that period shall arrive.'

Scoffing devil! Again do I vow vengeance; again do I devote thee, miserable fiend, to torture and death. Never will I give up my search until he or I perish; and then with what ecstasy shall I join my Elizabeth and my departed friends, who even now prepare for me the reward of my tedious toil and horrible pilgrimage!

As I still pursued my journey to the northward, the snows thickened and the cold increased in a degree almost too severe to support. The peasants were shut up in their hovels, and only a few of the most hardy ventured forth to seize the animals whom starvation had forced from their hiding-places to seek for prey. The rivers were covered with ice, and no fish could be procured; and thus I was cut off from my chief article of maintenance.

The triumph of my enemy increased with the difficulty of my labours. One inscription that he left was in these words: 'Prepare! Your toils only begin; wrap yourself in furs and provide food, for we shall soon enter upon a journey where your sufferings will satisfy my everlasting hatred.'

My courage and perseverance were invigorated by these scoffing words; I resolved not to fail in my purpose, and calling on heaven to support me, I continued with unabated fervour to traverse immense deserts, until the ocean appeared at a distance and formed the utmost boundary of the horizon. Oh! How unlike it was to the blue seasons of the south! Covered with ice, it was only to be distinguished from land by its superior wildness and ruggedness. The Greeks wept for joy when they beheld the Mediterranean from the hills of Asia, and hailed with rapture the boundary of their toils. I did not weep, but I knelt down and, with a full heart, thanked my guiding spirit for conducting me in safety to the place where I hoped, notwithstanding my adversary's gibe, to meet and grapple with him.

Some weeks before this period I had procured a sledge and dogs and thus traversed the snows with inconceivable speed. I know not whether the fiend possessed the same advantages, but I found that, as before I had daily lost ground in the pursuit, I now gained on him, so much so that when I first saw the ocean he was but one day's journey in advance, and I hoped to intercept him before he should reach the beach. With new courage, therefore, I pressed on, and in two days arrived at a wretched hamlet on the seashore. I enquired of the inhabitants concerning the fiend and gained accurate information. A gigantic monster, they said, had arrived the night before, armed with a gun and many pistols, putting to flight the inhabitants of a solitary cottage through fear of his terrific appearance. He had carried off their store of winter food, and placing it in a sledge, to draw which he had seized on a numerous drove of trained dogs, he had harnessed them, and the same night, to the joy of the horror-struck villagers, had pursued his journey across the sea in a direction that led to no land; and they conjectured that he must speedily be destroyed by the breaking of the ice or frozen by the eternal frosts.

On hearing this information I suffered a temporary access of despair. He had escaped me, and I must commence a destructive and almost endless journey across the mountainous ices of the ocean, amidst cold that few of the inhabitants could long endure and which I, the native of a genial and sunny climate, could not hope to survive. Yet at the idea that the fiend should live and be triumphant, my rage and vengeance returned, and like a mighty tide, overwhelmed every other feeling. After a slight repose, during which the spirits of the dead hovered round and instigated me to toil and revenge, I prepared for my journey.

I exchanged my land-sledge for one fashioned for the inequalities of the frozen ocean, and purchasing a plentiful stock of provisions, I departed from land.

I cannot guess how many days have passed since then, but I have endured misery which nothing but the eternal sentiment of a just retribution burning within my heart could have enabled me to support. Immense and rugged mountains of ice often barred up my passage, and I often heard the thunder of the ground sea, which threatened my destruction. But again the frost came and made the paths of the sea secure.

By the quantity of provision which I had consumed, I should guess that I had passed three weeks in this journey; and the continual protraction of hope, returning back upon the heart, often wrung bitter drops of despondency and grief from my eyes. Despair had indeed almost secured her prey, and I should soon have sunk beneath this misery. Once, after the poor animals that conveyed me had with incredible toil gained the summit of a sloping ice mountain, and one, sinking under his fatigue, died, I viewed the expanse before me with anguish, when suddenly my eye caught a dark speck upon the dusky plain. I strained my sight to discover what it could be and uttered a wild cry of ecstasy when I distinguished a sledge and the distorted proportions of a well-known form within. Oh! With what a burning gush did hope revisit my heart! Warm tears filled my eyes, which I hastily wiped away, that they might not intercept the view I had of the daemon; but still my sight was dimmed by the burning drops, until, giving way to the emotions that oppressed me, I wept aloud.

But this was not the time for delay; I disencumbered the dogs of their dead companion, gave them a plentiful portion of food, and after an hour's rest, which was absolutely necessary, and yet which was bitterly irksome to me, I continued my route. The sledge was still visible, nor did I again lose sight of it except at the moments when for a short time some ice-rock concealed it with its intervening crags. I indeed perceptibly gained on it, and when, after nearly two days' journey, I beheld my enemy at no more than a mile distant, my heart bounded within me.

But now, when I appeared almost within grasp of my foe, my hopes were suddenly extinguished, and I lost all trace of him more utterly than I had ever done before. A ground sea was heard; the thunder of its progress, as the waters rolled and swelled beneath me, became every moment more ominous and terrific. I pressed on, but in vain. The wind arose; the sea roared; and, as with the mighty shock of an earthquake, it split and cracked with a tremendous and overwhelming sound. The work was soon finished; in a few minutes a tumultuous sea rolled between me and my enemy, and I was left drifting on a scattered piece of ice that was continually lessening and thus preparing for me a hideous death.

In this manner many appalling hours passed; several of my dogs died, and I myself was about to sink under the accumulation of distress when I saw your vessel riding at anchor and holding forth to me hopes of succour and life. I had no conception that vessels ever came so far north and was astounded at the sight. I quickly destroyed part of my sledge to construct oars, and by these means was enabled, with infinite fatigue, to move my ice raft in the direction of your ship. I had determined, if you were going southwards, still to trust myself to the mercy of the seas rather than abandon my purpose. I hoped to induce you to grant me a boat with which I could pursue my enemy. But your direction was northwards. You took me on board when my vigour was exhausted, and I should soon have sunk under my multiplied hardships into a death which I still dread – for my task is unfulfilled.

Oh! When will my guiding spirit, in conducting me to the daemon, allow me the rest I so much desire; or must I die, and he yet live? If I do, swear to me, Walton, that he shall not escape, that you will seek him and satisfy my vengeance in his death. And do I dare to ask of you to undertake my pilgrimage, to endure the hardships that I have undergone? No; I am not so selfish. Yet, when I am dead, if he should appear, if the ministers of vengeance should conduct him to you, swear that he shall not live – swear that he shall not triumph over my accumulated woes and survive to add to the list of his dark crimes. He is eloquent and persuasive, and once his words had even power over my heart; but trust him not. His soul is as hellish as his form, full of treachery and fiendlike malice. Hear him not; call on the names of William, Justine, Clerval, Elizabeth, my father, and of the wretched Victor, and thrust your sword into his heart. I will hover near and direct the steel aright.

Walton, in continuation.

August 26th, 17—

You have read this strange and terrific story, Margaret; and do you not feel your blood congeal with horror, like that which even now curdles mine? Sometimes, seized with sudden agony, he could not continue his tale; at others, his voice broken, yet piercing, uttered with difficulty the words so replete with anguish. His fine and lovely eyes were now lighted up with indignation, now subdued to downcast sorrow and quenched in infinite wretchedness. Sometimes he commanded his countenance and tones and related the most horrible incidents with a tranquil voice, suppressing every mark of agitation; then, like a volcano bursting forth, his face would suddenly change to an expression of the wildest rage as he shrieked out imprecations on his persecutor.

His tale is connected and told with an appearance of the simplest truth, yet I own to you that the letters of Felix and Safie, which he showed me, and the apparition of the monster seen from our ship, brought to me a greater conviction of the truth of his narrative than his asseverations, however earnest and connected. Such a monster has, then, really existence! I cannot doubt it, yet I am lost in surprize and admiration. Sometimes I endeavoured to gain from Frankenstein the particulars of his creature's formation, but on this point he was impenetrable.

'Are you mad, my friend?' said he. 'Or whither does your senseless curiosity lead you? Would you also create for yourself and the world a daemoniacal enemy? Peace, peace! Learn my miseries and do not seek to increase your own.'

Frankenstein discovered that I made notes concerning his history; he asked to see them and then himself corrected and augmented them in many places, but principally in giving the life and spirit to the conversations he held with his enemy. 'Since you have preserved my narration,' said he, 'I would not that a mutilated one should go down to posterity.'

Thus has a week passed away, while I have listened to the strangest tale that ever imagination formed. My thoughts and every feeling of my soul have been drunk up by the interest for my guest which this tale and his own elevated and gentle manners have created. I wish to soothe him, yet can I counsel one so infinitely miserable, so destitute of every hope of consolation, to live? Oh, no! The only joy that he can now know will be when he composes his shattered spirit to peace and death. Yet he enjoys one comfort, the offspring of solitude and delirium; he believes that when in dreams he holds converse with his friends and derives from that communion consolation for his miseries or excitements to his vengeance, that they are not the creations of his fancy, but the beings themselves who visit him from the regions of a remote world. This faith gives a solemnity to his reveries that render them to me almost as imposing and interesting as truth.

Our conversations are not always confined to his own history and misfortunes. On every point of general literature he displays unbounded knowledge and a quick and piercing apprehension. His eloquence is forcible and touching; nor can I hear him, when he relates a pathetic incident or endeavours to move the passions of pity or love, without tears. What a glorious creature must he have been in the days of his prosperity, when he is thus noble and godlike in ruin! He seems to feel his own worth and the greatness of his fall.

'When younger,' said he, 'I believed myself destined for some great enterprize. My feelings are profound, but I possessed a coolness of judgment that fitted me for illustrious achievements. This sentiment of the worth of my nature supported me when others would have been oppressed, for I deemed it criminal to throw away in useless grief those talents that might be useful to my fellow creatures. When I reflected on the work I had completed, no less a one than the creation of a sensitive and rational animal, I could not rank myself with the herd of common projectors. But this thought, which supported me in the commencement of my career, now serves only to plunge me lower in the dust. All my speculations and hopes are as nothing, and like the archangel who aspired to omnipotence, I am chained in an eternal hell. My imagination was vivid, yet my powers of analysis and application were intense; by the union of these qualities I conceived the idea and executed the creation of a man. Even now I cannot recollect without passion my reveries while the work was incomplete. I trod heaven in my thoughts, now exulting in my powers, now burning with the idea of their effects. From my infancy I was imbued with high hopes and a lofty ambition; but how am I sunk! Oh! My friend, if you had known me as I once was, you would not recognize me in this state of degradation. Despondency rarely visited my heart; a high destiny seemed to bear me on, until I fell, never, never again to rise.'

Must I then lose this admirable being? I have longed for a friend; I have sought one who would sympathize with and love me. Behold, on these desert seas I have found such a one, but I fear I have gained him only to know his value and lose him. I would reconcile him to life, but he repulses the idea.

'I thank you, Walton,' he said, 'for your kind intentions towards so miserable a wretch; but when you speak of new ties and fresh affections, think you that any can replace those who are gone? Can any man be to me as Clerval was, or any woman another Elizabeth? Even where the affections are not strongly moved by any superior excellence, the companions of our childhood always possess a certain power over our minds which hardly any later friend can obtain. They know our infantine dispositions, which, however they may be afterwards modified, are never eradicated; and they can judge of our actions with more certain conclusions as to the integrity of our motives. A sister or a brother can never, unless indeed such symptoms have been shown early, suspect the other of fraud or false dealing, when another friend, however strongly he may be attached, may, in spite of himself, be contemplated with suspicion. But I enjoyed friends, dear not only through habit and association, but from their own merits; and wherever I am, the soothing voice of my Elizabeth and the conversation of Clerval will be ever whispered in my ear. They are dead, and but one feeling in such a solitude can persuade me to preserve my life. If I were engaged in any high undertaking or design, fraught with extensive utility to my fellow creatures, then could I live to fulfil it. But such is not my destiny; I must pursue and destroy the being to whom I gave existence; then my lot on earth will be fulfilled and I may die.'

My beloved Sister, September 2nd

I write to you, encompassed by peril and ignorant whether I am ever doomed to see again dear England and the dearer friends that inhabit it. I am surrounded by mountains of ice which admit of no escape and threaten every moment to crush my vessel. The brave fellows whom I have persuaded to be my companions look towards me for aid, but I have none to bestow. There is something terribly appalling in our situation, yet my courage and hopes do not desert me. Yet it is terrible to reflect that the lives of all these men are endangered through me. If we are lost, my mad schemes are the cause.

And what, Margaret, will be the state of your mind? You will not hear of my destruction, and you will anxiously await my return. Years will pass, and you will have visitings of despair and yet be tortured by hope. Oh! My beloved sister, the sickening failing of your heart-felt expectations is, in prospect, more terrible to me than my own death. But you have a husband and lovely children; you may be happy. Heaven bless you and make you so!

My unfortunate guest regards me with the tenderest compassion. He endeavours to fill me with hope and talks as if life were a possession which he valued. He reminds me how often the same accidents have happened to other navigators who have attempted this sea, and in spite of myself, he fills me with cheerful auguries. Even the sailors feel the power of his eloquence; when he speaks, they no longer despair; he rouses their energies, and while they hear his voice they believe these vast mountains of ice are mole-hills which will vanish before the resolutions of man. These feelings are transitory; each day of expectation delayed fills them with fear, and I almost dread a mutiny caused by this despair.

September 5th

A scene has just passed of such uncommon interest that, although it is highly probable that these papers may never reach you, yet I cannot forbear recording it.

We are still surrounded by mountains of ice, still in imminent danger of being crushed in their conflict. The cold is excessive, and many of my unfortunate comrades have already found a grave amidst this scene of desolation. Frankenstein has daily declined in health; a feverish fire still glimmers in his eyes, but he is exhausted, and when suddenly roused to any exertion, he speedily sinks again into apparent lifelessness.

I mentioned in my last letter the fears I entertained of a mutiny. This morning, as I sat watching the wan countenance of my friend – his eyes half closed and his limbs hanging listlessly – I was roused by half a dozen of the sailors, who demanded admission into the cabin. They entered, and their leader addressed me. He told me that he and his companions had been chosen by the other sailors to come in deputation to me to make me a requisition which, in justice, I could not refuse. We were immured in ice and should probably never escape; but they feared that if, as was possible, the ice should dissipate and a free passage be opened, I should be rash enough to continue my voyage and lead them into fresh dangers, after they might happily have surmounted this. They insisted, therefore, that I should engage with a solemn promise that if the vessel should be freed I would instantly direct my course southwards.

This speech troubled me. I had not despaired, nor had I yet conceived the idea of returning if set free. Yet could I, in justice, or even in possibility, refuse this demand? I hesitated before I answered, when Frankenstein, who had at first been silent, and indeed appeared hardly to have force enough to attend, now roused himself; his eyes sparkled, and his cheeks flushed with momentary vigour. Turning towards the men, he said, 'What do you mean? What do you demand of your captain? Are you, then, so easily turned from your design? Did you not call this a glorious expedition? And wherefore was it glorious? Not because the way was smooth and placid as a southern sea, but because it was full of dangers and terror, because at every new incident your fortitude was to be called forth and your courage exhibited, because danger and death surrounded it, and these you were to brave and overcome. For this was it a glorious, for this was it an honourable undertaking. You were hereafter to be hailed as the benefactors of your species, your names adored as belonging to brave men who encountered death for honour and the benefit of mankind. And now, behold, with the first imagination of danger, or, if you will, the first mighty and terrific trial of your courage, you shrink away and are content to be handed down as men who had not strength enough to endure cold and peril; and so, poor souls, they were chilly and returned to their warm firesides. Why, that requires not this preparation; ye need not have come thus far and dragged your captain to the shame of a defeat merely to prove yourselves cowards. Oh! Be men, or be more than men. Be steady to your purposes and firm as a rock. This ice is not made of such stuff as your hearts may be; it is mutable and cannot withstand you if you say that it shall not. Do not return to your families with the stigma of disgrace marked on your brows. Return as heroes who have fought and conquered and who know not what it is to turn their backs on the foe.'

He spoke this with a voice so modulated to the different feelings expressed in his speech, with an eye so full of lofty design and heroism, that can you wonder that these men were moved? They looked at one another and were unable to reply. I spoke; I told them to retire and consider of what had been said, that I would not lead them farther north if they strenuously desired the contrary, but that I hoped that, with reflection, their courage would return.

They retired and I turned towards my friend, but he was sunk in languor and almost deprived of life.

How all this will terminate, I know not, but I had rather die than return shamefully, my purpose unfulfilled. Yet I fear such will be my fate; the men, unsupported by ideas of glory and honour, can never willingly continue to endure their present hardships.

September 7th

The die is cast; I have consented to return if we are not destroyed. Thus are my hopes blasted by cowardice and indecision; I come back ignorant and disappointed. It requires more philosophy than I possess to bear this injustice with patience.

September 12th

It is past; I am returning to England. I have lost my hopes of utility and glory; I have lost my friend. But I will endeavour to detail these bitter circumstances to you, my dear sister; and while I am wafted towards England and towards you, I will not despond.

September 9th, the ice began to move, and roarings like thunder were heard at a distance as the islands split and cracked in every direction. We were in the most imminent peril; but as we could only remain passive, my chief attention was occupied by my unfortunate guest, whose illness increased in such a degree that he was entirely confined to his bed. The ice cracked behind us and was driven with force towards the north; a breeze sprang from the west, and on the 11th the passage towards the south became perfectly free. When the sailors saw this and that their return to their native country was apparently assured, a shout of tumultuous joy broke from them, loud and long-continued. Frankenstein, who was dozing, awoke and asked the cause of the tumult. 'They shout,' I said, 'because they will soon return to England.'

'Do you, then, really return?'

'Alas! Yes; I cannot withstand their demands. I cannot lead them unwillingly to danger, and I must return.'

'Do so, if you will; but I will not. You may give up your purpose, but mine is assigned to me by heaven, and I dare not. I am weak, but surely the spirits who assist my vengeance will endow me with sufficient strength.' Saying this, he endeavoured to spring from the bed, but the exertion was too great for him; he fell back and fainted.

It was long before he was restored, and I often thought that life was entirely extinct. At length he opened his eyes; he breathed with difficulty and was unable to speak. The surgeon gave him a composing draught and ordered us to leave him undisturbed. In the mean time he told me that my friend had certainly not many hours to live.

His sentence was pronounced, and I could only grieve and be patient. I sat by his bed, watching him; his eyes were closed, and I thought he slept; but presently he called to me in a feeble voice, and bidding me come near, said, 'Alas! The strength I relied on is gone; I feel that I shall soon die, and he, my enemy and persecutor, may still be in being. Think not, Walton, that in the last moments of my existence I feel that burning hatred and ardent desire of revenge I once expressed; but I feel myself justified in desiring the death of my adversary. During these last days I have been occupied in examining my past conduct; nor do I find it blameable. In a fit of enthusiastic madness I created a rational creature and was bound towards him to assure, as far as was in my power, his happiness and well-being. This was my duty; but there was another still paramount to that. My duties towards the beings of my own species had greater claims to my attention because they included a greater proportion of happiness or misery. Urged by this view, I refused, and I did right in refusing, to create a companion for the first creature. He showed unparalleled malignity and selfishness in evil; he destroyed my friends; he devoted to destruction beings who possessed exquisite sensations, happiness, and wisdom; nor do I know where this thirst for vengeance may end. Miserable himself that he may render no other wretched, he ought to die. The task of his destruction was mine, but I have failed. When actuated by selfish and vicious motives, I asked you to undertake my unfinished work, and I renew this request now, when I am only induced by reason and virtue.

'Yet I cannot ask you to renounce your country and friends to fulfil this task; and now that you are returning to England, you will have little chance of meeting with him. But the consideration of these points, and the well balancing of what you may esteem your duties, I leave to you; my judgment and ideas are already disturbed by the near approach of death. I dare not ask you to do what I think right, for I may still be misled by passion.

'That he should live to be an instrument of mischief disturbs me; in other respects, this hour, when I momentarily expect my release, is the only happy one which I have enjoyed for several years. The forms of the beloved dead flit before me, and I hasten to their arms. Farewell, Walton! Seek happiness in tranquillity and avoid ambition, even if it be only the apparently innocent one of distinguishing yourself in science and discoveries. Yet why do I say this? I have myself been blasted in these hopes, yet another may succeed.'

His voice became fainter as he spoke, and at length, exhausted by his effort, he sank into silence. About half an hour afterwards he attempted again to speak but was unable; he pressed my hand feebly, and his eyes closed forever, while the irradiation of a gentle smile passed away from his lips.

Margaret, what comment can I make on the untimely extinction of this glorious spirit? What can I say that will enable you to understand the depth of my sorrow? All that I should express would be inadequate and feeble. My tears flow; my mind is overshadowed by a cloud of disappointment. But I journey towards England, and I may there find consolation.

I am interrupted. What do these sounds portend? It is midnight; the breeze blows fairly, and the watch on deck scarcely stir. Again there is a sound as of a human voice, but hoarser; it comes from the cabin where the remains of Frankenstein still lie. I must arise and examine. Good night, my sister.

Great God! what a scene has just taken place! I am yet dizzy with the remembrance of it. I hardly know whether I shall have the power to detail it; yet the tale which I have recorded would be incomplete without this final and wonderful catastrophe.

I entered the cabin where lay the remains of my ill-fated and admirable friend. Over him hung a form which I cannot find words to describe – gigantic in stature, yet uncouth and distorted in its proportions. As he hung over the coffin, his face was concealed by long locks of ragged hair; but one vast hand was extended, in colour and apparent texture like that of a mummy. When he heard the sound of my approach, he ceased to utter exclamations of grief and horror and sprung towards the window. Never did I behold a vision so horrible as his face, of such loathsome yet appalling hideousness. I shut my eyes involuntarily and endeavoured to recollect what were my duties with regard to this destroyer. I called on him to stay.

He paused, looking on me with wonder, and again turning towards the lifeless form of his creator, he seemed to forget my presence, and every feature and gesture seemed instigated by the wildest rage of some uncontrollable passion.

'That is also my victim!' he exclaimed. 'In his murder my crimes are consummated; the miserable series of my being is wound to its close! Oh, Frankenstein! Generous and self-devoted being! What does it avail that I now ask thee to pardon me? I, who irretrievably destroyed thee by destroying all thou lovedst. Alas! He is cold, he cannot answer me.'

His voice seemed suffocated, and my first impulses, which had suggested to me the duty of obeying the dying request of my friend in destroying his enemy, were now suspended by a mixture of curiosity and compassion. I approached this tremendous being; I dared not again raise my eyes to his face, there was something so scaring and unearthly in his ugliness. I attempted to speak, but the words died away on my lips. The monster continued to utter wild and incoherent self-reproaches. At length I gathered resolution to address him in a pause of the tempest of his passion. 'Your repentance,' I said, 'is now superfluous. If you had listened to the voice of conscience and heeded the stings of remorse before you had urged you diabolical vengeance to this extremity, Frankenstein would yet have lived.'

'And do you dream?' said the daemon. 'Do you think that I was then dead to agony and remorse? He,' he continued, pointing to the corpse, 'he suffered not in the consummation of the deed. Oh! Not the ten-thousandth portion of the anguish that was mine during the lingering detail of its execution. A frightful selfishness hurried me on, while my heart was poisoned with remorse. Think you that the groans of Clerval were music to my ears? My heart was fashioned to be susceptible of love and sympathy, and when wrenched by misery to vice and hatred, it did not endure the violence of the change without torture such as you cannot even imagine.

'After the murder of Clerval, I returned to Switzerland, heart-broken and overcome. I pitied Frankenstein; my pity amounted to horror; I abhorred myself. But when I discovered that he, the author at once of my existence and of its unspeakable torments, dared to hope for happiness; that while he accumulated wretchedness and despair upon me he sought his own enjoyment in feelings and passions from the indulgence of which I was forever barred, then impotent envy and bitter indignation filled me with an insatiable thirst for vengeance. I recollected my threat and resolved that it should be accomplished. I knew that I was preparing for myself a deadly torture, but I was the slave, not the master, of an impulse which I detested yet could not disobey. Yet when she died! Nay, then I was not miserable. I had cast off all feeling, subdued all anguish, to riot in the excess of my despair. Evil thenceforth became my good. Urged thus far, I had no choice but to adapt my nature to an element which I had willingly chosen. The completion of my daemoniacal design became an insatiable passion. And now it is ended; there is my last victim!'

I was at first touched by the expressions of his misery;

yet, when I called to mind what Frankenstein had said of his powers of eloquence and persuasion, and when I again cast my eyes on the lifeless form of my friend, indignation was rekindled within me. 'Wretch!' I said. 'It is well that you come here to whine over the desolation that you have made. You throw a torch into a pile of buildings, and when they are consumed, you sit among the ruins and lament the fall. Hypocritical fiend! If he whom you mourn still lived, still would he be the object, again would he become the prey, of your accursed vegeance. It is not pity that you feel; you lament only because the victim of your malignity is withdrawn from your power.'

'Oh, it is not thus – not thus,' interrupted the being. 'Yet such must be the impression conveyed to you by what appears to be the purport of my actions. Yet I seek not a fellow feeling in my misery. No sympathy may I ever find. When I first sought it, it was the love of virtue, the feelings of happiness and affection with which my whole being overflowed, that I wished to be participated. But now that virtue has become to me a shadow, and that happiness and affection are turned into bitter and loathing despair, in what should I seek for sympathy? I am content to suffer alone while my sufferings shall endure; when I die, I am well satisfied that abhorrence and opprobrium should load my memory. Once my fancy was soothed with dreams of virtue, of fame, and of enjoyment. Once I falsely hoped to meet with beings who, pardoning my outward form, would love me for the excellent qualities which I was capable of unfolding. I was nourished with high thoughts of honour and devotion. But now crime has degraded me beneath the meanest animal. No guilt, no mischief, no malignity, no misery, can be found comparable to mine. When I run over the frightful catalogue of my sins, I cannot believe that I am the same creature whose thoughts were once filled with sublime and transcendent visions of the beauty and the majesty of goodness. But it is even so; the fallen angel becomes a malignant devil. Yet even that enemy of God and man had friends and associates in his desolation; I am alone.

'You, who call Frankenstein your friend, seem to have a knowledge of my crimes and his misfortunes. But in the detail which he gave you of them he could not sum up the hours and months of misery which I endured wasting in impotent passions. For while I destroyed his hopes, I did not satisfy my own desires. They were forever ardent and craving; still I desired love and fellowship, and I was still spurned. Was there no injustice in this? Am I to be thought the only criminal, when all humankind sinned against me? Why do you not hate Felix, who drove his friend from his door with contumely? Why do you not execrate the rustic who sought to destroy the saviour of his child? Nay, these are virtuous and immaculate beings! I, the miserable and the abandoned, am an abortion, to be spurned at, and kicked, and trampled on. Even now my blood boils at the recollection of this injustice.

'But it is true that I am a wretch. I have murdered the lovely and the helpless; I have strangled the innocent as they slept and grasped to death his throat who never injured me or any other living thing. I have devoted my creator, the select specimen of all that is worthy of love and admiration among men, to misery; I have pursued him even to that irremediable ruin. There he lies, white and cold in death. You hate me, but your abhorrence cannot equal that with which I regard myself. I look on the hands which executed the deed; I think on the heart in which the imagination of it was conceived and long for the moment when these hands will meet my eyes, when that imagination will haunt my thoughts no more.

'Fear not that I shall be the instrument of future mischief. My work is nearly complete. Neither yours nor any man's death is needed to consummate the series of my being and accomplish that which must be done, but it requires my own. Do not think that I shall be slow to perform this sacrifice. I shall quit your vessel on the ice raft which brought me thither and shall seek the most northern extremity of the globe; I shall collect my funeral pile and consume to ashes this miserable frame, that its remains may afford no light to any curious and unhallowed wretch who would create such another as I have been. I shall die. I shall no longer feel the agonies which now consume me or be the prey of feelings unsatisfied, yet unquenched. He is dead who called me into being; and when I shall be no more, the very remembrance of us both will speedily vanish. I shall no longer see the sun or stars or feel the winds play on my cheeks. Light, feeling, and sense will pass away; and in this condition must I find my happiness. Some years ago, when the images which this world affords first opened upon me, when I felt the cheering warmth of summer and heard the rustling of the leaves and the warbling of the birds, and these were all to me, I should have wept to die; now it is my only consolation. Polluted by crimes and torn by the bitterest remorse, where can I find rest but in death?

'Farewell! I leave you, and in you the last of humankind whom these eyes will ever behold. Farewell, Frankenstein! If thou wert yet alive and yet cherished a desire of revenge against me, it would be better satiated in my life than in my destruction. But it was not so; thou didst seek my extinction, that I might not cause greater wretchedness; and if yet, in some mode unknown to me, thou hadst not ceased to think and feel, thou wouldst not desire against me a vengeance greater than that which I feel. Blasted as thou wert, my agony was still superior to thine, for the bitter sting of remorse will not cease to rankle in my wounds until death shall close them forever.

'But soon,' he cried with sad and solemn enthusiasm, 'I shall die, and what I now feel be no longer felt. Soon these burning miseries will be extinct. I shall ascend my funeral pile triumphantly and exult in the agony of the torturing flames. The light of that conflagration will fade away; my ashes will be swept into the sea by the winds. My spirit will sleep in peace, or if it thinks, it will not surely think thus. Farewell.'

He sprang from the cabin window as he said this, upon the ice raft which lay close to the vessel. He was soon borne away by the waves and lost in darkness and distance.

# NOTES

## THE CASTLE OF OTRANTO

*Preface to the Second Edition.*

1 (p. 46) *Enfant Prodigue:* The Prodigal Son.

2 (p. 46) . . . *le mieux traité:* One sees here a mixture of seriousness and jesting, of the comic and the touching; often even a single event produces all these contrasts. Nothing is so usual as a house in which a father scolds, a daughter, absorbed in her passionate love, weeps; the son mocks the two of them, and various relatives take their different parts in the scene, etc. We do not infer from this that all comedy must have scenes of buffoonery and scenes of pathos: there are a lot of very good plays where only gaiety reigns: others are wholly serious; others are a mixture; there are others which are moving to the point of tears; it is not necessary to exclude any one type; and if I were asked which type is the better, I would reply, that which is best handled.

3 (p. 46) *toute serieuse:* wholly serious.

4 (p. 47 . . . *espece de simplicité:* All these traits of character are unsophisticated: here all is appropriate to those whom you introduce on the scene, and to the manners which you give them. These natural familiarities have been, I believe, well received in Athens; but Paris and our audience want another type of simplicity.

5 (p. 47) *parterre:* i.e. the audience.

6 (p. 47) *espece de simplicité:* type of simplicity.

7 (p. 48) *difficiles nugae:* troublesome nonsense.

*Chapter 1*

1 (p. 65) *officiously:* eagerly.

*Chapter 2*

1 (p. 75) *orisons:* prayers.

*Chapter 3*

1 (p. 97) *intelligence:* news.
2 (p. 101) *vitious:* legally unsound.

*Chapter 4*

1 (p. 116) *enlargement:* release.

*Chapter 5*

1 (p. 133) *vulnerary:* used for healing wounds.
2 (p. 134) *halidame:* a holy relic.

VATHEK

1 (p. 155) *discovered:* revealed.
2 (p. 159) *intelligence:* news.
3 (p. 164) *Divan:* a Council of State and Court of Justice in which the Ruler himself presides to dispense justice.
4 (p. 166) *Muezins:* in Mohammedan countries the public criers who proclaim the regular hours of prayer from the minaret or roof of the mosque. These hours are at daybreak, noon, midway between noon and sunset, sunset and half an hour after sunset.
5 (p. 170) *tapis:* carpet.
6 (p. 181) *the pre-Adamite sultans:* legendary monarchs who governed the beings who lived before Adam. One of the most noted of these rulers was Soliman Di Gian Ben Gian, who ruled over the Genii and Peris for two thousand years (see note 24). He was known for his warlike character, and he possessed a magic buckler which warded off the spells of the dives or giants. He was succeeded by Eblis (see note 30) who exiled the Peris to Dijinnistan, and remotest region of the earth (see note 14).
7 (p. 182) . . . *Of Mahomet:* Balaam was saved from being killed by an angel when the ass he was riding turned aside three times; when he beat the ass the Lord reproved him through its mouth (*Numbers* XXII). The seven sleepers were young men who fled from the persecutions of Decius in 250 A.D.; they hid in a cave guarded by a dog and slept there for many years.
8 (p. 184) *Moullahs:* moullah was the title given to those

learned in theology and sacred law; it was from their ranks that the judges of cities and provinces were taken.

9 (p. 184) *the sacred Cahaba:* the square stone building at Mecca which is the heart of the Muslim faith. It was said to have been built by Ishmael and Abraham on the spot where Adam first worshipped after his expulsion from Paradise.

10 (p. 185) *vulgar eyes:* the eyes of ordinary people.

11 (p. 188) *orisons:* prayers.

12 (p. 192) *manchets:* cakes.

13 (p. 193) *à la daube:* casseroled.

14 (p. 193) *the horrible Kaf:* the Caucasus mountains, which were supposed to surround the earth and to be founded on an emerald stone called *sakhrat*, which was the pivot of the earth. To reach the Kaf one had to cross a desert inhabited by giants and exiled Peris.

15 (p. 193) *the Simurgh:* a fabulous bird of great size, age and knowledge. It assisted famous warriors in their fights against the dives or giants.

16 (p. 194) *the relentless afrits:* the most powerful but one of the classes of devils in Mohammedan mythology. They are of enormous size, fearful appearance and malicious disposition: Solomon is said to have tamed one and made it obey him.

17 (p. 194) *the Abdest:* the highly ritualized ceremony of washing the hands, face and feet before prayer.

18 (p. 195) *Cafila:* a caravan. The camels composing it commonly wore bells.

19 (p. 195) *Deggial:* the Mohammedan version of Antichrist; he has one eye and on his forehead is written the word 'Infidel'. Traditionally he will destroy the whole world except Mecca but will himself be slain by Jesus at the gate of the church at Lydda in Palestine.

20 (p. 197) *Bismillah:* the initiatory formula of prayer, meaning 'In the name of the most merciful God'.

21 (p. 197) *officious:* eager.

22 (p. 198) *tecthtrevan:* a portable throne used only by those of highest rank.

23 (p. 202) *... calenders, santons and derviches ... bramins, faquirs:* Calenders were a mendicant order who had abandoned parents and possessions and who subsisted on what was given to them. Santons were monks or hermits, sometimes regarded as saints because of their tendency towards

ecstatic states. Derviches (dervishes) were holy men not bound by vows of poverty or chastity. They are sometimes called whirling or howling dervishes from the nature of their rites. Bramins were and are the highest Indian caste. They are strictly ascetic and observe rigid dietary laws. Their name derives from Brahma, who communicated the knowledge of science and religion to the priests. The faquirs (fakirs) were known for the severity of the mortifications with which they tormented themselves, such as supporting heavy burdens or dragging heavy chains for a long period of time.

24 (p. 205) *Peris:* the good and beautiful race of creatures which form the link between men and angels, the Persian counterpart of fairies; they were exiled to Dijinnistan by Eblis.

25 (p. 209) *cocknos:* a bird whose beak was used as a spoon.

26 (p. 217) *Imans:* the principal priests of a mosque.

27 (p. 217) . . . *Alla*'*:* 'there is no God but God'.

28 (p. 219) *Monker and Nekir:* the two black avenging angels who hideously torment the departed if his account of his faith is unsatisfactory.

29 (p. 239) *cadis:* the magistrates of a town or city.

30 (p. 241) *Eblis:* the prince of the rebel angels, the Arab equivalent of Satan.

31 (p. 242) *Balkis:* Arabian name of the Queen of Sheba.

## FRANKENSTEIN

### *Preface*

1 (p. 267) *Dr Darwin:* Erasmus Darwin (1731–1802), grandfather of Charles Darwin.

### *Chapter 1*

1 (p. 293) '*Schiavi ognor frementi*'*:* the slaves continually trembling (under Austrian rule); in *Lines written among the Euganean Hills,* (1818), Shelley addresses Venice

> With thy conquest-branded brow
> Stooping to the slave of slaves
> From thy throne,

where the 'slave of slaves' is the Austrian Emperor, Ruler of the Kingdom of Lombardy–Venice.

*Chapter 2*

1 (p. 295) *campagne:* a country estate.

2 (p. 296) . . . *infidels:* Roncesvalles, according to the eleventh-century heroic epic the *Chanson de Roland*, was the site of the battle between the French and the Saracen armies, in which Roland and Oliver died bravely, fighting overwhelming odds. The 'chivalrous train' was the army of the Crusades.

3 (p. 297) *Agrippa:* Cornelius Agrippa (1486–1535): German savant and writer on occult subjects; in his most famous work, *De Occulte Philosophia*, he argues that magic is the most perfect science, and leads men to a knowledge of God.

4 (p. 298) *Paracelsus and Albertus Magnus:* Paracelsus (1493–1541) was a Swiss physician and alchemist, who was responsible for some important discoveries in chemistry and pharmaceutics. Albertus Magnus (*c.* 1200–1280) was a German theologian, philosopher and scientist, who played a major part in introducing Aristotelianism into medieval Europe. He also enjoyed a legendary reputation as a magician.

*Chapter 4*

1 (p. 313) *than his nature will allow:* the theme of the danger of acquiring knowledge whose consequences cannot be controlled is also prominent in Mary Shelley's father's novel, *Caleb Williams* (1794), where the hero's 'crisis of fate' springs from a 'mistaken thirst of knowledge' (Vol. 2, ch. 6), and in his *Defence of Poetry* (1821), Shelley warns his readers that 'our calculations have outrun conception; we have eaten more than we can digest'. For a brilliant late Victorian treatment of this theme, see H. G. Wells's *The Island of Doctor Moreau* (1896).

*Chapter 5*

1 (p. 320) *discovered:* revealed.

2 (p. 320) . . . *tread:* Coleridge, *The Ancient Mariner*, Part 6.

3 (p. 321) *without Greek:* in George's account of his three years' wandering round Europe (*The Vicar of Wakefield*, ch. 20); the 'schoolmaster' is in fact the Principal of the University of Louvain.

*Chapter 6*

1 (p. 326) *Angelica:* in Ariosto's *Orlando Furioso* (1516), partly based on the Roland(Orlando)–Charlemagne legend, Angelica is pursued by many knights, including Orlando himself, but at length she marries Medora, a poor man.

*Chapter 7*

1 (p. 339) *Dear to me:* the vampire theme is a fairly common Romantic obsession; the best-known vampire story in English is Bram Stoker's *Dracula* (1897), and the earliest is probably *The Vampyre* (1819), by Polidori, Byron's doctor, who also translated *The Castle of Otranto* into Italian.

*Chapter 9*

1 (p. 358) *aiguilles:* peaks.

*Chapter 10*

1 (p. 361) *necessary beings:* William Godwin's pet theory was that the Principle of Necessity, which denies free will to man, rules the world. Peacock makes fun of the idea in Chapter 14 of *Headlong Hall* (1816) and Chapter 4 of *Nightmare Abbey* (1818).
2 (p. 362) ... *mutability:* the last lines of Shelley's poem *Mutability* (1816).

*Chapter 12*

1 (p. 379) *discover myself:* reveal myself. But the word 'discover' appears in its modern sense earlier in this paragraph ('I discovered that he uttered'), and elsewhere in the book.

*Chapter 13*

1 (p. 385) *Ruins of Empires:* the Comte de Volney wrote *Les Ruines, ou meditations sur les revolutions des Empires*, an essay in the philosophy of history, in 1719. The book added much to that aspect of the Gothic Revival which involved the love of decay.

*Chapter 15*

1 (p. 394) ... *Werter:* Carlyle, in describing the hero of Goethe's book (1774), wrote of 'that nameless unrest, the blind

struggle of a soul in bondage, that high, sad, longing discontent which was agitating every bosom'. The book was extremely popular, and G. H. Lewes, Goethe's nineteenth-century biographer, says that it found its way to China, where its chief characters were modelled in porcelain.

2 (p. 398) . . . *Creator:*

> Did I request thee, Maker, from my clay
> To mould me Man, did I solicit thee
> From darkness to promote me?
>
> *Paradise Lost.* Book 10, 743–5.

*Chapter 18*

1 (p. 425) *from the eye:* Wordsworth, *Tintern Abbey*; 'him' has twice been substituted for the original 'me'.

*Chapter 21*

1 (p. 453) *maladie du pays:* homesickness.